THE ACORN WINTER

THE ACORN
WINTER

Elizabeth Webster

This first world edition published in Great Britain 1994 by
SEVERN HOUSE PUBLISHERS LTD of
9–15 High Street, Sutton, Surrey SM1 1DF.
First published in the USA 1994 by
SEVERN HOUSE PUBLISHERS INC., of
425 Park Avenue, New York, NY 10022.

British Library Cataloguing in Publication Data
Webster, Elizabeth
  Acorn Winter
  I. Title
  823.914 [F]

  ISBN 0-7278-4643-4

Typeset by Hewer Text Composition Services, Edinburgh.
Printed and bound in Great Britain by
Redwood Books, Trowbridge, Wiltshire.

For Rog – and all the Cornfield Dancers

Who would have thought my shrivell'd heart
Could have recover'd greenness? It was gone
    Quite underground; as flowers depart
To see their Mother-root, when they have blown;
    Where they together
    All the hard weather,
Dead to the world, keep house unknown.

    These are thy wonders, Lord of power,
Killing and quickening, bringing down to hell
    And up to heaven in an hour;
Making a chiming of a passing bell.
    We say amiss
    This or that is:
They Word is all, if we could spell.

    And now in age I bud again,
After so many deaths I live and write;
    I once more smell the dew and rain,
And relish versing: O my only light,
    It cannot be
    That I am he,
On whom thy tempests fell all night.

George Herbert
from:- The flower.

PART I – THE EMPTY SEA

She stood at the edge of the sea, staring out at the horizon. A small, slim girl, – graceful too, probably, only now she was standing too straight and taut, staring out, straining to see something beyond her reach, beyond the horizon, beyond the sky . . . too far, too far away to reach . . .

The look on her face was one of bewilderment rather than loss – but loss was in it too, a puzzled disbelief that what she searched for was unreachable, was gone for ever, would never come back.

Never come back.

If I wait long enough, she told herself, he might come back. They both might. I think they are just out there, just round the corner, just round the point, searching for crabs, like they used to . . . They'll come back hand-in-hand, like they used to do – tall Robert, smiling and handsome as ever, and Little Mo, trying to keep up on his four-year-old legs, and smiling, too, at the father he adored . . .

They'll come, she said. They'll come round the corner together, and Little Mo will let go Robert's hand and come running to meet me, and everything will be all right.

She stood a little straighter and gazed out even harder at the cold grey sea, trying to pierce the veils of distance and see what could not be seen. But even now the tide was coming in. It wouldn't be safe round the point, they would have to come soon or it would be too late.

Too late?

Curls of white foam were breaking round her feet now, and spray rose up in rainbow plumes, encompassing her slight, lonely figure in a haze of glancing light. She looked drenched and cold, and somehow beyond recall.

But a sudden explosion of sound startled her, a burst of

1

cheering way down the beach near the jetty, and a cacophany of whistles and sirens from the small boats in the bay, a clapping of many hands and a chorus of excited shouts of encouragement. "Here he comes!" they shouted. "Well done!" "Here he is!" And the little boats hooted again even more loudly, and the cheering got even stronger.

The girl turned her head and looked down the beach to where a crowd of cheerful people jostled each other on the little harbour wall, all peering out seawards and pointing and laughing in excitement. Someone, or something, was clearly coming. But who? Or what?

The cheering broke out again, and the crowd all seemed to turn as one and line the edge of the jetty, just as a small, battered yacht slipped round the harbour entrance and came gently to rest at the end of the concrete pier.

The cheering got louder still, and the solitary figure of the yachtsman poised on deck raised a cheerful hand in salute, and then leapt ashore, mooring rope in hand.

So it was that Beth Halliday, cold and bereft and bewildered, first saw Finn Edmonson coming home in triumph from his lonely, single-handed voyage. And the brilliance of his coming seemed to spark in her a kind of desperate anger, it was so beautiful and so full of certainty.

He leapt ashore, and sunlight glinted on his golden beard, laid sparks of light on his tangled, sea-wet hair, and lit his eyes with sudden fire. He strode up the jetty like a Viking marauder, a hero of ancient legend, and the light of victory, the splendour of arduous achievement, were in his face as he walked through the cheering crowd of onlookers, past the TV cameras and waving flags and awestruck children.

And then the friendly press of people parted, leaving a pathway down the middle of the jetty, and at the end of the open space stood Finn's wife and small daughter, waiting to greet him. The pretty, young wife stood still, smiling and calm, but the little girl could not wait any longer and ran towards him, white-gold hair flying, calling out to him over the voices of the crowd as she ran: "Daddy-Finn, Daddy-Finn! You're home!"

He swept her up in his arms, and his stride scarcely lessened as he went on, straight into his wife's open embrace. His

2

home-coming was like a song – like something out of a film, said one of the enchanted onlookers – but something about that joyous, sunglided encounter seemed to pierce Beth to the core, and she turned away with tears in her eyes.

It was all very well for him. At the harbour end of the beach, the sea was blue and spangled with sunlight, and the little scene she had just witnessed seemed bathed in an almost mythical golden light. But here, where she stood, the sea was cold and grey, and empty – terribly empty – and no-one was coming home to her, no-one at all.

No-one at all. Not ever again. No tall, wind-browned Robert, no sturdy Little Mo. They would not come round the corner hand-in-hand. It was all a dream – a futile, self-deluding, cruel dream – and she was a fool to let herself believe it. Time to come to terms with reality, to put away fruitless longings and to leave the far horizons where hope laid a false brightness on the shadowed sea.

Stumbling a little, and shaking her head as if to rid it of visions and mirages, she began to walk furiously away along the shore, and tears of rage and grief mingled with the salt sea spray and blinded her as she went.

"Who is she, I wonder?" said Stephanie Edmonson, holding her breakfast coffee cup suspended in mid-air, and staring out of the hotel dining-room window at the slight, lonely figure on the shore.

Finn's gaze followed hers for a moment, but soon returned to his wife's expressive face with smiling affection. "How should I know? I just got here, remember?"

"She's been standing there since early morning, I saw her from our window and I think she was there most of yesterday too, only I was too excited to pay much attention." There was concern in the clear grey eyes, a lingering doubt in the gentle voice. "I can't help thinking – "

"You and your lame ducks," growled Finn. But he was too happy just now to protest very much, even when Stephanie left the breakfast table and went across to the reception desk in the foyer to ask discreetly if anyone knew who the solitary sea-gazer was.

"No," said the man at the reception desk, like Finn, unable

to stop smiling at Stephanie and her palpable happiness, but anxious to do his best for his most illustrious guests. "She's not staying here. But I think I've seen her coming out of the Harbour View – next door to the Grand." He looked up into Stephanie's puzzled face and went on to explain. "We use Harbour View as a kind of annexe when we're full, and so does the Grand. Mrs. Foster is very good with her guests, particularly with children."

"Thank you," said Stephanie, smiling back at him with absurd radiance. (The world was all smiles today.) "Maybe I'll enquire there."

She returned to Finn, who was busy explaining the intricacies of a sea-chart to his small daughter.

"You see, Chloë, that big dot is an island. But the little dots are reefs."

"Reefs?" It was incomprehensible to six-year-old Chloë, but she didn't mind. Anything her splendid hero of a father said was worth listening to, even if she didn't understand a word of it. She gazed up at him soulfully and basked in his attention.

"What are you doing today?" asked Stephanie, looking at the two of them with loving indulgence.

"Seeing to the repairs." Finn stretched in lazy contentment and got to his feet. "Coming, Sprat?"

"Yes, *please!*" Chloë put her hand firmly in his.

Finn twitched an enquiring eyebrow in Stephanie's direction, but she hesitated and then said in a curiously off-hand voice: "I'll follow you down. I want to make a call on the way."

Finn nodded amiably. He was used to Stephanie's determined independence. It was one of the things he liked best about her, and a blessing when he was so often away on his endless pursuit of new projects and adventures. "We'll be at the boatyard," he said, still alight with the same unquenchable energy, still sparkling with the same vivid happiness, and he strode off, with Chloë's warm brown hand in his.

Stephanie watched them go, an unfathomable expression that had more than a hint of hidden sorrow in it casting a faint shadow on her face. Then she turned and went out into the street, and walked briskly down the road past the

4

Grand and up the white steps into the sunny glassed-in porch of Harbour View.

It was an old-fashioned place, less pretentious than the Grand next door, though it had the same wide view of the sea, and there seemed to be an air of pleasant, not-too-smart tranquillity about it that Stephanie immediately liked. Mrs. Foster, who came from behind the reception desk to greet her, was middle-aged and, like her surroundings, pleasant and not too smart. She gave the impression of someone kindly and reliable, who had probably been running this discreet guest house for a good many years.

Stephanie approached her directly, reassured by that homely manner, somehow certain that she would not be rebuffed.

Like the smiling clerk in Stephanie's own hotel, Mrs. Foster clearly recognised her, (after all, she and Finn had been on the local telly only yesterday), and she seemed equally disarmed by Stephanie's warmth and friendliness. Finlay Edmonson was a very famous man these days, reckless and adventurous, always in the news, and (rumour had it) extremely rich. His wife was undoubtedly someone to be reckoned with, too. But she seemed so open and easy, so totally lacking in what Mrs. Foster privately called 'the usual arrogance of the rich' (like the people who stayed at the Grand) that it was difficult to refuse her anything she asked.

"Oh, you mean Mrs. Halliday – Beth Halliday." She looked up at Stephanie with genuine concern in her eyes. "Yes, I'm afraid she is very much alone now, poor young lady, and we don't know quite what to do for her."

"Why?" asked Stephanie bluntly. "I mean – why is she alone?"

The woman's cheerful face changed and became grave. "You wouldn't know, of course. They used to come down here quite a lot in the old days – the three of them."

"Three?"

"Her husband and the little boy. Such a lovely child. He and his father used to go out together, looking for crabs." She glanced at Stephanie, a faint smile softening the tired lines of her face. "He even brought me one once. It crawled all over the counter!"

5

Stephanie was staring at her hard. "You said they *used* to come – ?"

The woman nodded. "Yes. Quite often. He got a lot of short leaves, you see. He was an airline pilot."

"*Was?*"

Aileen Foster sighed. "Yes. Was. Some kind of accident, I believe, at some foreign airport." Her eyes strayed back to the sunlit beach beyond the guest house porch, and to the motionless figure at the edge of the water. "She was widowed very young, poor girl," she murmured, and then paused as if not quite sure how much to say. "But even after that, she came back with the little boy. I think she felt – " She hesitated again, and then turned back to Stephanie with a sudden rush of sympathetic feeling. "I think, maybe, she felt better, or something, in the place where they had been happy . . . ?"

Stephanie nodded silently. That made sense.

"And now – this," added the proprietress, as if driven by a kind of angry outrage she could not express.

"Now *what?*"

"The little boy – as if she didn't have enough to contend with. He died of meningitis."

"When?"

"Oh – only a short while ago, I think. She didn't say exactly. But she rang up to explain why she was coming down alone. Very brittle and sharp, she sounded. The hospital rang, too, the social worker, or something, to tell me what had happened and ask me to keep an eye on her. Very shocked, they said she was." She looked at Stephanie with helpless pity. "The poor young thing, she just stands there, all day. I had to send the lifeguard out to her once, she didn't seem to notice the tide coming in at all . . ." She shook her head sadly. Then she seemed to recollect that she was stepping outside her role of discreet guest house proprietress and sighed again. "I shouldn't be gossiping about my guests really, – "

"It's not gossiping," Stephanie told her roundly. "She needs help."

The wary, knowledgeable eyes looked at her anxiously. "Yes, well, – the Grand next door used to be a Hydro, you know, in the old days. People came down to convalesce.

6

They still keep a resident nurse." She went on looking into Stephanie's face. "I did wonder about asking her but I don't know what she could do?"

"No," said Stephanie. "Not a nurse. It's company she needs." She smiled at the woman with sudden warmth. "You've been very helpful. I'll see what I can do."

And such was the power of Stephanie's extraordinary gift of instilling confidence and reassurance in other people that the worried proprietress instantly felt better. It was out of her hands now. Something would be done for that poor girl out there, and she need not feel bad about it any more. Breathing a small, extra sigh of relief, she went back to work.

Stephanie had already left the sunny porch and was striding off along the beach.

"Aren't you cold?" she said, standing close to the lonely figure at the edge of the water.

"Cold?" The girl turned her head, the dark blue eyes, unfocussed and over-bright, stared blankly at the stranger beside her.

Cold? Yes, she was always cold now. There seemed to be no warmth left in the world that she used to know. None at all. Nothing but the cold seeping into her bones from the grey, empty sea, and the ache and pull of the tide as she waited for the two she loved who did not come.

"Yes, I'm cold." Her voice was cold, too, brittle and strange.

"Why not come and have a coffee?" suggested Stephanie, looking back into the brilliant, unseeing gaze with unspoken compassion.

Beth shook her head. "I have to wait," she explained reasonably to the kind face opposite. "You must see that." And then, since the face did not look convinced, she added very earnestly: "If I wait long enough, you see, they will come back."

"Do you think so?" The gentle voice was not sceptical, merely calm and quiet.

"They went round the point, you know," Beth told her. "They only went round the point."

"To look for crabs?" The voice was even gentler now.

7

Beth smiled, and the pinched, bewildered face was suddenly flooded with light. The change was so startling that Stephanie blinked. "Yes, that's it. To look for crabs. How did you know?"

"My daughter, Chloë, likes looking for crabs, too." Stephanie was watching her carefully. "Sometimes she goes on her own when the tide is low . . . I can see her from the hotel window."

"Can you?" The girl stood looking at her uncertainly, pushing the wet strands of her hair away from her face.

"Shall we go and see?"

Once more the girl's eyes turned to look at the sea, but it was still empty and cold – still dark with approaching rain clouds – and the tide was churning in black swirls round the point. There was no-one there. No-one coming back.

"Well, all right," she said, and then, more fiercely: "But I have to watch."

"Of course."

"You can't stop me." There was a sudden flash of childish anger in her voice.

"No," said Stephanie, and put a warm, comforting arm round her shoulders. "No-one's going to stop you." And she led her away towards the warmth and shelter of the hotel.

In the quiet lounge, they sat by the big picture windows that looked out on the bay, so that Beth could still watch the swirl of water round the point.

"Drink your coffee," prompted Stephanie, and carefully wrapped Beth's cold fingers round the warm china cup.

Obediently, Beth sipped at the hot liquid, and felt some of the icy numbness begin to thaw a little. She knew this friendly stranger was being extraordinarily kind, and she tried vainly to focus on the concerned face opposite, but somehow she couldn't seem to reach it. She couldn't seem to reach the world around her at all. There was this awful silence, this veil between her and reality, like an invisible pall.

Like a pall.

A pall . . . He lay in a pall, consigned to the cold, dark earth. His small body laid out neatly, stiff and cold. Cold as death . . . Death? How could he cope with death? He was only four, – so full of promise, so warm and loving, so brimming with life.

8

How could he deal with death, all on his own? I should be with him, she thought fiercely. I ought to be with him, helping him through. Through to where?

In her mind she saw a sudden, very clear picture of an enormous staircase, huge and dazzling-white and empty, empty, save for one tiny figure patiently trying to climb the stairs, tread by enormous tread, bravely struggling to master those massive, impossibly steep steps with his short brown legs . . . struggling on and on, alone . . .

"He was always brave," she said suddenly, and as she spoke those words, the whole distorted fantasy of her hopeless vigil by the sea collapsed, and she was through the veil and back in the real world again, and the tears (the tears she had not been able to shed) were running down her face.

"I know," said Stephanie, watching both sanity and pain return to the girl's face. "They are much braver than we are." And then, seeing how much that weight of sorrow needed to come out, she put a hand on Beth's arm and suggested quietly: "Shall we go upstairs? It's quieter there."

Beth nodded, not able to speak just now, and allowed herself to be led away to Stephanie's sunny room overlooking the bay.

"You can still look out," she said, standing near the window so that Beth could see the beach below, but she knew that this was not necessary now.

"No," whispered Beth, her voice choked with tears. "They won't come back . . . not now." And her shoulders began to shake.

"Oh, my dear girl," said Stephanie, and folded her in her arms.

When the storm of tears was over, Stephanie sent for more coffee and some brandy, and they began to talk. It seemed to her very important that Beth should tell someone – anyone – about what had happened. It didn't matter how long it took. She had all day to spare.

"I ought not to – " Beth began, already ashamed of her collapse.

"Yes, you *ought*," said Stephanie firmly. "You need to talk. And I want to hear it."

"Why?"

9

Stephanie looked at her with curious intensity. "Because . . . I need to know." She spoke obscurely, and when Beth did not go on, she prompted her gently. "Tell me about your husband first."

"Robert?" She sighed. "He was an airline pilot, older than me – and he was away a lot. So – so every leave was somehow exciting and special, like an extra honeymoon."

"Yes." Stephanie nodded comprehension. "Like Finn and me."

Beth glanced at her with sudden awareness. "Of course . . . on the beach yesterday. I saw him arrive." A faint smile touched her for a moment. "He looked like a Viking." But the smile faltered then. "I thought it looked such a – such a *joyous* meeting." The tears almost threatened to spill out again at the memory of that reunion, and she hurried on. "It reminded me so much of how it was every time Robert came home. But then, of course, one day he didn't."

Stephanie sighed. It could so easily happen to Finn. But she did not say it. "So – what happened exactly?" She knew she was pushing Beth, but she felt it was time things were said. And sometimes it was easier to talk to a stranger.

"It was such a senseless accident!" Beth exploded into sudden anger. "After all those flying hours – all those journeys all over the world, and never a mishap, never any trouble . . . "

"And – ?"

"He was just walking back to the airport for his next flight. He'd been shopping in the town. He was – they said he was carrying a toy for Mo . . ." Her voice shook a little. "And some car came round the corner too fast. It simply mowed Robert down – never saw him at all."

Stephanie looked shocked. "How dreadful."

"Yes." Her tone was dry. "There was a – a court case of some sort out there. And the company did their best to be helpful." She pushed the hair out of her eyes again in a childish, distracted manner. "I don't know why I'm telling you all this."

"Because I asked you to," said Stephanie, and then added her thoughts aloud: "Besides, it's sometimes easier to talk to a stranger."

Beth looked at her then in an odd, searching way and almost said: But you're not a stranger, are you? But it was too difficult to say, so she merely shook her head wordlessly and gave a shaky smile.

But Stephanie was not to be deflected. "How long ago was this?"

"Oh – about two and a half years. Mo was – was just two when it happened."

"It must have been terribly hard for you."

"Yes, I suppose it was." Beth paused, and then went on in a cool, light voice: "Though in a way it was easier to cope with than I thought because I had got used to managing on my own most of the time, and I had Little Mo to keep me company. Of course I missed Robert terribly, and so did Mo . . . Robert adored him – they were very close." She took a deep breath. "I knew Robert could probably cope with death – he lived with the possibility for so long, but – but somehow you never think it could happen to you." She drew another shaky breath. "It's the little things . . . not being able to say: 'Look, Robert!' when you see something beautiful . . . or having someone around who knows your thoughts without being told . . . or even – just someone to go out with . . ." She shook her head, angry at her own weakness. "Trivial things, really . . . Anyway, I thought I was coming to terms with it. Life was a bit bleak, but we managed, Mo and I. I suppose I concentrated everything on Little Mo, and I suppose I shouldn't have . . . He became the – the *focus* of my life." She was silent then, unable to continue.

Stephanie's comment was gentle. "That's only natural."

"Is it?" Beth swallowed hard. "He was such a – such a happy child. I never thought anything else could happen to us." She shook her head in helpless disbelief. "It – didn't seem possible."

Stephanie waited for her to go on, and when she failed to say anything more, gave her another quiet prod. "Then – what went wrong?"

Beth glanced at her rather wildly and shivered. "I – can't . . ."

"Yes, you can. Please?" Her voice was still soft, but Beth

11

could feel the steel behind it. Stephanie was difficult to resist when she was determined to have her own way.

"You know," Beth said, in a suddenly bright and brittle voice, "I spoke to a woman on the bus – a total stranger – on the way home from the hospital. *'My little boy is dead,'* I said. And she didn't know what to say."

Stephanie nodded. "I don't know what to say either. But I can listen."

The artificial brightness faded from Beth's voice and was replaced by sudden anger. "It's a bit much, you know, to lose *two* people you love in the space of two years. Extravagant, really."

Stephanie laid a hand on her arm, ignoring the anger. *"Tell* me."

Beth stared at her, seeming to return from bleak and sterile distance to a country of warmth and pain she dared not enter. "He seemed so well . . ." she said slowly, "so full of life that day . . ."

He had been running round the garden with her, laughing in the sun, looking for tadpoles in the little pond, chasing a dragonfly across the grass, climbing to the first branch of the hawthorn tree, his brown legs swinging on the rope ladder, and laughing, always laughing in the sunshine. *'Look at me, I'm high – high as a dragonfly!'*

There had been nothing to indicate disaster – no shadow on that bright spring day . . . And then nothing more than a headache, a tossing restlessness, a faint glaze in the blue, trusting eyes . . . And the fever rising, and rising . . .

"You'll feel better soon," she had said, laying a cool hand on his small hot head. And his answering voice, vague and drowsy, had faded on a sigh: *"Better . . . soon . . ."*

But he hadn't been better. He had been worse. And the nightmare had begun. The doctor – grave and concerned – the fever rising, and rising – the sudden, frightening convulsions and then the deep, dreadful unconsciousness, so sudden and so quick. The rush to the hospital, and the shocked, terrible wrench in her arms, in her heart, in the very fabric of her being, as they took him away from her. It felt like the stroke of death – even then.

"He just . . . got ill so suddenly," she said. "Meningitis is like that. I called the doctor as soon as – as soon as the fever rose . . . He did everything he could. So did the hospital. But it was too late. He just – never came round."

I never held him again, she thought. Never. And my arms will always feel empty. Always. As long as I live.

She had sat by the white hospital bed and looked at him in disbelief. His face was calm in death though, a little pinched and sharp, almost alien. It did not look like Little Mo any more. She had cried out once, she thought: *"He's not – ?"* Just that one cry. But then she had sat there, frozen. Utterly frozen. No feeling at all.

And then someone had come and led her away. She couldn't remember who. Couldn't remember anything, except that awful, wrenching sense of loss when they took him out of her arms. It was like dying, too, she thought. I wish it had been me – that would have been possible. But Little Mo – with a whole, wonderful new life to lead. Why him?

There was so much potential there – so much joy – such vivid imagination and incipient talent . . . so much loving delight in all things living . . . *'Look, Mummy, a rainbow!'*

'Look, I got a worm!'

'Look at me, I'm dancing!'

Dancing. Dancing across the lawn, twirling on a pattern of daisies in the grass, leaping over a dandelion, and laughing, always laughing, in the sun.

It won't do, she thought. I can't go on like this. I've got to come to terms with it somehow. Stop crying for the impossible. Stop remembering. Go on living. Go on. *But why?*

My life is utterly changed, and the gap is huge. Enormous. And the worst thing is, not knowing where he is – whether he can cope? Is Robert with him? Are they facing it together? Or is he alone? Terribly alone? What is heaven, anyway? Is it there at all? I can't see Robert twanging a harp. Nor Little Mo, either. He'd laugh . . . But is someone taking care of him? Is he safe now? Safe and warm and loved as he was on earth? How can I tell?

"Where do they go?" she said suddenly, turning a beseeching gaze on Stephanie *"Where are they now?"*

Stepanie looked at her sadly. "I don't know – I wish I

13

did." She paused, and then added, almost shyly: "Are you religious?"

"I don't know what I am." Beth shook her head. "I don't know what I believe – though I was supposed to have been brought up a Christian, I suppose . . . but – " the tears threatened again and made her voice shake, "I only know I'd like to think they went on . . . and that Mo was safe." She took another wavering breath and continued in a faintly puzzled tone: "I thought I might feel close to Robert, you know, after the accident that I might feel him nearby or something . . . But I never did. I got quite angry with him at times, for *not* coming back . . . But as for Little Mo – " again her voice shook a little, "He was too small to cope with eternity . . ."

"I don't know," repeated Stephanie, but in a different, altogether more certain tone: "I think a child might understand eternity better than we could. He wouldn't have any built-in conventions in his mind about what was real and what was not. Everything would seem possible to him."

Beth stared at her. "Do you think so?"

Stephanie smiled. "Yes. I think everything *is* possible. He'll be all right, he and your Robert. It's you we have to think about now."

Beth shook her head again, as if trying to see more clearly. "*I don't know who I am any more,*" she whispered, and there was despair behind her voice. *I don't know who I am. I was a wife, a wife and mother, a widow, a widow and child, and now I'm nothing. What am I? Who am I?*

"You'll find out," said Stephanie gently, and wrapped a consoling arm round her shoulders.

But at that point the door opened and Finn and Chloë burst into the room.

"You never came!" reproached Chloë, and Finn added, smiling: "We missed you!" Then, seeing Beth, he stopped short.

Stephanie looked up at him undismayed and said calmly: "This is Beth. She is coming to lunch with us downstairs."

"Oh, but – " began Beth.

"No buts." Stephanie got briskly to her feet. "Chloë can choose her favourite pudding. Shall we go?"

14

Finn shrugged broad shoulders and grinned with the greatest good humour. "Why not?" he said.

Over lunch, Finn was his usual brilliant self, and described in much hilarious detail the hazards of his single-handed voyage across the Atlantic. He was not a stupid man, and he knew without being told that Stephanie required him to keep things light and cheerful and cover for this distressed young woman's silence.

Chloë played up, too, tossing that lint-fair hair, plying her father with questions, chattering with excitement, spreading her own brand of private delight, her wide-eyed admiration of Finn's exploits like a bright cloak of many colours round their enchanted table. Stephanie sat back and watched them affectionately, and kept a quiet eye on Beth without saying anything, though she did wonder a little whether Chloë's exhuberance might upset her.

But even little Chloë somehow knew she ought to do something about that bewildered silence, and she turned to Beth suddenly with the utmost sweetness. "Would you like to come and see Daddy's boat? I'm sure he'd let you."

"I – " Beth tried to focus her flying thoughts on the bright, eager little face beside her. You can't snub a child, she thought. You can't quench that brightness with your own sorrow. It's not her fault.

"Yes," she said at last, summoning a smile, "I'd be honoured."

Beside her, Stephanie nodded quiet approval. It was a start. Trust Chloë to break the ice.

A waiter approached, looking concerned at Beth's untouched food, and wondering whether to take it away.

"Try to eat something," murmured Stephanie.

"I – I can't," Beth said. I can't. How can I eat when he is dead? How can I go on living and doing ordinary things? The world and its noise and clutter simply choke me. What's the point of it all?

"Never mind." Stephanie spoke softly. "It will come."

Beth glanced at her in mute protest and suddenly realised that she had never really looked at her new friend before, nor at Finn, nor Chloë, come to that.

Finn, with his golden beard and glinting mischievous smile, was just as her first impression had told her, a Viking, with a buccaneer's impish bravado disguising a steely courage. His small daughter had a smaller dose of bravado, and was – if anything – more outspoken than her father. But her eyes, grey and luminous like her mother's – were serious beneath the straight brows and wildly-flying ash-blonde hair. She was a forthright young six-year-old, but not without sensitivity.

Stephanie's face was an older version of Chloë's, but thinner and graver, with a clearcut bone structure, a rather determined chin, and the same clear grey eyes. Beth was rather afraid of those eyes. They probed too deep. The mouth, though occasionally stern, was full of the same quiet compassion as those disturbing eyes, but the set of her head was somehow alert and watchful despite its frame of fly-away hair (fair, but not the pale white-gold of her daughter's). And there was an odd hint of black courage, well hidden, and a sort of schooled and steady patience . . . (What need has she for patience, Beth wondered). But it was a face she could trust, she told herself. Even if she was frightened of all that compassion . . . And I have this extraordinary feeling that we know each other already, she thought suddenly. She didn't approach me like a stranger – and somehow I think our lives are already linked . . . Maybe that's why I'm frightened.

Stephanie was thinking much the same thing, looking back with an odd mixture of pity and recognition at the girl's pain-darkened blue eyes and the tense young head weighed down by the spiritless, honey-dark fall of hair. She looked almost like a child herself, she thought. A lost and centreless child. Somehow, we've got to help her.

"Let's go and look at the boat, then," she suggested. Since it was clear that Beth was not going to eat anything, they might as well do something else.

"But I haven't had my pudding!" cried Chloë, outraged, and Finn began to laugh.

"Oh, you must have that. What is it to be?"

And they all watched in fascination as the small girl's face puckered in concentration over the dessert trolley.

When she was successfully entrenched behind a mound of chocolate gateau and 'butterscotch ice cream with real caramel sauce,' Stephanie turned to Finn and said, smiling: "Beth saw you arrive yesterday. She says you looked like a Viking."

Finn grinned. "I felt like one. Except that I was setting foot on native soil, not a foreign shore."

Beth unexpectedly joined in here, trying hard to sound interested. "Does that make a difference?"

"Oh yes!" Finn wrinkled up his nose like a mischievous small boy. "Home ground. I know I didn't fall flat on my face and kiss it, but I felt like it."

Beth's voice was very light and cold – very brittle, still – but she was making a valiant attempt to keep her end up. "Why this place particularly? I would have thought you'd have chosen to arrive at somewhere bigger and more – "

"Spectacular?" murmured Stephanie, and lifted a roguish eyebrow in Finn's direction.

He laughed, and bright sparks of loving delight seemed to dance in his eyes. "Steph knows me all too well!" Then he became fractionally more serious for a moment. "No. I love this little place – always have. It's unpretentious, and still a small working fishing port . . . I suppose, while I was at sea, it became for me the epitome of, well, simple seaside England."

Beth nodded slowly. "Yes. Robert thought that, too."

There was a small, tingling silence, and Stephanie was beginning to wonder whether her carefully planned attempt at respite was going to disintegrate into disaster after all, when Chloë suddenly said – with her mouth full of chocolate – "Symbol."

"What?" Finn looked at his little daughter in astonishment.

"Symbol. Not simple." She took another large mouthful of chocolate gateau. "Mum told me."

Finn looked from Chloë to Stephanie, seeming even more astounded. "Did she now?"

But Stephanie was unperturbed. "Chloë wanted to know why you chose Tormouth, too."

"I see." His deep voice was warm with love. "Two minds with a single thought?" He looked at Stephanie, smiling, but she did not need to answer.

Chloë put down her spoon with a sigh. The mountain of

chocolate had diminished but not entirely disappeared – even so, she was defeated. "I'm ready now," she announced.

They got to their feet, all smiling – even Beth unable to resist the child's infectious happiness – and went to inspect the boat which was propped up on wedges high up on the slipway at the edge of the little boatyard.

"How long will it take?" asked Stephanie, eyeing the shabby paint with some respect. It had seen a lot of storms, she thought, that sturdy little boat. And it had brought Finn safely home.

"About a week," said Finn.

Stephanie looked at Beth and smiled. "We can potter about together then, can't we?"

Beth scarcely knew how to answer. She could not understand why this amazingly kind woman was taking so much trouble. "What will you do next?" she asked Finn, wondering if he would be off on some new adventure immediately.

"Oh, it's the family's turn," he said, smiling. "We're going to sail her down to the Greek islands. There's a project I have out there that wants looking at." He winked at Stephanie, and sunlight sparked in his golden, buccaneer's beard.

"When isn't there?" laughed Stephanie. But there was a plan forming in her head, only it was too soon yet to put into words.

"A family holiday," pronounced Finn, and hoisted Chloë up on to his shoulder. "How does that grab you, Sprat?"

"Magic!" said Chloë, and grabbed at her father's hair.

Stephanie's eyes met Beth's. But she did not say anything more just then. She merely laid a gentle hand on Beth's arm and led her into the boatyard office where there was coffee brewing.

All that week Stephanie kept it up, filling Beth's day with cheerful, unimportant excursions. She did not let her walk on the beach alone any more, but took her up on to the green hills beyond the town, and along the deep, leafy lanes of the Devon valleys.

At first she left Chloë with Finn, who was still haunting the boatyard, determined to supervise his repairs personally. It was good for the two of them to be together – Chloë saw little enough of her famous father as it was, and she was thrilled to keep him company. But there were family outings to be considered too – these weeks with Finn at home were precious – and time was probably short. Time was always short with Finn.

So one morning, Stephanie said suddenly to Beth: "Does having Chloë along with us bother you?"

Beth looked at her in amazement. "*Bother me*? She's enchanting."

"Yes, but – "

"No," said Beth firmly. "She doesn't remind me of Mo – not really. Except her zest for life. But then most children have that, don't they?" She looked at Stephanie, half-smiling. "After all, I used to be a teacher. I can't banish all children from my life for fear of hurt, can I?"

"No," agreed Stepahnie slowly. "You can't."

Beth was still looking at her, and wondering if she dared to ask a leading question. Things were unexpectedly easy between them now, especially since Beth herself was not quite so shocked and disoriented, and Stephanie had this strange capacity to instill confidence and trust.

"Can I ask you something?"

Stephanie lifted expressive eyebrows. "I should think so."

"Then – *why*?" She did not elaborate.

"Why not?" Stephanie smiled.

Beth shook her head, almost in exasperation. "Be serious. *Why* take all this trouble?"

Stephanie regarded her calmly. "I suppose . . . because I'm an interfering woman – and you remind me of me when young."

"But you're still young."

"Not as young as you." The smile still lurked behind her eyes.

Beth considered the matter. "Like you?"

"There are certain parallels!" But in spite of the smile, there was now a curious, reflective sadness in her gentle voice. "I married very young – like you. And I knew from the start that Finn would always be off on new ventures like your Robert."

"Didn't you mind?"

Stephanie sighed. "Oh yes, I minded. Just as you minded. But that's the way it is with men like Finn. He can't stay in one place for long. There has to be a challenge."

Beth nodded. "Yes, I know."

"Well, like you, I learnt to manage on my own." She grinned with sudden mischief. "And I've been managing ever since!"

Beth actually laughed.

But Stephanie was suddenly grave. "Of course, it's a bit hard on Chloë. She adores her father, and he's away more than half the time." She glanced at Beth and continued steadily: "It's like you said, each time he comes home it's like an extra honeymoon, and it makes everything a bit too . . . too important."

Beth agreed.

"And Chloë – " She broke off and then added in a softened tone: "'*The focus of your life*' you said, about your Little Mo. You're not the only one."

Beth understood her very well. But she did not speak.

"I sometimes wish – " went on Stephanie, and then paused, as if uncertain of her own thoughts.

"Yes?"

"Chloë would get attached to someone besides me . . . She relies on me too much."

"Isn't that inevitable?"

"Of course it is," agreed Stephanie, sounding almost angry. "But it's dangerous."

Beth looked at her then. "Oh, yes. It's dangerous."

Stephanie took a strange, long breath. "But I wouldn't have it otherwise. Would you?"

Beth looked bewildered. "What?"

"Every moment – every small happening – they are all extra special, extra precious, really." Her voice had taken on a soft, reflective resonance, filled with unexpressed thoughts. She seemed almost to be talking to herself, and the sadness was back in her voice. Then she turned to Beth with sudden insistence. "Weren't they for you?"

"Of course." Beth bent her head to hide the sudden tears.

"Don't you see?" persisted Stephanie. "You still have them – all those special moments. *You only have to remember*."

This time, Beth did not answer at all.

"There," said Stephanie, laying an apologetic hand on Beth's arm. "I've said too much, as usual!" She was smiling again a little, and Beth could not help responding. "But do you see now why you matter to me?" She tilted her head sideways in an interrogative way. "It could so easily have been me . . . But I have been much too lucky."

At this, Beth looked up and smiled with sudden generosity. "Well, thank God one of us has," she said.

After this, Stephanie often brought Chloë along too, and Beth found herself curiously drawn to the outspoken, fair-haired child with eyes so like her mother's.

It was while they were all three sitting on the springy turf of a nearby clifftop, finishing a picnic lunch, that Stephanie dared to talk of the future. She looked at Beth's profile, still saddened and shadowed with unceasing grief, and wondered if it was too soon. But the days were slipping by, and she needed to know what could be done to help.

"What will you do now?" she asked.

"Do?" Beth looked panic-stricken for a moment, and then seemed visibly to pull herself together. "I don't know – go back to work, I suppose."

Stephanie prompted her gently. "You said you were a teacher?"

"Yes." She hesitated, and then continued in a small, cold voice. "I went on working after I got married, till Mo was born . . . It seemed sensible, with Robert away so much."

Stephanie nodded.

"And – and after Rob was killed, I went back part-time, to – to have something to do. I took Mo with me then – the school had its own nursery."

Again Stephanie inclined her head. It made good sense.

"I was going to go back full time in the autumn, when Mo went to school." Her voice wavered suddenly. "He would be five in October . . ."

Stephanie pretended to ignore the break in her voice. It was probably better to keep her talking. "What subjects?"

"Subjects? Oh, general – junior school stuff. And music."

"*Music?*" Stephanie sat up straight and looked at her with sudden attention. "What kind of music?"

Beth looked surprised. "Any kind, class music, singing, piano and all that . . . And some of them started a pop group once! . . . I could just about teach the violin, though I wasn't very good myself . . . And the recorder, of course – a must in junior school life." There was almost a glimmer of a smile on her pale face. "And, of course, percussion. For all the duds who liked banging things."

Chloë, following the conversation in spite of the egg sandwich half in and half out of her mouth, said suddenly: "Tubular bells."

"What?" Stephanie was mystified.

"Tunes," explained Chloë, swallowing more sandwich. "Not only bangs. Like xylophones."

Beth smiled. "You're right. Not only bangs."

"We're not all duds," stated Chloë flatly, and looked at Beth with challenge.

"Of course not." Beth was ashamed of her generalisation. How could she be so stupid? She knew very well that percussion could be both subtle and intricate and immensely skilled . . .

"Do you know anything about Music Therapy?" asked Stephanie, sounding oddly off-hand and casual all of a sudden.

"Music Therapy?" Beth considered for a moment. "No. I don't." Then she went on more slowly: "Though I suppose all music is a kind of therapy . . ." She turned to look at Stephanie and caught a strange, speculative gleam in her eye. "Why?"

"Oh, it's just something I'm interested in." She spoke carelessly. "I'll tell you about it later."

At that point they saw Finn climbing up the cliff path to meet them, and Chloë leapt to her feet and went running across the grass to meet him.

"Daddy-Finn!" she shouted, a mixture of joy and reproach in her voice. "You're late, and we've eaten all the sandwiches."

"Never mind," he said, hoisting her up in the air and swinging her round. "I've brought a pork pie."

Stephanie looked at Beth's still face and knew she was seeing another summer's day and another joyful meeting, and desperately trying to stave off hurt. But it would not do. That way, she would never mend.

Gently, she broke into Beth's dark dream. "Don't shut them out," she said.

"Why?" asked Finn, unconsciously echoing Beth as he and Stephanie sat in their room to discuss the day.

"Oh Finn – *think*! She's lost everything in the world she loved. There's nothing left. How would you feel if you lost Chloë? . . . Or me, for that matter?"

Finn went pale. The thought was unendurable.

Stephanie looked at him curiously. "Didn't you ever have a moment of doubt that you'd get home, out there in the Atlantic?"

Finn's eyes met hers. "Yes," he admitted. "Once or twice." He reached for her suddenly and held her very close and hard. "But for the most part," he added honestly, "there was no time to worry."

"Not for you, perhaps," murmured Stephanie. How many long hours had she lain awake, she wondered, picturing that little boat cowering under twenty-foot waves or running before those tearing Atlantic gales?

"Steph?" he said in wonder, holding her away to look at her.

"Oh, it's all right," she told him, smiling at his air of disbelief. Did he really think she was so invulnerable? "I've learnt to live with it."

For once in his wildly adventurous, go-getting life, Finn felt faintly ashamed of himself. I'll make it up to her, he thought. We'll have a really good holiday together – and teach Chloë how to snorkel.

"I wanted you to myself," he grumbled.

"You can still have me to yourself," said Stephanie, laughing. "There's room on the boat for four. We won't get in each other's way.

"That's what you think!"

"And anyway, she can help to look after Chloë, if we should want to go out on our own to a taverna, or something."

"Would you trust her?"

"Oh yes," said Stephanie at once. "Of course."

23

"Even though she's still so – ?"

"Shocked? Yes, but she's coming out of it." She looked into Finn's face with sudden appeal. "Please, Finn. It's important."

"Is it? Why?"

She looked at him strangely and said in an oddly shaken voice: "Because we're so happy."

Finn was silent for a while, but he knew very well what Stephanie meant. Wasn't his whole life lived as a hostage to fortune?

Sighing, he acquiesced, and laid his tawny head close to his wife's in perfect accord. "Have it your own way," he said.

But Stephanie didn't have it her own way. When she made her offer, Beth flatly refused.

"No." She sounded unexpectedly firm and decisive, but then she smiled at Stephanie with sudden warmth to mitigate her refusal. "It's wonderful of you to suggest it – especially when I know your time with Finn is so precious! But I can't."

"Why not?" Stephanie was surprised and not a little impressed by Beth's new air of decision.

"I have to – have to get what's left of my life together. There are decisions to take about the house and I've got to find a job for the autumn term. That means applying now, really. And – " she hesitated, and then went on in a rather breathless voice: "I've got to stop crying and get on with living, I suppose."

"I don't think you ought to stop crying – yet," said Stephanie seriously. "Grief can't be turned off like a tap."

Beth made a face at her. "You're not to encourage me. I'm weak enough as it is." She paused, and then added in a voice that did not know whether it was laced with tears or laughter: "I must be out of my tiny mind to refuse a yacht trip to the Greek islands! But no, Stephanie – though I can't thank you enough for asking."

Stephanie knew when she was defeated. So, being a practical woman, she promptly discarded Plan A and prepared to put forward Plan B. But, being skilled in negotiation, she went about it in a roundabout way. There were things she needed to know first.

"What about your parents, Beth? Are they still alive?"

Beth sighed. "My father is. My mother died a few years ago. She never saw Mo."

Stephanie did not comment on that, but pursued her own path. "Would your father help?"

"I shouldn't think so. They split up when I was ten, and he married again. We've never really kept in touch. I believe he lives in the north of England somewhere."

"What about Robert's people?"

"They are living in Australia. They wrote, of course, when Robert was killed – and offered to have Mo and me out there. But somehow I couldn't face it." Her glance wavered a little and then settled on Stephanie's face with painful honesty. "To tell you the truth, I rather clung to the places where Robert and I had been happy . . . and I thought I could do the same about – about Little Mo. But it was a mistake."

"I don't think so," said Stephanie gently. "Remembered happiness is never a mistake, is it?"

Beth bent her head to hide the swift rise of tears. They still overcame her much too often. "I – I didn't know them very well," she went on, as if making excuses to herself. "Rob's people, I mean. They didn't come over for the wedding, it was too far. And anyway, it was one of Rob's rushed short leaves – very sudden and swift. We didn't have time to let anyone know."

Stephanie nodded quietly. She had got the picture now. "What about the house? Will you keep it?"

"No." She sounded even more definite than before. How could she go on living in that house, with the ghost of Little Mo in every corner – his toys lying idle on the floor, the empty swing in the garden, and the silence – the awful echoing silence all around her? "No," she repeated, and shivered. "I must start again. Somewhere else."

"Then maybe what I've got to say might interest you," said Stephanie, and waited for Beth's haunted gaze to come back into focus.

"Yes?" Beth asked at last.

"We live in Gloucestershire," began Stephanie carefully. "That is, Chloë and I do, and Finn when he is home And there's this very nice school that Chloë goes to – not far away.

It has an ordinary curriculum, but it also has extra remedial classes for children with problems of one kind and another."

"A special school?"

"No. It's an ordinary junior school. They don't approve of special schools any more. They like to have the children integrated into the normal system. But sometimes they need a lot of extra help to fit in."

Beth nodded.

"They are very keen on music," said Stephanie, eyeing Beth with hopeful speculation. "And Music Therapy is one of their special interests."

"I see." Beth was beginning to get the drift.

"Don't freeze up," said Stephanie hastily. "I think you might like it – and I know they are wildly looking for someone to take it on. Not many general teachers today seem to include music in their skills."

"That's true," admitted Beth. "And there are no funds for specialist teachers.

Stephanie shot her a grateful glance. "Exactly. Well, I know the headmistress, Margaret Collier – quiet well. I'm on the board of governors."

"Oh, *honestly*, Stephanie!"

"No, it's only because of Finn being famous, damn him! I get asked to do all sorts of weird things." She paused, and then added, with intent: "But I care about this one."

Beth was silent. The idea was beginning to interest her. And what had she got to lose? It didn't matter where she went, or what she did.

"A few of the children are quite badly disturbed," Stephanie warned her. "They need a lot of care and patience, and a certain toughness too, all of which Margaret Collier has got in good measure, I might add!" She glanced at Beth sideways. "It would be a challenge . . ."

Beth did not reply to this. She was still thinking it out.

Stephanie watched the thoughts chasing themselves across Beth's expressive young face, and went on quietly: "I know it sounds unlikely, Beth, after what you've been through, but I have a strange feeling you'd be just what they are looking for. And getting those mixed-up kids to fit into this sorry world would be something worth doing." She gave Beth another shrewd, half-humorous glance. "Is that too corny?"

"Yes," said Beth, smiling. "Much too corny. But it does sound interesting."

Stephanie heaved an exaggerated sigh of relief. It was all very well to admit to Beth that she was a managing woman – but she was rather terrified of trying to order someone else's life. But Beth was smiling. It would probably be all right. "I'll give you the address – and ring Margaret about it, if you like? You could go over to Gloucestershire and have a look for yourself."

"Yes, I could." She still sounded doubtful.

"No obligation!" protested Stephanie, also smiling now. "You don't have to take it on if you don't like it, do you?" She looked at Beth's hesitant face and then added: "But one thing I do know, you'll like Gloucestershire, whatever else!"

Beth laughed. "You're a scheming, conniving woman, d'you know that?"

"Yes," agreed Stephanie smugly. "Isn't it fun?"

Beth stayed on until Finn's boat was ready for the trip to Greece – partly because she was dreading the decisions ahead of her at home, and partly because she found herself very reluctant to leave Stephanie and cheerful little Chloë. They had somehow become important to her, and she was ashamed to find how much she had come to rely on their company, and their unfailing kindness.

But in the meantime, Stephanie had fixed things with Margaret Collier at Aschcombe School, and since Beth was already in Devon, it seemed sensible to call in on Gloucestershire before she returned to her suburban London house.

"I suppose you did come down by car?" Stephanie asked, for she had never seen Beth in or out of a car since they met.

"I – I think so." Beth sounded absurdly uncertain.

"What d'you mean, you *think*?" Stephanie was half-smiling at her.

"I mean, I don't remember how I got here." Beth pushed the hair out of her eyes in a gesture of pure confusion. "I think I just got in the car and drove until I got here." She tried to answer Stephanie's smile. "I know it sounds ridiculous – but I wasn't very rational at that time." She looked at Stephanie's sceptical face and began to laugh. "Anyway, the car is here in the hotel car-park, and I have the keys, so I suppose I must have driven it down!"

Stephanie did not express surprise. She merely shook her head at Beth and remarked cheerfully: "Well, at least it'll make the journey back more of an adventure and less of a chore!" She understood very well how difficult life was going to be for Beth in the near future. It would have been better, she thought, if the poor girl had agreed to go with them to Greece. It would have postponed all these painful decisions until later, when she would be feeling less shocked and distressed. But, at the same time, Stephanie respected Beth's determination to be independent. It meant, after all, that her natural courage and resilience was coming back – and maybe that was more important for her future than a few extra weeks of holiday. But even so, Stephanie's all-too-sympathetic heart ached for Beth and the lonely life she would have to face.

Surprisingly, even Finn seemed concerned, though secretly very relieved that she was not going with them on the boat. He knew his reasons were selfish ones, but he had been brought up short when Stephanie said "How would you feel if you lost Chloë – or me?' – and he now understood a little more about what Beth was going through.

"I rather hope you like the idea of Ashcombe School," he said to her suddenly when they were following Stephanie and Chloë down a lane to yet another picnic. "It would be good for Stephanie to have a friend nearby."

Beth looked at him in astonishment. "She must have lots of friends."

Finn regarded her oddly. "Not like you," he said, and did not elaborate.

Beth could find no answer to this. She could not deny that curious sense of recognition and warmth between Stephanie and herself – as if they were already old friends, tried and trusted through long experience and many vicissitudes. She could not explain it. She was not sure she even wanted to put it into words at all.

"She's lonely, you know," said Finn, pursuing his own thoughts. "And I'm a rotten husband!"

Beth laughed. "I don't think she'd agree with that!"

"Maybe not," growled Finn. "But it's true."

"Come on," urged Chloë, dancing up to them in the speckled sunlight of the lane. "The sandwiches are getting hot."

And both Beth and Finn put private thoughts away.

All too soon, it seemed, the day of departure came. Dancing Lady was loaded with stores and luggage, and it was time to go.

A small group of wellwishers came down to the jetty to see them off – not the excited crowd that had welcomed Finn home – and Beth stood alone, just in front of them, looking up at the gleaming newly-painted hull of the sturdy boat.

"Good luck," said Finn, smiling down at her. "I hope things work out for you," and he gave her a swift, comforting bear hug.

"Goodbye," said Chloë, and then added obscurely: "Remember the tubular bells."

Both she and Finn leapt on board the yacht and stood waving down at her.

And then it was Stephanie's turn. She simply put her arms round Beth and held her tight and didn't say anything at all. And Beth, not knowing how to express all she felt about the extraordinary care and kindness she had been given, could only stumble into incoherent thanks whispered into Stephanie's ear. "I can't tell you – what it's meant to me . . ."

"Hush," murmured Stephanie. "You'll be all right. I know you will." She gave her an extra hug of reassurance and then pulled away, and climbed rather swiftly on board to stand beside Finn.

They cast off. The sails filled with the gentle west wind and the tide began to take hold of the smooth white hull. Gently, quietly, the graceful boat nosed her way out of the harbour towards the open sea. The little crowd cheered and waved her off, and the three figures on board waved back.

Beth lifted her hand to them once, and then stood like stone to watch them go. It seemed to her that the only bit of light and warmth in her grey, centreless days was going from her with those three bright figures in their charmed circle of family happiness. The world seemed very bleak and empty without them, and she knew it was going to be very hard to fill it with other things.

For a long time she stood there, watching the little boat get smaller and smaller, and then at last she turned away from the sunlit sea. Time to go. Time to face facts. Time to stop retreating into dreams, and put her own life in order. No more dreaming of Robert and Little Mo. They were gone – and she was left. That was how it was, and somehow she had got to make some sense out of it. How, she did not know.

I'll drive up to Gloucestershire now. *Today*, she told herself. No point in delaying. I'll go there now – before I have time for second thoughts. I'll ring Margaret Collier. *Now*.

Taking a long breath of resolve, she began to walk back towards the town.

PART II – THE BEEHIVE

Beth arrived in Gloucestershire on a golden summer day which seemed to smile and pose no threat. Her first impression was one of space – high hills and open skies, and wide fields of wheat that moved in a continous green-and-gold dance, like silken water under the gentle wind. The land dreamed in a haze of light, spread out and calm beneath blue air and slow-moving cloud.

But then, as she drove on, the bare hillsides, awash with bleached summer grasses, and the liquid wheat fields, gave way to deep wedges of beechwood that curved and sloped in great masses of green, down into hidden valleys and steep, shadowed lanes.

Here, though the beech woods were tall and thick, sunlight still glanced through them, casting harlequin patterns on the forest floor, and the massive strength of the trees seemed to hold no menace, but only a smooth and lofty serenity. Beth had been dreading this journey and the difficult decisions ahead, but somehow she was already disarmed by the timeless beauty of her surroundings.

The village of Ashcombe stood on the curving south-west slope of a hill, the grey spire of its church reaching for the sky above a close-knit jumble of mossy stone-tiled roofs. Grey stone dominated the houses, too – at least, Beth thought, it was grey, but in this bright wash of sunlight it was a grey laced with many soft shades of weathered gold, and the stone seemed to radiate a kind of luminous warmth that cloaked the whole village in slumbrous well-being.

The sturdy houses stood foursquare with their backs to the slope, sheltered from the fierce north-east winds that raced across the hills in winter. They looked settled and sunk into their natural protection in the arms of the hills, as if they had

31

been there for ever, and as if nothing would ever shake them out of their somnolent calm.

I could like it here, she told herself, trying to summon up a courage she did not have. It feels peaceful and – and undemanding. It doesn't expect too much. And she drove on through the narrow village street in search of her destination. Past the church . . . first on the right up the hill . . . past the playing fields and the cricket club . . . The school is on your left beside a group of pine trees . . . Stephanie's voice came back to her, making her suddenly long for the friendly comfort of her unfailing support. If she was here, it wouldn't be so bad, she thought. And then shook herself mentally and told herself to get on with it and stop dithering. You've got to do this by yourself, she said. No sense being nervous. No-one can help you now.

She came to the school before she knew she was there. It was a long, neat building, made of the same gold-grey stone, with tall windows under pointed Victorian eaves, and a narrow porch with some sort of inscription carved into the lintel above the door. There were other buildings scattered round the tidy green lawns, a couple of modern portacabin extensions, and what looked like a converted stone barn. On one side there was a wide playground with climbing frames, and a kind of low-built tree house fixed to the sawn-off trunk of a chestnut tree that had probably died of old age some years ago.

The grounds looked cared-for – even the drive was somehow well-brushed – and there were flowers all round the main schoolhouse in neatly tended beds. Clearly, someone took a pride in its appearance, and for some reason this comforted Beth a little. Someone loved this place, whoever it was.

As she drew up in the drive near the front of the school, the door opened and a woman stood there, smiling a welcome. Margaret Collier was about forty-five, squarish and sturdy, with a hawk nose and a wide smile, and telltale flecks of grey at the edges of the thick dark hair on her strong, fighting head. She could be formidable when roused, but she was also immensely patient and immensely kind, pre-requisites for the job she had to do.

Now, she looked at Beth with frank, assessing eyes, and held out her hand. "Welcome to Ashcombe School.

You must be tired after that long drive. There's coffee brewing."

Before she could say one word, Beth found herself being led into a sunny staffroom where she was firmly guided into a comfortably shabby armchair and left to look around while Margret got busy with the coffee.

While she was still clattering about with the staffroom china, she said, with her back to Beth: "If it makes things easier, Stephanie Edmondson has told me all about your circumstances, so you needn't go in for a lot of background explanation unless you want to. I should just like to say how sorry I am – how truly sorry – and I hope maybe we can come to some arrangement that will help us both." Having said all this, she turned round, smiling, and came towards Beth with two steaming mugs of coffee in her hands.

"Thank you," said Beth, meaning more than just the coffee. It was a relief not to have to say anything – just to sit and wait for this curious interview to take its course.

"I must tell you a bit about the school," began Margaret, giving Beth time. "It is a local authority primary school, of course, but it also has an old Victorian trust fund which was set up long ago by the school's founder, a certain Josiah Madley. This enables us to add a few extras to the school curriculum, and music is one of them." She glanced at Beth, smiling a little grimly, but did not wait for any comment. "I expect you are all too aware that music is always the cinderella where school time-tables are concerned. Well, all the arts, really, I suppose. They are the first to go when cuts are imposed."

"Yes," Beth nodded a rueful admission. "I know."

"Well, here we are lucky. We are allowed to use the extra funds for outside activities, and we have a good board of governors who administer the cash and argue for us with the local authority when they try to impose more cuts because they think we are better off than most!"

Beth smiled. "They sound very useful."

She's really quite pretty when she smiles, thought Margaret, watching the tension ease a little in the pale, haunted face before her. But aloud she merely said: "Believe me, they are. Invaluable."

Beth said shyly: "I gather Stephanie Edmondson is one of them?"

"Yes. One of the best. A real fighter. And Finn – her famous husband – lends his support when he's home." She paused, and then went on more seriously: "I think Stephanie has told you of our special programme of Music Therapy?"

"Yes. But she didn't enlarge on it."

"Well, inevitably there are some difficult children in any school. But we have built up some kind of reputation for being able to deal with them, so we get extra problem cases sent to us as well as our normal intake. We never refuse a child if we can help it, and we seem to have considerable success in resolving their problems."

Beth looked into the tough, committed face before her with sudden sympathy. "It's – quite a responsibility."

"Oh yes," agreed Margaret at once. "It is – but it's worth while."

"I can see that." Beth met the shrewd, kind eyes with an unexpected sense of cameradie. "Tell me what you do?"

Margaret leant back in her chair and looked at the ceiling. "Well, mostly we just let them make a frightful noise!"

Once again Beth's face lit with amusement. "That sounds easy!"

Margaret grinned. "On the surface, yes. But you have to watch them." She hesitated for a moment, and then continued with her explanation. "We realised, from bitter experience, that the worst scenes and tantrums usually occurred at the beginning of the day – and worst of all, at the beginning of the week. Some of them hated coming to school, some of them hated being told what to do and where to go, some of them just hated everyone and everything."

Beth nodded. She had met some of that before.

"So we decided to have the special music class first, before the serious work of the day began." She glanced at Beth again, half apologetically. "Not that we think music isn't a serious subject – please don't think that." Her smile faded "In fact, as it turns out, it is probably the most important one in the whole curriculum – at least for some."

It was Beth's turn to grin. "I'm glad you see it like that!"

There was a comfortable silence. They were beginning to understand one another.

"So you would be plunged in head first, as it were, if you took it on. I can't pretend it would be easy. It never is. But you could try any kind of music-making you like – let them work out their frustrations in any way they can. Let them sing let them dance – let them shout . . ."

"Let them bang?"

"Exactly. We're not afraid of noise."

"Do you have a lot of percussion instruments?"

Margaret laughed. "Yes. Quite a lot. You can come and see in a minute. But there are funds available for more, if you need them." She turned back to Beth, still smiling. "That's one of the things Finn Edmonson did when he was home – set up a Music Fund. He was very generous."

"He didn't tell me that," said Beth, remembering his curious insistence that she should try for the job at Ashcombe School.

"Oh, there's more to Finn than meets the eye," said Margaret drily. "And Stephanie prods him too, when she gets the chance!" Then she grew serious again. "You would have to take on some of the ordinary subjects as well, you know that? The local authority won't fund the salary for a 'music teacher' per se, but they will 'allow' music to be part of your time-table."

"Big deal," said Beth, and then wondered if she had sounded too disapproving.

But Margaret simply grinned again and said: "Quite so." Then she went on: "So, what other subject would you be willing to offer?"

Beth pushed the hair out of her eyes nervously. "Oh – English? History? Not maths, unless I have to!" She paused, and then added in a tentative voice: "I used to teach art sometimes, but I expect that's outside the curriculum, too!"

"It is," agreed Margaret. "But, even so, it might come in very handy. Do you paint or anything yourself?"

"No," said Beth. "Not seriously. I used to – daub some wishy-washy landscapes. She stopped suddenly. Those were the days when Robert was away and she needed to fill her time – and Little Mo would climb on her knee and dab

35

at her sketch pad with a wobbly brushful of improbable colour.

'Look, Mummie, a cloud. That's a cloud.'

'Purple?'

'Yes. A purple cloud.'

"I – I wasn't very good," she said, trying to steady her voice, "but at least it made me look at the countryside." She took a shaky breath, grasping at normality. "It's very beautiful round here."

"Yes, it is." Margaret noted that silent struggle for composure. "You could take small sketching parties out sometimes, if you liked . . . They love any excuse to get out of doors!"

Beth saw the pattern of her days beginning to emerge. They would be full enough – but still the world felt empty. Her arms felt empty. It was like a dreadful unassuageable ache. It wouldn't go, she knew. It would never go. But maybe she would learn to live with it, somehow. Fill her days with ceaseless activity – that was the only way.

"Let's go and look round the school," suggested Margaret, with surprising gentleness. "There's quite a lot to see – before you make up your mind."

But Beth's mind was made up already. She had to take this job – she knew she had.

"I'm sorry the children aren't here," explained Margaret. "We broke up last week. But some of their work is still on the walls."

They walked round the classrooms, stopping to admire a lot of weird and colourful drawings, and inspected the gym and the school hall with its small working stage, and Beth took note of the sound system, the tape decks and record player and speakers, and privately breathed a sigh of relief. At least she could play them some real music from time to time – if she could get them to listen – and hope it would weave its own magic spell for them when they needed it.

"What happened to your last music teacher?" she asked, wondering if it was tactless to enquire.

But Margaret seemed unperturbed. "She left to get married. It was all rather sudden. Her fiancé got offered a job up north." She sighed. "It's still a man's world, isn't it? She went where he went – not the other way round . . . We missed her very much."

Beth was surprised at this remark. Had it happened some time ago, then? "When did she leave?"

"Last Christmas. We've been without anyone for two long terms."

Beth was concerned. "You will have lost the routine."

"No." Margaret gave a decisive shake of the head. "We kept it up, somehow. As a matter of fact, I took some of the classes myself."

Beth looked at her with respect. "As well as everything else?"

"Oh well," Margaret laughed, "that's an occupational hazard – being a headmistress."

They were strolling now round the playground and the scattered portacabins, and Beth commented on the flower-filled borders round the house.

"Yes, we're rather proud of those. The children do a lot of it themselves. We began it as a punishment – weeding the flowerbeds – but they loved it so much, we had to turn it into a privilege!"

Beth laughed, and stooped to look at some bright marigolds with their faces turned to the sun.

"But Beech keeps the place in order. He's a born gardener. I don't think there is anything that wouldn't grow if Beech told it to!"

"Who is Beech?" asked Beth.

Margaret Collier smiled. "Who is Beech? How can I answer you? He's as much part of this place as the hills – or the ancient beech trees themselves. He used to be head gardener on a big estate round here. Then I think he was a kind of honorary game-keeper when he got too stiff to bend. Now he lives in a cottage up at the edge of the beech woods – along with a menagerie of stray animals that come to him for shelter. He's a bit of a legend round here." She glanced at Beth with sudden warmth. "You should meet him – I think you'd like him. He still does most of the gardens round here – though he is choosy where he goes, they tell me." She stopped suddenly in her tracks, and banged a hand against her forehead, exclaiming: "What a fool I am – I forgot to tell you about the Beehive."

37

"The Beehive?"

"It's a small house – well, a cottage, really – and it goes with the job, if required." She looked into Beth's mystified face and went on to explain: "It belongs to the old Madley Trust, and they allow it to be rented out to any of our staff who need accommodation."

Beth stared at her. "Would – would it be available?"

"It's standing empty now." She saw the glimmer of interest in Beth's shadowed eyes, and said quickly: "Let's go and look at it, shall we?"

Silently, Beth agreed, and followed Margaret's brisk steps past the clump of pines and up a narrow, overgrown path at the far end of the school grounds. The little cottage stood alone in a patch of sunlight between two tall beech trees, and looked away from the path over the sloping valley below and out to the hills beyond. It had a curious, oval-shaped dome for a roof, the old stone tiles cut into small, overlapping layers that formed subtle downward curves – hence the name 'The Beehive', and the little house seemed to crouch in comfortable disarray in its tiny, tangled garden.

"Oh," breathed Beth, "isn't it lovely!" And something about the rounded curves of that dome-shaped roof seemed to offer warmth and shelter.

I would feel safe here, she thought. I could dream dreams and they would not hurt me. Mo would have loved it. And so would Robert . . . all that space to look out at, but somewhere small and safe to be in when you needed comfort . . . Yes, they'd have love it. I might – I might almost feel close to them here . . .

"Mornin', Missus," said a deep, slow voice behind her. "Dozy ol' day, ent it?"

Beth turned sharply, just as Margaret answered the voice with a warm one of her own. "What are you doing here, Beech?"

"Thought I'd keep an eye," he said, laying down the sickle with which he had been attacking the nettles at the edge of the overgrown little lawn. "Can't let 'er go to rack and ruin, can we?" He leant against the tallest of the two beech trees, which were standing just inside the garden wall, and patted it like an old friend. "Need a bit of air, like, don't 'ee? And so

38

do you, an' all," and he stooped to pull some bindweed off a rose that was struggling to survive in the neglected border. Then he straightened up and turned his faded blue eyes in gentle enquiry on Beth's startled face.

"This is Beth Halliday," said Margaret. "She might be needing the cottage – so we've come to look it over."

"Ar," said Beech, nodding a wise head. "Dusty, I dessay. But she'll stand till doomsday, she will."

He turned back then to the nettles and picked up his sickle, as if deliberately leaving the inspection of the cottage to Beth and Margaret wwith instinctive courtesy. It was not his place to persuade, for or against – he was simply there to serve. But whether he was serving the people or the green and growing world of the garden, he wasn't sure, even in his own mind.

Beth looked back once at his gnarled, stiff back stooped over the clump of nettles, and had the strange fancy that he was part of the landscape, like a bent old tree.

Then Margaret put the key in the lock and led her inside. Sunlight poured through the windows in dusty shafts and laid gold fingers on the bare oak floor; outside, beyond the unpolished windows, there was a tantalising glimpse of trees and distant hills. The room itself was smallish and almost circular under the beehive dome of the roof, with an extra bulge at one side for the little kitchen, and at the other for a kind of extension that housed a narrow dining table and four plain chairs. At the back of the room, set in the curve of the wall, was an open fireplace within a rounded arch, and on one side of this was a steep spiral staircase made of open ironwork, leading upwards to the two tiny rooms and miniature bathroom in the roof space above.

"It's very small," said Margaret, looking round with affection, "but it has the basics, and it's very warm and cosy in the winter."

"It's enchanting," Beth answered, in a hushed voice of dream. And then, trying to be practical: "What about the furniture?"

"Oh, that goes with it – if you think it will do. Though, of course, you could always bring some of your own."

"No." Beth was firm. "It's perfect as it is."

There were a couple of good old rugs on the floor, dark-coloured and glowing with a faded richness, and the small sofa and two equally small armchairs looked lived-in and comfortable, all covered in creamy-coloured linen. There was one free-standing hexagonal bookcase-table near the window, but the curving walls made it difficult to place any heavy furniture against them.

Just as well, thought Beth. I like it empty and the honey-coloured stone of the walls makes everything look warm and spacious.

"Well?" said Margaret gently, watching the thoughts chase themselves across Beth's vulnerable face. "What do you think?"

"I think I'll come," said Beth, and then added humbly: "If you'll have me."

Margaret laid a hand on her arm and led her outside. "I am so glad," she said.

Out in the tangled garden, Beech straightened his back again to watch them go. "I'll get 'er shipshape," he said to Beth as she passed, "afore you come. She'll come together with a bit o'care, given half a chance." Then he turned away and went to put his sickle in the toolshed behind the cottage wall.

Beth did not think to ask how he knew she was coming. Or why he was up there tidying the garden already without being asked. It all seemed part of the magic of this dream-like place. She merely smiled and murmured: "Thank you," as she followed Margaret down the path.

And Beech turned back to look after her, with quiet satisfaction in his rheumy eyes. To him, she was just another wounded creature who had found sanctuary in his gentle hills.

It took longer than Beth had expected to get things sorted out in London. It was difficult to sell the suburban house, and even more difficult to make up her mind what to take with her and what to leave behind.

In the end, she had to leave the sale of the house, and its contents, to the agent, and just hope the matter would be resolved one way or the other sometime soon. She had got rid of all the clothes and personal things she did not want to keep (after much heart-searching) and was left with a small pile of necessities which included her books, all the photos of Robert and Mo that she could find, her violin and set of recorders, and the best of her records, C.D's and tapes. The piano, which was a good one, she had to sell. It would not go into the Beehive. She would have to see if she could buy a small one down there.

At the last moment, she reached down Robert's favourite old tweed jacket from behind the door where she had forgotten to look (whether deliberately or not, she could not tell) and put it in the suitcase with Mo's two favourite toys, a stuffed horse called Toggle, and a furry squirrel called Squiggle, because Mo couldn't get his tongue round the 'r's. She knew this was sentimental of her, but somehow she had not been able to bring herself to part with them, and maybe they would make both Robert and Mo seem a little closer . . .

But she did not allow herself to pursue these thoughts any further. She snapped the suitcase shut and carried it out to the car before she could change her mind. For a moment she stood looking back at the empty house – the bare, echoing rooms and the silent garden. Could she still hear an echo of Mo's laughter across the lawn, the sound of his small feet running down the path? . . . Or Robert's deep voice saying: 'Come on, Mo. I'll be the horse . . .' And Mo, upright and sturdy, riding high on his father's shoulders and laughing, always laughing in the sun . . .

No, she told herself. This will not do. I am going away. I am going to begin again. I must. I know I must . . . And, shivering a little, she turned her back on the empty garden, climbed into her car and drove away.

It was almost dark when she got to Ashcombe, but the village was still bathed in golden light, and still seemed quietly welcoming. She drove through it thankfully, almost with a sense of home-coming, and made her way to the little Beehive cottage at the top of the lane. Late evening sunlight glanced off its windows and made gleams of gold on its old stone walls. It almost seemed to be smiling at her as she approached the door.

She found the key under the flower-pot in the porch, as directed, and went inside. The place looked swept and scrubbed, and shining with polish. Someone had been busy. There was a fire laid in the hearth, and a neat stack of small logs tucked in under the stone arch of the fireplace. There was even a box of matches laid strategically nearby, though in this summer weather there was little need for a fire.

She went into the tiny kitchen and found a box of groceries on the table, together with a loaf of fresh, crusty bread, a pint of milk and some brown eggs. There was also a glass jamjar filled with late summer wild flowers – ox-eye daisies and scabious and purple knapweed and delicate harebells – placed carefully in a shaft of sunlight where she could see them.

As she stood looking round her, touched by these signs of thoughtful welcome, a shadow crossed the window and there was a gentle tap at the open door. She turned and found the old man, Beech, looking in at her.

"Everything all right, Missus?" he asked, smiling a creaky smile.

"Yes, Beech, thank you. Did you put the stores there – and the flowers?"

"Ay. Thought they might cheer you up, like. Flowers is cheerful things, given half a chance." He glanced round the little garden, which showed signs of improvement but was still very choked and tangled. "I done a bit, Missus, but she needs a sight more."

Beth nodded. "I'll be able to have a go myself soon. You must show me what to do."

The creaky smile got wider at this. "Some good stuff in there – under the rough. Worth saving."

Beth looked out at the fading twilight and saw other shadows in the garden. But, she suddenly thought, they are not unhappy shades. They are laughing together out there, I do believe . . . and I must learn to laugh with them, not weep at their absence.

Aloud, she said: "What do I owe you for the groceries?"

Beech shook his grizzled head. "Nay, Missus Collier fixed all that. She said to tell you she'd be up directly, and you was to arsk me if there's anything else you wants?"

Beth smiled at him, and the old eyes blinked a little at the sudden transformation in her pale, shuttered face. "No, Beech, thanks. You've thought of everything."

42

He stood looking at her for a moment and then said in his slow, quiet voice: "Well, I'll be gettin' on, then. You can usually find me at the school, come term-time – or leave word at t' post office. I allus calls in there for messages." He hesitated and then added as he turned away: "She's a happy place, this – given half a chance."

Given half a chance, thought Beth, as she watched him stump off down the path. It seemed to be the old man's catchword – his philosophy, probably. Give everything and everyone half a chance, and they'd be all right. Would she?

A happy place, he had said. Well, it was up to her now, she supposed, to make it true. She could probably do it, given half a chance.

Beech was old now – he had to admit it. Nearly as old as the trees he loved, but not quite. The beeches of Swift's Wood had stood there for more than a hundred years – at least, some of them had. Their girth was massive, and they spread smooth solid arms outwards in a wide embrace of their vibrant, growing world, carpeting the earth with gold and brown in autumn, lightening the dark woods with slender furls of young green in spring. Beech didn't feel he had any green shoots left, but sometimes he was tempted to spread his arms like the trees, embracing the whole tingling landscape, the whole life-springing cycle of green and gold.

He didn't, of course. He was not given to extravagant gestures. But his heart inside the gnarled, rheumaticky frame didn't feel old at all, and sometimes – especially in early spring when the green was especially furly and translucent – it felt too big inside the frail walls of his chest and as if it might burst.

It was not so bad in autumn. The turn of the year was a gentle time, usually. Golden and drifting with wood-smoke and dreams . . . curving downwards, like the falling leaves, in a spiral of quiet melancholy. It soothed him with its promise of winter fires and close-drawn curtains, its pattern of slow descent into sleep and untroubled death . . . But spring, now that bothered him. It was too full of newness – too bright – too sharply beautiful. It made him ache.

However, it was nearly autumn now, and he felt tranquil, if a little sad, as he collected firewood among the tall beech trunks in the heart of the wood. There had been a tree down in the first of the autumn gales, and the timber men had left a useful residue of broken branches and off-cuts, with a sprinkling of sawdust and chips from the chainsaws, which would all come in very handy.

He hated to see a tree down, though. When he had heard it crash, something inside him had bled and died with it. He had felt the weight of its death on his soul, and went out to have a look, even in the teeth of the gale. It had lain crosswise, its great smooth trunk resting against a couple of saplings, its ancient roots uplifted into the air above a shallow grave of sandy soil. The wide grey arms had been spread out in helpless defeat – a golden pall of leaves still clinging to every twig. It had seemed to Beech, standing there, that the whole living world mourned the fallen giant – even the very wind that had brought it down, which was still crying like a banshee through the fretted trees of the listening wood.

He shook his head sadly and addressed the tree in his soft warm voice: "Too shaller, them roots o' yourn. Should-a dug deeper, my friend." He reached out and gave the silvery trunk a valedictory pat. "Sleep sound now. They'll put you to good use." And he turned away then, with the wind in his face making his old eyes water.

That was only three days ago. But the loggers had come with their tractors and chainsaws, and now there was nothing left of the tall old beech tree but its stump and a scattering of sawdust . . . and the useful kindling.

Nothing was ever wasted of a tree, he reflected. The leaves went back into the soil, the beech mast made a winter covering for the frozen bluebell bulbs and fed many a scampering squirrel. The twigs got snatched by scroungers like him, or waited for the springtime birds to turn them into nests. Even the uprooted stump left a splendid hollow with an inviting hole at the bottom among the broken stones and sandy rubble – just right for a wandering badger looking for a new sett, or a fox, maybe . . .

"Something will come of it," he said to himself. He often talked to himself out here among the trees. "Someone will use it."

He looked down at the hollow below the uprooted stump

and smiled a cracked and creaky smile. Then he picked up the bundle of firewood, straightened his bent back as much as he could, and made for home.

On the way, he caught a glimpse of some of the school children again. He often saw them scampering about the edges of the wood, especially in the holidays, and their laughter echoed through the trees above the sound of birdsong and tapping woodpecker . . . He liked children, provided they weren't too noisy for the creatures in the wood – or his own special charges up at the cottage. They even came to see those sometimes, especially that little one, Chloë Edmonson, and her mother. He liked Mrs. Edmondson, she was quiet on her feet and didn't fuss, and the little girl, 'the Littl'-un' he called her, was mad about the wild creatures in his care. He had shown her a pheasant's nest with some chicks in it, and she had laughed with delight and said: "So small – like a fluffy ball," and danced about singing it. They had stayed quite a while, that time, admiring everything. It was only after they had gone that he admitted to himself that he was lonely. He hadn't seen them for a while, though, and they said in the village that they had gone off with the father – the famous Finn Edmondson – on his boat to some foreign part. He missed them though, and when he went down to see to their garden at the old Mill House, it seemed very empty and quiet. Still, he supposed they'd come back soon, now that it was nearly term-time.

He wondered if the new young woman at the Beehive would come up to see him and the animals. He liked the look of her, though she was sad, of course, very sad and lonely at present, he knew. But that would pass. They told him at the post office (they always knew things at the post office) that she had recently lost her little boy, and her a widow as well, poor young thing, and all but destroyed with grief, so they said.

Beech knew about grief, too. He had watched his own wife die, slowly and painfully, of cancer, and nothing anyone could do about it either. And his only son had gone and got himself killed in some far-off war he did not understand . . . But those were old stories now, and the grief had sunk down and gone deep, like a dropped acorn buried fathoms deep in leaf-mould. It was still there, but it didn't hurt any more.

That young woman, though. He was sorry about her. He would have liked to tell her about the way feelings sank down and settled into a dark, slow, waiting time before the new growth began . . . He would like to show her the shrivelled seeds in the brown earth waiting for spring, and the fragile, crimson curl of new life in a sprouting acorn . . . But it was too soon, of course, and it was not for the likes of him to tell her what to do.

Still and all, he might be able to show her the animals if she came, like he did with the Littl'-un. Maybe he could even ask her into his cottage to have a cup of tea or something. He had never asked Mrs. Edmondson or the Littl'-un inside either, yet. But he might dare if they came in the winter. He'd have had time to tidy it up a bit inside by then . . . What did children like to drink these days, he wondered? Probably Coke or something fizzy. But, with a vague memory of frosty days and cold hands, he decided to make a special journey to the village on his creaky legs and buy a tin of cocoa.

Maybe, if he got the place shipshape and welcoming, then they would come.

When Beth arrived to take her first special music class, she walked into chaos. One boy was lying on the floor, kicking and screaming in a furious tantrum. He was quite big, about ten years old, she thought, and far too old for tantrums of that kind, but at that moment he was clearly quite beyond reason. Three other boys were fighting in a heap on a pile of mats in one corner. A small knot of anxious girls were clinging together, watching the action with obvious trepidation, and several other children (who, presumably, had attended these classes before) had seized the noisiest of the percussion instruments, including a large bass drum and xylophone, and were making a determined effort to drown out the screams of the tantrum boy on the floor.

"That's Mark," said Margaret Collier, who had come in with Beth to see her through the first few chaotic moments. "He does this every other Monday."

"Why?" Beth looked down at the wildly flailing legs and purple, outraged face.

46

"Family split." Margaret's voice was dry. "Spends the weekend with his father.

Beth nodded. "I see." It made sense, of course, and she could well understand how the boy's grief and rage had to come out somehow.

She looked round the room and wondered which problem to tackle first. As her glance took in the other children and the array of different instruments waiting to be used, she suddenly remembered little Chloë's cheerful, matter-of-fact voice saying: *"Remember the tubular bells." Tubular bells*, she thought. Yes, that's it.

She went up to the little group of scared girls and asked them if they knew where the bells were kept.

"In the cupboard," said one, looking up at her with large, frightened eyes.

"I'll show you," volunteered another, risking a small, tentative smile.

Beth smiled back. It was a start.

Together, she and the girls got out the long, silver tubes and their frame. But instead of setting up in the normal fashion, Beth carried the frame over to where Mark still lay yelling on the floor, and set the framework half on its side across two chairs and fixed the bells so that they hung down right over the boy's frantically flailing legs. Then, with a gentle push to one of the chairs, she lowered the whole contraption a little further so that the silvery tubes made instant contact with Mark's angry feet.

A wonderful cacophany of chimes rang out, and the rest of the class – even the fighting boys – crowded round to enjoy the effect.

For a moment, Mark went on kicking and screaming, but then he seemed to become aware of the extra noise his feet were making, and he paused in mid-scream, took a bewildered, sobbing breath, and looked up at Beth in amazement.

"Well done," said Beth. "That sounds lovely. Do it again."

But though he obediently kicked out at the bells again, the heart had gone out of his rage, and he slowly got to his feet, looking confused.

Margaret, watching all this with a distinct quirk of amusement touching her stern headmistress demeanour, murmured:

47

"You'll do, Beth, you'll do" and went quietly out of the room.

"What we need is an earthquake," said Beth to the class. "Do you think you could manage that?"

They looked at her doubtfully.

"Come on," she urged. "You could make enough noise for an earthquake, couldn't you?"

"Yes!" said the boy with the bass drum, and began to demonstrate his ability with enthusiasm.

I could do with a timp, she thought. And a tam-tam. Nothing makes quite such a lovely rumble as a timp and a tam-tam. But where would I find those in a village school?

"And a tidal wave," she added, aloud. "We could use the gongs for that – and the piano. Look, I'll show you . . . And then we want a fire. A fierce fire. How can we do that? You could *dance* a fire, couldn't you? Flames dance . . ."

She looked at their puzzled faces and smiled. "You see, there's this story – a true story, about an island and what happened to its people . . . It all began one hot day in Japan . . ."

Before the class was over, she knew she had got through to most of them. The musical story grew, the noise was tremendous – and the young faces were enthralled.

Later on, she told herself, I'll be able to put on a record or a tape. I'll get them to listen, too . . . Something peaceful and quiet. They'll calm down in the end . . . But at first, what they need is this. More violence than their own – larger events than they have ever seen – dangers much greater than they have had to bear . . . It will all come down to normal size then. Their own lives won't seem so terrible. And maybe, somehow, I will begin to feel the same . . . Maybe we'll learn together how to accept disaster.

She sat down at the piano and began to play them a tidal wave.

That evening, after her first difficult day, Beth went for a walk on the hills. She needed to clear her head of noise and turmoil – both emotional and physical. For she had to admit to herself that she was already involved in the frustrations and anxieties of the children she had been teaching.

But the high hills received her calmly, reducing all her problems to human size, and she found herself walking in blue air on springy turf, looking out at climbing ridges of beech-clad slopes on one side, and the silvery curves of the winding Severn river below her in the mist-laden vale of Gloucester. It was still early autumn, and the beech trees had not yet turned to their fiery brilliance of russet and amber, but even so there was a faint wash of gold on the thick green leaves, a hint of changing colour to come in the dying fall of the year, when the first frosts would sharpen the soft summer nights. But now it was only the merest promise of change, and the gilded curves of the landscape drowsed in richness and plenty; cornfield and orchard heavy with ripeness, hedgerows alight with hawthorn berry and rose hip, glistening with blackberry and sloe.

Beth had never seen so much burgeoning life spread out all round her, and stopped to admire this golden, fruitful world with new eyes. Unexpected things caught at her attention, like tugging briars, suddenly springing into focus before her startled gaze; one vivid blackberry leaf, already turned scarlet in the late summer sun; the brilliant pink-and-orange symmetry of the ripe spindleberries on a little incandescent tree growing near the edge of the woods; a blue drift of late harebells, fragile and airy among the bleached summer grasses on the hillside, and a small blue butterfly with wings to match; the jewelled gleam of a dewladen cobweb stretched between two tall stems of cow parsley, and the sudden swift uprising of a lark from behind it, almost at her feet, spiralling upwards in a high, sweet burst of song . . . All this seemed to be laid before her in extraordinary brilliance, demanding notice, as if each item had been new-turned in mint-bright clarity especially for her delight.

How Little Mo would love it, she thought, and Robert, too. He never had much time to stop and stare. But then a curious thought came to her, stirring all her held-down grief into breathless uncertainty. *Maybe they can see it all? Maybe they can enjoy it – through me? Or by themselves? . . .* Maybe, she explained to herself, they are here beside me, and I am just too shut-in to my own grief to realise it? . . . I can imagine them running down the green curves of these hills hand-in-hand . . . And if I can imagine it, maybe it is true?

I don't know, she thought. I don't know anything any more. But I am willing to keep an open mind . . . Stephanie told me anything is possible . . . I must let them in, if I can . . . And she walked on across the hills, arguing with herself as she went.

As the sun finally sank into a golden haze far in the west behind the Welsh mountains, and twilight began to cast a blue shade over the hills, Beth turned for home and took the path that led through the edge of Swift's Wood on the way down to the village. The primrose afterglow from the sky still made shadows under the trees, so that her feet walked in dappled patterns of green and gold, and the scented wind sighed in the beeches so that the leaves seemed to have a thousand voices. The path curved round, skirting the wood where the grassy flanks of the hill met the first tall trunks of the beech trees in a golden mixture of light and shade, and it was through this dazzle of gleams and glooms that Beth saw the cottage. It stood alone in a small clearing, and the door stood open to the quiet evening, and the scent of wood smoke drifted across in a blue haze from its single chimney.

Beech saw her standing there, and straightened up from his cluster of sheds and cages, and stood waiting for her to come forward.

"Good evenin' to you," he said, mustering a creaky smile. " 'Tis a pearly old time for walkin'."

For a moment, Beth stood looking from the grey stone cottage to the shadowy trees and the deepening sky beyond, and decided he was right. It was a pearly old time. "So it is," she asknowledged and smiled back.

"I wus just feedin' the critturs," he explained, holding a bucket of scraps out for her to look at.

"Can I come and see?"

The old man nodded briefly. "Wunt do no harm. So long as you'm quiet-like."

Beth followed him, feeling she ought to walk on tiptoe. They came first to a small wire pen with a kennel-like box at one end and a heap of golden-brown bracken at the other. At least, Beth thought it was just a heap of bracken, but when they got close she saw that there was a small russet-coloured fox cub curled up asleep on top of the heap. When the cub heard Beech coming, her ears twitched and she leapt to her feet and skittered foward eagerly to meet him, thrusting her little pointed muzzle at him through the wire in ecstatic welcome.

Beech shook his head at her reprovingly. "Never get you back to the wild, will I?"

"Isn't she pretty!" breathed Beth, enchanted by that small, inquisitive face framed in its soft ruff of baby fur.

"Ar. Handsome is as handsome does," growled Beech darkly. "She's too forward by half!" and he opened the cage to let the cub out. It was only then, when she sprang out and made straight for the safe protection of Beech's arms, that Beth saw that she had one very crooked, mangled leg.

"A trap, that was," muttered the old man, allowing a glint of anger to show in his faded eyes. "Not allowed, they aren't, but they still puts 'em down, the b – " But he changed that into a sort of snort, in deference to present company.

Beth grinned. "Why won't you be able to get her back to the wild?" she asked.

Beech sighed, and stroked the little rufous head with blunt but loving fingers. "She'm too fond," he explained. "Had to be handled a lot, see, because of her leg . . . That meant she'm bonded to me – like to her mother. T'will be hard for her to manage on her own."

"What will you do with her, then?"

"Go slow," said Beech, sounding slow already. "Takes time for a crittur to mend . . ." He looked up at Beth with a sudden sharp gleam of awareness in his eyes, and then turned back to the task in hand. "When she's right agen," he murmured, "then we'll see . . ." Beech was confident that he could call on the expertise provided generously by a local vet, should it become necessary. The donations box in his surgery's reception was regularly filled by contributions from the villagers.

He let Beth touch the soft baby fur, and then put her carefully back in the pen with a small handful of food scraps to keep her happy.

"Got an owl over there," he said, and led Beth over to another, rather taller wire enclosure with an upright tree branch placed carefully inside. There was a wooden nesting box fixed in the angle of the branch, and sitting just inside it on the enclosed piece of tree was a large tawny owl, fast

51

asleep with its head sunk down into its shoulders in a soft haze of feathers.

"Broken wing," said Beech succinctly, eyeing the bird with an assessing gaze "Can't hunt for herself, see? But her'll get away easy enough when the time comes. He looked at Beth and then back at the sleeping bird reflectively. "Wings need air, not cages . . . She'll go when she's ready."

"What do you feed her on?"

"Mice, mostly," said Beech, and fished one out of his bucket. "I puts down a trap or two near the house . . ." He dangled the dead mouse by its tail and dropped it inside the owl's enclosure.

"Had a barn owl once," he remarked, as they moved away. "Rare, they are, these days – and you needs a licence to keep 'un . . . Not enough barns left for 'em, see? And not enough hedgerows for huntin' . . ." He sighed. "It's a tough old world out there," he said.

Beth agreed, feeling rather like one of her own pupils on a visit to the zoo. "How many other charges have you got?"

The old man laughed. It was a sound rather like a blunt saw on a piece of very knotted wood, but it was a laugh, nevertheless, and Beth was curiously reassured by it. "Well now, let's see. There wus two hedge'ogs got run over, but they're both mendin'. They runs to and fro now and just comes back for food. And then there's Blackie, but he's free to come and go, only he *wunt* go."

"Who's Blackie?"

For answer, Beech gave a slow, surprisingly tuneful whistle, and almost immediately a cocky blackbird with a bright yellow beak flew down and settled on his shoulder.

"Reared 'im," he told her. "Fell out of the nest. Never thought 'e'd live, but 'e did." He reached up one gnarled finger and softly scratched the bird's head. "They tells you not to try to save 'em, but some'ow this one just wouldn't die. And now 'e wunt go, the varmint." He turned to Beth, smiling. "If you bangs a spoon on a tin plate, he'll come down to eat from almost anywheres."

Beth looked impressed. "Shall I bang one now?"

"Could do. I got a worm or two." He delved again into his inexhaustible bucket of scraps.

Feeling even more like one of her music class, Beth banged the spoon on the old tin plate Beech offered her, and at once the perky little blackbird sailed down on outspread wings and settled on the ground to inspect Beech's latest offering. Bright-eyed and clever, it cocked its head on one side and considered the matter. Then it seized the worm in its beak and hopped off across the grass to a secluded corner where it could swallow this new titbit in peace.

Beech nodded approval. "Now it's only the reg'lars."

"Who are they?"

The rusty-saw laugh came again. "Well, there's Juniper, the goat. I keeps her for the milk, see? She'll eat anything, including the washing on the line, if I don't watch 'er!" He waved one brown hand at an enclosed piece of green grass where one very white goat was tethered and munching happily at a low branch of hawthorn. Beech gave her a reproving glance, and moved on across the clearing. "Then there's the hens – six o' they – Rhode Islands – and one's setting on a clutch of pheasant's eggs as was abandoned." He took a small plastic scoop of mixed-up mash over to the boxed-in hencoop in the corner of the shed, and lifted up the lid. Inside was a warm brown mound of smooth feathers and, peering up from it, a couple of sharp enquiring eyes in a neat brown head.

"All right, old girl," he said, and moved her a little to one side with a calm, unhurried hand so that Beth could see the clutch of pale, olive green pointed eggs under the hen's ample breast. Then he allowed the proxy mother to settle back over her brood, clucking in vague disapproval at the intrusion.

Beech shut down the lid and turned away. "A good mother, she is – and I'll show you another. Though she's more of a long-termer than a reg'lar."

He took Beth this time through another wire enclosure to a thick clump of bushes – mostly bramble and hawthorn in a tangle of overgrown bracken – at the edge of the main stretch of beechwood, and put his finger to his lips, cautioning Beth to move quietly. Once more, she felt like going on tiptoe, and wondered what to expect.

The old man bent down and lifted one hawthorn branch and one frond of bracken with infinite slowness and care. Then he stood back a little so that Beth could look down. The

53

hawthorn bush and the overhanging brambles had formed a perfect enclosed hollow space, like a green cave, and there in the centre on a soft bed of grass and bracken sat a velvet-coated deer, and beside her, curled up very small, was a tiny fawn. The doe looked up at Beech and his companion with big, anxious eyes but she did not move.

"There then," crooned Beech, "we won't moither you – you're safe enough here," and he let the branch slide gently back to cover their safe haven, and moved away with Beth beside him. "Chased by dogs, she wus," he said, when they had moved far enough. "Dropped her fawn right there almost on my doorstep, you might say. And there she stayed." He smiled his crinkly smile and added softly: "Don't seem afraid o' me, so long as I move *slow*."

Beth thought he probably couldn't do anything else but move 'slow'. Everything he did was slow and quiet.

"Do you feed her too?"

"I do, that. Needs her strength, a nursing mother." He was leading Beth back towards the cottage now, and as he got near the doorway, a sandy-coloured mound of fur lying on the step began to wave a feathery tail. "That's my Jess," he said, a hint of extra warmth creeping into his voice. "And she's going to be a mother too, any day now."

"Puppies? How lovely." Beth stooped to touch the gentle head. She liked dogs. And Little Mo had always been on at her to get one. She wished she had, now.

"Would you like a cup o' tea?" asked Beech, hardly daring to offer such a thing – but he had to try. He had promised himself he would, if she came. And if she said no, well then, there was no harm done.

But Beth didn't say no. She saw the sudden brief flick of anxiety in those blue, faded eyes, and thought to herself with sudden recognition: Why, I do believe the old man is lonely – just like me."

"I'd love one," she said, smiling, "if it's not too much trouble."

Beech grunted amusement. "We've fed them," he grunted. "Now it's our turn!"

So they sat companionably in the deepening twilight beside

54

the open doorway, and sipped hot strong tea out of chipped china mugs.

"Are there other deer in these woods?" asked Beth, wondering about the soft-eyed doe and her fawn.

The old man shook his head. "Nay. Not here. Over to the big estates, there's a herd or two in the parks. She'm just a stray run-away – and she probably wouldn't 've run if she hadn't bin frit." He sighed. "Dogs, you know, when they gets together on the loose, they turns into a pack. No stoppin' them then."

Beth looked out across the quiet clearing round the little cottage. "She seems safe enough up here."

Beech's expression was a little grim. "I wired a goodish piece round her. Not s'posed to, mind." He turned the grimness into a fairly wicked grin. "But I'll take it down when she'm ready to go."

"Will she find her way back?"

"Oh, she'll do that all right. Travel for miles, deer can." He took a noisy swig of tea. "Any road, I told one o' the gamekeepers – a friend o' mine – and he says to leave 'er be till 'er's reared the littl'un. Then maybe he'll come over and take a look."

Beth nodded. It was growing dark now and it was time she went if she was to see her way home. She put her mug down on the step and got to her feet. "Thanks for showing me round,' she said shyly. "They're lucky to have you to look after them all."

Beech shrugged creaky shoulders, but he was clearly pleased. "Ar, well, I reckon most things mend theirselves in time, given half a chance," he said, and the smile behind the old, hazy eyes was warm and full of quiet understanding, but he did not say any more. He just pointed Beth's way down the stony path to the village, and stood in the deepening shadows to watch her go.

Beth took her time to sort out in her own mind the various children and staff at the school, but each day she notched up a few new names, or put names to faces she had already begun to know. With the children from the extra music class it was easy, for they were so individual with their quirks and hang-ups and special problems.

Besides Mark, the Monday tantrum boy, who she discovered was ten now and ought to be behaving more like an adult, there was Lisa who hit every blonde in sight and was caught trying to cut off one small girl's golden ponytail. (It turned out, her father had gone off with a dizzy blonde bombshell.) There was Melissa, who was quite docile until someone tried to play Greensleeves on the recorder, when she went rigid and held her breath until she was blue in the face and then fell on the floor and screamed. (Beth hadn't got to the bottom of that one yet.) And there was Paul, who was always running off to the playground gates where he threw stones at any red car that came along. (That one was easy – his mother had an 'uncle' with a red car and was always zooming off somewhere with him. Paul informed Beth in cold tones that all uncles were bad and he'd *kill* them all if he could.) Then there were the twins, James and Ann, who fought everyone who came near or tried to separate them, and refused to do anything at all unless they could do it together. There was also one small girl called (ridiculously) Lulu, who sat in a corner and rocked herself to and fro singing softly to an ancient rolled-up sleeping bag which she refused to give up, and brandished a pointed pencil at anyone who tried to take it away. (Her beloved elder brother had run away from home.) And there was George, who was large and lumbering, older than the others but not considered ready yet to go on to the big comprehensive school in the town, so he was staying at Ashcombe a year too long. He was mostly slow and quiet, but would suddenly fly into violent rages when he smashed everything in sight, including any of his own work that had shown signs of being successful. (He was good with his hands.) No-one could reason with him then, but he usually subsided in the end, though Beth could sense a deep and awful frustration inside him. There were others in that special class, too, whose needs didn't seem quite so pressing, but none of them were easy to manage, and several of the larger boys were sometimes very stroppy, (one even waved a pen knife once) until Beth suddenly got tough, and then they looked at her with grudging respect and subsided.

But through all this mayhem and bedlam (as it sometimes seemed to Beth's battered senses) the dramatic story of the Japanese island was growing, the noise was slowly turning into something approaching music, and the class – even the worst misfits – were beginning to co-operate. "I believe we are writing an opera," she told them. They weren't impressed. But they were getting more and more involved, and some of them could sing like angels.

As to the rest of the school, whose different forms she taught from time to time, they were easy to deal with on the whole, and friendly, and the faces were becoming individuals one by one, especially when she taught them the violin or the recorder, or got them to write their own extraordinarily inventive adventure stories.

Then there was the staff, easier to sort out, as there were fewer, but perhaps not so easy to get to know. There was Bill Lewis, the oldest, known affectionately as Old Bill, who had been with the school for years and taught maths with fierce, old-fashioned discipline, and ruled his own form with a rod of iron, but who was, inexplicably, popular with everyone (though the more mischievous boys watched him somewhat warily). Then there was little Miss Brown (no-one seemed to call her Ruth, though it was written clearly on her coatpeg behind the staffroom door), who was birdlike and wispy, and looked after the Reception Class with enormous patience and no sign of dismay even at the most copious tears. Her cheerful colleague with the Kindergarten, Laura Fredericks, was the opposite – large, positive and friendly, rather like a well-meaning St. Bernard. She seemed to tackle all crises with unflagging energy and good temper, and everyone – children and staff alike – called her Freddie. (Beth did not go near the Reception and Kindergarten classes any more than she could help. The smallest ones were too near Mo's age – too like him in their firm young limbs and unblunted joy in living. She was afraid she might do something stupid and her arms might go out and clasp those sturdy little bodies in a fierce, possessive embrace, trying to escape an emptiness that could never be filled. So she mostly stayed away from them and concentrated on the other children who needed her more and offered no such immediate temptation.) Beside these, there was young Peter Green, yellow-haired and athletic, in charge of a lively form of ten-year-olds, and who also taught games when it was fine and chess when it was not. He was nearly always friendly and approachable, except when the weather spoilt a football match with a rival junior school, or ruined a cricket match just when his side was winning. He also sometimes joined forces with Debbie Arnold, the other fourth form teacher, who liked taking parties on 'history delving expeditions' and was keen on archeology and Roman villas. The children called her 'Digs' behind her back (which she well knew and secretly rather liked) and 'Yes, Miss Arnold' to her face, because she was quite strict and stood no nonsense from anyone.

Beth found them all quite welcoming and easy to get on with, though she was a little scared of Debbie Arnold, and went a bit cautiously with old Bill Lewis who was known to be short-tempered, though she hadn't seen any sign of it yet. The only thing that slightly puzzled her, as she gradually got all these new faces clear in her mind, was that there was no sign of little Chloë Edmondson in any of the classes, and no welcoming word from Stephanie, who had been so keen for her to take this job. But, on reflection, she supposed they must have stayed on in Greece while they had the chance, and would probably return later in the term.

She was actually thinking about this one evening as she pottered about the little Beehive garden, trying to work out which bit needed her attention most, when she saw her headmistress, Margaret Collier, coming up the path.

"How nice," she said, straightening up and laying down the fork she had been too undecided to use.

"Are you busy?"

"Not really – I don't know where to start!" She laughed. "I need Beech to tell me what to do." She glanced at Margaret's face, and added swiftly: "Let's put the kettle on," for it seemed to her that Margaret was looking far too grave and troubled for this scented autumn evening.

Together they went inside, and Beth made some coffee, wondering with increasing uneasiness what was behind Margaret's silence. She seemed as kind and friendly as ever, but something was clearly wrong, and she looked at Beth now in some distress, as if not knowing what to say. Had Beth's unorthodox methods with her special music class been too noisy and chaotic even for her? Was she, perhaps, having second thoughts about Beth's appointment?

Beth carried the cups over to the two armchairs near the empty grate, and said awkwardly: "I'm sorry I haven't lit the fire yet."

Margaret looked up from the deep armchair and took the cup from her gravely "Sit down, Beth. I'm afraid I've got some rather awful news for you."

Beth sat down and waited. She was used to awful news. What else could happen in her life that was awful enough to matter?

"It's about Stephanie," began Margaret. "Stephanie Edmondson." She paused, and seemed to draw a long, steadying breath.

"Stephanie? What about her?"

"I – I'm afraid she's dead, Beth. She died in Greece a week ago."

Beth looked at her in utter disbelief. "She can't be. They were going off on such a lovely holiday together." Her voice trailed off as she saw Margaret's sorrowful, compassionate expression. "What happened?"

Margaret sighed. "Well, the Greek doctors said it was a brain tumour which caused a massive stroke, and the post mortem confirmed it." She shook her head. "Whatever it was, it happened very suddenly. And the worst of it is, Finn was away at the time, inspecting some site or other on one of the smaller islands nearby, and the little girl, Chloë, sat beside her mother for three days alone until he returned."

"Oh, my God." Beth's voice shook. "How absolutely dreadful." She thought of the bright, eager child, Chloë, sitting alone in that silent room beside a mother who did not stir, and shivered. "Where was everyone? Why did no-one come?"

"A rented villa, on the main island away from the town . . . The girl who cleaned it only came once a week . . . Chloë spoke no Greek, so she just sat there.

Tears stung Beth's eyes. "How – ? How has she taken it?"

"That's the trouble," said Margaret grimly. "That's where you come in. She won't speak."

"*Won't speak?*"

"Won't, or can't." Margaret shook her head again in helpless sympathy. "It's the shock, they think. She is –

Finn says she has totally cut off from everything, and she won't even let him touch her."

Beth stared at her. "That means she probably blames him – ?"

"I think so, yes."

"Oh, the poor child." She paused, trying to assemble her own shocked thoughts. "Will she – ? You said that was where I come in?"

"Yes, I did. She will have to go into your special class, you see. Finn is bringing her home. He has taken her to see the appropriate medical specialists. Apparently, it has been recommended that she continue her schooling in the normal way. He asked specially if you would be there to look after her. He seemed to think you might be able to get through to her, having been so close to her mother."

Beth looked doubtful. "I don't know . . . She might hate me too, because I couldn't prevent what happened."

A sudden, awful thought came to her, then. If she had gone to Greece with them, as Stephanie had planned, would she have been able to prevent it? Probably not – but at least she could have been there for Chloë, and maybe avoided this latest catastrophe. "Oh," she murmured, agonised, "*I should have been there.*"

Then she began to think back to those strange conversations that had taken place between her and Stephanie while they walked on the Devon hills or sat looking out at the sea from the hotel windows . . .

"Why?"

"Because I need to know . . ."

"Sometimes I wish Chloë would get attached to someone besides me . . ."

"It's dangerous."

Yes, it was dangerous. Love was always dangerous. You thought life was safe and full of happiness, and then it was suddenly quenched and you were in the dark . . .

"I wonder," she said slowly, and looked into Margaret's face with painful intensity, "do you think Stephanie *knew* this was likely to happen?"

Margaret hesitated. "I don't know. She didn't confide in me to that extent. Perhaps not to anyone." Once more there was a fractional hesitation. "But – something our local doctor said when I told him made me wonder."

Beth was still looking at her. "Yes?"

Margaret looked back with frank uncertainty. "He said it was very sad, *but not altogether unexpected.*"

Beth nodded, confirming her own thoughts. "Then she knew . . ." She sounded suddenly quite certain. "That's what this was all about."

Margaret did not contradict her. She simply sighed again, and said: "Well, the child will be home tomorrow – in time for school on Monday . . . Finn thought she would be better occupied, even if she doesn't communicate."

"Yes, that makes sense." Beth was in agreement with that, though she too blamed Finn for his incurable rest-lessness which always took him away from his family when they needed him most. "How is Finn coping?" she asked, seeing that careless buccaneer's smile quenched in sudden, bewildering grief.

Margaret shrugged. Clearly, she had the same reservations about Finn and his wandering. "I haven't seen him yet, of course. He sounded – shattered." Then she added honestly: "And very concerned about Chloë."

"I should hope so," snapped Beth, and then was sorry to sound so disapproving.

Margaret looked at her with understanding. But if she felt the same way, she did not say so. Instead, she quietly went on to practical matters. "I'm so sorry to spring this on you. But I thought you'd rather know about it before seeing Chloë on Monday."

"Yes, of course."

Margaret's pleasant voice slowed a little. "And there's the funeral next week, too. I expect you'll want to go to that – unless you would find it too upsetting?"

The poor girl, Margaret was thinking. She's had all this before – twice over. It really is most unfair.

"No," said Beth bleakly, "it's no good being upset, is it?" No good. Generous, warm-hearted Stephanie, whom she had grown to love in so short a time, was gone, like the other two she loved – and there were no tears left to shed, no words left to say.

But then she remembered suddenly the rest of that curious conversation, Stephanie's gentle voice insisting: *"But I wouldn't have it otherwise, would you? Every moment – every small happening. Don't you see? You still have them – all those precious days . . . You only have to remember . . ."*

Yes, Stephanie had known then how precious the days with Chloë and Finn were. But she hadn't wept about it, and she hadn't been afraid. She had simply rejoiced in the moments she had, and still found the time to offer Beth consolation. *You only have to remember.*

"I'll be there," she said slowly, but I'm not sure Chloë should be."

"No," agreed Margaret. "We'll keep her in school that day." She was eying Beth's startling pallor with some misgivings. But again she thought it better to keep to practical arrangements. "Stephanie already had a housekeeper, since they were away such a lot with Finn. They needed someone to keep an eye on the place. And no doubt Finn will keep her on. But I don't know how much comfort she will be to Chloë."

Beth stirred out of distant thought. "What's she like?"

"Mary Willis? Oh, kind enough, and very practical. A real village home-body. But – " One more she hesitated a little. "A bit lacking in imagination, I should think she'd be way out of her depth with this."

Beth sighed. "Aren't we all?"

Margaret agreed, still worrying about that pale, strung look of inexpressible grief. "I'm sorry, Beth," she said again. "You must think life is nothing but blow after blow at the moment."

Beth's answering smile was dim and fragile. "Oh well," she said, keeping her voice surprisingly steady. "If we can help little Chloë, perhaps something good may come out of it."

When Beth saw Chloë sitting alone in the corner of the music room, with the rest of the class milling noisily around her, it was difficult to believe it was the same bright-eyed, independent little girl she had known before. The flower face was closed and pale, as if blanched with sudden frost, the fly-away, silver-gilt hair hung lank and flat on her head, and the wide grey eyes had somehow lost their luminous distance and looked strangely veiled and opaque. She did not show any sign of recognition when Beth came towards her, and did not answer in any way when Beth said gently: "Hallo, Chloë."

The only time there seemed to be a flicker of response was when Beth mentioned the tubular bells and suggested that someone should get them out. Then, it seemed to Beth's watchful gaze, some faint spark of recollection came into the small blank face, but Chloë did not move or make any attempt to speak. She just sat there, docile and quiet, and let the activities of the class flow round her unnoticed.

But there was one rather curious result in all this hidden, unspoken drama. The tantrum boy, Mark, suddenly decided to take Chloë under his wing. "It's all right," he said to Beth, in a firm, no-nonsense sort of voice. "I'll look after her." And from then on, he did. He led her by the hand when she needed to go from one class to another. He left her sitting quietly close to the window, and positioned himself beside her or in front of her to fend off persistent intruders asking awkward questions. He joined in the music class activities himself when asked, (he sang rather well, and could cheerfully tackle small solos without shyness) but he always kept a weather eye on Chloë's small, lost figure and never left her alone for too long.

Beth was amazed at the transformation. Here was a boy who had been almost unbearably sunk into self-centred anguish and rage over his parents' quarrels, now suddenly becoming the most thoughtful and sweet-natured boy in her class, with absurdly chivalrous kindness oozing out of every pore. She couldn't really believe what she was seeing, but she was thankful for it while it lasted. Though Chloë didn't exactly respond, Beth noticed that her hand went quite readily into Mark's, and she went where he told her without demur.

There's no accounting for what children will do, she thought. We always under-estimate them. Then she got on with the day's work, and tried not to let the pale, sad shadow of Chloë haunt her too much.

When the time came for the children to go home, Beth wondered if Finn would come to collect his little daughter, but the housekeeper, Mary Willis, came instead. Beth did not see how she could discuss Chloë's condition in front of the child herself, so she did nothing more than say: "Do let me know if there is anything I can do," and smile as encouragingly as she could at the silent child beside her.

Mary Willis was briskish and plumpish and competent, with a cheerful disposition and kind brown eyes that were probably a lot more observant than they let on. But she had no idea what to do for the small girl in her charge. "Fair flummoxed, she was," she told her friends, being more used to practical things than such bewildering patterns of behaviour. She could only make the little girl's life as pleasant as possible, with nice hot meals that usually went uneaten, and nice clean clothes that the child allowed herself to be dressed in but showed no interest in at all. It was hard for someone like Mary, who knew how to make people comfortable and liked to have her efforts appreciated, but she did her best and tried not to mind when even Finn Edmondson failed to give her a single smile, let alone a word of thanks.

Now, she looked at Beth with sudden gratitude, for here was someone who clearly understood what a difficult time she was having, and actually seemed to want to help. "Thank you, Miss – ?" she began, sounding almost shy.

"Halliday," said Beth, smiling. "Mrs. Halliday – but most people call me Beth." She watched the shyness begin to recede from Mary's round face, and went on encouragingly. "I'm living in The Beehive just now. D'you know where that is?"

Mary nodded.

"You can always come and see me there," Beth suggested. "And bring Chloë. We've met before, you see, – on holiday." She smiled again, noting with an odd flick of detachment that her face ached with smiling – almost as much as her heart ached for Chloë and Finn, and for her friend Stephanie who was no longer with them. "I think Chloë might like the Beehive," she added gently, and waited while Mary Willis nodded briefly again, and took Chloë's limp hand in hers and turned away.

Well, I've done what I could, thought Beth. But I wish I could talk to Finn. He ought to know what to do, if anyone does . . . Then she collected her belongings from the staffroom and walked the short distance from the school to her little house at the top of the lane.

She was getting to like living in the Beehive, as much as she liked living anywhere at present. It was a welcoming

64

little place, warm and compact, and no trouble at all to keep in order. But even so, going home after school was still an ordeal. The world was still terribly empty when she dared to think about it, and the silence of her lonely evenings still echoed round her even in those small rooms. Mostly, she went out again, walking on the hills or in the depths of the turning beechwoods, or tried to tame the jungle in her tiny garden. It was better to get tired – tired enough to sleep and not lie awake aching for Little Mo and his laughter, and for Robert's comforting arms. She found herself sometimes getting confused in her own mind about the timing of those tragic events, and saying to herself with irrational anger: Robert ought to be here to comfort me. And then being ashamed of her own weakness and muddled thinking.

She had hoped that working with the children of Ashcombe School would help to assuage the long ache for Little Mo, and to some extent it did. There was plenty to do, plenty of sympathy and affection to give. The needs were there, she knew, and clearly evident. But though she was already getting involved with a number of children, she was aware deep down that the awful hole in her own life was not really becoming filled, perhaps would never be filled. She had just got to learn to live with a permanent ache inside, and use her days as fully and usefully as she could. Perhaps some kind of peace would come in time. And perhaps she would not always feel so alone.

But this time when Beth got home, she found that she was not alone. The old man, Beech, was in the garden. He was stooping over a tangled flowerbed at the far end of the bumpy grass that was supposed to be a lawn, and patiently disentangling some half-choked late chrysanthemums that were trying to bloom, in spite of the couch grass that was trying to smother them. He had already cleared a small space in front of the boundary wall, and had dug a clean-looking patch of freshly-turned earth in the opened-up area.

The old man straightened up when he saw Beth, and touched one finger to his unruly thatch of white hair in a curiously old-fashioned salute. "Arternoon," he said, and then added in his soft old voice: "I wus hopin' you'd come – I brung you a tree."

65

Beth went across to him, startled. "A tree?"

"Only a little 'un," he explained, and then paused, as if the phrase reminded him of something. "Missus, I heard about the trouble at Edmondson's – and about the little 'un Chloë. Really sorry I wus to hear it." He sighed. "A lovely lady, Missus Edmondson, if ever there was one."

"Yes," agreed Beth slowly. "She was."

"That's why I brung the tree," he said, and stooped to pick up a small flower pot with a seedling beech growing sturdily in it.

Beth looked puzzled. But she put out a finger and touched the green, furled leaf at the top of the tiny sapling.

"I allus plants a tree," said Beech softly, "when there's a gap, like." His creaky smile rested on Beth. "That way, there's allus something new."

Beth looked at him with tears in her eyes. It was such a simple philosophy but today, in this sungilded autumn garden, it made sense.

"What a good idea," she said, and smiled at him through a dazzle of tears. "Where shall we put it?"

Beech pointed to his newly turned patch of earth. "Her won't block the view here, however tall she gets, and she'll have plenty o' room to grow." He looked into Beth's face for a moment, and then quietly handed her the seedling in its pot, and a small, shabby trowel.

"What do I do?"

"Just make a hole," he said, gently guiding her hand to the right spot, "and put in a handful of this here leaf-mould . . . It'll feel like home, then." He watched tranquilly as Beth obeyed him, and then nodded approval. "Now, jest tap 'er – she'll come out easy-like, and you wunt disturb 'er."

Beth did as she was told, and the tiny tree with its neat rootball of soil was transferred to the hole and stood bravely upright."

"Firm 'er in a bit," instructed Beech, "or she'll loosen in the wind. But not too much, hers got to breathe."

Obediently, Beth followed instructions, and knelt back on her heels to admire the vivid green of the new young leaves.

"There!" crooned Beech, in his most caressing voice.

"You'll do nicely now." And he smiled at Beth again over the head of the little tree.

"Would you like a cup of tea?" asked Beth, remembering how anxiously Beech had offered her one, and wanting to return the compliment. It seemed to her, somehow, that a ritual was being established that might be important.

"Ar, I wouldn't say no," agreed Beech, and followed her politely up the path.

It was still a golden afternoon, and Beth brought a chair out into the sun. But when she turned back for a second one, Beech protested sturdily: "Nay, I'll sit in the porch," and lowered himself creakily on to the wooden seat by the small front door.

So once again they sat drinking tea together, and found the companionship unexpectedly pleasant.

"What do you think we ought to do about Chloë?" Beth said suddenly, not quite knowing why she asked.

Beech considered. "Wunt speak, is it?"

"Won't, or can't. She seems . . . totally cut off, somehow."

"Ar." The old man nodded. "Too much to bear, for a little 'un." He paused, as if thinking of things a long way off. "Had a dog once that grieved," he said at last. "When my missus took ill and died . . . wouldn't eat. Laid in 'is basket all day – turned 'is face to the wall, like . . ."

He was silent so long that Beth prompted him gently. "What happened to him?"

He sighed and turned to look at Beth out of misted blue eyes. "'E mended in the long run. Like me, 'e got used ter things . . . Came a day when the sun shone and 'e decided it was good to be alive arter all." He shook his head slowly. "You can't order it, Missus. It jest comes when the time is right . . . And she's young. She'll mend – *given half a chance.*"

Beth smiled. That phrase again. It was becoming almost a catchword in her mind. Said in that tranquil, slow voice of Beech's, it sounded like a spell.

"I hope you're right," she said.

It was later that evening when Finn came. He stood in the doorway, looking haggard and grim, and Beth was shocked

67

at the change in him. Gone was the wicked buccaneer's grin, gone was the light of adventure in his blue, sailor's eyes. Even the hair on his head and his curly golden beard seemed to have lost its spring.

"Can I come in?" he said.

And Beth, almost without thinking, put her arms round him and answered: "Oh, Finn, I'm so sorry – " and drew him inside. But she felt his strong, wiry body stiff and unyielding within her swift embrace, and withdrew at once. Finn was far out on a tide of private desolation – like she had been – and could not be reached at present.

However, he managed a faint attempt at a smile, and said gruffly: "Yes. Well, now I begin to understand what you have been going through."

Beth did not comment on that. She went through to her tiny kitchen and made some coffee.

"How was Chloë when she got home from school?" she asked, bringing in two mugs of coffee. "Did it seem to have upset her at all?"

"No." Finn shook his head. "There was no change." He sighed, and sipped gratefully at the scalding coffee. "That was really what I came to see you about . . ." He paused, and looked vaguely round the room, not really seeing his surroundings. "I expect you'll be at the funeral," he added, with apparent irrelevance, "but there won't be much time to talk afterwards." He made a face of some distaste. "It will be full of gushing friends."

Beth was a little shocked. "Finn, they all loved her."

"Oh, I know, I know." He shrugged helplessly. "But they all go on so."

Beth thought it best not to answer that, so she waited for Finn to get back to Chloë. But when he failed to say any more, she gave him a gentle nudge. "Tell me what has been happening to Chloë, since?"

Finn rubbed a weary hand over his face. "Well, nothing really. That's the trouble. When I – when I got back from the Spirios site and found them . . . His voice shook for a moment and then steadied itself, "Chloë was just sitting there, holding Stephanie's hand, staring at nothing. She did not seem to be distressed exactly – just blank."

"Did she know you?"

Finn's face darkened. "Yes. I think so. Though she didn't speak. But she – she shrank away from me, as if I was an enemy." Once again his voice shook, and once again he controlled it. "She's been like it ever since."

Beth looked at him in wordless sympathy. It was a pretty awful situation for Finn, whichever way you looked at it. Then she said carefully: "How is she at home? What does she do?"

"Nothing much." Finn's voice was still rough with anxiety. "She does what she's told to do – gets up when Mary wakes her in the morning – goes to bed when Mary takes her upstairs in the evening."

"Does she do anything for herself – like dressing or undressing?"

"No. She just sits there, quite passively, with her hands in her lap, waiting to be ordered about. It's so – unlike her."

Yes, Beth thought sadly. It was totally unlike the lively, independent little girl she had known that summer.

"Doesn't she – play with her toys, or read, or anything?"

"No. Mostly, she sits staring out of the window at the garden. Occasionally she does wander out into it on her own and drift about out there, rather aimlessly. But she shows no interest in anything – and she positively hates me."

"Oh Finn, that can't be true."

"I'm afraid it is," said Finn, and once again his hand went up to his face, covering his eyes. "She blames me for Stephanie's death – and I can understand why. I blame myself, too. I wasn't there when I was needed." There was a world of self-reproach in his deep voice now. "Maybe, if I *had* been, I might've been able to save her."

Beth knew she had to protest at this. Finn must not be left with this dreadful weight of guilt on top of everything else. "Finn, from what Margaret Collier has told me, there was nothing you could have done to prevent it. You might have protected Chloë from extra stress, but you couldn't have saved Stephanie. You must believe that."

Finn shook his head, unconvinced. "I don't know – I just don't know . . ."

"There was no indication that anything was wrong, was there?"

For a moment Finn hesitated, and then looked up at Beth with piercing directness. "Nothing specific – no. But I might've guessed, if I hadn't been so wrapped up in my own affairs."

"Why?"

"Oh – there were small clues – if only I'd noticed them. She had sudden fierce headaches, which she put down to migraine. And she complained once or twice of numbness in her hands. Steph was very practical. She hated anything hampering her fingers . . ." He hesitated again, as if remembering forgotten things. "And she did go to see her own doctor, and got herself sent on to a specialist, but she told me it was nothing to worry about." He paused and then added in a voice of bitter condemnation: "And I believed her."

Beth nodded slowly. It only confirmed her own suspicions that Stephanie had known what was likely to happen – if not when it might occur.

"I always used to think," said Finn, in a strange, cold voice, "that something might happen to me – though I didn't worry about it much." He drew a sharp breath of pain. "It was only recently that I came to realise Stephanie worried about me. Something she said made me wonder – and I was ashamed of putting her through all that every time I went off on some jaunt or other . . . But – but it never occurred to me that it might be Stephanie – that something might happen to *her*." He shook his head again, appalled by his own selfishness. "And now there's Chloë – and I'm failing her, too." His eyes glittered with self-contempt as he stared at Beth. "D'you know, she won't even eat at the same table? Not that she eats much at all these days . . . I tried having us both in the dining room together, but she would only eat in the kitchen with Mary. Then I tried having Mary in to eat with us, but that didn't work either. Chloë just sat there refusing to eat with us, waiting to be taken back to the kitchen." He rubbed a weary hand over his sparkless hair in despair. "I've tried talking to her, coaxing her – or ignoring her and leaving her alone. Nothing seems to register. I don't know what else to do." There was despair in his voice, too.

"You have to be patient," said Beth, remembering Beech

70

and his gentle certainty. *"She's young. She'll mend – given half a chance."* But she did not think Finn was ready to accept the old man's tranquil philosophy yet.

Finn almost snorted, but turned it into a sigh. "That's why I came to you. Mary Willis is kind enough, but she doesn't really understand the situation."

"And you think I do?"

A glimmer of a smile touched his gaunt face. "At least you have an inkling. I just – I would be so grateful if you would keep an eye on her. Mary told me you'd spoken to her, and asked her to bring Chloë round. She was very pleased – " He looked at Beth with sudden fierce entreaty. *"Please*, Beth help her if you can. There's no-one else who understands as well as you – "

Beth was distressed that Finn expected so much of her. "I'll do anything I can, of course. But I can't promise to be successful." She was regarding Finn with some anxiety. "I think it has to come from you, in the end."

Finn got up, almost violently, and began to pace up and down. "No. I only make things worse. I'm just an added source of stress – and anger." He took a deep breath and turned round on Beth. "That's why I'm going away again."

Beth was horrified. "You *can't*! Not now. She needs you, Finn. You're all she's got."

"She doesn't need me." His tone was clipped and dry. "She dislikes me intensely – and she's better off without me."

Beth looked at him in helpless disapproval. "I think you're wrong."

"Probably," he snapped. "Everything I do is wrong, as far as Chloë is concerned." Then he tried valiantly to sound calm and reasonable. "No, I'll keep out of her way for a bit. She's got Mary, and if you will just – just watch over her a little, I think she'll have more chance of recovery." He gave Beth an awkward, appealing glance that reminded her of a nervous schoolboy. "I – I'm not being callous, Beth – I really do think it's best . . ."

Beth shook her head at him sorrowfully. "Very well. But things are never that cut and dried, Finn. Can't you wait a while and see what happens?"

"No," he said violently. "I can't. I can't bear to see her like this – and to know that I'm making it worse."

Then Beth understood that nothing she could say would make any difference. Finn had to go away and work out his own hurt and grief, – and find his own salvation – before he could be any help to his little daughter. She reflected with some bitterness that it was typical of a man to shrug off responsibility and go off on his own. A mother wouldn't be able to do any such thing. She would feel bound to stay, whatever happened. And, with a real spurt of anger, she added to herself, at least he's *got* a child to worry about, whereas I . . ." But she would not go on with that. Instead, she found herself trying to reassure him.

"I'll do my best," she promised. "But you will have to come back in the end.

Finn nodded briefly. "I know that. Just give me time – give Chloë time. And try not to blame me too much."

"I don't blame you at all," said Beth roundly, not being entirely truthful. "I just hope we can put some of it right."

"Oh, so do I," said Finn, 'So do I." And he walked away from her out of the door and didn't look back.

Beth went to the funeral, willing herself not to be upset or to think of her own past tragic events, and managed to get through the simple service without becoming visibly distressed. But when a grave-faced Finn, looking taut and grim, invited her up to the house with the other mourners, she gently refused.

"No, Finn, thanks. Chloë's still waiting at the school. I'll take her home and give her some tea. She's better out of harm's way till this is all over."

Finn nodded gratefully and said no more. But Mary Willis, overhearing, came up to her and said shyly: "Shall I come and fetch her, then?"

Beth shook her head. "I'll walk over with her later on. You'll have enough to do."

They smiled at one another, like shy conspirators, and Beth walked away from the village church with its tall, silver-grey spire, and made her way back to Ashcombe School. The children were just going home for the day, but Chloë was still sitting passively in the classroom, waiting for someone to tell her what to do next. And standing protectively beside her, also waiting, was the tantrum boy, Mark.

"No-one came," he said, in accusing tones.

"It's all right," Beth reassured him. "Chloë's coming home with me today. Just for a while," she added to Chloë's blank face, in case the idea seemed too alarming.

But Chloë made no protest. She simply looked up at Beth out of grey, sparkless eyes, and allowed herself to be led away.

Mark came with them as far as the end of the school drive, still looking anxious, and Beth turned to him there and asked: "How are you getting home?"

The boy shrugged careless shoulders. "On my own. Mum's at work."

"I see," said Beth. "Well, go carefully." But a plan was beginning to form inside her head, only she would have to talk to Margaret Collier first. "Chloë'll be all right now," she added, to those anxious eyes of Mark's, and went off up the path to the Beehive, with Chloë's hand in hers.

If it was Mo, she thought, I'd be talking to him all the way home, pointing out things and enjoying things – that is, when he wasn't doing the same to me! Maybe, if I keep talking to Chloë, she will begin to respond. Anyway, I have to try.

So she stopped to admire the bright red berries of a rowan tree, and stood underneath a chestnut tree, admiring the new-turned gold of the leaves and waited for a shiny conker to fall down. When one landed to her feet, she stooped and picked it up, turning it in her hand to let its glossy brown shell catch sparks in the sunlight. "Look!" she said to Chloë. "Isn't it smooth? Just like polished maghogany." And she put it into Chloë's slack, uncaring hand. But she fancied that the small fingers tightened a little round their latest prize.

Small things, she said to herself. Keep to the small things. Small beginnings. Don't expect too much.

She kept it up all the way to the Beehive, and then left Chloë sitting in the sunny porch while she fetched some tea and a couple of rock-buns she had made earlier. She didn't bother much with cooking these days, since Margaret Collier had wisely insisted that she ate a school dinner every day, there wasn't much need for anything else. But lately, people had

73

begun to arrive on her doorstep at teatime, with the flimsiest of excuses – she suspected that it was a bit of a conspiracy among the staff, and even among the villagers, so she kept a cake-tin full of buns just in case.

First of all it had been little Ruth Brown, fluttery and shy, explaining that she was 'just passing' and couldn't stay long, but in fact staying for nearly two hours of gentle, enthusiastic chit-chat about Ashcombe village and the various children she cared for in her classes. Then came her cheerful colleague, Freddie, bearing a plate of fairy cakes covered in sickly green icing – the product of her cookery class – and chattering happily about nothing in particular, and managing to make Beth laugh at her description of the culinary disasters of her class.

After her, it was young Peter Green's turn. He told her, somewhat bashfully, that he was very good at fixing things if she had any problems with shelves and such, and asked whether she would like to join the Ramblers on their sponsored walk next Saturday. To this Beth bravely agreed, having determined within her reluctant mind sometime earlier that she must try to accept every invitation offered at present.

Next came the bouncy 'Digs' Arnold, with yet another invitation, – this time to join an expedition to look at a local Roman villa – and a present of some prickly sweet chestnuts to roast on the fire. "Just stick 'em on a shovel and push it in – they taste marvellous with a bit of salt." Beth accepted that invitation, too.

Last of all, shyer and more awkward than the others but just as well-meaning, came old Bill Lewis. He did not bring gifts or offer invitations, but he sat gravely in her deep armchair sipping tea, looked round him and sighed: "It's nice here, isn't it? Peaceful." Then he came to the anxious point of his visit. "You know, I'm not much good at socialising. But one thing I am good at is money."

Beth looked confused. "Money?"

"The market. Stocks and shares. You know. Keep tabs on it. Play it a bit."

"Oh." Beth was still mystified.

"Make a bit here and there. In a modest way." He eyed Beth with hopeful speculation. "What I'm getting at is – if you ever wanted any advice or anything, don't hesitate. Ask

Uncle Bill. Everyone does." He took a gulp of tea, nearly scalded himself, and choked.

Beth smiled at him with sudden warmth. He was so clearly offering the only help he knew how to give. "Thanks, Bill," she said. "That's very kind of you. I'll bear it in mind."

That was the last of the school visitations for the time being, but besides these, various villagers turned up on various pretexts, bringing small gifts of one kind or another.

"Thought you might like some lettuces . . ."

"I've got too many apples, you see . . ."

"This is local honey from Charlie's bees."

"We were wondering if you'd like to join the local history society?"

And lastly, and most hesitantly, came a young woman with shadowed eyes who said: "I hope you won't think I'm intruding . . . but I wondered whether you'd be interested in joining the Meningitis Trust?"

Beth looked at her with sudden swift sympathy, understanding the shadows under those anxious eyes. "You too?" she said.

The girl sighed. "Not exactly. My little boy survived – but he's partially deaf."

Beth's face softened. "I'm so sorry . . . It's a terribly cruel disease." She took a deep breath. "What can I do to help?"

The eyes grew a shade less anxious. "Oh dear, I was so afraid I'd upset you by asking . . ." She dared a small, shy smile. "Welcome to the club . . . We try to raise funds for research . . . lobby people . . . make as much fuss as possible to get something done about it . . . Not enough is known about it, of course, or what triggers off these local outbreaks. But there have been some important break-throughs lately in identifying the different strains . . ." She looked up at Beth earnestly. "I could tell you more if you came round to the Trust offices some time . . . ?"

"Yes," agreed Beth firmly. "I'd like to do that."

"I'm Jean," said the girl, holding out her hand. "Jean Shaw." She looked into Beth's face, and added softly: "Sometimes it helps – to be doing something useful about it."

Beth nodded. "You're absolutely right."

But the girl did not push her luck then. The time, she judged, was not right for more than one small overture. So she merely handed Beth a few pamphlets, and risked a slightly wider smile and said: "Well, I'll look forward to seeing you. The address is in there. Please come – and ask for me." And she hurried away before Beth could say anything else.

But she knew she must take up the girl's offer and go to see her. In fact, she knew she had to say yes to everything – while still amazed at everyone's kindness and generosity. She realised the word had gone round and that everyone was going out of their way to be helpful, but somehow she did not mind. They were so open and friendly about it, and who was she to be proud and stand-offish, anyway? It was clear that her time would be filled with useful activity and cheerful company if she wanted it – and she rather thought she did at present.

But now it was little Chloë who needed useful activity and cheerful company, and someone patient and observant to watch for any signs of return – and Beth was determined to be that person if she could. Not only for Finn's sake, she told herself, but for Stephanie's too. She owed it to her to do what she could to put things right.

It occurred to her, over the tea and buns, that she didn't really know exactly where Finn's house was. She knew it was called The Old Millhouse, and that it was at the bottom of the valley, where the old millstream still ran through the steep-sided meadows, – but which of the many lanes from the village led to it, she had no idea. On consideration, therefore, rather than ringing up her headmistress to ask for instructions (which would seem a bit irresponsible and feeble, anyway) she decided to take Chloë up to see Beech on the way home. He knew the house, since he did Finn's garden too, and would tell her which path to take. And Chloë might like the animals – they might even trigger some response. In any case, Beth felt curiously certain that Beech would be good for Chloë. It was worth a try . . . So after tea, Beth took Chloë's hand in hers again, and walked firmly up the hill to the edge of the woods to look for Beech.

They did not have to look far. He was stooping over one of his cages, inserting some scraps of food for its eager occupant. When he saw the two of them approaching, he stood up and waited for them, not saying anything until they came and stood beside him. Then he turned gravely to Chloë and said: "I'm glad to see you, Little 'un. I've something to show you." And he led the way over to a new wooden box set down on a spread of fresh straw close to the house.

"There!" he said, and there was a note of pride in his voice. "What d'you think of that!"

Beth still had Chloë's hand in hers, and now she looked down into the wide, straw-filled box before her, not knowing what to expect. And there, lying peacefully spread out on the straw was the golden retriever, Jess, and nuzzling close to her in small wriggling heaps were a tawny litter of tiny puppies.

"Oh!" breathed Beth, "how lovely. Six of them!" and she went down on her knees and stretched out her hand to touch them. "Look, Chloë! Jess has got six new babies to look after." Her hand went first to the proud mother, rubbing the velvet head with gentle fingers, and then Beth looked up at Beech for permission to stroke the puppies. Sometimes the mother did not like it, she knew, and she did not want to do anything to upset her.

Beech approved of this, but he nodded easy permission and stood looking down with a smile at his favourite animal and two of his favourite people. "She's a good mother," he said in his soft, warm voice. "See, Little'un, they'm very small and new just now, need a lot o' lookin' arter. But she wunt let 'em come to harm, not one of 'em."

Beth was still on her knees beside the straw pen, and Chloë was still standing beside her, but no longer holding her hand. At first she had paid no attention whatever to Beech or Beth or the retriever bitch and her new litter, but now something like a flicker of realisation seemed to come into her eyes and she looked down. She stood there for a long time, just staring down at the wriggling puppies all fighting blindly for their mother's teats full of milk, and then, very slowly, one of her hands stretched out towards them.

Beth and Beech loked at one another in triumph. It was the first spontaneous gesture Chloë had made since she came home, as far as Beth knew.

"That's the way," said Beech gently. "Go slow, so as not to let 'em get frit . . . Feel how soft they are."

And they both watched, breathless, as Chloë's small hand

77

actually reached out and touched one warm, squirming body. Every movement she made seemed very slow and hesitant, but her hand did move and linger, and then withdraw carefully to its usual passive position by her side. For a moment she looked up into Beth's face and seemed almost to be struggling to find words. But then the faint urgency in her expression seemed to fade, and it returned to its look of closed disinterest. But Beth was sure from then on that the child really could not speak, and was not – as Beth had vaguely suspected – just staging her own private protest. Whether it was shock, or disillusion over her hero of a father, or the sheer desolation of life without her mother, or whatever trauma had triggered her present condition, Chloë could could not help it, even *wanted* to speak and return to some kind of communication – but somehow she could not. There was some kind of desperate barrier which she could not cross.

"There now," said Beech, still in the same soft, reassuring voice. "It's a start. When you comes agen, they'll be bigger, and you can pick 'em up." He glanced again at Beth, and a small, quiet smile passed between them.

Yes, it was a start. And Beth must be content with that. If this was a beginning, maybe the rest would follow in time.

"We must go home now," she said gently to that closed flower face. "Beech will tell us the best way to go."

Beech might be slow in movement and in speech, but he was not slow in the uptake. "Well now," he said, "maybe I could walk along o' you a bit of the way . . ." and he set off down the path, with Beth and Chloë beside him.

Was it her fancy, Beth wondered, or did Chloë's hand seem to grip hers in a slightly more confident way? In any case, it's a start, she repeated to herself. A start. But we've got a long way to go yet.

PART III – YONDER . . . ?

Finn did not want to go back to the Spirios site, especially after what had happened on the main island – but he knew he had to before he could hand it all over to someone else. He hadn't tried to explain to Beth why he had to go back. It didn't seem possible at the time, and her horrified face only made him feel guiltier than ever at leaving Chloë. He was sure he was right to keep out of his small daughter's way, at least until the initial shock had worn off, but that didn't make him feel any better about it. How could he explain to her that Stephanie's death was not his fault? Especially when he wasn't even sure about that, either. He blamed himself bitterly for not having been there when he was needed, but if he had been, could he have prevented it? Or could he have persuaded Chloë then that no-one was to blame?

He did not know. Being without Stephanie somehow meant that he didn't know anything any more. All certainty was gone. She had always been his rock, the fixed point on his compass to which he always returned. Now there was no fixed point – no-one to return to, except Chloë, who did not want him.

It was a new experience for Finn not to be wanted, not to be admired and fêted. Maybe, he reflected, it was good for him, maybe he had been a bit spoilt and arrogant. Certainly, he had taken too much for granted. And Stephanie – brave, uncomplaining Stephanie – had never reproached him, never made him feel selfish and insensitive, which he now realised he was.

Yes. Selfish and insensitive. And now it was not only little Chloë's blank, pinched face that haunted him, but Beth's accusing stare of disbelief as well. So he was going back to the Spirios site, unhappy associations and all, with something like a sense of relief. Out there, in the simplicity of Greek island life, no-one would be getting at him. There was a lot of work to do, and he would be glad to get on and do it, unhampered by doubts and regrets and the awful anguish that Stephanie's absence left in his centreless life.

There were problems with the Spirios site that were difficult to solve. He had failed to explain it to Beth, he had even failed to tell Stephanie all about it, but there were decisions to take, and a number of people dependent on his judgement. The initial trouble was the actual placing of the hotel complex. The original promoters of the scheme had been pushy and uncaring about local tradition and custom. They had planned a huge, brash five-storey complex right in the middle of the island's most beautiful bay, on its wildest and most unspoilt coastline. It would also interfere with an archeological site still being explored by a mixed team of experts from the Athens Museum and from several American universities who were putting up the money. Everything was wrong about the scheme, but the building began and a forest of metal struts went up before the concrete structure was poured into place, making the lovely pale gold bay look like a scrap metal dump waiting to be demolished. And then the promoters went bust, the metal struts stayed pointing at the blue, flawless skies of Greece, and nothing more was done.

Here, Finn stepped in and bought the whole concern. He drew up new plans, arranged for all that awful structure to be removed (no easy task) and for the raw, sandy site to be filled in. Instead, a new, separate complex of low-storey buildings was to be constructed around the corner in the next, slightly less spectacular bay. It was a good scheme, and the local villagers were pleased about it and very anxious to help. But before that could happen, Finn had to find a more intelligent site manager, and persuade his new, imaginative architect to come down from Athens and oversee the building process, making sure that everyone – including the archeological team – was happy.

In the middle of all this, Finn had meant to go back to Athens to consult everyone and fix things up satisfactorily, but the awful events surrounding Stephanie's death had overtaken him. Now, he knew, he had a lot of arranging to do, various people to placate, and at least a couple of weeks on the spot making sure that his plans were being put into effect without upsetting anyone else. It would be difficult, a task requiring tact and good humour, but Finn usually liked that kind of challenge. Only, now he was so shaken by his own private grief that he did not feel in the least confident about being able to sort things out. However, he had to try.

So he took a plan to Athens, arranged with his new architect, Theo Koussalis, to meet him on site in three days' time, and went down to Piraeus, where he got on a boat for the islands, and finally took a caique from the last port of call on the shipping run to the small island where the Spirios site lay waiting for him in the bright Greek sunshine.

It was a little island, with a little port – too small for the Piraeus boat to visit – and only the caiques had a shallow enough draft to pull up at the tiny jetty. This meant that it was not over-run with summer tourists, and the steep, narrow streets and neat white houses of the miniature town were largely untouched by the taint of western commercialism. Further inland, it was a place of high, herb-scented hills, small stony fields and wandering goats, sudden deep valleys filled with olive groves and vines, and unexpectedly lush crops of sunflowers, lilies (in spring) and vegetables. And beyond all this, the sea again, on every side.

The Spirios site was on the far side of the island, away from the port, the idea being that it should create an exclusive, quiet resort only to be reached by boat. With this end in view, the plans included a new jetty and a couple of waterside tavernas, as well as the new long-shaped hotel and its modest complex of separate small villas. Gardens were planned, too, with some imported trees for shade, since the island coastline had very little tall vegetation, only the fragrant scrubby slopes of herbs and arbutus and a few bent olive trees and stunted vines. And three special cypress trees guarding the little church of St. Spiridion on the slope above the village.

Finn did not wait for the island bus or the one and only taxi, but set out on foot to cross the island. It was no great distance, only four miles across, though the going was steep in places. But he could do with the exercise, and the familiar scent of the sun-warmed clumps of sage and thyme, juniper and basil, went to his head like wine. So did the gentle warmth of the

October sun and the extraordinary brilliance and clarity of the light. He had forgotten how marvellous that light was – how every late wayside flower seemed to glow with colour, every leaf and twig shine with its own incandescence – and the sky, that cloudless burning blue, seemed to reach to eternity.

How Stephanie would love it here, he thought. I meant to bring her, as soon as the site was fit to look at, and safe for Chloë to run about on . . . I only meant to leave them there in the villa on the main island for a day or two, until I could come and fetch them . . .

He quickened his stride, trying to walk away from his thoughts. But they pursued him. In Greece, he thought, the Furies are never very far away . . . that's why all this burning beauty seems so perilous . . .

"Kirios Finn, you are back early," said a voice beside him, and the smiling brown face of his foreman, Yannis, was looking up at him.

"It is good to see you, Yannis," answered Finn, and grasped him by the arm. Indeed, it was curiously good to see this tried and trusted friend standing solidly beside him on the white stones of the path. "How are things?" he asked, as they fell into step together.

Yannis spread out his hands in his usual gesture of comic dismay. "But dreadful, Kirios Finn, of course. There was rain, and the bulldozers got stuck. The pile-driver struck rock and broke a blade . . . The taverna ran out of food and the fish did not come in, so the men grumbled . . . But," and here his infectious smile broke out again, "the boats brought some squid, and the farmer, Andreas, killed some chickens, so everyone was happy."

Finn laughed.

Yannis's seamed brown face was grave again by now, and his merry brown eyes looked suddenly shadowed. "I am sorry, Kirios Finn, about your sadness. I would not mention it, but we are all most sorry. We would like you to know that."

Finn looked down at his old friend and nodded. "Thanks," he said briefly. And they strolled on together to look at the site.

It was a long day by the time Finn had inspected everything

– even the abandoned site in the next bay which was being filled in and slowly returning to normal – and he was tired, tired and dispirited when he sat down at a small table near the water's edge in Georgios' taverna. It was dusk now, and night came down swiftly in the islands. A late glow from the sunset still hung in the west, but lights were beginning to prick on the other islands in the shadowed sea, and a small, cool wind carried the scent of herbs from the sun-warmed hills to the edge of the shore. It was beautiful and quiet, and he wished most passionately that Stephanie was beside him and his little daughter was dodging the lazy waves at the edge of the sea and chattering happily up at them as she used to do.

Once again, doubts began to assail him. Had he been wrong to go away again? Should he have stayed, no matter how it distressed the child to see him? Wasn't it his duty as a responsible father to watch over her, however painful it was for both of them? He did not know. He was too confused and unhappy to know anything. But it suddenly began to dawn on him that he was now that curiously bleak modern phenomenon: a 'single parent', and Chloë must rely on him totally for all the decisions of her present way of life. It frightened him when he thought of it. Until now, Stephanie had taken almost all the responsibility, made all the decisions for him. The only thing he had to do was provide a lovely home and plenty of money – and that was easy, being the kind of man he was. Too easy, he realised now. He had never needed to worry about Chloë's happiness – Stephanie provided it all. And he had never worried much about his own wife's happiness and safety, either, he told himself in anguished remorse. He had taken for granted that she was content with the way of life he had given her, security and independence, but a wandering husband who came back in snatches and brief interludes of precious joy – and was gone again on some other adventure before they had time to come down to earth . . . Had Stephanie minded? She never said so. But did she get lonely when he was away so much? Did she long for a more settled, ordinary existence with a steady, supporting husband who was always there when he was wanted. *Always there when he was wanted?*

He did not know the answer to any of these questions – but his tortured mind was full of doubt.

"Finn," said a voice at his elbow. "Good to see you back. Can I join you?"

Finn looked up, startled, and saw that it was one of the archeologists from the exploration site round the corner. He was a quiet, bearded young man, from London, Finn thought, with some connection with the British Museum, and his name was Bob Furness, if he remembered right.

"Hallo, Bob. Yes, do. I could do with some company."

Bob looked at the carafe of local wine on the table and signalled to Georgios to bring another bottle and another glass. Then he sat down comfortably beside Finn and stretched out his long legs under the table.

"We were sorry to hear about your wife," he said, feeling it was better to get it out in the open.

"Yes," Finn growled. "It was – it was rather sudden."

Bob nodded silently. "How is the little girl now? We heard she was – very shocked?"

"Yes," said Finn again. "Very." He sighed and took an incautious gulp of wine. "She's much the same, I'm afraid." He was staring out at the darkening sea, but now he turned his head and looked at the concerned face beside him. Bob was a gentle sort of person, and his brown eyes were kind and anxious. "To tell you the truth," said Finn suddenly, "I don't know if I ought to have left her, but I . . . I just seemed to make things worse for her, somehow."

Bob grunted, understanding. "Blames you, does she?"

"Yes." Finn's mouth was grim. "And she's not the only one."

Bob poured out some of the new wine that Georgios had brought. Then he said in a mild, judicious voice: "One always blames oneself when tragedy strikes – but it doesn't do you or anyone else any good."

"I know," said Finn heavily. "I know . . ." And he shook his head in helpless acquiescence. But then he seemed to realise that he was being extremely self-centred and gloomy, so he took a deep breath and changed the subject.

"What about the dig? Have you turned up anything interesting?"

Bob smiled at him gratefully and began to talk about antiquities. He also signalled to Georgios, who brought them two plates of fish without being asked, and while Bob talked he also kept a weather eye on Finn and made sure that he ate something.

They did their best, Finn's friends, to cheer him and comfort him, and if they did not altogether succeed in dispelling the shadows, it was not for want of trying.

Later that night, Finn stumbled up the steps to the little whitewashed room above the taverna where he usually stayed, and found his bed made ready, a jug of fresh water on the table, and a bunch of the wild island flowers in a glass jar on the window ledge.

He looked at the flowers with a faint reminiscent smile touching his tight, grim mouth. The red poppies, said to be the blood of the heroes of Marathon, the blue-bell flowers, almost as blue as the Aegean skies, and the gold and orange, tightly-closed petals of the hawksbeard that only opened with the sun . . . He remembered that Georgios' wife, Marina, had taught him the first word of Greek that he ever learnt. He had paused to touch the crimson petals of a poppy and looked up to find a pair of dark, sympathetic eyes regarding him with approval. Anyone who respected and admired the island flowers merited her approval. "Orea . . ." she murmured.

"*Orea*?" He did not know the word yet.

"Beautiful," she translated, and smiled at him. It was the beginning of a love affair, really – not with the wife of Georgios, though she was pretty enough, but with her countryside, its herb-scented hills and wayside flowers and deep blue encirling sea . . .

From then on he set himself to learn a little of the language, a smattering that would make it possible to communicate (though many of the islanders spoke a bit of English, for the sake of the visiting tourists). That was the trouble with his wandering life, Finn thought suddenly, it was full of smatterings. A bit of Greek here, a bit of Arabic there . . . a few words of Turkish, an attempt at Urdu and even Hindustani, but he never stayed long enough to become fluent, or to get to know the people really well.

Still, here he was again, in the familiar small bedroom above the taverna; plain white walls, the simplest of furnishings, a goatskin rug on the floor, and it felt like coming home.

"Kirios Finn," said Marina's voice at the doorway, "I have brought you some tea." She smiled at him, welcome in her tranquil brown eyes, and held out a steaming cup of green, fragrant tea. "It will help you to sleep," she added in a matter-of-fact, no-nonsense tone.

"Thank you, Marina." Finn took the cup from her. "You are very kind."

She stood looking at him judiciously for a moment, as if assessing the emotional state of her most favoured guest.

"The island mends sadness," she said, in careful English. "But you must wait. Agios Spyridion takes his time."

Then she turned and went out of the room before Finn could answer.

Beth had meant to go and talk to her friendly headmistress about the idea she had been considering concerning Mark and Chloë, but before she had got round to doing so, she saw Margaret Collier coming up the path to the Beehive one golden evening just before dusk.

"I can't remember such a lovely autumn as this," said Margaret, smiling at Beth over the tangle of roses beside the door.

Beth smiled back. "I thought perhaps this corner of Gloucestershire was always drenched in sunlight."

"Not on your life!" grinned Margaret. "You wait till winter."

They stood for a moment admiring the afterglow in the western sky, and the curious sheen of mellow light it seemed to cast on the dreaming hills.

"So *quiet*," breathed Beth, who had had a very noisy day at school.

Margaret laughed. "That sounds heartfelt. Are you finding the racket insupportable?"

"No," Beth protested. "Of course not!" She glanced at Margaret with a sudden gleam of mischief. "As a matter-of-fact, I believe I love every minute of it – tantrums and all."

"That's what I wanted to hear!" said Margaret, and laid an approving hand on her arm.

They went inside then, leaving the last of the sunlight to fade into blue dusk, and Beth set about producing the usual cup of coffee.

"I hear Finn's gone off again," remarked Margaret, accepting her coffee with a nod of thanks.

"Yes." Beth frowned as she sat down opposite her in the second-best armchair by the hearth. "I think he's quite wrong."

"Did you tell him so?"

"Yes, I did." She pushed the hair out of her eyes in a faintly impatient gesture. "But it didn't make any difference."

"He's an obstinate man when he gets an idea in his head."

Beth nodded. "He seems so full of guilt – so convinced he is to blame." She sighed. "And so certain Chloë is better off without him."

"Do you think she is?"

"No. I think he ought to be there – in the background, whatever the child feels. After all, he's all the family she's got now – even if she doesn't seem to want him at the moment. I think she must feel even more bereft when there's no-one there, no-one, that is, except Mary Willis."

It was Margaret's turn to sigh. "It's a difficult situation."

Beth agreed, and went on to her request about Mark. "He seems to have taken Chloë under his wing," she explained. "In fact he's becoming absurdly protective. But it seems to work, and I have the curious feeling that he actually knows what Chloë wants."

Margaret did not look very surprised. "I've always thought children understand a lot more than we give them credit for."

"Yes." Beth was relieved to find no scepticism in Margaret's observant gaze. "And I think it's good for Mark, too, in some obscure way . . . He seems a lot less tantrum-prone – a lot more adult, really, now he's taken on some responsibility for someone else."

"That's good news." Margaret looked at her questioningly, knowing that this was leading to something else.

"I don't know exactly what his family situation is," Beth went on. "But he told me he went home on his own because his mother was at work."

87

"Yes, he does. So?"

"So, I wondered – when I was taking Chloë home with me the other day, he was clearly longing to come too . . . I was wondering whether I could keep them both for tea some days, and arrange to get them home, of course. I just have a feeling Mark may be the – the *link* Chloë needs to bring her back to us."

Margaret nodded again slowly, pondering the idea.

"I'd have to go and see Mark's mother," Beth continued anxiously. "And I wanted to know how you would feel about that? I think Mary Willis would be no problem. She's at her wit's end to know what to do for Chloë anyway. But Mark's situation might be tricky?"

"No, I don't think so." Margaret was making up her mind as she spoke. "No, I think it's a good idea . . . And I suspect Mark's mother will be only too pleased to have him taken care of for a bit longer during the day. She's another one at her wit's end, I rather fear."

Beth looked at Margaret's thoughtful gaze enquiringly. "Then – I can go ahead?"

"With my blessing? Yes. But don't expect it all to be plain sailing. Mark is an unpredictable boy. He might relapse quite suddenly and be a handful."

"I realise that."

"You're prepared to take the risk?"

Beth said in a suddenly weary voice: "I don't think any crisis would seem too alarming now . . ."

Then she pulled back from her sudden lapse, and offered Margaret another cup of coffee.

Mark's mother, Lucy Reynolds, was youngish, thinnish, harassed and tired. But she had a smile like her son's, warm and genuine when it flashed out, and the permanently anxious look in her brown eyes softened a little when Beth explained her mission.

"Oh . . . I thought you were coming to tell me that Mark was being unmanageable again."

"On the contrary," said Beth, and turned to smile at Mark who was supposedly not listening from his perch on the sofa in front of the television screen. "He is actually being extremely co-operative and helpful with a little girl who is in deep trouble."

Lucy looked astounded. "That doesn't sound like Mark!"

Beth laughed. "It may be a surprise, but it's the truth." She went on to describe how Mark had adopted Chloë as his own special charge, and the effect it seemed to have on his own behaviour.

Lucy listened in silence, a look of painful understanding gradually dawning in her face.

"I'm afraid he is left alone too much," she confessed. "When my husband walked out, I was obliged to go back to work . . . He does contribute something *now* – after I went to court to sue for maintenance. But it is somewhat grudging." She looked at Beth a little grimly. "And of course it's all tied up with him having what they call 'reasonable access', whether I like it or not." She lit a cigarette with nervous fingers, and Beth could hear the suppressed anger in her voice.

"And whether Mark likes it or not?" murmured Beth, reflecting that in these cases it was often the child's own wishes that came to be considered last – if at all.

Lucy sighed. "It's not that simple for him. He misses his father. One part of him wants to go and stay for that weekend, – and one doesn't. He's not sure what he wants really . . . But when he gets there, with the new girlfriend in residence and all that, he finds that he doesn't like it after all. He tells me they are apt to ignore him, or get what he calls 'too sexy' which embarrasses him, or they take him out to an expensive restaurant and talk over his head . . . And then they try to load him with expensive presents . . ." She ran those brittle fingers through her hair. "He's too intelligent to be bought, you see . . . It just makes him mad."

"I can understand that."

"Can you?" Her eyes met Beth's with a kind of angry appeal. "Most people can't. But Mark's a proud boy. He doesn't like being patronised." She drew fiercely on her cigarette, and then looked at Beth again, still with that unspoken appeal behind her glance. "I suppose . . . he will come to terms with it in the end." There was a question in the light, careless voice.

"Oh yes," Beth spoke with certainty. "I think that is beginning to happen already."

Lucy's smile flashed out briefly again. "You're very encouraging."

Am I? thought Beth. Encouraging? When I can see no pattern, no purpose for encouragement in my own centreless existence? How can she say that?

But aloud she only said quietly: "I think he deserves encouragement. And so does little Chloë."

Lucy nodded tiredly so that her heavy, straight-cut bob swung round her face, and the small gold earrings flashed in her ears.

She would be quite good-looking really, thought Beth, if she wasn't so tired. I wish I knew how to help her.

"Can I take it that you approve, then?" she asked, returning to the point of her visit.

"Oh God, yes. Anything that helps Mark and keeps him occupied. I can't ever be home much before six . . . It's a long time to have to wait for home comforts – and I don't really approve of latch-key kids, anyway."

"I'll make sure they have some tea."

"You won't have much problem with that!"

Beth grinned. "Maybe not with Mark. But Chloë is difficult . . . I fancy, though, she'll probably eat if he does."

"Well, then – " Lucy was actually laughing, "sounds like you can't lose."

Beth got to her feet. "I'll fix it for next week." She hesitated, and then added with sudden shyness: "By the way, if you are ever at a loose end at weekends, I'm usually there."

Lucy stared at her for a moment in silence. "D'you know," she said, in a curiously bright and brittle voice, "people are apt to avoid a divorced woman, as if you were some sort of pariah, or a threat to their husbands, or something.

"Well, I haven't got a husband now," said Beth calmly, putting on a resolute smile. "And I'm not sure I know what a pariah is."

The two women looked at one another, and the smile between them seemed to grow.

"Mark," Beth said as she passed, "you can come out of there! You're going to help me to look after Chloë. Your Mum will tell you all about it."

90

"Smashing!" grinned Mark, and turned a neat cartwheel on the living room floor.

So each weekday after school, Beth took Mark and Chloë home with her. She did not mind the encroachment on her free time – why should she? There was too much free time in her life already. The long evening hours still hung heavily on her hands, and there was still that echoing silence to fill, the unceasing ache for little Mo and his laughter, for Robert and his warm protection – to be kept at bay somehow or other . . . So it was better to be busy, and her concern for Chloë was very real, and for Mark too, as he struggled to come to terms with his warring family loyalties and turn himself into a responsible young person, not a disruptive child. Besides, Beth told herself again, she had promised Finn to do what she could to help, and, deeper than that, she had made a silent promise to the loving spirit that was Stephanie who had somehow left her small daughter's welfare in Beth's hands.

She talked to them both as she walked home with them, just as she would have done to Mo, pointing out anything that seemed to catch their attention. Mark listened and responded, Chloë did not. Though Beth sometimes fancied that the small girl's face was not quite so closed and blank as before. Mark knew what Beth was trying to do, and played up valiantly.

"Look at the butterflies, Chloë. They're using up the last of the nectar, Mrs. Halliday says . . ." He faithfully followed up all Beth's leads with a running commentary of his own. "That's a tortoiseshell. And the one with rings on its wings is a peacock. This is a special butterfly tree, you see, it's called a b – ?"

"Buddleia," smiled Beth.

"Buddleia," repeated Mark. Chloë did not reply, but her hand stayed in Mark's, and she stood looking up at the late butterflies swarming round the long purple fingers of the buddleia tree with eyes that were not quite so veiled and distant as before.

They ate Beth's buns and drank tea in the garden on the days when it was fine, as it usually was this golden autumn – or on the rare wet evenings they sat round the fire and toasted bread on a long brass toasting fork.

91

Mark continued to talk cheerfully, and to play scrabble or do a jigsaw, or even play chess with Beth if she set it up for him. He described every move to Chloë. "Look, that's my knight, see? . . . And that's my queen . . . If I move it here . . ."

But Chloë did not seem to see the chessboard. Or the jigsaw . . . The only time she actually made any kind of response was when Beth was showing Mark how to plant some winter pansies in the flower bed near the front door.

"Look, Chloë's that's a pansy – a yellow one – and here's a sort of red one . . ." Mark held it out for her to see, still in its little plastic pot, and waited, bright-eyed and challenging, to see what she would do. And slowly, very slowly, as if in a dream of wonder, Chloe':'s small fingers came out and stroked the jewel-coloured velvet face of the flower.

"Would you like to plant this one?" asked Mark, blithely suggesting what Beth had not dared to ask.

But that was too much to hope for. Chloë did not move. She just stood there, looking down, while Mark's strong, competent young hands put the little plant in its place and pressed it firmly home.

"Never mind," he said cheerfully, "you can do it next time," and he took her down the garden path to look at Beth's late roses in the sun.

It was slow, and not always obvious, but by these small signs and tiny victories, Beth knew that Chloë was gradually returning to the world she had shut out.

Mark, understanding a lot more then he said, grinned at Beth one evening and remarked with startling confidence: "She's coming back, you know."

Beth looked at him in astonishment, but then admitted to herself that she had under-estimated Mark's intelligence, as usual. But she made no other comment than: "Yes, I think you're right."

So far, Beth had not taken them up to see Beech again, though she was sure it would be a good idea, if she could manage it. But by the time they had got home to the Beehive and had tea and wandered about the garden a bit, it was usually time to go home. Sometimes, Mary Willis came for Chloë herself, and then Beth only had to walk home with Mark to his house on the other side of the village (though he assured her fiercely more than once that he was perfectly all right on his own.) But sometimes Beth had to take Chloë back to Finn's house herself, and since it was quite a way outside the village, she usually got the car out and dropped Mark off on the way. The friendship with Mary Willis had progressed comfortably during this time, and the two of them would often end up drinking tea together, either in Finn's roomy Millhouse kitchen, or in Beth's tiny one.

Finn's house – or rather, Stephanie's, for it was clear to Beth that Stephanie's hand was in all the elegant furnishing and ordering of that lovely building – remained empty and silent, except for the cheerful kitchen and Chloë's small, white-painted bedroom. Beth, looking round at it all rather wistfully, felt angrier than ever with Finn for being away and refusing to let these quiet rooms come to life again. She felt sure Chloë would respond more quickly if there was cheerful company and colour and movement all around her, instead of this tidy, sparkless existence. Mary herself was kind enough, and full of warm-hearted attempts at home comforts, but she had no idea how to talk to Chloë, or how to interest her in what went on around her. The only person who seemed able to do that around the Millhouse was old Beech, when he came down to the garden. He would talk quietly on as he worked, rather like Mark did, and not wait for Chloë to answer, but he somehow managed to include her in whatever he was doing. Beth had seen him with her a couple of times, and she always felt a surge of extra warmth and confidence about Chloë's future when she saw how the old man handled her.

She was thinking about this one Saturday morning, when she saw Beech himself approaching her along her garden path.

"Missus," he said, giving his usual half-serious salute with one work-stained hand, "could I have a word?"

"Of course." Beth looked at him enquiringly, and motioned him to sit down in the little porch.

But he shook his head. "Nay, I'll not stop long. 'Tis about the little 'un. Chloë, I mean . . ."

"Yes? What about her?"

He seemed almost to be apologising for something, even before he spoke. "I'm allus glad to see her, Missus. You knows that. But I reckon she'm a bit young like, to be wandering about they woods on 'er own."

Beth looked startled. "*On her own?* Does she? When?"

The old man looked uncomfortable, as if he felt like a child telling tales out of school. "Weekends, Missus. I know you keeps an eye on her, weekdays like – and good it is of you, an' all – but weekends, I reckon she gives Mary the slip somehow, and there she is, up by my pen, crouching down like a fritted rabbit in the grass."

Beth was horrified. "*Frightened?*"

"Nay, not exactly, Missus. More – folded up small like, so as not to be noticed . . . She were by my Jess and the puppies – twice I found her there."

Folded up small so as not to be noticed. But she had shown an interest in the puppies. And clearly she was still interested . . . That was surely something.

"Oh Beech, I'm sorry. I'd no idea she went on her own."

"It were all right, Missus. I was there, see, and I took her back when she'd had a bit of a look round. Mary was that grateful." He paused, and then went on, pushing his battered old hat further back on his head. "It's just that I'm not allus there, see? . . . I goes hither and yon a bit, odd jobs and gardens and the like . . . She might be up there all alone, and me not come to see her home safe – if you follows me?"

"I follow you very well," said Beth. She too paused for thought before going on. "The trouble is, it's difficult to forbid Chloë to do things or to give her orders. We're none of us sure how much she takes in. I expect Mary Willis finds it hard to know what to do."

"She does that," agreed Beech. "Told me so." He hesitated, and then seemed to pluck up courage to make a suggestion. "I wus just wonderin' . . . ?I know you gives her a lot o' time as it is – ?"

"Yes?" Beth waited a moment, and then when the old man still seemed unsure how to continue, she added gently: "I have plenty of time, Beech, if it helps Chloë."

He looked immediately relieved at that, and proceeded with slow caution to his plan of campaign. "If, maybe, you could bring her up once on a weekend, like . . . and she could stay

94

a bit to look at the animals . . . Maybe she'd not need to run off on her own?"

Beth smiled. "That sounds a very good idea. I might even get through to her that it's safer to have someone with her." A thought struck her then, and she added in a tentative voice: "Would you mind if I brought someone else along as well? A boy who is rather good with little Chloë?"

Beech managed a creaky smile, too. "So long as 'e's quiet with the animals.

"Oh yes, he'll be quiet all right." She had a sudden vision of Mark lying on the floor, screaming and beating his heels against the floor in a paroxysm of fury. "He's a good boy, really," she said, hoping to God it was true.

"Ar, well then," agred Beech, as if it were all settled. "Termorrer? Would that suit?"

"What sort of time, Beech? You can't wait all day."

He pondered briefly. "Noonish? I feeds the animals then. They might like that."

"I'm sure they would. Noon it is, then." A curious unspoken camaradie seemed to grow between them as they looked at one another and allowed their smiles to get wider.

"If we can see after her, like, I reckon she'll come through," said Beech, "given half a chance."

Beth almost laughed. But instead herself solemnly repeating Beech's catchphrase like an incantation. "Yes. *Given half a chance.*"

Beech was waiting for them when they arrived by his cottage door, and took them, with no preamble, to see his latest arrivals. He appeared to pay no special attention to Chloë, though he watched with approval how she held on to Mark's hand and followed willingly wherever he led. As for Mark, he was so entranced with all the animals, he scarcely said a word, and just gazed at everything in fascinated silence.

"This here," said Beech, stooping over a new little cage, "is a ferret. Got hisself caught in a snare, see, and the wire near took his head off, 'e wriggled so bad." He took out the long, lithe creature and smoothed its golden-brown fur with a gentle hand. "But 'e's mendin' nicely now, see? And not a bit afraid o' me."

"Where did he come from?" asked Beth, wondering whether the old man himself kept ferrets and did a bit of quiet poaching on the side. It didn't somehow seem quite in character for an ex-gamekeeper.

"Boy in the village," replied Beech succinctly. "A pet, see? Not used to the wild. Ran straight into a snare. Didn't know as 'e couldn't trust everywhere to be as safe as houses."

"Poor thing," said Mark, and also reached out a hand to stroke the golden fur.

"Mind, there shouldn't 'a been a snare there," Beech told him severely. "Not allowed, them wires – lethal, they are." He put the young ferret back in its cage with careful slowness, and put a few scraps of food inside to keep it happy. "You'll be ready to go home soon, won't you?" he told it in his soft, caressing voice.

"Do you always know what to do?" asked Mark, awestruck at all this unspoken knowledge and expertise.

"Nay, that I don't. Sometimes, if it's bad, I gets the vet out – or I takes the crittur in, if I'm able . . . There's things I can't do, see? . . . and medicines to give, like . . . If there's bones broken, or a bad wound, and they needs antibiotics, I has to get 'em from the vet then."

Mark nodded sagely.

"Now, this 'un, for instance," said Beech, leaning down to a wire enclosure where a big grey bird lay curled up asleep, with its long black neck and white face half-hidden under one curved black-and-white wing. "She's a barnacle goose – on her way to winter at Slimbridge, where it's safe and warm and there's plenty o' food. All the way from the Arctic, she came, and what did she do? Flew straight into a power-line. Near killed herself, she did, and broke a wing an' all . . . Someone picked 'er up, all limp and floppy like, thought she was a goner. But she came round, see? So he brought 'er along to me."

"Will she mend?" Mark sounded quite anxious.

"Ay, she'll do fine now. But I got the vet to set 'er wing. It were too bad for me to handle."

After that, he took them to see the owl, which was so much recovered that it was now flying in long sweeps inside its wire enclosure, practising its flight paths, and would clearly soon be able to hunt again in the wild. "Another day or two," he said, looking at the smooth feathers with a judicious eye, "and she'll be ready to go. She should be asleep by rights, it being daytime, but she's gettin' restless." He turned to Mark seriously. "Mustn't keep 'em, see, if they'm ready to go. They belongs out there." And he waved a vague brown hand at the blazing autumn beechwoods all around them.

Beth had watched the trees slowly turning from green to gold and then to fiery red and all the colours of flame that burned in the October sun, but she had not seen them at quite this point of brilliant perfection until today. Now, as she gazed along the woodland rides, every leaf and branch seemed to glow with incandescent red-gold light, like living embers from a thousand fires . . . And as her eyes looked beyond the nearby woods to the hillside beyond, she saw that all those tree-clad slopes were afire with the same vivid wash of smouldering colour.

It's so beautiful, it hurts, she thought, with a strange catch at the heart. A world transformed, a jewelled fairyland . . . How Mo would love it. And Robert? Yes, Robert had loved every place they had gone to on those special short leaves . . . With him and Little Mo beside her, everywhere had seemed like fairyland . . . But it is still beautiful, even without them, she told herself. I mustn't shut it out just because it makes me sad . . . I ought to rejoice that it is here and I am here to see it . . .

"Here," said Beech. "Here be something to be glad about," and he led them over to see the gentle fallow deer and her fawn. "She be going home soon, and her little 'un." He turned to Beth and smiled. "Remember, I said the keeper would come and take a look?"

"Did he?"

"He did that. Reckons she be one o' his herd."

"How will he get her back?" It was Mark, sounding anxious again.

"Bring a truck. She'm pretty tame by now. I dessay she wun't be too moithered by it." He shrugged broad, bent shoulders. "But I shall go with 'er, to see 'er safely in."

"I'm glad of that," said Beth.

But Mark was working something out in his mind, and now he said in a rather angry voice: "Is it always *our fault*?"

Beech looked at him gravely, and did not misunderstand him. "Nay, that it's not. Not always." He considered for a moment. "Take Blackie, now. He just fell out o' his nest – an accident, like . . ." The old, clever eyes strayed now to look at Chloë's closed, upturned face, and then to Beth's, where they lingered with reflective gentleness. "Sometimes," he said softly, "it en't nobody's fault. It just happens . . . Animals get sick, just like people. Without warning. You can't go on blaming it on other folks all the time – that don't help to mend 'em, do it?"

There was a silence, while Mark thought about a lot of things that he could not put into words. If Chloë thought anything, she did not show it, but she was still looking up at Beech with her face turned to the light.

"No," agreed Mark at last, very slowly "I suppose not."

"Let's have a look at my Jess afore you goes," suggested Beech. "The pups are growin' fast."

He went back to the cottage door, where Jess and her wriggling litter of golden puppies lay in the sun.

It was true, thought Beth, the pups were growing fast. Their eyes were open, and their baby fur was coming in a soft gold fuzz on their fat little bodies.

Chloë had let go of Mark's hand, and was crouching down by herself to look at them. She really was looking, too – and the blankness was gone from her eyes for a little while.

"Come Christmas," murmured Beech to Beth, "they'll be wantin' homes . . ." He did not say any more just then. But Beth understood him very well.

Yes, it might be just the thing to bring Chloë out of her shell . . . She would have to talk to Finn about it. Then she remembered that Finn was away and could not be talked to at present. It made her suddenly angry. He ought to be here. But I'll get hold of him, she told herself. He can't stay away for ever. He simply can't.

She looked up to find that Beech had produced two glasses of fizzy lemonade for the children, and was offering her a ceremonial cup of tea.

"Can we come again?" asked Mark, who seemed as enchanted as ever by all that he had seen.

"Surely," smiled Beech. But he looked down at Chloë, and

added firmly: "Along o' Missus here, mind. Not on your own. Too far from home, it is, for a little 'un." Then he allowed his creaky smile to grow a little, in case he sounded too stern. "But I'm allus here about now of a Sunday, and allus pleased to see you."

"That's good," grinned Mark, looking suddenly cheerful. "Isn't it, Chloë?"

She did not answer, but she put her hand in his without being asked, and walked quietly between him and Beth through the tawny woods towards home.

Finn woke to the sound of bells – goat bells on the high hillside, the tinny single bell of St. Spyridion's little bell-tower on top of the white-washed church, and some kind of summoning bell being struck to call the builders on to the site for the morning's work. (Better than a factory whistle, anyway, he thought.) He lay for a few moments listening to the sounds of the early morning . . . A donkey braying somewhere, and the strident voice of a cock crowing above a comfortable clucking of hens – the rest of Andreas the farmer's flock? A couple of women calling to one another across the tiny village street: 'Kalemere, Anna . . .' and the laughter of children as they waited for the island bus to take them to the school in the little port.

But the laughter of children brought recollection to Finn's dreaming mind, and he sprang out of bed, determined to get on and do something practical – anything hard and useful that would serve to keep his thoughts at bay.

At one of the taverna tables, his foreman, Yannis, was having coffee and a hunk of bread before starting work, and he called Finn over to join him.

"You must have coffee, Kirios Finn. You cannot start the day without."

Reluctantly, Finn sat down beside him. He had a great, almost ungovernable urge to push on and get started, but that was not the way they did things out here in the islands. Georgios, seeing his favourite customer looking frustrated, brought him coffee and a large lump of the island's greyish-brown bread, still hot from the local bakery. Like Yannis, Finn broke off some bread and absently dunked it in his coffee, while watching the rest of the village beginning to wake up and prepare for the long day's toil. Several of the women were going into the bakery with their own covered dishes of lamb and herbs to be baked for them in the big, slow ovens, for tomorrow was a special saint's day – in fact, Saint Spyridion's own – and everyone would be eating a festive meal. As he watched, the village priest came out of his house near the little church on the hill, and walked down the winding path in his long black robes to join the queue in the baker's shop. Presently he came out, carrying a long loaf under his arm, and seeing Finn and Yannis, came over to join them.

"Good morning, Father," said Yannis dutifully and got to his feet.

The old priest nodded kindly and turned to Finn. "Kirios Finn, I am glad to see you back," she said gravely. "But I am grieved at your loss." He spoke good but rather too formal English, and had the beautiful, old-fashioned manners to go with it.

Finn inclined his head, and said briefly: "Thanks."

And Yannis, with supreme tact, gave them both one swift glance and muttered something about 'getting the men started' and went off down the street to the site near the jetty, leaving Finn and the old priest alone together.

"It's a good morning for work," said Finn hopefully, looking up at the flawless blue of the sky.

But the old priest was not to be deflected from his duty. "The little one – your daughter – she is better?"

"No," growled Finn, avoiding the priest's observant gaze. "I'm afraid not."

"You have not brought her with you this time?" Was there unspoken criticism in that innocent question?

Finn glanced rather wildly around him, almost as if looking for escape. "No . . . I thought it might upset her – even more." He hesitated, and then something compelled him to go on. "She is better without me at present."

"But not for ever," said the priest, and it was not a question this time.

Finn sighed. "I hope you are right."

The old priest was looking at him with some concern. "You

are not the only one, Kirios Finn, to blame themselves for the happening – "

Finn looked startled. "Not the only one?"

"No. We all felt it – especially the girl, Sofia."

"But," protested Finn, "she couldn't have known . . . She wasn't due back at the villa till the Friday. It was not her fault."

"It was not your fault either, Kirios Finn."

The two pairs of eyes met then, the black ones challenging and bright, Finn's blue ones still clouded with grief and self-reproach. But he understood what the old man was saying.

"I – I wish I could believe that."

"We islanders are proud of our hospitality," explained the priest, going about things in a roundabout way. "We like to look after our friends – especially a friend like you, Kirios Finn, who brings work to the island and takes away the ugliness of the other site from our beautiful bay . . ." He paused, and then continued with slow deliberation: "So it was very bad for all of us when something so terrible happened to your family – especially for those on the main island. They felt responsible."

"But they weren't."

"No, Kirios Finn. They were not. And you were not. But in the eyes of God we are all one family, are we not? And we must share in each other's griefs and each other's joys, must we not?"

Finn was silent at this, not quite knowing where it was leading. He looked down at his hands clutching his cup of coffee, and waited.

"We will all be waiting," said the priest gently, "for news of the little one. We will all be praying to Saint Spyridion tomorrow, for your wife, Kyria Edmondson, God rest her, for you, Kirios Finn, and for the child, little Chloë. We will all ask that she be well, and you will be together again soon."

Finn did not dare raise his head, for fear the tears in his eyes would actually spill out and disgrace him in front of everyone in the taverna. Life was so simple to these people. Ask Agios Spyridion and the good God to take care of things, and all would be well. Stephanie would be all right. Chloë would be all right. Even he, with his load of guilt, would be all right. You only had to ask . . . *If only,* he thought, *oh if only it was true!*

But the old priest seemed to know he had said enough. Now he merely leant forward and patted Finn's shoulder kindly. "You will go home when the time is right," he said, with strange certainty in his voice, and then he got to his feet and wandered off down the village street without saying any more.

Finn looked at Georgios, who was hovering anxiously nearby, and rolled his eyes in comic dismay. "For God's sake, give me a cognac and let me get to work!" he said.

But the old priest's words haunted his mind all day, and had the curious effect of making him feel more guilty than ever for having deserted Chloë – for whatever well-intentioned reasons. All day, tramping about the site with Yannis, inspecting the cutting off of the awful forest of metal struts and the infilling on the other abandoned site, and discussing with Bob and his colleagues on the archeological site how best to leave their work unimpeded, he was conscious of the war within himself. Chloë's pinched little face seemed to stare up at him out of every closed-up flower waiting in the shade for the sun to reach it. And Beth's face too, shocked and accusing, her voice – usually so gentle and shy – saying urgently: "You *can't! She needs you!*

In the end, driven by guilt and anxiety, he walked back over the island hills to the little port, and went into the small shipping office that held the only phone. Communication was always difficult from the islands, and the lines were almost always bad, but even so he had to try.

He rang Mary Willis first, and after a lot of waiting and arguing with telephonists in Athens, he finally got a creaky line. Between the crackling and whistling, he managed to gather from Mary that Chloë was all right, she was eating and sleeping, but she was still as shut in as ever – except with Beth Halliday and the old man, Beech, who both reported signs of improvement. Mary then asked if he wanted to try to speak to Chloë. Finn hesitated, and then said awkwardly: "Ask her." But after a pause, Mary returned to say that Chloë had simply

102

sat there where she was 'like stone,' Mary told him, and refused to move. Sighing, Finn rang off after a few further words of instruction, and decided to try to get through to Beth.

After more frustrating delays, he finally heard Beth's breathless voice on the line.

"It's Finn," he said. "Did I make you run?"

"I – I was in the garden." She paused, and then said shyly: "How are you, Finn?"

"All right." His voice was abrupt, and though Beth did not know it, equally shy. "I was worried about Chloë."

"Of course." Beth tried not to let her disapproval sound too apparent. After all, communication was what they all needed now, not recriminations.

"How does she seem to you?" He also paused, and then added: "Mary told me you have been very good to her."

Beth sighed. "We do our best, Finn, but it's slow progress. I think she does show signs of improvement now and then." She hesitated, wondering how much to say about Beech and the boy, Mark, and his staunch protection of little Chloë. "There's a boy here called Mark who seems to know how to handle her. Very supportive . . . I have them both to tea most days, and she seems to respond a little."

"That's wonderful of you."

"No," said Beth honestly. "It's just practical. Mark needs help, too – and they seem to get on together somehow." Once again she hesitated, considering "And then there's Beech – you remember him?"

"I do, indeed. Does our garden. Nice old fellow."

"And pretty wise in his way. He's got the two of them interested in his animals."

"Even Chloë?"

"Even Chloë. Particularly in his retriever puppies. She actually stretched out to stroke one. We – we all felt it was a tiny breakthrough."

"Yes." He sounded both relieved and sad at once. She heard him sigh down the line. "Yes, it was."

"Beech thinks she might like to have one of her own."

"A puppy?"

"One of his. It might be a good idea, Finn. She seems to respond better to animals than humans at present."

"Could she manage it on her own?"

"No," said Beth, almost explosively. "But Mary said she would help. And you – when are you thinking of coming home?"

"Not yet, Beth." His voice was still sad. "I asked if Chloë wanted to speak to me on the phone and she refused. 'Sat like stone,' Mary said."

Beth took a deep breath of resolve. "All the same, Finn, I think you should be here. She has no roots at present – no-one of her own. And your house feels so empty."

"Yes," he agreed grimly. "It does."

"But you could change that," she insisted. "You could make it come alive." She took another perilous breath. "I think you ought to come home for Christmas at least. You should be here then – and you could give Chloë the puppy yourself."

There was a long silence. At last Finn said, rather hoarsely: "I'll consider it."

"*Please*," begged Beth. "Please do, Finn. It's important."

He made no reply to that, and the tenuous line between the Greek islands and Gloucestershire began to crackle and fade even more.

"I'll think about it," he repeated. "Thanks, Beth, for all you're doing . . . I do appreciate it. This line is terrible, I'll ring off now."

"Come home soon," Beth urged, to the fizzing telephone. "She needs you, Finn . . ." and then she heard the click of the receiver cutting off.

Oh well, she thought sadly, pushing the hair out of her eyes in a familiar gesture of frustration. I did my best . . . And she went back to her garden and the last of the evening sunshine, with Finn's grim, unsmiling face far too clear in her mind . . .

As for Finn, he put down the phone with the same sense of guilt he had had when he picked it up, swallowed a quick Metaxa at the cafe on the quay, and strode off back up the darkening hills to the Spirios site and his own quiet room above Georgios' taverna. But the Furies still pursued him.

It was a day or two after the trip to see Beech, when Beth was having a five minutes breather between classes, that

Mark came rushing into the staff-room, white-faced and out of breath.

"George is on the roof," he said. "And he won't come down."

Beth leapt to her feet, and so did the other two staff in the room, who happened to be young Peter Green and fluttery Ruth Brown. They all rushed out into the playground to have a look, and found a small group of children standing in a huddle, gazing up at the steep pitch of the roof. At the top of the ridge, with one arm round a chimney stack, stood a wild-eyed George. His hair seemed to be on end, his face was red with rage, and his eyes, looking down at the little crowd on the ground, were somehow beyond reason.

"How did he get up there?" asked Beth swiftly. "Can we reach him?"

"There's a skylight in the top attic," said Peter, and began to run. "I'll go."

"No!" Beth followed him urgently. "He's my responsibility, Peter . . . I know how to handle him."

Peter glanced at her over his shoulder, but he did not stop running. "We'll both go, then. Come on."

"I'll fetch Miss Collier," said Mark from beside them, sounding extraordinarily sensible and helpful. Beth shot him a grateful glance and followed Peter Green up the stairs to the top floor.

The rooms up there were mostly used for stores, or occasionally for extra craft lessons, and were full of old papier-mâché models, bags of clay and piles of materials for the sewing classes. In the last one, a collection of wooden boxes had been stacked together underneath the open skylight where George had managed to climb out.

Without hesitation, Peter climbed out too, and reached down a hand to help Beth. But he hesitated before he let her follow. "Are you sure? It's none too safe out here."

"None too safe for George, either," retorted Beth, and kicking off her shoes, she grabbed at his hand and clambered out on to the roof after him.

George saw them coming, and began to back off on to the far slope of the roof. "Keep off!" he shouted. "Keep off, or I'll jump!"

105

"George," said Beth reasonably, "there's no need for this. What's the matter?"

George glared at her, daring her to come any nearer. "I told you," he hissed. "I'll jump!"

"Why?" asked Beth, hoping to get him interested in telling her what his grievance was, and edging a little nearer as she did so.

Peter did not try to approach the boy from the front where he could see him. Instead, he began to work his way round to the back of the house, hoping to come up to George from behind, and at least stop him slipping on the steeply-raked tiles.

"Why?" shouted George, even more wildly. "I'll tell you why! They hate me, see? I'm no good. No good at *anything* – and they hate me, all of them." He backed a little further, and Beth saw his foot slide a little on the tiles beneath him.

"Who hates you, George?" she asked softly. "Who are you talking about?" And she edged a little nearer.

"Everyone!" yelled George. "All of them!"

"That's not true, George," said Beth, still sounding reasonable and calm, though she wondered fleetingly if George could be the victim of school bullying of some kind. She thought not, when she considered it. Margaret Collier was very strict about such things, especially with her 'special' children, who might get picked on. "I don't hate you, George . . . None of us here hate you – so who are you talking about?"

"Them!" screamed George, and took another unwary step backwards. "Ask *them*! They'll tell you! They'd rather I was dead!" And he teetered wildly on the roof-ridge and began to slide backwards down the slope.

Beth acted then. It was too late for caution. She flung herself forward and grabbed George's flailing arm as he lost his balance and fell sideways, spread-eagled on the slanting roof. Her hands caught one arm and held on, but she thought desperately: He is too heavy. I won't be able to hold him.

"Hang on," said Peter's voice, from the other side of the chimney stack. "I'm coming."

Beth found herself looking straight into George's mad, frantic gaze, and as she stared, the red rage seemed to die in his eyes and he looked suddenly like an ordinary, rather frightened boy who had begun to realise the danger he was in.

106

"Just keep still," said Beth, seeing that look of dawning realisation. "I've got you, George. You can't fall. We'll soon have you safe and sound." She did not dare shift her position, but her own arm was beginning to feel as if it was being pulled out of its socket. "Reach up your other hand," she told him. "Try to catch hold of me – can you?"

But George could not move. His hand was clamped on the edge of a tile like a frozen claw, and he could not get it off.

"All right," said Peter, close to Beth now, and within reach of George's prone body. "Take it easy . . . We've got you . . ." and his arm went round George and held him firmly against the slippery tiles. "Now . . . when I say 'heave' – push yourself up a little . . . We'll pull you back bit by bit – understand?"

George gulped, and tried to nod. But he was too terrified to move his head, let alone anything else.

"Try, George," coaxed Beth. "You're very brave to come out here all on your own – I'm sure you can do it."

"*Now*," ordered Peter. "One, two, three – HEAVE!"

Peter pushed, Beth pulled, and George at last made an effort and moved upwards.

"That's it!" said Peter, sounding cheerful and approving.

"Well done, George," Beth encouraged. "Try again!"

"*HEAVE!*" commanded Peter, and something in the sharpness of his voice made George obey.

Once again Beth pulled and Peter shoved the boy upwards, and he was suddenly safe again on the ridge of the roof.

"There!" said Peter, breathing hard.

"I knew you could!" smiled Beth. "Now, all we have to do is wriggle backwards." She waited to see an answering glimmer of a smile on George's face, and then edged slowly away towards the skylight, still holding on to the boy's arm. Peter followed, holding the other arm in a firm and none-too-gentle grip.

In a few moments they were all safely down on the attic floor, where Margaret Collier was quietly waiting for them.

"I think we all need a cup of tea," she said.

It was when George's mother came to fetch him that Beth began to understand the trouble. Mrs. Warner was small and dainty, where George was large and clumsy, and she was blonde and pretty where George was dark and plain. She was also, Beth suspected, vain and rather stupid – and George was neither of those. To add to the bitter contrast, she had brought her daughter, George's sister, with her. Germaine Warner was fourteen, small and blonde like her mother, with long, elegant legs and small neat feet beneath a too-tight, too-short skirt, and a supercilious manner that did not make much attempt to disguise her contempt for her bumbling hobbledehoy of a brother.

"What's he done *now*?" she groaned to her mother, casting her blue eyes to heaven.

"I asked Mrs. Halliday to be here when you came," said Margaret Collier steadily, "since she was instrumental in getting George safely out of trouble."

"Very grateful, I'm sure," said Eve Warner, not sounding particularly pleased.

"And she probably knows more about the cause of his outburst than any of us," added Margaret, and waited for Beth to speak.

"He said," Beth told them deliberately, "'*they all hate me. They'd rather I was dead.*'"

Eve Warner flinched, and even Germaine's pert face looked suddenly uncertain.

"I don't know who he meant," added Beth, looking from one to the other of them with the greatest innocence.

"Oh, the poor boy," wailed Eve and began to cry.

"There's no harm done," said Margaret Collier briskly. "He'll be all right after a good night's sleep." She paused, and then went on with firm intent. "But he is rather highly strung – like most clever boys."

"*Clever?*" Eve sounded incredulous.

"Oh yes. Very." Margaret turned blandly to Beth. "Ask Mrs. Halliday."

Beth smiled. "One of the most intelligent boys in my class – except when he's upset."

They did not rub it in any more just then. It seemed to them that they had done enough to help George's cause for the time-being. Beth went to fetch a somewhat chastened George, and gave him a swift hug of reassurance before she handed him over to his mother. "It'll be all right," she murmured to him.

"Don't worry," and smiled as comfortingly as she could into his bewildered brown eyes.

"Oh *George!*" said his mother, and then somehow could not think of anything else to say in front of Margaret Collier's grave, carefully neutral gaze. She gave Beth one nervous glance, and then hurried out of the room with her hand on George's unwilling arm. Germaine followed, looking bored again at what she privately called 'all this fuss' – but she did not say anything unkind to her brother. At least, not then. About what would happen when they got home, Beth was not so sure. She just hoped they had got the message, that was all.

"Sit down, Beth," said Margaret close behind her, "before you fall down."

"Thanks," said Beth, suddenly aware of her shaky legs. "I don't mind if I do!"

Beth hadn't realised she was so shattered till she got home. Then she collapsed into the nearest chair and allowed the shaking of her limbs to take its course until she felt steady enough to get up and make a cup of tea. She was just settling down again with the mug of tea in her hand, when someone knocked on her door. Sighing, she struggled to her feet and went to see who it was. Peter Green stood in the porch, looking shy.

"I just came to see how you were," he said, sounding even shyer than he looked.

"Recovering." Beth stood back to let him come inside.

"It was quite an experience," he remarked, and began to grin.

"You can say that again!" Beth went back into the kitchen and poured out another mug of tea.

"Have you been down to look at the river yet?" Peter was nothing if not direct.

"The Severn? No. Why?"

"Very soothing." His grin was somehow infectious. "Very restful." He took a cheerful swig of tea. "There's a nice pub right by the river. Thought you could do with a breather?"

Beth was on the point of refusing, on the grounds of total exhaustion after the day's traumatic events, when she suddenly thought: Well, why not? A peaceful drink beside a slow-moving river sounded very tempting.

"You'd like it down there," he coaxed. "Lovely and quiet."

That did it. Beth's head was still singing with George's hysterical shouts, and her heart (she supposed it was her heart) was still clenching with the fright she had not dared to show.

"All right," she agreed suddenly. "Why not? It sounds a great idea."

They sat peacefully at a wooden table on a green slope of rough grass, with the silver Severn spread out before them. Beth had not realised it was so wide, but the silken water seemed to stretch for miles, and the mudflats at the edge made it look even wider. There were hundreds of birds flying up and settling in ceaseless clouds of white wings on the sandbanks in the middle of the river downstream, and across from Beth on a small sandy spit of shore was one solitary heron standing motionless like a sentinel in the shallows. He stood so still that his reflection came up to meet him on his tall stilted legs in perfect clarity. Even the reeds at the water's edge had their own double image below.

It was close to sunset now, and over all this silvery spread of water the sun, sinking behind the far Welsh hills, laid a patina of gold and rose, and a shimmering pathway of fading crimson light from its own bright disc across the smooth stretch of water at Beth's feet.

"Thought you'd like it," said Peter, sounding as pleased as a magician who had just produced a rabbit out of a hat.

Beth turned to him, smiling. "You're very clever. It was just what I needed."

Peter nodded a cheerful yellow head. "Often come here myself when things get fraught."

Beth laughed. She couldn't imagine Peter getting worked up about anything. "You were pretty cool on the roof."

"So were you," he retorted, grinning again. Then his smile faded and he looked at her curiously. "Weren't you scared at all?"

Beth considered the matter, wondering how to answer

110

truthfully. Yes, she had been scared – but mostly about George and whether he would fall, whether she was strong enough to hold him, or whether there would be another young life wasted? . . . She hadn't really been scared for herself – for one thing, there wasn't time, and for another, she had to admit she didn't really care an awful lot what happened to her nowadays. She supposed it was wrong to be so negative, and she ought to be thankful to be alive, but she still found it hard to be glad about anything much.

"For George, of course," she said carefully. "But for the rest – " she just shrugged and left it there.

Peter, with surprising tact, did not pursue it, but went to fetch her another drink and a supper menu. In the meantime, Beth was scolding herself for being an ungrateful wretch with all this tranquil beauty burning away to blue dusk in front of her eyes.

"Look!" said Peter, "the birds are going home for the night," and pointed down river to where flight after flight of white-winged water birds wheeled and turned in the sunset afterglow before fanning out into flocks and skeins of drifting flights homing in to the west.

"Where are they going?" Beth wondered.

"Mostly to Slimbridge – to the Wildfowl Trust," explained Peter. "The tide's coming up fast now. The feeding grounds will be covered."

Spellbound, Beth watched the bird-clouds grow faint in the west, and the incoming thrust of the tide make swirling eddies on the rose-coloured surface of the sleeping river.

"Magical!" she murmured, admitting to herself at last that this was something she was glad to be alive to see. It would have been better if Little Mo and Robert had been here to see it, too. But even without them it was worth seeing. She was suddenly reminded of Beech talking about his grieving dog and saying: '*Came a day when the sun shone and he decided it was good to be alive after all . . .*' Was that happening to her? Perhaps not quite yet – there was still too much aching sadness in beauty when she dared to look at it. But even so, it was coming back . . . the will to stay alive . . .

"Magical!" she repeated, and smiled at Peter in sudden gratitude.

111

And Peter smiled back and raised his glass to her, and carefully did not say a single word.

Beth knew what she wanted to do about George, and she got busy organising it as soon as she could. She was going to make him into the star of their Japanese opera, and what's more, she was going to make him so good that the whole school, and particularly his idiotic mother and sister, would be filled with admiration.

"But I can't sing," growled George, when she put it to him.

"You won't have to. You are Hamaguchi, the Village Grandfather, the one everyone looks up to and obeys. You are an old man, see? You wouldn't be able to sing anyway, but you can speak, can't you?"

"I s'pose so . . ." He still sounded very dubious.

"We'll give you a beautiful long robe – a kimono, they call it – and a long, thin beard. You'll look smashing."

"I'll look right silly."

"No, you won't, George. You'll look tall and dignified. You're much the tallest in the class, and the oldest. You're the only one sensible enough to act like a wise old man."

George looked at her in amazement. "Me?" He sounded totally disbelieving.

But Beth was determined. "Please, George. No-one else could do it."

He shifted uneasily from one clumsy foot to another. Tall and dignified? . . . Wise and old? . . . Could he be? It didn't seem likely. He'd be sure to fall off the stage, or trip over his k- thing and fall flat on his face.

Unexpectedly, Beth found an ally in Mark, who had already agreed to sing the solo part of the young fisherman, Ojotaki. "Go on, George," he urged, suddenly appearing beside him. "Have a go. I'm going to."

George looked at him suspiciously. "So what?"

"So it's no worse for you. At least you haven't got to sing." Mark glared at him with fierce challenge.

For some reason this made George begin to smile. "Oh, all right," he said grudgingly. "But I'll make a proper mess of it."

"No, you won't." Beth grinned back. "I won't let you."

She went off to tell Margaret Collier about her plan and to enlist her help. "I know they've never done anything like it before," he said, trying to sound persuasive and entirely reasonable both at once, "and they're apt to be unpredictable – "

"You can say that again," agreed Margaret, smiling.

"But I – I'd like to try." Beth looked at her with urgent appeal. "It would be so wonderful for them to do something really well that everyone else admired."

"Yes." Margaret thought about it. "Yes, it would."

Beth saw her approval and sighed with relief. "Then – I can go ahead?"

Margaret nodded. "Of course. Though goodness knows what you're letting yourself in for."

"If it's a flop," said Beth slowly, "you mustn't blame them. It'll be my fault for being too ambitious."

"Quite so," agreed Margaret, an unmistakeable glint of humour dancing in her eyes.

Beth saw it and began to smile back. Then she remembered a question she wanted to ask – something that seemed to her very relevant to her present problems. "What is George's father like?"

Margaret laughed. "Like George – only more so."

"Large?"

"Very."

"Clumsy?"

"I should think so – bumbling, at least."

"Henpecked?"

"Almost certainly."

Beth sighed. "Yes. That figures." She paused and then added: "Clever?"

"Probably – but not as clever as George."

"Would he be an ally?"

Margaret did not hesitate. "Oh yes. If we enlisted his help." She looked at Beth and then away out of the window, and murmured: "I daresay a quiet word wouldn't do any harm."

Beth thought she had said enough, and got up to go.

But Margaret said suddenly: "How is Chloë getting on?"

"Slowly," Beth admitted. "But there are signs . . . and

113

young Mark is a great help." She hesitated, and then went on with sudden shyness: "Finn rang up to ask about her – and I tried to get him to come home."

"Did he agree?"

"No." Beth was honest. "But he said he'd think about it."

"Poor man." Margaret spoke with quiet pity. "Without Stephanie's guiding hand, he finds it hard to know what to do. He was never very good at being a family man."

"But he's got to learn!" Beth sounded absurdly belligerent.

"Oh yes," agreed Margaret mildly. "He's got to learn. But it will take time."

When Beth got back to the empty classroom at the end of the lunch break, Mark was waiting for her.

"Mrs. Halliday," he said seriously, "what can Chloë be?"

Beth sighed. What could a totally silent, totally unresponsive little girl be? A piece of scenery?

"What do you think, Mark?" she asked, telling herself that sometimes children were wiser and more inventive than you expected.

"My sister," he said with flat certainty. "Then she could hold my hand. She'll go where I go, then."

Beth nodded. "Good idea."

Mark was working it out carefully in his mind. "A fisherman could have a little sister, couldn't he?"

"Several, I should think, in a Japanese village. But I don't know whether he'd take her out fishing in his boat."

"Well, I don't go out in my boat, do I? I mean, not on the stage . . . I only sing about it." His logic was infallible.

"So you do," agreed Beth, and smiled at his concern.

But Mark had not done with her yet. He seemed to hesitate with painful shyness before he spoke again. "My Mum told me what happened to Chloë . . . it's worse for her. I mean, my Dad's gone away, but I know where he is, and I see him sometimes. But Chloë . . . ." He hesitated again, and then rushed on. "And now her Dad's gone away, too, hasn't he? And she doesn't see him at all."

Beth sighed. "I know, Mark. It's very sad." Then, for some unexplained reason, she felt obliged to defend Finn. "But her

114

father will be back soon, I'm sure, and by then, perhaps, Chloë will feel more like talking to him."

Mark said slowly, understanding a lot more than he let on, as usual: "Beech said *you can't go blaming it on other folks all the time . . .*"

"Yes, he did." Beth's voice was gentle. Can this be the same boy that lay on the floor and screamed his frustration to the world, she thought – this calm, rational being who understands so much about human frailty, and shows so much concern about someone else's grief?

But the honest eyes were still looking into hers with some kind of unspoken appeal. "Could we go and see him again soon?"

"Who?" Beth asked, startled.

"Beech."

"Oh." She smiled at him. "I don't see why not."

His face lit up for a moment, and then grew absurdly grave again. "It's – it's for Chloë, really," he explained, with great earnestness, "not me." He took a nervous breath. "He might know what to say – " he added lamely, not quite knowing how to explain.

But Beth understood him very well. "He might, indeed," she said, and hoped most passionately that he would, for she herself did not. She could barely come to terms with it herself, let alone know how to comfort one small, bewildered child who could not accept the enormity of death, or the awful sense of loss and loneliness it left behind.

"We'll go and see him on Sunday," she said to those anxious eyes. "It can't do any harm."

Finn had forgotten about St. Spyridion. The festival did not really start till the evening, but when it did, it erupted with a bang. A volley of fire-crackers went off in the street and on the quayside, lights sprang up in all the little houses, everyone who could move at all flocked to the little church on the hill, and everyone who could play any kind of instrument played it loudly all the way up the road. In the church, the statue of the Saint was lifted on to his ceremonial float, bedecked with late flowers and bunches of herbs from the hillside. The bearers, dressed in their best black suits, stooped their shoulders to the platform handles and lifted Saint Spyridion aloft. Everyone lit a candle and began to sing, following the Saint in a long, glowing snake of pinpoint lights down the winding hill to the village streets below.

Finn had been sitting alone at a taverna table, not feeling that he belonged in such joyful festivities, but now the crowd all began to spill out round him into a singing, purposeful mob that swept him along with them and would not let him be left behind. Someone grabbed his arm, and someone else thrust a lighted candle into his hand, and several of the children seized him by his shirt-tail and dragged him along, singing and laughing as they went.

The procession wound its way along the front of the village to the edge of the sea and the little jetty with its few small boats, and here it stopped for a breather. The Saint was set down while his bearers rested their shoulders. Here the village Priest, in his best festival robes and carrying a tall silver cross, blessed the tiny quayside and the boats which brought fish to the islanders, and the sea itself which provided them with riches as well as winter storms. Finn noticed then that every boat had a light swinging from its bows and sometimes another lantern hanging high on the mast of the bigger ones.

"Kyrios Finn," said Marina's voice close to him, "you must have some herbs to give the Saint," and she handed him a bunch of fragrant silver-grey leaves tied up with yellow ribbon.

Finn looked round and saw that everyone was carrying some kind of small offering, mostly flowers or herbs, or small laden branches of arbutus with their pink strawberry-fruit. One or two had bunches of grapes, or a tiny basket of olives, or even a loaf of bread. He smiled at Marina and thanked her in careful Greek, and resolved to watch what everyone else did with their gifts for the Saint, and do likewise.

The procession now re-formed and moved off along the edge of the sea, all round the small, sandy bay to where Finn's new site was beginning to take shape close to the rocks at the furthest end of the cove. And here the priest signalled to Finn and Yannis, his foreman, to come forward and stand beside him facing the neat clearance where the first signs of the new structure were visible in the growing dusk.

116

"We will bless the new site," the old priest said gravely, "that it may bring prosperity and happiness to our village, and not destroy the beauty of our shore . . ." And when he had lifted his hand and waved his silver cross, the singing rose up louder than ever, and the Saint on his flowery platform seemed to nod and smile in the candlelight as the bearers turned round and began to move off in another direction.

This time, the procession left the edge of the shore and wound its way over the hill path to the next bay where the false site was being cleared away. It was a beautiful bay, long and curving, with very white sand lapped by a gentle surf, and surrounded by sheltering rocks beneath shallow ochre-coloured cliffs. The sea beyond that pure white line of surf was a deep and glowing blue, almost as dark as lapis lazuli out in the open water where it was deepest, and shading to indigo and purple near the black rocks at the edge of the encircling cliffs. But where it still reflected the grassy herb-strewn clifftops, the strange, luminous blue seemed to change to the clearest green.

How beautiful it is, thought Finn. I am glad we could save it. He glanced round at the abandoned site and saw with relief that all the metal struts had now gone, the bulldozers had already covered the worst area with earth and most of the remaining clutter had been either flattened or filled in. The wild plants will soon come back, he thought. But if I'm going to turf it all (and I *am*,) we'll need rain. He looked up at the flawless sky, now darkening into starlit night, and said somewhat wryly to himself: St. Spyridion, you'd better do your stuff!

Then the procession stopped again, and this time the priest blessed the bay itself and the sea once again. (After all, the sea dominated their lives – it was all round them on every side, and its moods, its fierce tempests and sudden calms, governed all their going out and coming in).

"May the flowers of the field return," said the Priest in his most musical voice, "and the herbs and grasses of the hills clothe our bay anew."

(He's quite a poet in his way, thought Finn)

" . . . And let us also thank Kirios Edmondson that he has returned our land to us," the Priest added, confounding Finn

117

with his honeyed tongue, and various of the villagers clapped their hands in agreement.

After this, the whole gathering moved off again and came to a halt at the edge of the archeological site on the farther hill. The archeologists were standing together in a small, anxious knot, wondering if all these feet were going to trample on their careful digging, but the Priest was the only one who came forward to meet them. Everyone else stayed quietly beside the Saint, with their lighted candles forming a bright halo round him.

(How will the old priest reconcile St. Spyridion with the ancient gods? wondered Finn. For the archeological site was unearthing the remains of a temple to Apollo on the seaward-looking slope of the hillside.)

"May the Saint protect you in your labours," said the priest, in his courtly old voice. "For all that you discover here is to the glory of Greece . . ." He lifted a gentle hand, and added softly: "and the ancient ones were but other faces of the One."

(Well done! thought Finn. That will please everyone). He saw Bob and the rest of the workers turn to each other and smile, and then they all came down with the priest to join the long lines of the procession as it began to move off again back to the village and the little church on the hill. The singing started up again, supportedly by a motley collection of bouzoukis, guitars, pan-pipes and one-string fiddles, and the line of lights gleamed like fireflies in the deepening night.

When at last the weary Saint-bearers desposited their burden back in the church, the singing grew loudest of all, the candles were all stuck into spikes round the Saint so that his gold paint glistened all over, and the villagers gave him their presents one by one before they left for the more lighthearted festivities in the village below.

Finn, too, went up and left his small bunch of silvery herbs, and was not ashamed to whisper a small prayer to match. *"Help Chloë to come back,"* he breathed – and such was the power of all that village faith and homage round him that he found himself almost believing in miracles.

True to her promise, the next Sunday morning Beth took Mark and Chloë up to see Beech again. Mark's eyes were curiously full of hope as he walked beside her, and Beth found herself wishing most fervently that the old man would find a way to keep that spark alive and not let the boy be too disappointed in his eager plans for Chloë.

This time, Beech had some different charges. The owl had gone by now, and so had the mother doe and her fawn. The fox cub was still there, and Blackie was still singing small snatches of song to them from the nearest beech tree, and the Rhode Island hen had hatched her pheasant foster babies, and the chicks were tumbling about the straw like small speckled balls of fluff. The puppies had grown, too, and did even more tumbling than the chicks. But in one quiet pen, a hare lay prone in a concealing heap of bracken, and scarcely even moved when Beech came near.

"Shot, she was," he said, his voice rough with anger. "Not clean-like – one-two-gone – but raggéd. Pellets all over the place." He bent down to smooth the bedraggled fur with gentle fingers. "We got most of 'em out, but the shock near killed 'er."

"Will she get better?" Mark's voice was anxious.

Beech looked down at the hare, and then at the boy beside him, and gave a non-committal shrug. "Maybe – if she'm not too frit."

Mark did not say any more just then, and Beech led them over to another, smaller pen where a chattering grey squirrel was running up and down a small tree-branch inside the wire, sounding very angry at being kept in.

"Cross with me, aren't you?" grinned Beech. "You get that paw o' yourn better and I'll let you go, see?"

Then Beth saw that the angry little creature was running about on three legs, and the joint of one front paw was missing so that it ended in a half-healed raw stump.

"What happened to him?" asked Mark, sounding shocked, and Chloë seemed to cling on to his hand a little tighter.

Beech sighed and shook his head. "They'm braver than us, critturs are. I reckon he got it stuck somewhere – a trap or some wire, like – and he just bit it off, to get free."

Beth expected Mark to look even more horrified, but to her surprise he just nodded, and waited for Beech to drop some nuts and an apple core into the cage, with the cheerful

119

words: "Stop frettin' now. You'll soon be free agen." He turned gravely to explain to Mark: "Infected, see? Has to be treated. But he's a tetchy customer – bite you as soon as look at you, he will." He laughed – the same creaky-old-saw laugh – and dropped in a final titbit to cheer the squirrel up.

Chloë was actually tugging at Mark's hand to make him go over to look at the puppies, but for some reason Mark held his ground, and stood looking from the angry squirrel and the sick hare to Beech's seamed, compassionate face.

"*Do they ever die on you?*" he said.

Beech stopped short and looked down. Something about those clear grey eyes disturbed him. He hesitated. "Sometimes they do, young 'un, yes."

"Can't you make them better?"

He understood then what was behind the question, and knew he must go carefully now. But he also knew, without question, that he must be honest with that uncompromising stare.

Beth, standing beside him, held her breath for his answer.

"Not always," he said slowly. "Sometimes they just don't make it. Sometimes . . . I reckon their time is up."

"*Why?*" Mark demanded, and took a tight grip of Chloë's hand. And in that fierce question was a whole world of bewilderment and rage against a world that was cruel and unfair.

Beech paused for thought. Go easy now, he said to himself. This is important. And not only for the boy and the shocked little one who cannot speak, either. There's the young woman, too, as full of sadness as all of 'em put together, though she don't say so . . .

He looked down into Chloë's upturned face with a kind of aching pity. Was she listening, he wondered? Certainly, the boy was. But how do you answer a child who has asked you the most difficult question in the world?

"Well," he began slowly, "I don't rightly know how to answer that, young 'un, but I reckon it's like this. Some of 'em – like this here squirrel, or my fox-cub – they has to get knocked about a bit afore they grows up, so's they can cope with the world out there – " He jerked a broad thumb at the golden beechwoods and the huddle of grey stone houses below the hill. "Wicked ol' place, the world is, young 'un, and you needs to be tough, see, to get through . . ." He looked into Mark's

120

face enquiringly, and saw the boy nod quick comprehension. Yes, the boy had been knocked about too by life, one way or the other, Beech guessed. He understood that all right.

"And in the end," he went on, "when you've mostly learnt what there is to know and done what there is to do, like – then you're old, like me, and it's nearly time to go home, all natural like." He took a long breath into his tired old lungs and wondered if he was making any sense to his listeners at all.

"But there's some," he went on, and now there was an odd thrill of authority in the old voice, as if he knew what he was saying had the ring of truth, "there some as is well-night perfect already, see? Not when they're old with the corners knocked off at all, but young-like . . ." And now his glance strayed to little Chloë's closed flower face, and then to Beth's still one which was watching him with such breathless attention, " and they be ready to go home much sooner, see? . . . So that's what they do, you see, young 'un – go home where they're safe and free."

He wasn't sure if he knew what 'home' was exactly, but somewhere in his mind's eye, home was a green place where the sun shone – and maybe a sprinkle or two of good spring rain – and no creature, whether man or beast, was ever frightened or hurt ever again . . . That was how it seemed to him, and he wondered if the boy, Mark, and the little one, would understand.

"D'you know what I do?" he said, and this time he spoke very softly and gently to those vulnerable faces turned towards him. "When one of 'em goes home, I goes out and plants a new tree."

"A new tree?" Mark was straining to understand, and to make it clear for Chloë.

"Come and I'll show you," said Beech. "The Missus here, she knows. I gave her a tree once."

Beth nodded, smiling, but the tears stood in her eyes and she dared not let them fall in front of the children.

"I keep all the seedlings, see, safe where the rabbits can't chew 'em, and then I plants 'em out. That way, there's allus something new comin' up."

He stumped over to his small patch of tilled land at the back of the cottage and pointed to a row of little flower pots at the

121

side of the path. "See? This here's a new beech. One day it'll be as tall as that one there – and as gold – but now it's just a twig. And this here's an oak. There's not lot of oaks up here – but when there is, he grows mighty." He looked into the young faces and added cheerfully: "Sometime, I'll take you to find where the acorns fall. Then you can grow an oak all by yourselves. Would you like that?"

For a moment, Mark did not answer. Then he looked from Beth to Chloë and back again, beseechingly, to Beech, and said in a quiet, clear voice that somehow understood everything: "I think Chloë would like to plant a tree *now*."

Beech nodded tranquilly. "Well then, so she shall. You can choose one for her. Which is it to be?"

Beth stood spellbound beside the old man and looked down as Mark bent over the little pots, pulling Chloë after him to look at them, too. And somehow the silent little girl did at last seem to be aware of her surroundings and to be looking at the tiny trees as if she really saw them. Mark's hand hesitated over each pot, not knowing which one to choose. The beech seedlings were very green and furly, with minute, pleated leaves on a thin, twiggy stem. But the oak seedlings were somehow sturdier, with strong indented leaves, and a miniature version of knotted bark on their upright stems. Mark thought the oak looked tougher. But the beech looked prettier.

And then he saw the right one. It was an oak seedling, smaller than the others but very sturdy, and its leaves were extra bright and extra curly, standing bravely spread out in three horizontal fingers of new green. And Beth, watching the process of choice through eyes that were still too full of tears for safety, was instantly reminded of Little Mo. So strong, so sturdy, so full of life, so brave . . .

"That one!" said Mark, and as he pointed, Chloë's small brown hand reached out and touched the tiny, perfectly-shaped leaves with one shy finger.

"Right then, that one it is," agreed Beech, and his eyes met Beth's in quiet triumph above the children's heads.

He gave Mark an old, battered trowel, and showed him where to plant the little tree at the edge of the woodland where it would have space to grow 'mighty', and helped him

122

to dig down into the centuries-old layer of leaf mould on the forest floor. Mark made a hole and set the little tree in it, and then patted the earth firmly round it – *and Chloë leant forward and patted it, too.*

Then Beech showed them how to put a small wire cage round it to keep it safe. "There you are then, my lovely," he said, smiling a little. "Safe and free to grow . . ."

He looked at them then, out of his shrewd old eyes and said suddenly: "I reckon they'm all runnin' about out there, right as rain, the safe-home ones – all on 'em, out yonder – dancin' about like hares in a cornfield." And he waved a gentle hand at the golden woodland around them. "What do you think?"

Mark did not answer, but he turned slowly to stare out into the dreaming spaces of the woods. Chloë looked too, with eyes that hoped to see miracles. She wanted to ask the old man where 'yonder' was, but then she suddenly felt sure she knew. 'Yonder' was out there, just past where you could see, in those bright and hazy places between the trees, where the hills grew misty and blue before they reached the sky.

And then Chloë spoke the first word she had uttered since her mother's death. "*Yonder?*" she said, and pointed towards the dazzle of sunlight beyond the trees.

PART IV – CORNY

The small break-through with Chloë did not develop into a major cure, though there were increasing signs each day of returning awareness. She did not speak very often yet, only if words seemed imperative, but she was less shut in behind walls of resistance, and even tried to co-operate with Mark and the rest of the class in the rehearsals for the little Japanese opera.

Beth did not try to push things. It was enough to see her actually holding up a lantern and swinging it in time to the music when the others did, and humbly standing to one side when Mark climbed up the central rostrum (alias the hillside) to sing his solo. And sometimes on the way home to tea at the Beehive with Mark, when Beth as usual chattered and pointed things out to them, Chloë's eyes would come back into real focus and she would stop to admire the late chrysanthemums or the scarlet rose-hips in the hedge.

It was November now, and the woods had almost lost their golden autumn clothing. The trees stood gaunt and dark against the evening sky, with every branch and twig etched in fine tracery, while the ground beneath them was springy and rich with the red-gold of fallen leaves. It was a time for wood fires and lamplight and drawn curtains, and crumpets and toast for tea. Beth did her best to make these tea-times warm and happy. Mark, she knew, enjoyed them, but Chloë was still too withdrawn to show much enthusiasm. However, she did at least sit by the fire and help to make toast on the long brass toasting fork, and then eat some of it herself, which was an improvement. So maybe, Beth told herself, the rest would come.

What with the weekday tea-times and the Sunday morning visits to Beech, it left little enough time for Beth to be lonely or at a loose end. Especially as, since the rooftop episode with George, young Peter Green had become a persistent Saturday visitor, with always some new excuse or some new place to show her. Beth did not mind. She rather liked his company. He was easy and undemanding, and seemed to like the kind of quiet pubs and wayside cafés in small unpretentious villages that also appealed to Beth. She did wonder once or twice if she ought to let him waste his time with her, knowing that she was still much too shocked and sad to enter into any kind of serious relationship with anyone, but it was somehow so soothing and pleasant to be taken out by this friendly, cheerful young man, that she hadn't the heart to refuse.

She was therefore half-expecting it one Saturday morning when there came a knock on her door. It was a bit early for Peter really, but still, she had nothing better to do. She went through from her little kitchen, crossed the front room and opened the inner door to the porch. But it wasn't Peter who stood there, it was Mary Willis from Finn's house across the valley.

"I'm so sorry to bother you," she began, almost wringing her hands in her distress, "but is Chloë with you?"

"Chloë? No. Should she be?"

"Oh dear. Oh dearie me." Mary looked about to cry. "Wherever can she have got to?"

Beth put a hand on her arm and led her inside. "Sit down a minute, Mary, and tell me what's happened. It can't be as bad as all that."

"Oh my goodness, I hope not," said Mary, and took a deep breath of attempted control. "I left her playing in the front room while I went upstairs to do some cleaning. I had the hoover on, so I didn't hear anything. When I came down, the French windows were open and she was gone." She looked at Beth with fearful apology. "I didn't leave her for long – but I have got other things to do sometimes . . ."

"Of course." Beth smiled at her encouragingly, and waited for her to go on.

"I went out to look for her in the garden, but she wasn't there, nor in the sheds nor the summer house where she sometimes goes . . . I did wonder if she might've gone up to see old Beech again, like she did before –

but I didn't think she'd do that, since you told her not to?"

Beth looked doubtful. "She might . . . I'm never sure how much of what I say she takes in . . . especially if she doesn't want to!"

The two women looked at each other, and both smiles were a little grim.

"And she is very keen on those puppies . . ." Beth added, thinking it out.

She had made Mary a cup of tea by this time, and now she handed it to her and waited while she tried to drink it, though her hands shook so much that the tea spilled in the saucer.

"I'll tell you what," Beth decided, "I'll walk up to Beech's cottage and see if she's there."

"Shall I – should I come with you?"

"No." She patted Mary's arm with gentle reassurance. "You go on home and wait there. She may come back of her own accord anyway. And a nice warm fire and a good hot meal will be just what the doctor ordered!"

Mary's face lit up. This was something she could understand. Warm fires and hot meals were exactly what she was good at. If only looking after little Chloë was always as easy as that.

"Don't worry," said Beth, seeing the relief in Mary's round, worried face. "I'll find her. She won't have got far."

Together they went out into the grey November day, and while Mary hurried back to the old Mill House, Beth climbed the hill to the edge of the woods and the clearing round Beech's cottage.

As she reached the top of the path, she saw the old man himself hurrying towards her.

"Missus," he said, still just remembering that small, polite salute with his hand, "I'm glad you've come. I didn't rightly know what to do."

"Why, Beech? Is Chloë here?"

He hesitated a little, and then shook his head. "Not here, exactly, Missus, no – but not far-off like." He fell into step beside her then, and led her past his cottage and on towards the first of the lofty beech trees in the wood. "Best go quietly, Missus . . . I didn't know if it was right to disturb her."

126

Beth looked at him, mystified, but did not ask any more questions.

"I came on her by chance, like," he explained, and now his old voice sank to a whisper, "and she looked so – happy, like . . ." He shook his head again, as if words failed him. "And I wus in two minds – whether to leave 'er be and go for you – or to stay by her in case of trouble . . ." He scratched his grizzled thatch of hair with one brown finger, as if still confused by the choice he had to make.

"Not fur now," he told her, and led her round a thicket of blackberry bushes and back on to the forest path.

Ahead of them, the trees grew closer and thicker, but just to one side there was an unexpected clearing. It was where the great old beech tree had come down in the storm, and its huge ancient stump still lay on its side, its roots dangling over the deep and hidden hollow its upheaval had left in the sandy soil. And as they came close to it, Beth heard a small voice talking softly to something – *talking freely and without restriction in a quiet, happy way* . . .

Beech put a finger to his lips, and Beth leant over the edge of the hollow to look inside. It was like a cave down there, under the roots of the tree stump, with steep shaly sides and a litter of small stones and wood chips at the bottom. And curled up on the ground, looking down and crooning softly to something warm and wriggling on her lap, was Chloë, with one of Jess's puppies cradled in her arms.

" . . . and you'll grow big and strong," she was saying, "and run about everywhere, won't you? . . . I'll take you in the fields . . ."

Beth looked at Beech in a mixture of dismay and relief. Chloë was *talking*! Not to them, of course. Not yet. But to the puppy, she could say anything. And it was clearly of enormous importance to her already – this small bundle of fluff – a release and joy they had none of them anticipated. Now what were they to do?

But Beech was beckoning to her to come away out of earshot. "Let's leave 'er be a little longer," he said, and his smile was wide and gentle.

"What are we going to do?" Beth said aloud.

127

The old man shrugged tranquil shoulders. "I said as they'd be needing homes . . ."

"Yes, but – isn't it too soon?"

He considered. "Nine weeks would be better – that's just into December."

"I haven't even got permission from her father."

Beech's expression was calm. "Seemingly, she's chosen already – "

Beth's smile met his. "Well, you'll have to explain to her about waiting." She thought, rather desperately: How do we tell her the puppy still needs its mother, when she hasn't got Stephanie any more at all?"

"Ar," agreed Beech, following her thoughts, "it'll be hard for her – but I reckon she'll understand."

They stood there for a little while, each pondering on the best way to approach her, when suddenly they saw the top of her head appearing above the edge of the hollow. As they watched, not knowing what to do, Chloë climbed carefully out, still cradling the puppy in her arms, and came directly towards them, looking not at all shame-faced or put out.

"She needs her mother," she said, quite calmly and clearly, and handed the puppy back to Beech without any fuss at all.

"Well, now," said Beech, "let's go and put her back then, shall we?" He took Chloë's hand in his, and gave Beth a slow, mischievous wink as he went past with the puppy tucked under one arm. Beth, speechless with surprise, followed meekly behind, and did not try to interfere.

"You can allus come and talk to her agen, can't you?" said Beech, as they stooped over Jess and laid the wriggling puppy back among her brothers and sisters. "Is she the one you like best?"

Chloë put her hand in the warm box and unerringly stroked the right small head. "Oh yes," she told Beech. "She's *mine*."

Beth stood looking down at Chloë and wondered what to say.

"When she'm ready, little 'un, you can take her home," Beech said. "But not yet."

"No," agreed Chloë gravely. "Not yet."

"You'll have to think of a name for her," smiled Beech, trying to give her something to hold on to.

Chloë looked at the pale gold bundle of fur, and then away through the trees, as if remembering something. "Cornfield . . . ?" she said in a questioning voice.

Dancing about like hares in a cornfield, remembered Beth, and looking into the old man's faded eyes, knew that he remembered, too.

"Corny?" murmured Chloë.

"Corny would do fine," said Beech, his voice suddenly warm with approval.

And Beth had another sudden memory, of Stephanie saying, half-laughing, '*Is that too corny?*' '*Much too Corny!*' Beth had replied. '*But it sounds interesting . . .*'

"Corny?" repeated Chloë, and bent down to pick up the puppy and have one more look. "Are you Corny?" And the squirming puppy reached out and licked her on the nose.

"That settles it!" smiled Beth, and Chloë actually laughed.

Then she carefully put the puppy back, got to her feet, and put her hand into Beth's, seeming perfectly ready to go home.

Beech stood still to watch them go, and then turned back to his litter of puppies, and picked up Chloë's choice to have another look at her.

"You'd better keep it up, young Corny," he told her. "I think you're doing the little 'un good."

That afternoon, Peter turned up as usual, and took Beth walking on Ashcombe Beacon. It was a place of short, springy turf and wide spaces, and the path climbed to a crest at the edge of the escarpment, so that the whole of the Severn valley was spread out below them, fields and woodlands and towns, with the silver river snaking through them down towards the Bristol Channel and the sea. And beyond the river, in a blue haze of distance, were the Welsh mountains, with the famous Sugar Loaf standing high.

"Lots of sky!" said Beth, taking great gulps of the spicy air.

"Room to breathe," agreed Peter.

"You always seem to turn up with a new kind of respite just when I need it!"

She had told him about the morning's panic about Chloë,

and his only comment had been: "No wonder you look pale!"

Now, glancing at her sideways, he said half-seriously: "I can think of worse ways of spending my time."

Beth was troubled by this, and began to protest: "You shouldn't – "

But he cut her short. "Yes, I should. I like it." His smile was open and ingenuous. "I just wish I could make you laugh a bit more, that's all." "Perhaps I should turn cartwheels or something." And he promptly did just that on the perilous slope and fell over backwards in a tangle of limbs on the grass. He lay there, laughing up at her, with the westering sun in his eyes.

"You are a fool," said Beth, laughing too, and stretched out a hand to help him up.

"That's better," he approved, watching the light grow in her face as the sadness retreated for a moment. "You should do it more often."

Beth did not make any comment on this, and they walked on companionably, until Peter said it was time for tea and they'd be caught in the dark if they didn't hurry.

"Hurry where?" asked Beth.

"I don't know," he admitted, grinning. "The Ritz is a bit far – though it does a good tea, I believe." He struck a ridiculous pose and put up a hand to his eyes in an exaggerated gesture of search. "Now, let's see, which way is London?"

"Stop clowning," laughed Beth. "You'd better come back to the Beehive – at least it's nearer."

"I thought you'd never ask," said Peter, his grin growing even wider, and led her skilfully down the darkening hillside to the friendly lights of the village.

They sat over the fire and made toast, and Beth felt herself relaxing in the comfortable glow. But she was still a little anxious about letting Peter expect too much, though she had no idea how to say so.

However, Peter took matters into his own hands, and being a forthright young man, came straight to the point. "Beth – does it bother you, having me hanging around?"

Beth looked at him and smiled. "Of course not. I love being taken out to all these new places . . ." She hesitated, and then

130

went on slowly: "It's just that – I'm not a very good bet at present, company-wise."

"You're doing all right," he told her, rescuing another piece of toast from the fire, and carefully not looking at her.

She sighed. It wasn't easy to make things clear to Peter. He was so incurably optimistic and cheerful, and so clearly believed in the dangerous doctrine that 'everything would turn out all right in the end.' How could she tell him that without Robert and Little Mo she was only half alive? The gap was still enormous. Maybe, one day, she would be able to contemplate having someone else in her life. But not yet. Not now. It was too soon . . . And then there was all this dark tension surrounding Finn and Chloë, and the constant struggle to resolve it. She badly needed to talk to Finn, to tell him about Chloë's latest small victory over her isolation. It was somehow essential to see their problems solved before she could think of any new happiness . . . Life was never that simple, was it?

"It's okay," said Peter, with surprising gentleness. "I know how things are. You don't have to worry." He handed her the latest piece of buttered toast. "Just take things as they come – like this!"

He smiled at her with impish affection, and waited for her to laugh.

It was not long after this that Beth decided to talk to George's father. She didn't know quite how to engineer this without involving the awful mother and daughter, too. But here Peter proved to be an ingenious ally.

"He's quite good at football," he said. "George, I mean. He's got the bulk for it." His infectious grin flashed out. "I'm sure his Dad would come to watch a game if I asked him."

"Peter, you're a genius."

"Thanks," he said modestly. "I'll talk to George."

So it was that Beth found herself on the edge of the cold football pitch at the end of the game, waiting to talk to George's father while the boys were in the changing room.

"Mr. Warner," she said, looking up at the tall, burly man with some trepidation, "could I have a word with you about George?"

131

The round, friendly face looked instantly anxious. "Of course. Is he being a nuisance?"

"No," said Beth firmly. "Far from it. He's being a very stalwart and co-operative member of my team."

The tough, red face relaxed, and the eyes – brown and warm like George's – began to smile. "Well, that's good news, at least."

"Yes." Beth tried to marshall her arguments into some sort of coherence. "I think he's much under-estimated, your son."

"You do?"

"He's very intelligent, Mr. Warner. Especially over maths and anything constructional that requires tricky calculations. Maybe he takes after you?"

Stan Warner laughed. "Not my wife's line, you mean? Or my daughter's." He was not slow off the mark, Beth thought. "Well, I am a builder. I suppose those sort of skills do come into it."

"He needs someone who understands his kind of ability, Mr. Warner. Someone who might give him a bit of praise now and then. I'm afraid he has a very low opinion of his own worth."

"Does he?" The kindly face looked puzzled.

"Yes. The crux of all that roof business – "

"What roof business?"

Beth looked at him in astonishment. "But – didn't they tell you?"

"Who?"

"Your wife and daughter . . ." Beth took a deep breath of outrage. How could they say nothing about it? Were they, perhaps, too ashamed when they realised what George's outburst had meant? "I think I'd better tell you myself, then," she said, and promptly did.

The effect on Stan Warner was immediate and fierce. "They should've told me!" he growled, and his face went redder than ever.

"It was a near thing, Mr. Warner," said Beth, allowing herself to rub it in a little. "If it hadn't been for Peter Green – "

"And you, Mrs. Halliday, by the sound of it." He smiled

at her with sudden warmth. "I'm – I'm more than grate-ful."

Beth nodded, dismissing it. "The reason I'm telling you is that it showed what was bugging George."

"Yes." His mouth grew straight and grim. "So it seems."

"So, I was wondering if you could – as it were – *counteract* the criticism at home with some extra praise of your own? . . . Your wife is very pretty, Mr. Warner, and so is your daughter, and they are both so . . . small and neat. George is the opposite, and I think he feels . . . rather like a bull in a china shop among all that daintiness."

Stan Warner laughed. "He's not the only one!"

Beth met those warm brown eyes and smiled. "Couldn't you take him fishing or something? . . . Or out with you on your building projects? . . . Let him do something special with you that the others can't do?"

He nodded slowly. "That makes sense . . . Should've thought of it before."

"He's growing up fast now," said Beth, thinking of George struggling to be the wise all-knowing Village Grandfather in her Japanese story. "He'll be good company."

Stan grinned apologetically. "I'm sure you're right."

"And then there's the school play – well, music-drama, I suppose you'd call it," Beth went on. "I've given him the leading part – for special reasons which you will understand." She paused, and waited to see him give another quick nod of comprehension. "And he's doing it very well – surprisingly well . . . I am hoping that you will all come to the performance at the end of term, and clap him like mad!"

Stan's grin got wider. "It'll be a pleasure!"

And then they both saw George coming towards them, looking anxious.

"Well done, George!" said Stan, going over to him and giving him a hearty slap on the back that would have felled a lesser boy. "That was a damn good game."

George looked up at his father in amazement and actually smiled. It was clear to Beth that he was not used to such praise, but he did not reject it. Instead, he looked all pleased and shy and muddled, and said in a stifled voice: "Oh well . . . it wasn't

133

bad . . ." Then he added honestly: "I could've tackled a bit harder . . ."

Stan winked at Beth over the top of George's touselled head, and said judiciously: "No. Just right. You need to know your strength . . ." and they went off together down the school drive, arguing happily.

Beth heaved a sigh of relief, and turned to find Peter beside her. "Looks like you did the trick," he said, watching them go.

"I hope so." Beth sighed again, and gave herself a mental shake, realising that she was almost trembling. She had been way out of her brief as a teacher, she knew, in all she had said to Stan Warner, but she didn't regret it. She glanced at Peter somewhat ruefully and said: "Parents! I sometimes think they need educating more than their own children!"

Peter laughed. "Bringing up kids is no easy task. I'd be terrified myself."

Beth made no comment on this, though she privately thought he would make a very good father. Instead, she said fervently: "I hope, after all this, George will come up trumps on the day!"

"He will," said Peter confidently, "with you to push him!"

"He's not a perambulator," protested Beth, laughing. "But I'll do my best."

Finn's architect, Theo Koussalis, came out to inspect the work on the Spirios site, and expressed himself satisfied that it was going according to plan. He also went with Finn to look at the old site, and promised to send a friend out to landscape the whole torn-up area and return it to the villagers better than before.

Then Finn broached the subject of a site manager – explaining unnecessarily that neither he nor Koussalis could be there all the time, and someone would have to take responsibility.

But here Theo Koussalis surprised him by saying: "Your foreman, Yannis, seems very reliable. I should think he could handle it, that is if he really understands the plans."

Finn looked startled for a moment, and then the idea took shape in his mind. "I *have* been over the plans with him while we were discussing the foundation digging – the rock was very

134

hard . . ." He looked at Theo searchingly. "Would *you* be satisfied to leave things in his charge?"

Theo temporised. "Let's talk to him and see what he says."

"He's got quite a lot of experience, I believe," said Finn slowly. "Though I doubt if he can boast many qualifications."

"A site manager doesn't need qualifications so much as good relations with his work force," said Theo crisply. "And I can keep an eye on things myself from time to time." He smiled at Finn, offering cheerful reassurance. He was a calm young man, with the kind of dark, solid good looks that somehow engendered confidence. And, Finn knew, he had a high reputation for good, original work that caused few structural problems in the completion of his plans.

"Does that mean you would come out here quite often?" he asked hopefully.

"Of course." Theo's eyebrows went up. "You don't want to be bothered with it, do you?"

Finn hesitated. "Not when it's safely under way – no. But the islanders have had a basin-full of bad building practice . . . I don't want it botched up again."

The young architect nodded. "I can understand that. I think you can rely on me to see it through."

Finn laid a friendly hand on his arm, afraid he had offended him. "I'm sure I can. Let's go and talk to Yannis."

They strolled on down to the site, where the men were already busy pouring concrete. Yannis, seeing them approach, left the little knot of workers and came across to speak to them.

"Yannis," said Finn, smiling, "we have a proposition to put before you." He turned to Theo, instinctively realising that the suggestion would come better from him.

Theo took his cue. "How would you feel about being site manager?"

Yannis looked astonished. "Me?" He stared at them both, and then turned to look at the laid-out lines of the hotel complex with an experienced but anxious gaze. "Would I know enough?" he murmured, seeming to ask himself as much as the other two.

135

Finn smiled. It was that kind of humility that endeared these sturdy island people to him. They didn't pretend to be more than they were – but they would tackle anything if they thought they could do it.

"I am sure you would," said Theo, speaking for Finn as well. "Why don't we go into the site office and discuss it?"

A large, shy grin came over Yannis's rugged face. "I would be honoured," he said.

It was while they were still poring over the plans, that the shout went up. Yannis, understanding the call better than the other two, went quickly outside and started running down to the little jetty, accompanied by most of the able-bodied men of the village.

Finn, when he got outside, was amazed at the change in the weather. Five minutes ago, it had been the usual brilliant sunshine and clear blue skies, but now the horizon was inky-dark, the sea was rising into black choppy waves, and a fierce squall was sweeping across the surface, bringing a high, screaming wind and lashing rain.

"What is it?" asked Finn, close beside Yannis.

"A boat out there – " Yannis pointed a brown finger into the extraordinary darkness across the sea. "A yacht in trouble – can you see her?"

Some of the men were already launching the biggest and sturdiest of the caiques and getting ready to go to the rescue.

"We do not have a life-boat service," Yannis explained. "Out here, we make our own."

Finn looked at the solid, rounded hull of the fishing boat with a practised eye. "Can she survive in that?"

The storm seemed to be increasing in power with every second, and now lightning played round the clouds rolling in across the angry sea, and thunder began to growl above the howl of the wind.

"The storms are very sudden here," Yannis said, watching the approaching squall anxiously. "But yes, she can weather it. I must go. I am one of the crew." And he sprang away down the tiny slipway and leapt into the rocking boat.

Finn, after a swift glance of apology at Theo, who was standing there uncertainly, followed Yannis at a run and leapt on board as well. "Used to yachts," he said briefly to Georgios the taverna owner, who also seemed to be the skipper of the caique. "Might come in handy . . ."

The others looked at him with brief, swift assessment and then nodded agreement. They set off into the teeth of the gale. Rain swept across them, whipped up into stinging needles by the wind, and waves, already looking mountainous and dark with menace, broke over the bows in ever-increasing power, jolting the boat with a continuous battering. Finn was used to storms, and the men beside him seemed used to them, too – but he knew that the caique was quite likely to turn turtle in such a sea. As for the yacht, what they could see of it between gusts of rain and spray, the white hull seemed deep in the water, and listing heavily in the swell, and the tall, central mast seemed to be gone altogether.

"You're right," he growled to Yannis, "she's in real trouble." But he doubted if Yannis even heard him in the increasing chaos of the storm.

The caique was making little headway against the driving force of the wind and tide, in spite of its powerful engine, but it ploughed steadily on, making a half-circle round the stricken yacht so that the actual power of the storm might bring them nearer to its wallowing side. But it was a perilous operation, and twice they were swept even further away by an unexpected gust and a larger-than-usual wave.

"We'll never get near enough," Yannis murmured, shaking his head.

"Might get a line on board," answered Finn, and edged his way foward to help uncoil the rope. The others looked at Finn hopefully. He was much the tallest – the Greek islanders were not tall men – and would be likeliest to throw a long line successfully.

They came up suddenly quite close to the ailing yacht, and now Finn saw a couple of dark shapes crouched helplessly on the deck. One, he guessed from his position, was injured somehow and would be unlikely to catch anything, let alone a snaking wet rope in this tearing wind, but the other seemed more alert, and waved an arm that seemed to know what it ought to do.

Finn threw. But the caique gave a sudden lurch, and he

137

missed. Twice more he threw and watched the line fall uselessly back into the sea, but the third time it fell across the yacht's heeling deck, and the dark wet shape of the man fell on it and grabbed it before it was too late. Finn saw him stumble to his feet and manage to lash the rope on to a cleat before another wave broke over the bows and knocked him off his feet. But he staggered up again, and began to haul the thin rope in until he reached the joined thicker line that would be strong enough for a tow. Lurching wildly on the slippery deck, he managed to secure it somehow to the nearest solid-looking stanchion in the bows. And then, to the horror of the watching crew of Georgios' boat, the sodden figure on the yacht seemed to slide sideways in the retreating wash of the last huge wave, and before he could grab at anything else, he was swept overboard.

"Throw a line!" yelled Yannis, and one of the others seized a life-belt and flung it overboard. But though it floated on the black surface of the boiling sea, the waterlogged figure of the man did not respond. He lay there, tossed to and fro like a piece of flotsam, and made no attempt to help himself.

Finn, cursing under his breath at the storm and the helpless vulnerability of inexperienced sailors, stripped off his jacket and his shoes, and plunged overboard.

"No!" shouted Yannis. "Kirios Finn – it is too rough!" But Finn did not hear him. He was a good swimmer, and he knew from experience that the islanders mostly were not. They managed their boats and they fished their seas when they had to – but they did not waste time swimming in the sea like the tourists. They respected it too much to take liberties with it, and anyway, they were too busy.

So it was Finn or no-one, he thought. And it might as well be him; he had nothing to lose. He struck out strongly, but the waves were very fierce and kept carrying him away from the sodden body in the sea, so he turned sideways into the swell and tried to drift down towards the drowning man, using the power of the surge to sweep him forward, as Georgios had tried to do with his boat. At last he got a grip on the man's hair and yanked him upwards so that he could breathe, and then reached out to grab the life-belt as it floated by. He had just succeeded in getting the rubber ring round the man's body, when a sudden

138

lurch of the yacht brought the white-painted side heeling over almost on top of him, submerging him in a flurry of spray and sucking water. He went under, still clutching the man in his life-belt, and thought, very clearly and distinctly: *This is it. What a fool I am.* And then he thought something else, with piercing clarity: *I can't drown now. What will happen to Chloë?*

He did not hear Yannis shout, or the splash as his devoted foreman plunged in after him, but all at once there was someone else flailing about in the water beside him, and he was coming up for air.

"The line," gasped Yannis, "take the line," and sank like a stone under the next huge wave.

Finn didn't know then whether he was rescuing Yannis who was a poor swimmer, or Yannis was rescuing him, or whether the limp body still inside the life-belt was worth rescuing at all, but somehow or other, he hauled Yannis up again and wound the trailing line round all three of them. Then all he could do was tread water and wait for the crew of the caique to pull them in.

It seemed to take forever, the waves were so tall and smashed down on top of them so hard, but at last he was near enough to the wildly-dipping side of the caique to push Yannis into the strong waiting arms of his friends. Then it was the turn of the unconscious man in the life-belt, who was harder to get on board because he was a soaked dead weight and could not help himself. And last of all, the same strong, friendly arms seized Finn and dragged him on board just before another wave smashed over them, nearly pulling the boat's gunwales down to sea-level.

"My God," spluttered Finn, coughing up half the Aegean, "some storm!" Then he looked round to see how the other two were doing. Yannis was also coughing up sea and grinning with relief, and one of the crew was working on the prone figure of the other man, trying to pump the water out of his lungs.

What about the yacht? thought Finn, and the other crouching figure on the slippery deck? Was he still there? He peered out through the sleeting rain, and thought he caught a glimpse of something dark still huddled on the slanting deck-boards, but he couldn't be sure.

"The line's still holding," shouted Georgios. "We'll try to tow her in." He turned his boat away from the pounding swell and began to let it run with the wind and tide. But he cast an anxious eye at the dim shape of the yacht, hoping the sudden jerk as they took up the slack would not snap the line altogether.

Finn looked up at the sky and thought he could see a lightening at the edge of the purple-black stormclouds over the sea. "Squall's going over," he said to Yannis, and got to his feet to go and help the others keep the line clear and the brave little caique afloat.

It was a slow, painful process, bringing the two boats in, but at last the caique bumped awkwardly against the little jetty and managed to tie up, leaving the stricken yacht lying sluggishly in the deep water some way off. Finn hoped it wouldn't drift helplessly in further before they could secure it, for the lone figure on its deck still lay unmoving, unable to help his stricken boat, and the seas were still almost too mountainous for anyone to board her. But as he thought this, he realised no-one else knew how to handle a yacht as well as he did, and it was clearly up to him now to bring her in and get her safely anchored. If she came on, out of control, she would smash herself to bits and probably break up the fragile little jetty as well as any other small boats in her way.

"Yannis," he said. "I must get aboard. Can you get me there?"

His foreman grinned cheerfully. "Sure, Kirios Finn. We take the *varka* – the little boat."

So they climbed down into the smallest boat with an outboard motor and shot across the choppy bay to the side of the wallowing yacht. The storm was sweeping away eastwards now, and had almost blown itself out over Spirios bay, but the sea was not subsiding yet, and the little *varka* bobbed about like a cork. But Finn had spotted a rope ladder dangling from one streaming side of the yacht, and now seized it as Yannis came close under the white hull, and swinging wildly, managed to climb aboard.

After that it did not take him long to get things straight and to get an anchor down to prevent her drifting any further. But how he was going to get the injured man ashore, he did not know. He stooped over him now, and grasped a wet shoulder in his cold hand. "Are you all right?"

For answer, the man groaned but did not open his eyes, and Finn saw that he had a deep gash on his head, probably from some falling bit of timber, and judging by the awkward position he was lying in, he had probably broken a leg as well.

But now Yannis was shouting something from the other side, and Finn went across to see that he was struggling with a rescue-harness and hammock and trying to climb the rope-ladder with it in his hands.

"Don't come up," shouted Finn. "I'll pull it in," and he found a long boat-hook that could just reach Yannis and the tangle of wet canvas and straps. Everything was wet – the rain and spray got everywhere – but that couldn't be helped. Just get the injured man strapped in, and he could lower him over the side.

Eventually, he got him dangling over the edge above a black abyss of water, but Yannis managed to keep the little boat steady, and Finn was just strong enough to lower the cradle slowly and not let it fall with a rush. He debated whether to stay on board and try to bring the yacht in further, or whether to abandon it until calmer weather. The electrics had failed, he knew, and the pumps weren't working, but though a lot of water was slopping about down below, he thought she was not in imminent danger of sinking. Maybe she would last out until the sea went down. He cast one more assessing glance round the splintered deck-housing and litter of broken mast and torn canvas, and decided it could all wait.

"Hang on," he yelled to Yannis over the side, "I'm coming." And he clambered down into the wildly pitching little boat and let Yannis head for the shore.

After that, the island routine took over. Someone had already ridden over to the little port on his motor scooter and sent messages to the rescue service. It was still too rough for a boat from the main island to get round the point, but a helicopter would come and ferry the injured men to hospital on the mainland. In the meantime, the local islanders produced vast quantities of hot coffee, and wrapped the half-drowned men in blankets, and someone who said she was a nurse put

141

some disinfectant on the head-wound and covered it with a neat bandage.

Yannis and Finn were plied with endless coffee and Metaxa, and slapped on the back by everyone who could get near them, and Theo Koussalis looked at them affectionately and said: "I didn't realise I was dealing with heroes."

Yannis laughed and was clearly pleased, but Finn frowned a little and kept his thoughts to himself. That moment of blinding truth about little Chloë had shaken him to the core. He knew now what kind of man he was. He would rather take foolish risks and plunge into boiling seas than face up to his responsibilities. He would rather be seen as a hero, admired and fêted as usual, than go home and look after his own bereft small daughter who needed him more than she knew how to say.

He was ashamed when he thought about it, and kept his head bent and let the cheerful rejoicing flow round him without paying any heed. He also reflected that Yannis, who could scarcely swim and did not much like the sea anyway, was much more of a hero than he was. So he laid a comradely arm round his foreman's broad shoulders and gave him a swift, surreptitious hug as the taverna talk grew loud and merry.

Tonight, said Finn to himself, I'll borrow a scooter and ride over to telephone home.

The telephone lines were even worse than usual after the storm, and Finn spent a long and frustrating time trying to argue his way through the stone-walling Athenian telephonists, but at last he got through to Mary Willis and heard Chloë was actually improving and beginning to come out of her shell. He was so relieved by this that he knew he must talk to Beth and find out exactly how the improvement had come about, and how much of an advance it really was. Mary had said something about a puppy and some word Chloë had come out with that sounded like 'wander' – but he couldn't catch exactly what Mary was trying to tell him over the crackling line.

So he went through another long and tiresome mixture of argument and waiting before he finally heard Beth's voice on the line. He was surprised (and rather shocked, he had to admit) to discover how much the sound of Beth's voice meant to him and what a curious lurch of pleasure it gave to him.

"Finn? Where are you?"

"Still in Greece. But I'm finishing up here now, Beth, and then I'm coming home."

Beth at the other end of the line also felt an unexpected little jolt of pleasure – or was it relief? – when she heard these words. But she did not say so. "I'm glad to hear it." She knew she sounded too prim and severe, but she couldn't help it. There was so much she needed to discuss with him about Chloë, and it was impossible to say any of it over this fading, uncertain line.

"Mary says Chloë is getting better. Can you tell me what's been happening?"

"It was the puppy, Finn. I told you she ought to have one of them – she seems to relate to them somehow."

"Yes?" Finn sounded almost impatient.

"Well, she chose one all on her own, and went off with it. We found her talking to it."

"*Talking to it?*"

"Yes. Exactly. It was the break-through we had been hoping for. I don't know why, except perhaps it was something of her own to love and care for, without any connotations of grief or anything . . ."

"I see." Finn's voice was suddenly near and deep. He did see, too, and was ashamed at what he saw. He had given her no help, no chance to find a way out of her world of bewildering loss and hurt. It had to be a small, inoffensive puppy that gave her the comfort she needed. "I'm sorry," he murmured, aloud. "I should have known . . ."

"We none of us knew, Finn. She found her own way out."

He grunted agreement at this, and then went on: "What was this word she came out with? Mary said something about 'wander' . . . ?"

Beth hesitated, and her voice became suddenly gentle, too gentle, probably, for this difficult line. But how could she explain that strange conversation with Beech which had somehow reached the heart of one small girl?

"Not 'wander,' Finn. It was '*yonder*.' I'll explain when you come home. The old man, Beech, gave her somewhere to put Stephanie, that's all."

Somewhere to put Stephanie? *Yonder*? . . . Finn was not stupid, not lacking in imagination, either. And, God knows, he thought, I've been trying to find somewhere to put Stephanie where I can reach her, too . . . (Even if I couldn't quite accept St. Spyridion and the islanders' simple beliefs) . . . He saw then with instant comprehension just what that word 'Yonder' meant to little Chloë, and what that clever old man had done for her.

"Beth," he said abruptly, "something happened today that brought me to my senses . . . I'm sorry to have been so dense . . ." He wasn't being very coherent, he knew, but somehow he felt sure Beth would follow him. "I'll try to find some way to reach her when I get back, but, but can I ask one more favour – among the many you've already done for me?"

"Of course." Beth sounded entirely calm and sure.

"It's just . . . I don't know how Chloë will feel about me coming back – or whether it will throw her all over again?" He sounded absurdly humble. "Can you – could you sort of prepare the way a bit? See what she says – if she says anything – or how she reacts? I mean, I don't want to send her back into retreat just when she's coming out."

Beth sighed. "I'll do what I can, Finn, of course. But I don't know either which way she will react . . ." She wanted to tell him how cautiously and carefully she had been going with Chloë, how she watched and waited for every small sign of returning awareness, and how hard she tried – how hard they all tried, Mary and the old man, Beech, and even Mark, as well as Beth herself – to put some positive thoughts of the future into that small, closed mind.

But she could hear the anxiety in Finn's voice, and knew she must try to reassure him now. Time enough for discussion later. "I'll sound her out gently, Finn – I don't think it will upset her. She's a lot less fragile now. Some of that sturdy independence of hers is coming back at last."

"Is it?" There was such hope and heart-break in his voice that Beth could have wept.

"Oh yes. I think it will be all right. But you must come home soon, Finn. There are a lot of things to talk about."

"I know." Finn's voice faded on the line and seemed to grow near again. "I know there are – and I know I've been avoiding them . . . I'm an awful coward, Beth."

She smiled a little at that, having a very clear picture of that brave buccaneer, Finlay Edmondson, striding up the jetty after his famous single-handed voyage across the Atlantic . . . A coward?

"I think we all are, Finn, when it comes to human relationships. Stephanie is the only person I've known who wasn't afraid of them."

There, she thought. I've said it. Sententious and pious, it sounds, but it's true. Maybe it will make Finn feel a bit better, or at least make him less shy about his emotions.

"You are absolutely right," Finn said, sounding suddenly warm and close. "And I'm coming home. Give – give Chloë my love . . . if you can, that is." He seemed to waver then, once again unsure and far too humble. But all at once his voice came clear and strong as he added: "Beth – *I think 'yonder' is awfully close* . . . Maybe you could tell her?"

And before she could reply, he had rung off.

It was not long after Finn's telephone call that young Mark said suddenly: "I can't come to tea any more – " and then added, trying to soften his bald statement: "not for a bit, anyway."

"Why, Mark?" asked Beth, seeing that the boy was clearly unhappy about it.

"My Mum's ill," he explained. "I have to get the tea for her."

Beth looked at him with concern. "I'm sorry to hear that. A bout of winter 'flu?"

Mark seemed uncertain. "It's sort of wheezy – on her chest." He gave Beth a lopsided grin. "The doctor said she should've given in sooner."

"I can imagine." Beth smiled back encouragingly. "Tell you what, when I take Chloë back after tea, I'll call in to see how your mother is. Will that do?"

"Smashing!" said Mark, his face lighting with relief. "I'll tell her you're coming." And he went off quite cheerfully, with that promise for reassurance. But even so, he turned in the doorway and looked back, sudden doubt in his eyes. "Will it bother Chloë – me not coming?"

"I don't think so. I'll explain it to her." Beth breathed a secret sigh of thankfulness that she could explain things to Chloë now.

Mark understood her very well, and gave a satisfied nod. "See you then," he grinned, and went on his way.

Beth reflected, watching him go, how much the boy had changed lately. Who would have thought that screaming heap of self-destructive fury would have turned into anyone so responsible? He was fast becoming her most reliable ally in the special music class. She suspected he was a born leader, underneath all that family confusion. And his concern for Chloë was real and touching, – he had, in fact, done more to help her to come back than any of them. Now, it seemed, he was trying to be the mainstay and prop of his own little household, taking care of his mother as a good son should. But it was a lot for a ten-year-old to cope with, especially one who was already being torn apart with divided loyalties . . .

Beth sighed, and wished – not for the first time – that children did not get so damaged by the mistakes and traumas of their parents. Then she remembered Finn's plea for help over Chloë, and decided that this tea-time without Mark might be a good opportunity to approach the problem. Would it do any harm, she wondered? The child's new grasp on reality was so tenuous and so fragile. Was it safe yet to risk destroying it with an incautious word?

Chloë did not seem particularly worried about Mark's absence, though she did look at Beth enquiringly when they set off for the Beehive without him.

"Mark's getting tea for his Mum today," said Beth, answering that unspoken question. "She works too hard, and she gets tired." It seemed important not to say that his mother was ill. There was no knowing what anxieties that might evoke in Chloë's mind. She might even ask, in innocent cruelty: 'Is she going to die, too?' No, much better to say nothing that could cause alarm, and to keep this tea-time as cheerful as all the others . . . There were so many things to avoid, so many concessions to make, in the handling of Chloë at present.

146

So they went home hand-in-hand, with Beth talking gently about anything that came into her head, as usual, and Chloë listening – yes, really beginning to listen – in grave and thoughtful silence. They lit the fire, and made toast as usual, and again Beth wondered if this was the right moment to mention Finn's home-coming.

But Chloë unexpectedly moved closer to her as she knelt on the hearthrug by the fire, and leant her head against Beth's shoulder in a gesture of confiding trust. It was the first time she had shown any sign of returning warmth or affection, and now she seemed to let go of the awful tension that had kept her so stiff and unapproachable, and to rest tiredly against Beth in a kind of weary surrender. She was not fighting the world any longer, not trying to keep it at bay, but just admitting exhaustion, as a small child suddenly could, and asking mutely for comfort.

Greatly daring, Beth put an arm round her and drew her close. It was something she had often longed to do, and told herself sternly that she must not. She knew all too well that her own dreadful sense of loss over Little Mo could make her all too eager to grab at another child's affection. Once or twice, on bad days, she had even wondered if she was the kind of woman who might snatch a baby out of someone else's pram. And knowing this about herself, she had perhaps been more scrupulous than need be about offering any physical comfort to Chloë.

But now, it seemed, the child herself was making overtures, and that being so, how could she refuse? . . . And, what's more, how could she spoil this fragile advance by broaching the subject of Finn? . . . She felt, instinctively, that this moment was far too important to lose – she simply could not risk it. Chloë was only now beginning to trust her – and to turn to her for consolation. She could not destroy that frail trust, not now – not yet. So she simply tightened her arm round Chloë's suddenly yielding little body and said softly: "Tomorrow we can go and see Corny again, can't we?"

And she was somehow unsurprised when Chloë just nodded and sighed and suddenly fell asleep beside her in front of the fire.

*　　*　　*

147

Beth was late getting to Mark's home, and when he opened the door he looked at her reproachfully and said: "I thought you weren't coming."

She could see the anxiety in his expressive face, and wondered how many times he had been promised something by his father, and then been disappointed.

"Mark," she said sternly, "when I say I'm coming, I come!"

He grinned his relief and led her into the living room to see his mother. Lucy Reynolds was propped up in a chair, looking feverish and exhausted, but she smiled at Beth with real welcome in her overbright eyes.

"Shouldn't you be in bed?" smiled Beth.

"I'm better like this." Lucy's voice was hoarse and rather breathless. "I can breathe more easily sitting up." She rightly interpreted Beth's doubtful look, and added hastily: "The doctor agrees – he's given me antibiotics."

Beth nodded, wasting no more time on argument. "What can I do to help?"

Lucy's answering smile was fragile but full of tired gratitude. "Just stay and talk to me for a bit. I get blue sitting here." She glanced at Mark affectionately. "And that rubs off on him."

Mark said, with sturdy protest: "I'm O.K. Shall I make some more tea?"

"What have you had to eat?" asked Beth, keeping to practical matters.

Mark looked worried. "She wouldn't have anything except a cup of tea."

"And what about you?"

He shrugged and avoided Beth's eye. "I had some bread and butter."

Beth sighed. "I suppose you have an oven?"

"Of course." Mark glanced rather warily at his mother. "And a microwave."

"Well," Beth grinned at him encouragingly, "it just so happens that I brought some supper with me. Let's warm it up."

Lucy began to protest vaguely, she seemed too tired to make much of a fuss, and Beth went swiftly over to her chair and said in a firm, no-nonsense teacher's sort of voice: "It

148

makes good sense, Lucy. I've got to eat. You've got to eat. We might as well do it together."

Lucy looked suddenly as if she was going to cry.

"And besides," added Beth hastily, "I get blue on my own, too."

The two women looked at each other and laughed. Lucy had capitulated. It somehow became a cheerful evening from then on, in spite of the fact that Lucy was clearly ill and ought to be resting. But she did eat some of Beth's supper, and did begin to look better before Beth decided it was time to go.

"If it's all right by you," she said to Lucy's tired figure, which had slid down a little lower in her chair, "I'll come again tomorrow evening."

"Beth, there's no need – "

"Yes, there is." Beth's voice was oddly insistent. "Mine – as much as yours."

Lucy was silent for a moment. Then she said in a stifled voice: "You make me ashamed."

"Why?"

"You have so much more reason for – for grief than I have."

Beth considered the matter. "I don't know . . . A failed marriage is a kind of death, I suppose . . ."

Lucy looked at her. "But I have Mark."

Beth smiled. "Yes, indeed you have. You are very lucky."

Once again, Lucy looked near tears. "Getting ill is so – *dangerous*. I mean, I get terrified that I won't be able to cope – and then what would happen to Mark?"

Beth nodded.

"You and your little boy were left on your own . . . Did you ever feel – ?"

"Vulnerable? Afraid? . . . Of course."

"But you coped."

"Well, *you're* coping." She gave Lucy's shoulder a little shake "This is just the bronchitis talking. You know that, really."

Lucy sighed. "I hope so."

Beth got to her feet. "Time you were in bed. Mark is making you a hot drink."

"On your instructions?" Lucy was smiling now.

"Of course."

"You're an awful bully."

"Aren't I? It must be the teacher in me." She turned to Mark, who was coming in with a cup of ovaltine held carefully in his hand. "You'll make her go to bed, won't you?"

Mark made a face. "If I can!"

"That reminds me," said Beth obscurely, "I've promised to take Chloë to see Corny tomorrow. Would you like to come too?"

Mark turned to look at his mother doubtfully. "I – "

"You go," said Lucy swiftly. "It'll do you good. You can't stay cooped up here all day."

"There's the shopping – "

"Do it first." She looked enquiringly at Beth. "You won't be going up there very early, will you?"

"No." Beth smiled reassuringly. "And not for very long, either." She paused and then suddenly asked Mark the question that had been in her mind all day. "Chloë's father is coming home, and I'm not sure how to tell her. What do you think would be the best way?"

Mark's eyes grew dark with thought. "Beech might know," he said at last. He looked at Beth and then at his mother. "I mean, he knew about not blaming people . . ."

"Yes," agreed Beth, surprised. "So he did." She saw the sudden swift glance of understanding pass between mother and son, and knew that Beech had done his work well. "We'll ask him tomorrow," she said, and smiled at them both. "And now it's time for bed."

She left them then, aware that they had things to say to one another, and that Lucy had the comfort that she needed.

That night Beth dreamed of Little Mo with extraordinary clarity. She often dreamed of him, and of Robert, too, but usually the dreams were muddled and anxious, or the old nightmares of loss and terror were back and she was afraid – so afraid that she woke, sweating, in the dark of the night. But this time it was a clear, vivid picture that she saw, and there was no fear in it at all. She saw Mo running down a steep, grassy slope between two dark wedges of winter beechwoods. The grass was short – like sheep-grazed turf – and very green. Mo

150

was careering down it with arms outspread as though he was almost sailing on the air, and he was laughing in the sun as he ran.

He is all right then, thought Beth in her dream. He is having the time of his life out there. It is all so green and pure, and so full of space, that steeply-falling curve of sunlit hillside . . . I wonder which hill it is? And Mo looks so happy, so entirely free and happy. Nothing could cloud that joy.

But what about Robert, she thought? Where is he in all this light and space? Shouldn't he be with Mo, flying downhill like a bird on the wind? Why isn't he there?

And then she saw him, waiting at the bottom of the green hill, with his arms outstretched to catch Mo when he came – and he was laughing, too.

So they're both all right, Beth told herself, feeling oddly matter-of-fact and sensible in her dream world. I needn't worry any more.

She did not wake then, as she usually did when the dreams became too real. This time she merely sighed a little and smiled to herself as she drifted further into untroubled sleep.

"Yes, you can take Corny out, Little 'un," said Beech, smiling at Chloë and Mark as they bent over the puppies. "Show her the wide world, like. She'll have to get used to it soon."

Beth watched them take the golden-haired retriever pup out of its box and set it down a little way off under the trees, where it scampered about chasing leaves and shadows. Then she turned to Beech and said rather anxiously: "Her father is coming home. She'll be able to have the puppy soon."

Beech looked at her, not missing the doubt in her voice. "They're good pups," he said slowly. "I knows the father – they'm not come-by-nights."

Beth laughed. "I know that, Beech. That's not what's worrying me. It's how Chloë will react to her father."

Beech nodded. "I dessay we could do summat about that." He went across to the two children and said cheerfully: "I got someone new to show you. Bring Corny with you, then," and he led them a little way down the path to where the grassy hillside met the edge of his own smallholding. Here he had extended his fence to include what had been the roe deer's

151

secret refuge, and a bit more grass besides, and there was now a small lean-to shed at one end of the little paddock. He led Chloë and Mark, with Beth close behind them, towards the little shed, where they could see a shaggy grey mound standing motionless with its back to the open door.

"This here is Moses," he said, and laid a quiet brown hand on the rough furry flank. "And he's mortal sad and lonely, so we've got to be extra kind to him."

"Why is he sad?" asked Mark, who already realised that Beech was up to something, and knew he ought to ask the right leading questions.

"Well, there's two reasons really," Beech paused and looked down at Chloë with a speculative gaze. "One is, he's lost his Jenny – his wife, like. They wus together a long time, see, and donkeys are faithful critturs. But his Jenny died at the end of the summer, and he can't seem to get over it, seemingly." Once again he paused, still with his eyes on Chloë's listening face. "And then there's the children, see – he misses them, too."

"What children?" Mark was still asking the right questions.

"Why, on Weston sands," explained Beech. "Moses was a riding donkey, see, and so was his Jenny, too. All summer long, the children came to have rides, and they used to pat him and make a fuss of him, like, and give him sugar lumps (which they didn't ought to!). Come winter, all the donkeys go to have a rest in some farmer's field and such . . . I usually has one or two . . . Then, when spring comes and they'm fattened up a bit on the new grass, they goes back to work on the sands – and meets all the children agen, see?" He gave the shaggy coat another gentle pat. "But old Moses here, he's grieving for his Jenny, and there's no children to take his mind off things . . . He needs a lot o' cosseting just now."

"Cosseting?" said Chloë, very distinctly.

"Ar. Cosseting." He took Chloë's hand and led her a little nearer to the donkey's warm flank. "When people miss someone bad, Little 'un, they needs a lot o' cosseting. Would you like to give him an apple? Moses likes apples."

"Yes," said Chloë, and held out her hand.

Carefully, Beech put the apple into her hand and showed

her how to hold it out on the flat of her palm to the sensitive velvet muzzle.

For a moment the sorrowful donkey did not move, but then the scent of the fruit seemed to reach him, and he lifted his drooping head a little and nibbled delicately at the apple in her hand.

"That's it," encouraged Beech. "Try talking to him, Little 'un. He likes the sound of young voices, see?"

"Moses?" said Mark, close behind Chloë, and urging her on. "Don't be sad, Moses . . . We've come to talk to you, Chloë and me . . ."

"And Corny," added Chloë firmly. "Look, Corny, this is Moses . . ." and she held the small puppy up to see what a furry old donkey looked like.

Mark smiled in triumph at Beech and asked him for another apple. And when that had been crunched up, both children put an arm round the shaggy grey neck and began to whisper into the twitching, intelligent ears.

Beech and Beth stood a little aside and watched this without making any further comment. But at last Mark said regretfully: "I've got to go now, Moses. My Mum's got flu, you see, and she needs looking after, too."

"Cosseting?" asked Chloë, trying out the new word.

Mark grinned at her. "Something like that." Then he glanced at Beth in mute enquiry, aware that he was somehow helping to reinforce Beech's argument.

Beth did not miss his unspoken question and gave a quick nod of approval. Satisfied, he turned back to the old donkey and gave him a last, consolatory pat. "Cheer up then, Moses. I'll come and see you again soon."

"I'll come too," added Chloë, not to be outdone. She turned away then, still clutching little Corny under one arm, and went rather unwillingly to put her back with her brothers and sisters.

Beech noted her reluctance with satisfaction. It suited him very well. "You'll be able to take her home soon," he told her, smiling. "Missus here says your father's on his way home." He did not wait for her to reply, but went on smoothly: "Need a lot o' cosseting, an all."

"The puppy?" asked Chloë, innocently.

153

"Nay," said Beech. "It wus your father I wus thinking of . . .
Like Moses, he is, sad and lonely." His faded blue eyes were
regarding Chloë with gentle understanding. "Only, o' course,
he's got a little girl of his own to talk to."

Chloë gazed at him in silence. Then she nodded once, and
put her hand firmly into Mark's and started for home.

There was no need to say any more, Beth knew. Skilfully,
the old man had prepared the way for Finn's return. There
would be no trouble now. Chloë had a rôle to play in his
home-coming.

"Thank you, dear Beech," she murmured, as she turned to
follow them down the path.

And Beech just winked and muttered "Cosseting!" as she
passed.

Finn had meant to slip away from the Spirios site quietly without any fuss, but in the end the villagers made it impossible.

To begin with, he had to arrange things with Theo Koussalis
and Yannis so that the building would go on smoothly, and
once they knew he was going home to England, the rest of
the village soon knew too. A party ensued – the islanders
loved an excuse for a party – and friends and relations seemed
to come from far and wide to give Finn a royal send-off. He
had become something of a hero to the villagers, what with
the restoring of the old site to its original unspoilt state, and
the well-paid work available on the new site, not to mention
the rescue of the yacht and its helpless crew, and Yannis and
Finn as well, though no-one was quite sure who rescued who
in that tumultuous sea. It all made Finn feel worse than ever,
but he hadn't the heart to rebuff their friendly admiration or
spoil the fun.

He said as much to his friend, Bob the archeologist, who
had joined him at the taverna when the merriment was at its
height.

"The Greeks are used to pedestals," said Bob, grinning at
Finn's discomfiture.

"I know," growled Finn. "But what they don't know is, it's
easier to be a hero than to face up to one's responsibilities."

Bob patted his arm kindly, and poured out some more
wine. "You're going home, aren't you?" He glanced round

154

at the lively crowd in the taverna, and then beyond to the rose-coloured sea lying calm beneath a sunset sky. "I should think it's probably a lot braver than staying here . . . ?"

Finn sighed. He loved these islands, too, but he knew it was time to go. "How much longer have you got on the dig?" he enquired. He rather liked the team of archeologists and the work they were doing. It was an interesting site, and they had already found quite a few artefacts which had pleased the Greek authorities.

"Another six months, I should think, before funds run out." He shrugged philosophical shoulders. "Then – who knows?"

Finn was immediately tempted to offer them financial help, but he sternly resisted the impulse. He had more than enough projects on his plate already – and he was going home. His future lay at home with his small daughter, both duty and inclination demanded it. There must be no more distractions to make him turn aside or loiter on the way.

"Ah well," he said, allowing a certain amount of regret to creep into his voice. "I'd like to have seen the final result."

"There's never a final result in our kind of work, Finn – you should know that." Bob waved the wine bottle at him. "We just go beavering on finding bits and pieces, but think of all the things we miss!" He laughed and waved the bottle some more. "Drink up. You're getting sad."

Finn dutifully emptied his glass, but the sadness was too profound to shift, and he knew it.

"Kirios Finn, they want you to dance with them," urged Yannis, coming up with Georgios the proprietor behind him, "and Marina has made you a garland which you must wear, or she will be most offended."

Finn got to his feet and smiled. He knew better than to say no to these affectionate people. It was their night, and he must cast no shadow upon it. So he danced, arms linked with the men of St. Spiridion, while the bouzoukis and guitars strummed like mad, and the one-string fiddles squealed and the accordions groaned, and the rest of the onlookers clapped and sang and cheered and let off a few fire-crackers for good measure.

And last of all, when the dancing was over and even the drinking was slowing down and turning into dreamy demands for café-cognac, the villagers came to Finn with their parting gifts.

First of all came the priest, with a candle from the shrine of Saint Spyridion. "For your wife, Kyria Edmondson," he said gently, "but we will burn one for her here too, of course." He fingered the soft, honey-coloured wax and added: "It is made from the wax of our own bees on our own hills. We hope it will bring you peace."

Finn accepted it gravely, and could think of no words to say in reply. But then came Georgios with a bottle of his best island wine, saying with more than a twinkle in his observant black eyes: "And this is made from the grapes on our own vines on our own hills also – and maybe it will also bring you peace." And when Finn laughed, both Georgios and the priest laughed with him. Then, while they were still laughing, Marina came, with a small leather bag filled with herbs "also from our hills," and there was even more laughter.

Next came one of the village children, bringing him a pure white pebble of pendellic marble from the beautiful, unspoilt beach by the restored site, and said: "Because you have left it pure," as he had been told, and then looked shy and ran away and hid.

After this, one of the villagers gave him some Greek worry beads with one blue eye to ward off evil, and the fisherman from the smallest caique brought him a polished sea-urchin shell to give to his small daughter when he got home. This prompted one of Marina's friends to come forward with two small dolls dressed in exhuberant Greek costume – a boy and a girl – also for Chloë, if she would like them? "My mother dresses them," she explained, "so they are – ?" She turned shyly to Marina, having lost her words.

"Correct?" suggested Marina.

"Authentic," pronounced Bob, the archeologist, smiling. And then he too produced something for Finn to take home. "It is not a shard of pottery, for we have to give all that to the museum," he said, "but it is from the site, and it is even older." He held the small object out on the palm of his hand, and Finn, looking down, saw that it was a perfectly formed ammonite fossil, newly scrubbed so that its strange, pinkish colours shone under the taverna lights.

"It'll remind you that you left us undisturbed!" he added, and laughed.

And last of all came Yannis, carrying two beautifully polished olive-wood shepherd's crooks with carved dolphin heads, one large and one small, for Finn and Chloë to take walking on the hills of home. "My father carved them," he said. "He was a shepherd once, but now he sits at home and carves!" He grinned and added rather ruefully: "They mass produce them now in Athens for the tourists – but these are truly carved with love." He looked at Finn and murmured softly: "They go with the blessing of all at Agios Spyridion.

By this time, Finn was altogether too overcome to think what to say, so he called loudly for Georgios to give everyone an extra drink all round, and the party broke up in cheers and laughter.

But when everyone had gone wandering home, Finn walked alone by the sea and looked at the lights of the bigger island beyond the bay, and the myriad bright stars burning above it, remembering that this lovely coastline at the edge of the restless Aegean was the last place that his young wife, Stephanie, had looked at before death overtook her . . . But then he had taken her home, he told himself, where she could rest among her own quiet hills . . . Well, he was going home now, and if he could not find her there, at least he could try to make young Chloë happy again.

"I'm such a coward, Steph," he said to her. "And you knew it all along – though you never blamed me. But I'll try to make a go of it. I really will."

There was no answer in the quiet night, but the sea made a gentle hushing sound on the shore as if saying 'Sleep."

Beth was in two minds about Finn coming home. One part of her was anxious and full of misgivings about how it might affect Chloë. In spite of the clever suggestion put forward by Beech, Beth was still not entirely sure how the small girl would react. Would she remember that important word 'cosseting' and really want to look after her father? Or would she close up and grow silent and pale again, refusing all overtures? Could Beth herself make it easier for her by suggesting some kind of hopeful preparation for his homecoming? She only knew that she wanted to put things right for Chloë and for Finn, too. Somehow, she still felt she owed it to Stephanie, and she ought not to fail her . . . And thinking about all this, she was troubled.

But then, another part of her seemed to be unexpectedly relieved and glad that Finn was coming home. There was a curious warmth – almost a feeling of safety – about his return into her life. He was so strong and cheerful, so full of energy and high endeavour. But then she rememberd how she had seen him last, – sad and self-accusing and somehow quenched, and she sighed at the memory and hoped, unreasonably, that he would have recovered some of his sparkling optimism. But would he have? Why should he, when she herself was still caught in the same inextricable web of grief and loneliness.

Loneliness? That word brought her up short. And she knew she must not try to use Finn to cure her own sense of loss. Or Peter, either. For it was becoming clear to her that young Peter was trying very hard to fill the gap for her, and she knew she must not let him. It was too soon to think of any such thing, especially as she had nothing to offer in return.

With these thoughts very much in mind, she therefore decided to go off on her own that Saturday, and not wait for the persistent Peter to come knocking on her door. So she got in her car and drove off to look at the hills, and decided to visit the small Saxon church at Elkstone which someone had told her she must see.

It was a grey late November morning when she set out, with the hills looking cold and clear, and the nearly-leafless trees standing gaunt and beautiful against a pearly sky. But when she got to Elkstone a gleam of winter sunlight pierced the clouds and suddenly bathed the ancient stone of the little church in a pale wash of gold.

Beth looked up at the thrusting heads of the gargoyles and down at the solid, sturdy little building set foursquare against the fierce wind and weather of these high hills, and then made her way round the path and pushed open the heavy oak door.

Inside, it was cool and quiet under the timbered roof, but as she looked up the tiny nave past the old wooden pews to the chancel arch, she became aware that the shaft of winter sunshine outside seemed to have got into the church, and the whole of that inner sanctuary beyond the double stone arches and their dog-tooth mouldings seemed to be swimming in golden light.

Astonished, she walked slowly towards the shimmer of brightness behind the miniature wooden altar rail, and saw that the small windows set either side were furnished with a special amber-yellow glass which transformed all the light pouring through them to translucent gold, and laid a gentle, glowing ambience on the honey-coloured stone of the walls, and even reflected back from the stone-flagged floor. It felt to Beth as she stood there, as if she was enwrapped in warmth and light, and an extraordinary sense of timeless tranquillity seemed to encompass her. There was no need to think anything, to do anything, to go anywhere – it was enough just to be – to be here at this moment in the midst of sunlight and peace . . .

But when she looked up at the central small window above the altar, set into yet another small golden arch, she saw that this glass was not amber-coloured but blue, the clear and brilliant blue of a Madonna's robe, and the light shone through her blue veil and the plain white wraps of the Child in her arms. It was a simple window, and the figure was small and unpretentious, quietly standing in its unadorned stone frame, but it caught Beth unawares, and something about that serene and patient mother, waiting there through the years of eternity, made Beth's own unguarded heart clench with sudden pain. I can't look at you, she said, a sudden spurt of irrational anger seizing her. The perfect mother and child. How can you stand there, looking so calm and good? . . . How could you bear it, knowing what you knew?

She began to turn away then, as if the vivid glowing colours of the little window actually hurt her eyes, but something about the very simplicity of that quiet figure made her pause. She was not aware of any change in her own feelings – any lessening of grief and loss – but the atmosphere of the little church seemed to reach out to her, the radiance of that golden chancel seemed to fill her with a curious sense of rightness and acceptance.

For the first time since Little Mo's death – and since Robert's death, too, which she had shut away inside her for fear of more hurt – she could look back to all that past happiness without flinching. And, perhaps, look forward, too – to a life that had to go on somehow, and had to find a purpose and some kind of peace . . . And for the first time – in broad and golden daylight, not in dreams – she began to feel that they were not far away, the ones she loved. Not far in this dazzle of gold – she need only stretch out a hand . . .

She stood there, gazing, for a long time – and even after the fitful sun had gone behind another veil of cloud, the golden light in the chancel still persisted. But at last she turned away from the blue Madonna window, and stumbled rather blindly down the aisle into the porch.

"Are you all right?" said a gentle voice beside her, as she sank down onto the stone seat beside the door and closed her eyes against the dazzle of tears.

Sighing, and making a vague effort to collect her flying thoughts, Beth turned her head to the light and looked up. The face she saw before her was long and scholarly and pale, – with the parchment-thin frailty of old age giving it a luminous transparency. It was also compassionate and concerned, and the faded blue eyes were kind and reminded her of Beech's tranquil gaze.

"Er – yes," she answered, somewhat doubtfully. "I think the atmosphere rather threw me."

The old man nodded, and sat down beside her companionably on the stone seat. "It is a bit overpowering."

Beth glanced at him in surprise. "You feel it too?"

"Oh yes. I think most people do – especially if they have some private grief on their mind."

She looked at him in continuing disbelief. "Does it show that much?"

He smiled at her, and she was astonished at the sudden transformation. The face looked instantly younger and stronger – and somehow happier – as if it could not contain its own private source of joy.

"Only to the initiated."

Beth's eyes opened wider. She was about to say: "You too?" when she noticed that the stranger was wearing a clergyman's dog-collar under his unremarkable jacket, and her heart sank. Now he will preach at me, I suppose, she thought, like the one

160

who came when Mo died. Stupid platitudes that didn't help at all . . . But he had been kind, so she had better be polite. "Are you the vicar of this little church?"

"Oh no," he said and laughed. "I have long since retired from active work. I'm just a visitor – like you." His observant gaze rested on her for a moment, and then he said briskly: "I think you'd better have some of my coffee. I always carry a flask when I'm walking."

She saw then that he was carrying an ordinary hiker's rucksack from which he produced a thermos flask, an extra plastic cup and a packet of biscuits. Apparently undismayed by sitting in the church porch, he proceeded to pour out a cup of very hot coffee for Beth, and insisted on putting in two lumps of his small store of sugar and finding her a spoon.

"Shock," he pronounced, "requires sugar. Many people have been hit on the head, as it were, by little Elkstone church."

Beth met his eyes over the rim of her cup and began to laugh. "You seem to know a lot about it."

There was a distinct fleck of amusement in his friendly glance now. "I come here quite often – and it always gets to me." He paused, and added in a reflective tone: "There's something about ancient places of worship – an aura of holiness, perhaps? It seems to cling to them through the ages. Generations of prayer has gone up from these old stones . . ." He paused again and then added with apparent irrelevance: "Have you ever been to Delphi?"

Beth stirred from her thoughts and looked at him with attention. "Delphi? In Greece? No, I haven't."

"It has the same feeling," he said dreamily. "Two thousand years of prayer to the ancient gods – two thousand years of sanctuary and peace – the very stones seemed steeped in it . . ." He glanced sideways at Beth and smiled again. "And, after all, I think the concept of the ancient ones was only another facet of the same eternal belief . . ."

"Belief in what?" asked Beth, and there was a real need for an answer in her voice.

"A merciful God?" suggested the soft old voice. "The power of good . . . ?" He glanced at her again, and there was much understanding in his quiet gaze. "*A life beyond our own?*" He hesitated and then added gently: "We have always searched for such reassurance – all through history."

Beth bent her head to hide the swift, too-easy tears. "And never found proof?" she said.

The old man's tranquil stare did not change. "You can't prove light," he said. "But it's there." He waved a transparent hand towards the little church behind him. "That golden chancel – you can explain the yellow glass and the position of the sun – the warmth of the Cotswold stone in the arches – but can you explain what you felt in there?"

"No," said Beth. "I can't." And she kept her head bent.

"I think they are in all of us," murmured the old voice, as if speaking half to himself, "the seeds of eternity . . . binding us all together . . . The links can never be broken . . ." He did not say any more, but sat on quietly beside Beth until she had mastered her tears and began to smile again.

"You are very clever," she said at last, "and very comforting. I feel as if I'd known you all my life."

"You probably have," he agreed, and his glance was distinctly roguish now. "More coffee?"

"No, thank you. I'll be all right now."

"I thought you were," he nodded, and patted her hand with paper-dry fingers. "And in that case, I'll be going."

He got to his feet, shouldered his battered rucksack, and prepared to walk away.

"I – I don't know how to thank you," Beth began.

But he cut her short. "Thank Elkstone," he said. "It's not my doing. *Remember the light.*" And he went off down the path, past the ancient, lichened tombstones, and disappeared among the trees.

Beth was too shaken to go home straight away, so she drove on through the winter hills until she came to a small, quiet pub in a sunny courtyard just outside a village. It seemed a good place to stop, and there was a cheerful fire and a blackboard announcing bar food.

She had just got herself a drink, when someone turned round from a shadowy corner and remarked without surprise: "Oh, there you are."

162

"Peter?" She went across to him in astonishment. "What are you doing here?"

"Waiting for you." He looked up impishly, and his grin was infectious.

Beth began to smile, too. "Honestly, you're incorrigible. How did you know I'd be here?"

"Saw you go off. Just missed you." His grin was a bit uncertain now. "As a matter of fact, Digs told me she'd suggested Elkstone." He paused, and added honestly: "She also told me to stay away and let you see it by yourself!"

Beth's smile softened. "She was quite right."

"I know," said Peter gloomily. "Digs usually is!"

Beth took a gulp of her drink and actually laughed. "But that still doesn't explain – ?"

"Feeling phased – make for the nearest pub – stands to reason." He also took a long swig of his drink. "And this is the nearest – on the way home."

"It was a long shot."

"I like long shots." He screwed his eyes up at her like a naughty small boy. Then he allowed himself to look mildly serious for a moment and added: "Thought you might be needing a bit of support."

Beth sighed, and sat down beside him. It was time she made a few things clear to young Peter, but she hated to hurt that too-casual kindness.

"Peter, I – "

"Oh, I know, I know," he said, keeping his voice light. "No intrusion intended. Nothing required – except an occasional smile or two." He lifted his glass to her and smiled over the rim.

Reluctantly, Beth smiled back. "You're hopeless."

Peter glanced up at the blackboard and then looked at her enquiringly. "Let's order something to eat. First things first. Then you can lecture me all you want."

Beth shook her head at him helplessly, and allowed him to order home-made steak and kidney-pie, which he assured her was extra special here.

Then she tried again. "Don't you have a girlfriend of your own?"

"Not now."

"Why not?"

"She went off with someone else."

"Oh." She glanced at him warily. "Was that – traumatic?"

"A bit. At the time." He was still looking away, still frowning a little. Then he turned back to her, smiling again, if a trifle lopsidedly. "Usual scenario. We were planning to get married, but my best friend beat me to it." He took a quiet sip of his drink. "I was rather angry at the time," he added, in a cold, detached sort of voice.

"I can imagine," agreed Beth. She paused, and then went on, carefully pursuing her point: "But that doesn't mean – "

"Oh no. Plenty of fish in the sea, and all that." The smile was still a bit crooked. "But, like you, I'm not in the mood for any more emotional upheavals." He was suddenly quite serious again. "You're very scrupulous, Beth, but you needn't worry." His eyes, looking into hers, were absurdly clear and honest. "I happen to like your company a lot – and I'm the kind of idiotic bloke that likes to feel useful . . . For God's sake, why else would I be a teacher?"

Beth laughed again. "Why indeed?"

"So that's all right then," said Peter, as if everything necessary had been said. "We both need company at present. Stands to reason. Have another drink." Beth met his eyes with unwilling acceptance, but could not resist that impudent grin. "All right, then," she said, and knew she had capitulated to that endearing boyish charm once again.

But Peter understood her very well. "No danger here," he said, getting to his feet. "Safe as houses." And he went to fetch her another drink.

Finn's way of life was paved with good intentions, but somehow they always got sidetracked. He had planned to go straight home from the Spirios site, knowing it was high time he did, but there were still a lot of loose ends to tie up if he was going to arrange his working life round his family commitments. And he *was*, of course he was. From now on – once he had got things sorted out and could run his various projects from home – he was going to devote his time to Chloë and learn how to be a proper father.

So he went first to Athens, where he saw a couple of banks

and arranged finance for the Spirios development, and then paid a brief visit to another site on the northern coast above Sounion, where he had somehow got involved in the building of a convalescent home overlooking the sea. Then he went to Italy where a firm of shoe manufacturers had nearly gone bankrupt but had decided to become a co-operative for its own work force (with financial assistance from Finn). After that, he visited a printer in Spain where he had a stake in their expansion progamme, and then Paris and Stuttgart, where he simply talked more money. Finally, he took a plane to Bonn for more banking talks, and from there, certain at last that he had got everything in order, he rang Beth to announce his return. He did not ring Mary first this time, wanting to be sure that his coming was not going to cause a major upset with Chloë before he spoke to her. So he waited to hear what Beth had to say about the situation and how he ought to proceed. He sounded absurdly humble and anxious on the phone, and Beth was touched by his desperate concern to do the right thing.

"It's going to be all right," she told him. "Chloë's got a role to play now. You're going to be cosseted."

"What?"

"It was old Beech who put the idea into her head. You'll need to play up a bit, Finn, that's all."

"How?"

"Oh – just be a bit sad and lonely. That's what Beech said you were."

"He's not far wrong," admitted Finn, still not quite understanding the situation.

"She needs to be useful, Finn – to feel wanted."

"Don't we all," growled Finn, but he was beginning to follow what Beech's skilful suggestion had done for Chloë.

"So – you think she won't mind my coming?"

"*Mind*?" said Beth, realising that Finn needed as much reassurance as Chloë. "If you handle it right, she'll revel in it."

Finn sighed. "Tell me what to do?"

Beth thought for a moment. "I think you'd better come here, Finn. At tea-time. Chloë and Mark will be here then, so it will break the ice. We can arrange a special tea – she'll enjoy that

. . . And then you can take her home, and she and Mary can fix a special supper!"

Finn laughed. "It sounds like one long party."

"Yes," agreed Beth. "That's the idea."

"Shall I – ought I to ring Mary and tell her when I'm coming?"

Again Beth thought carefully. "No," she said at last. "I'll tell her – and I'll tell Chloë. That way there's be no awkward moments . . . Just tell me when you *are* coming, that's all!"

"The day after tomorrow," said Finn, sounding humble again. "Will that be all right?"

"Lovely." Beth's voice was suddenly warm with approval. "Tea-time. At the Beehive. We'll be waiting for you."

Finn did not know whether to laugh or cry with relief. So he did neither. He just said: "Bless you, Beth," and rang off.

After some serious thought, Beth decided to go round and see Mary herself, not trusting the phone to iron out all the hidden tensions and anxieties that might arise.

"He's coming the day after tomorrow, Mary, so I think you'd better lay on an extra special meal. And let Chloë help, if you can. Could she make a sauce or something?"

Mary's round face lit with enthusiasm. "Surely. I can think of something for her to do. We can get it ready tomorrow evening."

"And let her help to dust his room, or put flowers in . . . Anything that will make her feel she's preparing her own special welcome for him."

Mary nodded. She understood exactly what Beth was doing. After all, it was how she showed her own feelings of welcome, – cleaning and polishing things till they shone, and providing a celebration meal to mark the occasion. Much better than mere words, good food was – and a well-ordered house was the most welcoming thing she knew.

"Is Chloë asleep?" asked Beth, looking at the kitchen clock which said after ten.

"In bed," Mary corrected, smiling. "But I doubt she's asleep. She's started reading books again now – I have quite a job to get her to put the light out!"

Beth grinned. "That's a good sign! . . . Shall I go up and tell her the news? Or would you like to?"

166

"You'd better." Mary was nothing if not practical. "You'll handle it better." She looked round her warm kitchen and added cheerfully: "Tell you what, I'll make us all a nice hot drink, and there's a few buns left. She can come down just this once!"

"A midnight feast," agreed Beth, smiling. "I'll go and fetch her."

Chloë was sitting up in bed with a book on the duvet in front of her, but she looked up and smiled when Beth came into the room. Nowadays, Beth reflected, the child was much more ready to smile, and much less inclined to rebuff anyone who tried to come near to her.

"Can I come in?" Even so, Beth was still careful not to push her luck.

"Sit on the bed," commanded Chloë, and moved a little to make room for her. Then she looked into Beth's face rather searchingly, and said: "Is Finn coming home?"

"That's exactly it," answered Beth, not really surprised at Chloë's quick gasp of essentials. After all, it wasn't every day that Chloë's teacher arrived late at night and came to sit on her bed. She also noted that the old affectionate nickname 'Daddy-Finn' had not yet returned to Chloë's vocabulary. But maybe that would come in time. It was enough that the home-coming had been accepted without fuss. Now to get her involved in the preparations for Finn's return . . . "We thought – Mary and I – that you might like to come down and plan a good welcome?"

Chloë was still looking at her, and now she considered the matter seriously before answering. "Yes," she agreed at last, and began to climb out of bed. "What shall we do?"

They sat at the kitchen table with Mary and discussed the matter in detail. Menus were suggested and rejected, and finally decided upon. Plans for tidying and cleaning, for flowers and even a welcome banner were arranged.

"Will he be coming straight here?" asked Mary, and Beth knew she had got to go very carefully at this point.

"No." She smiled at Chloë, feeling all at once quite certain that her arrangement with Finn was the right one. "He says he can't wait that long! And he doesn't want to interrupt Chloë's usual tea-time arrangements." She turned then to

167

speak directly to Chloë, watching for any sign of doubt or anxiety in the small, wary face. "So he's coming to tea with you and Mark after school. And then you can take him home yourself."

Chloë's clear, uncompromising gaze was on her. She was not in the least fooled by Beth's strategy, but she seemed to approve of it. "Can we make some of your rock cakes?"

"Why not? We'll do it tomorrow afternoon."

"And get out the chess set? He likes chess."

"Yes, of course – though I don't think he'll want to stay too long. He'll want to get home."

Chloë nodded, thinking it out. "I suppose he might be tired?"

"I should think so – after all that travelling . . . You'll have to sit him down with a nice drink by his own fireside. That's what he'll like best."

Chloë and Beth looked at each other and smiled. They understood each other perfectly.

Mary, seeing that look of perfect accord, heaved a sigh of relief, and poured them all out some more hot chocolate.

It was going to be all right.

So Finn came home. And when he stood in Beth's doorway, looking in on the firelit scene before him, he was suddenly caught in such a wave of gladness that he was almost shocked. Beth, too, was overtaken by the same unexpected surge of feeling, and stood looking at him without quite knowing what to say.

Beth had planned carefully for this meeting, knowing that it was vitally important for Chloë that it should go well. So the fire was warm and inviting, the two children, Mark and Chloë, were crouched in front of it brandishing toasting forks, the table was laid for tea by the hearth, and the kettle was singing gently in the kitchen. The curtains were drawn against the cold November night, and the whole room had taken on a rosy ambience reflecting undemanding peace and comfort. And yet here they both were, Beth and Finn, almost tongue-tied at their meeting when they both needed to carry things off with the utmost tact and diplomacy.

But Chloë took things into her own hands. She did not run

168

into his arms crying 'Daddy-Finn, you're home!' as she had done on that golden day of arrival when Beth first saw her. (And Beth, remembering that joyous meeting, felt a small lurch of pity for the quiet too-serious little girl Chloë had become). But instead, she came gravely forward across the room, and stood looking up into Finn's face for a moment in silence. Then she said simply: "I'm glad you're back safe," and led him towards the fire. It was not exactly an effusive welcome, but it told Finn what he wanted to know.

And then the cosseting began. "We're toasting crumpets," Chloë told him. "Are you hungry?"

"Ravenous," admitted Finn, and somehow everyone was laughing and the dangerous moment was past.

Chloë did not ask any questions or make any demands upon him, but kept him plied with crumpets and rock buns and cups of tea, and afterwards she and Mark challenged him to a game of chess which he skilfully lost. And then it was time for him to take Chloë home, and he stood there wondering how he was going to manage to talk to Beth. For talk he must, soon – there were a lot of things about Chloë he did not understand yet, and there was a whole future different life to plan.

But here Chloë helped him too, for she suddenly made her first and most important request. "Can we go and get Corny from Beech now you're home?"

Finn looked at Beth in bewilderment.

"It's the puppy," she told him, smiling. "Chloë was just waiting for you to say yes."

"Then 'yes' it is," agreed Finn, nodding cheerfully so that the firelight glinted on his golden buccaneer's beard. "But wouldn't Saturday be better? Then you'll be home all the weekend to look after him."

Chloë saw the sense of that. But she hadn't finished with him yet. "Can Mark and Beth come too?"

"Oh but – " Beth began, and then she saw Mark's eager face and fell silent.

"Of course," said Finn. "We'll all go." Then, smiling a little apologetically at the three of them, he added: "I don't know much about puppies. But I'm willing to learn."

"Beech knows," stated Chloë, with sublime confidence. "Doesn't he, Mark?"

"Yes," agreed Mark. "Beech knows most things." But he was looking at Finn with the kind of expression that said: I bet you know a lot, too, whatever you say.

He misses that father of his, Beth thought. He does so need someone to look up to. Do all boys need heroes, I wonder? . . . And small girls, too? And she thought how strange it was that Finn Edmondson who could sail yachts round the world and climb impossible mountain peaks and run innumerable enterprises in different far-off places, could yet sound so humble and shy in front of his own small daughter.

"That was a splendid tea," Finn sighed, including them all in his thanks.

"Supper's next," announced Chloë, and put her hand into his without any hesitation. "We've got something *special*."

"Saturday then?" Finn was looking at Beth with some urgency over the top of Chloë's head. "At Beech's? When?"

"He likes to feed his animals about noon," volunteered Mark.

Finn looked from him back to Beth. "Noon?"

"We'll be there," smiled Beth, and followed them over to the doorway to watch them go.

"Now for our special supper," said Finn to Chloë, playing up like mad as he had been told to do. "Lead me to it, Chloë!" And they went off side by side down the path.

Beth and Mark looked at each other and smiled like conspirators.

"He's nice," said Mark, and there was a certain wistfulness in his voice. "Chloë'll be all right now."

"*Given half a chance,*" murmured Beth, unable to resist Beech's catchphrase.

And they both began to laugh.

Beech was indeed feeding the animals when they arrived, and they all found themselves caught up in the process, carrying buckets of food and bundles of hay. Chloë could barely contain her impatience, but somehow she knew the old man couldn't be hurried, and all his animals must be cared for before he would go back to the cottage where Jess and her puppies were waiting.

So they fed the fox cub and the frightened hare, scattered

170

corn for the Rhode Island hens and the pheasant chicks, put some chopped-up dog-food down for three injured hedgehogs, and a bale of hay for Moses the donkey.

"Is Moses still sad?" asked Mark, reaching up to rub the furry grey neck as he hung his head over the gate to look at them.

"Better ask him," said Beech, and delved into one of his capacious pockets for an apple. "Needs talking to some more, I reckon." His quiet, observant gaze went thoughtfully from Chloë's face to Finn's as he spoke. "Critturs are like people seemingly, they needs talking to when they're sad."

Chloë nodded gravely, and Mark put his arms round the old donkey's neck. "You hear that, Moses? Beech says you need a good talking to."

Chloë laughed and began to talk to him as well. But Finn looked from Chloë to Beth and did not say a word.

In a little while all the chores were done, and Beech led them back to the cottage, and allowed Chloë to run on ahead and pick up Corny from among the tumbling litter of puppies by the back door. When they came up to her, she was standing there with the golden bundle of fur in her arms, looking down at her with an expression of such loving delight that Finn's own heart seemed to contract with sudden pain . . . If only she would look at him like that! . . . But perhaps it would come back with time . . . ?

"I see why she needs the puppy," he said to Beth under his breath.

Beth smiled at him, well understanding the fleck of pain in his eyes. "It's a way of release," she murmured carefully. "Easier than human emotion . . . The rest will come."

He gave her a grateful glint of a smile and went forward to look at the puppy which Chloë was now holding up to him.

"This is Corny. Would you like to hold her?"

Finn took the eager little puppy in his arms and held her up close to his face. "So you're Corny, are you? Welcome to the family, Corny."

And Corny, seeming to know that this was an important moment, licked everything she could reach, and tried to bury her head in Finn's golden beard.

171

"She thinks you're as safe as her mother," explained Chloë. "Your fur's the same colour!"

And everyone laughed.

Then Finn handed Corny back to Chloë, and turned to negotiate with Beech.

"Nay, I don't want a lot for her," Beech told him. "Her father's a retriever too – belongs to a farmer I knows. The only payment he wants is two good pups. And I've found homes for most o' the others – except for Corny, of course."

"Why Corny?" asked Finn, turning to Chloë for clarification.

Beth waited somewhat breathlessly to see whether Chloë would answer, but when she didn't and shot Beth a glance of mute appeal, it seemed better to answer for her. "I think it's short for Cornfield," she said easily, "because of her colour." She paused and then added softly: "But Chloë will tell you why later on, I'm sure."

Finn was instantly aware that there were hidden meanings here, but he merely nodded as if quite satisfied with Beth's explanation and said no more.

Beech, too, ignored the conversation and went on to explain a bit more about puppy-handling to her new owners. "I've bin teachin' her a bit, like," he said, "while she was waitin'. She comes to 'Corny' now when she's called, and she'll walk a little way on a lead, but her legs is a bit short still for long walks." He fondled the puppy's silken ears with his kind, blunt fingers. "As for house-trainin', she'm nearly there, but I still puts newspaper down on the kitchen floor when I lets her come into the house . . . She won't be long, though, she's a clever little thing." He turned to Chloë seriously. "You must learn to take her out, see? Regular, like. And take her little walks – and teach her to bring sticks back, or a ball. She's very obedient, if you tells her clearly what to do."

Chloë nodded solemnly. "I'll tell her. She listens when I talk to her."

Beech smiled approval. "That's the ticket. She'll do all right with you." Then he produced a small collar and lead. "They'm a bit old, like, but they'll do till you can buy her some new 'uns." And he also provided a small bit of familiar-smelling blanket to wrap the puppy in on the way home if she got tired

172

of walking. "The wind's perishin' cold today, and Corny's not used to the big bad world out there!"

So at last it was all arranged, and Beech finally accepted Finn's money, admitting it would come in handy for feeding the other animals, and gave Corny a last valedictory pat on the head.

"You look after her, Little 'un," he said to Chloë, "and she'll do you proud." He looked for a moment as if he was going to give Chloë a farewell pat on the head as well. But instead he winked at her broadly and added in his soft voice: "Talking and cosseting – that's what's needed. Remember?"

"I'll remember," promised Chloë, and set off down the path with Corny pulling every which way on her lead.

The others began to follow her, but Finn suddenly turned back to Beech and murmured an extra thank you, adding: "I believe I owe you a lot more than the price of one small puppy!"

Beech did not answer, but he nodded and smiled, and watched them with tranquil satisfaction as they went down the hill. One more of his animals was safe, and if maybe a father and his small daughter were closer to understanding in consequence, it would do no harm at all.

PART IV – '. . . AND MAKE ANOTHER SONG.'

Finn still had not managed to have any private conversation with Beth, and for the rest of that day he was entirely occupied with Chloë and the new puppy. And for the next day, too. But late on Sunday evening, when Chloë was at last asleep, with young Corny curled up beside her (though it wasn't allowed), Finn left Mary in charge and walked over to see Beth at the little Beehive.

Light was streaming from the windows as he came up the path, and he thought how warm and welcoming it looked in the cold November night. Beth came to the door, looking both startled and pleased to see him, and stood back at once to let him come into the firelit room.

"I'm sorry to come so late," he began, "but I waited for Chloë to go to sleep, and it took some time!"

"I can imagine," laughed Beth, "with Corny to distract her . . . Would you like some coffee?"

"Lovely," sighed Finn, and stretched himself out in the chair that Beth drew up for him close to the fire.

There was silence in the room for a few moments while Beth fetched the coffee and Finn tried in a muddled way to marshall his thoughts. But at last he said abruptly as she came back into the room: "You've worked miracles with Chloë."

Beth handed him his coffee and smiled. "Not me only. Mary, and Mark – and most of all Beech. They all had a hand in it."

Finn nodded. "I did try to thank him – but words seemed somewhat inadequate."

"Not to Beech," said Beth, still smiling a little. "Words are very important to him, though he uses few enough himself."

Finn's smile was apologetic. "True. He certainly seems to have given them back to Chloë." He paused, and then asked

174

curiously: "What was it he said about 'Yonder'? And where does Corny come into it?"

Beth looked away from him into the fire and she answered. "He got Chloë and Mark to plant a tree. He told them he always did that when one of his animals died."

Finn glanced at her in swift comprehension.

"And then he said: *'I reckon they're all running about out yonder – dancing about like hares in a cornfield . . .'*" Beth turned her head then and looked straight at Finn. "And Chloë understood him. She pointed away through the trees, Finn, as if she could almost see them . . . And that was when she said her first word."

"*Yonder*," sighed Finn, understanding a whole lot of things in a very short space of time. He was silent again for a while, and then he suddenly seemed to recollect that Beth had her own problems to sort out as well as Chloë's, so he said gently: "And how has it been for you?"

Beth stirred and seemed to come back from a long way off. "Me? Oh . . . I struggle on." Her smile was a little fragile. But then she seemed to realise that Finn needed reassuring. After all, her own ability to cope was part of Chloë's recovery plan. She could not fail either of them now. "My days are full – thanks to this job. And not only Chloë's problems are absorbing . . ."

Finn caught the glint of humour in her eye, and grinned. "I can believe that."

"And people have been enormously kind," she added, thinking of young Peter, and the rest of the well-meaning staff.

"But – ?" Pursued Finn.

"I didn't say but."

"Your voice did."

She sighed. "Oh, you know it too, Finn. What's the point of saying it? The gap is still huge – one day, perhaps, it will seem less vast . . . I don't know. But in the meantime, I suppose we have to do the best we can!"

She got up then, a little restlessly, to put another log on the fire and fetch some more coffee from the kitchen.

Finn had not answered her this time, but at last he asked slowly: "What did Stephanie say?"

175

Beth paused in surprise. "About Mo and Robert?" Then her face softened as the words came back to her. "She said: *'You only have to remember.'*"

Finn nodded. "That sounds like her." He gave himself a rueful little shake of self-contempt. "I told you I was a coward. She faced up to everything." Then he seemed to pull himself together and come back to the questions of the day. "About Chloë . . . what ought we to do about these tea-times with Mark? They seem to be important."

Beth was ready for that. "I've been thinking – she'll want to get home to Corny now, as well as you, won't she? Why don't you walk down with the puppy to meet her? That way she'll just get in Corny's exercise while it's still light."

"What about Mark?"

"Well, as a matter of fact, the school rehearsals are getting intense just now, so I shall probably want to stay on late with Mark and George and one or two others . . ." She glanced at Finn, all at once alight with enthusiasm. "They're getting quite good, you know. You will come to it, Finn, won't you? Chloë's in it, too." She hesitated, and then added honestly. "I haven't given her much to do, but she couldn't *do* very much at first. But she's beginning to join in now. And she will do anything Mark tells her to!"

Finn laughed. "He'll have to give me lessons!" Then he grew serious again. "But I don't think Chloë will like not seeing you after school at all . . . It seems to me that she has got very fond of you, – and so she should!" He looked at her, half-smiling. "So I wondered if you would come over to supper – once or twice a week, or something? She could show you how Corny's getting on . . . I – I don't want her to feel cut off from you . . ." He stalled there for a moment, and then blurted out: "And I'd like it, too – if you'd come?"

Beth grinned. "Don't sound so humble. Of course I'll come. I'd love to."

Finn let out a gusty sigh of relief. "Phew! I'm glad that's over . . . I never was any good at begging for help!"

"I think you're doing splendidly," said Beth. "You've only got to look pathetic and everyone melts!"

Finn got up then, still laughing a little. "I'd better go, before you unravel me any further." But he had done what he set out to do, and Beth too, now, would have an excuse to fill one or two lonely evenings.

Steph, he thought, I'm doing what I can. And I have a sneaking suspicion that you planned this all along. But aloud he only said: "This is a lovely room. I only hope mine will be as welcoming." And he turned his back on the glowing firelight and went home in the dark.

The rehearsals were, in truth, getting intense in the couple of weeks before the performance, but both George and Mark were only too pleased to stay on after school. They neither of them wanted to get home any sooner than necessary, if for different reasons. One or two of the girls stayed on too, if they had tricky solos to sing, but the main chorus of Japanese villagers had to be content with the ordinary music classes. They knew what they were doing anyway by now, Beth told herself, and did not really need extra coaching. But George blossomed with the special attention he was getting, and was producing quite an impressive performance as Hamaguchi, the Village Grandfather. He had even found a strange, deep voice hidden somewhere in his gangling frame, and he had learnt to stand very tall and straight and still, holding on to his staff and gazing out like a true village seer. Mark's clear treble had mercifully not broken yet, and was as pure and true as a boy's voice should be, and he enjoyed the bit of dramatic acting Beth had given him to do.

But now she realised she had got to organise some scenery, and a bit of skilful lighting, too, if she could manage it. But, above all, she needed that tam-tam, and a timp as well, if she could get hold of one. But where from?

For the first two problems, she went to Peter. He was practical and reasonably inventive. He would be bound to think of something.

"Peter, could you build us a mountain?"

"Certainly. Everest or Snowdon?"

"Well, more like Fuji-yama, really." She answered his grin with a hopeful one of her own. "I'm trying to paint a backcloth a bit like a Japanese print – you know, all washy and cloudy, with islands floating in a sea of mist."

"Sounds wonderful."

"Well, it won't be, unless you can put a sort of slope for them to climb up in front of it. And then I want lighting for three different things."

"What things?"

"An earthquake, a fire and a tidal wave."

Peter scratched his head. "You don't want much, do you?"

"I know it sounds awful, Peter, but can you do it?"

"Of course," agreed Peter stoutly. "Leave it to me." Then he added cheerfully: "I daresay George and Mark will help me hammer?"

"They'll be delighted." Beth was laughing, too.

Then she went to ask Margaret Collier about the tam-tam and the timp.

"I think you'd better talk to Finn," said Margaret, smiling.

"Finn Edmondson?"

"He's back, I hear." Margaret was looking at her in a considering way. "He's in charge of the Music Fund, – and I'm sure he'll find the money if you ask him."

"I only want to hire them – not buy them!"

"I'm glad to hear it. They sound somewhat expensive to me." She was laughing now, and Beth was relieved to see that she did not really think the request too outrageous for a junior school production.

"Will he know where I can get them from?"

"If he doesn't, he'll find out. Nothing daunts Finn when he sets his mind on something."

Beth nodded, but it was not the picture she had of Finn as he was at present – shy and uncertain, and curiously lost without Stephanie's unswerving support.

She sighed a little, and said in an unconvinced voice: "All right, I'll ask him. I shall be seeing him and Chloë tonight."

Margaret did not miss the hesitation behind Beth's quiet manner, or the fact that there already seemed to be some kind of understanding between Finn and her young colleague, but she kept her own counsel about it, and merely added, with a glint of extra warmth: "It's a good cause, Beth – you can tell him that from me. You deserve all the help you can get."

Beth shot her a surprised, grateful smile and went back to work, somewhat reassured.

178

So that night when Beth arrived at the Mill House for supper with Chloë and Finn, she had an extra purpose for her visit. (And for some reason this made her feel less shy and awkward). The old house was ablaze with lights and smelt of beeswax and wood fires, and everything shone with Mary's devoted polishing. Chloë and the puppy came racing together down the hall as Finn opened the door, and the sound of laughter floated out into the cold night air.

It feels alive again, thought Beth, and smiled in genuine pleasure at the change in the atmosphere of the graceful rooms. Then she looked down at Chloë's small, glowing face and was amazed at the change in that, too.

"Look at Corny," said Chloë, giggling, "she's got Mary's knitting wool."

"Oh Corny, how could you!" protested Finn, laughing too. "What on earth will Mary say?"

But Corny merely pranced off a bit further down the hall, wreathed in purple wool, and Chloë ran after her, giggling even more helplessly as she tried to disentangle the wriggling furry legs from the tangled skein.

"Come into the sitting room," said Finn. "Supper's nearly ready." He gave one exaggerated glance of mock despair at Chloë and the puppy, and left them to unwind each other. But his eyes met Beth's and they both smiled with relief and undisguised gladness. It was wonderful to see Chloë laughing again.

"It's a great success," he said.

Beth nodded. "I can see that."

"I can't tell you – " he began, and then shook his head. "She's a different child . . ." He went over to the tray of drinks that stood on a corner table, and asked over his shoulder: "Sherry? Or would you rather have gin?"

"Sherry will do nicely."

He brought it to her, still smiling. "There's a lot to celebrate!"

"I know." Beth lifted her glass. "To Chloë and Corny – and Beech."

"And Beech," Finn repeated. "And Beth!"

This seemed to Beth a good opening for her request, so she said cheerfully: "If you include me, can I claim a reward?"

179

"Name it," grinned Finn. "The sky's the limit."

"I want a tam-tam."

"A what?"

"A tam-tam. An orchestral gong. A huge one. And a timp, if you can get one."

Finn looked at her in amazement. "This is for your school production, I take it?"

"Exactly. And Margaret Collier said you were the one to ask."

Finn thought for a moment. "To hire?"

"Of course."

"Orchestral Society," he said. "I'll see about it."

"Just like that?"

"Why not? It shouldn't be impossible." His grin was mischievous now. "And the impossible will only take a little longer."

Beth laughed. "Margaret said you'd fix it."

At this point Chloë ran in, with Corny skittering about on the polished wood floor behind her, and announced solemnly: "Supper's ready, and Mary says not to let it get cold." Then she added hopefully: "Can Corny come too?"

"No!" Finn's voice was stern. But then, seeing her face, he relented: "Well, only if you keep her quiet, under your chair."

"I will," promised Chloë, not knowing in the least how she was going to do it, and Corny skidded forwards in a blur of golden fur and started to kill the Indian rug in the hall.

It was a cheerful meal – and Chloë announced with pride that she had made the apple crumble herself, and then admitted honestly: "Well, Mary helped . . ." Mary, who usually ate with them these days, confirmed this, and added smiling: "She's becoming a right good little cook," – which pleased Chloë enormously. There were some home-made peppermint creams to go with the coffee, also of Chloë's invention, and even Corny was allowed to try one of these, but the peppermint made her sneeze and rub her nose on the carpet.

Finn did not insist on a specific bedtime at weekends, but he did remind Chloë that there was still school tomorrow, and Beth would not like her young singers to be yawning their heads off. To Beth's surprise, Chloë took this seriously and turned to her with earnest insistence. "I *am* singing now, aren't I? He'll be able to hear me, won't he?"

"Of course he will," Beth reassured her. "Especially if you stand in the front with Mark."

Chloë smiled in relief. "I'm Mark's sister, you see," she told her father. "In the play, I mean."

"I see," said Finn gravely. "Well, I shall be listening extra hard."

"That's all right then." Chloë suddenly sounded brisk and matter-of-fact. "Come on then, Corny. Bedtime." She started for the door, and then looked round at Beth. "I promise not to yawn," she said solemnly, and went off up the stairs with Corny tumbling up after her.

"I'll come up and say goodnight," Finn called after her, and turned back to pour out more coffee. "She seems happy enough," he said, and there was sudden anxiety in his voice, "don't you think?"

"Yes, I do." Beth sounded firm and decisive. Then, seeing the uncertainty in his eyes, she added gently: "What worries you about it?"

He sighed. "It's just – will it be enough for her – just me here, and Mary and the puppy? . . . She must still miss Stephanie dreadfully."

"She's beginning to talk to you again, isn't she? You'll soon build up a kind of working relationship . . ." She smiled at him encouragingly. "And Corny helps."

"Oh yes," he admitted, smiling a little himself. "Corny certainly helps! But then he grew serious again. "Though we've got a long way to go yet, before we understand one another . . ." He glanced at Beth and then went on in a voice that was suddenly shy: "She said an odd thing yesterday . . . out of the blue. Not about anything in particular . . ."

"Yes?"

"She said *'Sometimes it's nobody's fault.'*" He looked at Beth with anxious candour. "It was almost as if – as if she understood."

Beth nodded. "I think she does understand now, Finn."

"But how? I haven't tried to say anything."

Beth smiled at his concern. "I think it was our old friend, Beech, again. He and Mark between them. They got talking

181

about the awful things that happen to the animals. Mark asked: 'Is it always our fault?' And old Beech said: "No. *Sometimes it's nobody's fault. You can't go blaming other folk all the time.*'" She paused and added softly: "He knew he was talking to Mark about his family problems, and to Chloë about hers, too . . . and he knew she was listening, though she didn't say anything at the time . . . But I think it just simmered down into her mind, and came out when she wanted it to.

Finn was silent for a long time. Then he said slowly: "There seems to be no end to what that good old man has done for her . . ."

Beth nodded quietly. "It will be all right now."

Finn roused himself. "I'm going to work from home now," he told her. "I've fixed up an office, and phones and faxes and things . . . It'll be perfectly feasible to run it all from here. I needn't go away at all."

"But you must sometimes," protested Beth, alarmed at the thought of this restless, adventurous spirit entirely caged at home. "You can take Chloë with you."

He looked startled. "Could I? Wouldn't it unsettle her?"

"Not really." Beth sounded coolly certain. "There are the school holidays. Travel would be good for her – so long as you were with her." She looked at him seriously. "But you'd have to take her pretty well everywhere – on the site and so on . . ."

"Yes, I know that," he said, sounding a little grim. "After what happened, I could never leave her alone again . . ."

Beth silently cursed herself for allowing the past to creep back into his thoughts. "I think she'd like to feel part of your working life, Finn," she insisted. "You could talk to her about it, couldn't you?"

"If she'd listen!" Finn laughed a little.

"Try her," said Beth.

And then they heard Chloë calling to them to come and say goodnight. Finn insisted on Beth going up with him, and she stooped over Chloë rather shyly and patted the sleepy puppy on the way. She was wary of showing too much affection, of becoming too much involved with Finn and his demanding small daughter, even of admitting to herself her own need of simple human contact in a world grown grey without Little

182

Mo's loving presence in her life. But before she could draw back, Chloë's arms came up in a warm, strong hug, and she whispered into her ear: "Thanks for coming," before she let go.

Beth went out of the room rather blindly and left Finn to talk to Chloë alone. But he came out quite soon, and then took Beth to inspect his new office and the computers and fax machines, and the maps of his projects on the wall. And finally he took her downstairs, and Mary had produced more hot coffee, and he found some brandy and a couple of balloon glasses to go with it, and settled her down by the fire for a nightcap.

"Beth," he said suddenly, "do you feel . . . manipulated?"

Beth did not misunderstand him. "By Stephanie, you mean? Yes, a little."

"Do you mind?"

She paused to think it out. "No," she said at last. "Not really, I suppose. Stephanie saw very far ahead, didn't she? And she was a born manager – she told me so herself!" She was smiling now. "Somehow, this job – which she engineered for me, as you well know – and – and the problem of Chloë seemed to fall into place naturally. It wasn't forced on me."

Finn looked unconvinced. "I've used you, too."

Beth dismissed it calmly. "What else could you do?" Then, seeing the doubt in his eyes, she tried to reassure him. "I need to be used, Finn. That's the trouble!" She laughed a little, and then went on more seriously: "You know I'd do anything to help Chloë – that goes without saying. And not only because Stephanie was very good to me at a moment of crisis . . ." She paused and then added shyly: "I – I loved her too, you know."

"Yes," agreed Finn. "I know."

They did not talk of it any more after that, and presently they got up, warmed by the fire and the brandy and their companionable silence, and Finn took her home.

And then, all at once it seemed, it was time for the school performance. Peter had been as good as his word and made them a mountain to climb up, and his lighting was in place and magically effective – if the boy in charge of it didn't push the dimmer slides too fast.

Finn had found her a rather battered but perfectly usable timp for the earthquake, and an absolutely beautiful tam-tam whose deep reverberations were almost too soul-shaking to bear. Beth's own misty backcloth seemed to take on a kind of shimmering life of its own under Peter's lights, and the colours of the costumes looked unexpectly subtle against it.

The cast were ready, and not too nervous not even George who looked extraordinarily tall and dignified in his long robe and thin village-grandfather beard. And the gaggle of really wicked boys who were usually disruptive and unpredictable seemed suitably awestruck and ready to co-operate. The audience were in place, the lights in the hall were dimmed, and everything was in order. It was time to start.

Beth took a deep breath and put her hand on the piano keys. Oh God, let them make a success of it, she prayed. It matters so much to them, it will do them so much good to do something really well and be admired . . . ! Then she began.

The Japanese Villagers came on, singing about the rice crop, and began to hoe in long lines across the stage, watched over by a benign Hamaguchi, the Village Grandfather, to whom they bowed at the end of their work song.

Then Mark, as the young fisherman, Ojotaki, began his sad song about the missing fish shoals and the empty sea.

'We sail away – ' he sang, and his voice was clear and sweet as he lifted his head to look over the audience out to sea.

'Across the pearl and silver bay,
From dusk till break of day . . .'

And the chorus joined in softly and sadly with their repeated lament:

'The fish have gone . . .'

"But where they go we do not know . . ." sang Mark, sounding bewildered and sadder than ever.

'And we return with nothing, nothing, nothing to show!' lamented the chorus.

The light changed then, from the silvery magic of dawn to a flat and sultry yellow. (Well done, thought Beth, it's earthquake weather, and he's remembered to bring up the ambers!) And Mark's voice changed too, from that

184

sorrowful, melting treble to something ominous and full of foreboding.

'The land lies locked and spellbound in the heat . . .
We hear our own hearts beat . . .
O strange, uneasy day,
What heavy doom lies on our silver bay?'

The timp began a slow, menacing beat that grew slowly louder. And then the earthquake came. The timp and cymbals thundered, and Beth thundered too on the piano. The wicked boys banged everything in sight, the lights went dim and the villagers rocked on their feet and fell about the stage in terror, while little Chloë clung to Mark's hand and looked like an authentic frightened little sister.

'*Hamaguchi, save us!*' cried the chorus, falling on their knees.

Then George, in his new deep voice of authority, commanded:

'*Be still, my children. It is an earthquake. But it is far away.*'

For a moment there was almost stillness from the frightened villagers, but then all at once Ojotaki pointed over the heads of the chorus and cried:

'Across the bay! Look out across the bay!
The sea! Look at the sea!'

and he was answered by the wondering chorus of villagers, whispering in fear:

'The sea is receding . . . It is going away . . . The sea is gone . . .
Nothing is left except the empty crawling bay . . .'

But Ojotaki suddenly pointed again, his voice alight with triumph:

'The empty crawling bay, you say!
Look at the fish – the fish!

185

Leaping and tumbling like silver fire!'

And the chorus, wild with excitement now, repeated his words over and over again as they rushed off the stage:
    In vain Hamaguchi's deep voice rang out, trying to warn them:

'Wait, children of my village,

But the chorus went on singing, off stage, their voices faint and fading:

'The bay is alive with their dancing, dancing . . .'

(Keep it soft and far away, begged Beth, playing ever more softly, and knowing that once the chorus was off stage she could not reach them or direct them. They had to manage on their own now.)

'Wait!' thundered George, in his brand new voice.
'Wait till the anger of the earth is done.'

But they did not heed him, and their sweet, childish voices floated up to the stage, still singing far away: *'Dancing . . . dancing . . .'*
    Then Hamaguchi began to use Peter's mountain.

'Let us climb, boy, climb!' he urged.
Climb to the foot of the mountain!'

and round and round he went, moving upward on Peter's circular ramp, and Mark followed him, holding Chloë by the hand, and letting his voice become sad and puzzled again as he asked:

'What is it, honoured grandfather, that you fear to say?'
'Look far out, boy,' commanded Hamaguchi, on the top of Peter's mountain now. *'What do you see?'*
'I see the bay, all silver grey,
And all our people wading in the sea . . .'' began Ojotaki.

186

'Look farther, boy, look farther!' commanded Hamaguchi, sounding sterner than ever.

And this time Ojotaki sang, as sweet and true as ever, but even more puzzled: *'I see the sea – the wide and restless sea, 'tossing and churning, lifting and falling – '* and then he screamed.

"Ah!'

(Well done, said Beth, heaving a sigh of relief. That was a splendid scream.)

'Yes, boy what do you see? demanded Hamaguchi.
'I see a line – a dark, thin line,
Coming towards us over the sea . . .
Growing and mounting . . . What can it be?'
'A wave, boy, a wave!' said Hamaguchi, and his voice was deep and angry.
'A tidal wave, High as a hill. Strong as a hurricane.
I knew it must come.
After the sea goes back, it has to come.'
'Our people will all be drowned,' cried Ojotaki.
What shall we do?'

Hamaguchi lifted his hand with his long white staff in it and pointed:

'Ring the bells in the temple!
Beat and ring! They must hear us!'

Then Ojotaki ran about, beating all the gongs and bells (but not the tam-tam yet. That came later,) and even Chloë ran up and down hitting out with a gong stick at anything she could reach, including the tubular bells.

(Remember the tubular bells, recalled Beth. And a line of George Herbert flashed into her mind at that point: *'Making a chiming of a passing bell . . .'* as she watched Chloë's eager little face, entirely wrapped up in the action and not a telltale shadow upon it).

But the chorus, far away, were still singing: *'Like silver fire . . . '*

'They do not hear us!' cried Ojotaki in despair.

187

'Beat again, boy. Shout and ring!' commanded Hamaguchi.

And once again Mark and Chloë beat everything within reach.

Then Ojotaki pointed out to sea in terror;

'Look at the sea! It is rising like a mountain . . .

Hurtling towards us – higher and higher!

What shall we do?'

'We must burn the rice fields,' said Hamaguchi, and George put all the depth and power he could find into his brave new voice.

'They will see it burning and come running to help me save it.

Quick, boy, fire the rice fields!'

So Mark and Chloë ran about with torches in their hands. (Thank God the batteries are working, said Beth).

'It burns, it burns!' sang Mark, and beat at the bells and gongs again. Then the girls who were flames danced in waving their crimson and scarlet drapes, and Peter's lights went red and the fire-flicker wheel began turning so that the whole stage seemed to be on fire, and the chorus came running back, shouting and crying: *'The rice! The rice is burning!'* And as they rushed in, Beth and the timp began the roaring of the approaching water.

'Hurry, my children, up the mountain.

Leave the rice fields,' called Hamaguchi.

'We have our lives – our lives . . .'

'Our lives . . . we have our lives!' answered the chorus, running upwards round Peter's ramp in terror.

'The sea is coming, the sea is coming!' they cried, still running upwards in panic-stricken spirals.

And then the wave came. The voice of the tam-tam rang out, huge and deep and fierce. (Never had the boy playing it made such a glorious noise before!) and the girls who were waves surged up across the stage in their floating blue and green scarves, dowsing the flames, and then retreated, hissing like receding water against the dying reverberations of the splendid tam-tam, and Beth let her surging piano die down too, until there was almost a silence.

188

'Honoured Hamaguchi, Oji-san,
You have saved our lives,' sang the chorus, kneeling.
'But not our village, or our rice!' sang out one of Beth's
doubting boys.

George seemed to stand taller than ever then, and to draw
himself up very straight as he said, strong and clear:

'We have our lives
We can begin again.'

And that was the cue for the last, sentimental song that
everyone was going to sing. (They've done it, thought Beth.
They've got there! It's corny, all right, Stephanie, but you just
listen to them! Aren't you proud of them?)

The world goes on,' sang the whole company, softly:
'And we must live and die.
When terror comes and sea meets sky,
We pick the pieces up,
We do not cry.
Though all our lives are hard,
And toil is long,
We find another way,
And make another song.'

And now everyone was singing – even Chloë – and even
George, in a strange, new tenor an octave lower than everyone
else, but in tune!

'Though all our little world
Is wrecked and gone,' they sang, with all their hearts in it,
'We find another way,
And make another song.'

And the company lifted their hands then to the audience and
sang the last line again: *'And make another song!'*

And Beth brought the last chord to an end, and found that
she could not see the keyboard. Those wonderful children,
she thought. All of them with such frightful problems of their
own – all singing like angels! . . . But she was not the only one

189

with tears in her eyes. Many of the people in that hall knew what those children had been through in their young lives. The silence seemed to go on and on, and then the applause began. (Beth had asked them to clap, no matter what happened, good or bad.) But she need not have worried. It roared and surged like the sea. Like her tidal wave.

The cast bowed politely and went off, and came on again. George came forward, prodded by Mark, and the clapping became ecstatic, and someone – was it George's father? cried 'Bravo'. Mark came forward next, still holding Chloë by the hand, and the clapping was almost louder. After all, Mark had done most of the solo singing, and beautifully, too. And then the whole cast bowed again, and one of them came down and grabbed Beth from the piano, so she joined them, taking the timp player and the tam-tam smiter with her, and everyone bowed again.

(For God's sake, she thought, let me get out of here before I disgrace myself altogether.) But of course she couldn't go away and leave them all, not when they were all so proud and happy. So she stayed with her cast and listened to the fervent praises of the astonished parents. (At least we shook 'em! she thought).

George's father came up, and said under his breath to Beth: "I said I'd clap like mad, come what may, but I never expected anything like this!"

"Wasn't he splendid?" said Beth.

"He was that!" He turned to his wife and daughter beside him, who both seemed to be struck dumb with amazement. "Wasn't George grand?"

"Wonderful," said George's mother, sounding suddenly pleased and proud, as any good mother should. "Simply wonderful!"

Then Mark's mother, Lucy, was there, looking both tearful and happy at once, saying incoherently: "I can't tell you – I didn't know he could!" And Beth smiled, remembering her first sight of Mark lying on the floor and screaming out his private rage and frustration against all the world.

Behind Lucy, obviously waiting to get in a quiet word, Beth noticed the young mother from the Meningitis Trust, Jean Shaw, and she turned to smile at her.

"Did you know," said Jean, "that Tony was your tam-tam player? It's the only musical sound he can really hear!"

Beth nodded, still half smiling. "I knew he had hearing problems. But those vibrations can get through anything!"

"He says it's the most wonderful noise he's ever heard!"

They laughed together, in relief. But then Jean said, in a shy, tentative voice: "It's such a lovely piece. I was wondering . . . do you think they'd do it again for the Trust sometime? . . . I'm sure it would raise a lot of funds!"

Beth considered the matter. "I'd have to ask the head-mistress, of course. I'll see what she says."

Jean's anxious eyes lit up. "I won't bother you any more now. But – but thanks for Tony's big moment!" And she hurried off before Beth could answer.

And last of all came Finn, who had waited patiently till the throng of delighted parents and friends had stopped besieging Beth, and there was room to breathe. He simply grasped her by the arm and said, smiling: "Never was a tam-tam put to better use!"

Beth laughed, and Chloë, who was still clinging possessively to Mark's hand, looked up at her father and said: "I *was* singing – did you hear me?"

"I heard you," smiled Finn. "I heard you loud and clear! It was simply beautiful – all of it!"

"Hear, hear!" agreed Peter, who was standing close beside them. "Especially my Fuji-yama!" and everyone round them laughed.

Margaret Collier had not attempted to say anything to Beth while the excitement was at its height, but now she came over with a cup of coffee in her hand and said: "I think you'd better drink this before you pass out."

"Do I look that bad?" said Beth, laughing.

Margaret looked at her judicially. "For someone who has just broken the sound barrier, you don't look too shattered."

Beth grinned. "Was it all right?"

"*All right?*" Margaret glared at her. "I wonder if you know what you've done for those children? . . . But yes, of course you do." She shook her head at Beth, as if words almost failed her. "Stephanie knew what she was doing when she sent you to us!"

191

Beth said, looking round for Finn and Chloë in a confused way: "I think Finn was pleased . . . ?"

Margaret nodded. "Am I mistaken, or was the child actually *singing*?"

"She was," smiled Beth. "And so was George – after a fashion!" And they began to laugh again.

The last person to come up to her, rather to her surprise, was old Bill Lewis – gruff and shy and awkward, but determined to add his small quota of praise. "I hate you, Beth Halliday," he growled. "You have undone me. I haven't shed a tear for forty years!"

"I'm sorry," said Beth, not knowing whether to laugh or not.

"Don't you dare be sorry!" he barked. "It was splendid, and I hated every minute of it, so there!" And then he actually laughed himself, so Beth dared to join in.

But when it was all over and she was finally alone and walking back to the little Beehive under the December stars, she found herself thinking almost tranquilly of Robert and Little Mo. They'd have enjoyed it, too, she thought. Mo would have loved to join in the singing . . . He was so musical . . . And then, unexpectedly, she found herself smiling as a new thought came to her: *Perhaps he did.*

Soon after the performance of Hamaguchi's Harvest, the school broke up for Christmas, and Beth said a temporary goodbye to the rest of the staff.

Peter, of course, insisted on taking her out for a farewell drink, but he had the sense not to give her an expensive Christmas present. Instead he gave her a hand-made mahogany Chinese block to add to her percussion instruments and a toy clown on a stick who turned somersaults when pushed – "to make you laugh when I'm not here."

Beth laughed then and there, but she was touched at the thought behind the little gift. Peter was a lot more sensitive than he made out.

"Where will you be going for Christmas?" she asked, realising she knew very little about Peter's circumstances, or where he lived.

"Oh, home to the family hearth-stone," he said, grinning.

"My mother expects it. We all turn up, eat too much and quarrel like mad, and then we all go away again for another year. It's classic."

"Only once a year?" wondered Beth.

Peter looked a trifle embarrassed. "Oh well, no – I go back more often. The others don't." He gulped down some of his luke-warm beer. "But then I live nearer."

Beth was looking at him curiously. "Do you? . . . I don't even know where you *do* live."

Peter laughed. "It's no dark secret. I have a flat in a converted vicarage on the edge of town. Very respectable." He was regarding her now with a carefully casual gaze. "What will you do?"

Beth hadn't really considered the matter till now. "I'll probably ask Mark and his mother round – and no doubt there'll be a visit from Chloë and her puppy." She smiled. "I'll be occupied enough, if that's what's worrying you."

His grin remained cheerful, but he went over to the bar and fetched her another drink without being asked. "It's a short holiday," he said, when he returned. "We'll be back at work before we've had time to get over our Christmas dinners."

He knew very well that Beth needed to have her time filled – and that the grey empty days of winter were hard enough to get through. But he did not say so. Instead, he began to tell Beth about all the places she ought to visit while he was away, and waxed so lyrical about them that he made her laugh, which was what he intended anyway.

They walked back through Ashcombe under frosty stars, and Beth found herself admiring the honey-coloured stone under the streetlamps, and the glowing windows with their glimpses of warm interiors and lighted Christmas trees. It was a lovely village, she told herself, and it had a special magic after dark.

Peter did not try to get himself invited in this time. He just stood looking at her quietly in the porch, and then said: "Keep laughing till I come." Then he turned and went away down the path, whistling 'The Holly and the Ivy' as he went.

A couple of days before Christmas Eve, Finn and Chloë, with

Corny gambolling about on the end of a brand new red lead, arrived at the Beehive with questions to ask.

"Chloë wants to give Beech a Christmas present. What do you think he'd like?"

Beth considered. "Food for his animals?"

Chloë's smile came out like the sun. "He'd like that."

Finn looked doubtful. "How do we know what to get?"

"A pet shop," suggested Beth. "And – I know – ask Mark to come with you. He understands a lot about Beech's animals."

"Ask Mark," commanded Chloë, and Corny began running round in circles, chasing her own tail and tying Chloë up in knots. When she had been disentangled, Chloë looked up hopefully at Beth. "Will you come too?"

Finn looked hopeful, too.

"All right." Beth gave in to the pleading looks. "I was going to give Beech a little Christmas cake. We can take that up to him as well."

"Did you make it?" Chloë was getting interested in cooking.

"Yes. Only a small one. But I made you one, too." She was smiling at Chloë now, and somehow trying not to see the warmth in Finn's eyes.

They collected Mark and drove over to the town to the nearest pet shop. Once there, Mark seemed perfectly confident about what to buy.

"Dog food," he said. "The hedgehogs like it, and so does Foxy. And all the puppies and Jess . . . Corn for the hens, and wild bird seed for Blackie and the others . . . Moses likes apples and carrots – we can get those in a greengrocer's, and some lettuces for the hare if she's still there . . ." He paused, trying to think what else to get. "Nuts for the squirrel . . . I think the ferret's gone, but they'll know what ferrets eat . . . And as for Juniper, she'll eat anything!"

Before long, Finn was loaded with parcels, and everyone was heading back to the car.

"Tell you what," said Finn, juggling with the apples and a slippery bag of nuts, "let's dump these and go and get an ice-cream or something. It's Christmas, after all."

The day was frosty and bright for once, clear of the grey

194

fogs of November, and the town was alight with tinsel decorations, fairy lights and sparkling Christmas trees. On one street corner, a brass band was playing carols, and on another, a rival group of singers were trying to make themselves heard above the noise of the chattering shoppers and the traffic.

Finn made a despairing face at Beth, and led them all into a cheerful pink café where Mark and Chloë were allowed to order the fanciest ice-creams they could find.

"Beth," said Finn, looking at her over his cup of coffee and sounding absurdly tentative, "you will come on Christmas Day?"

Beth sighed. She had known this was coming, and she had also known that she couldn't refuse. Chloë was going to need all the care and kindness she could get this first Christmas without Stephanie – and so was Finn. And so, she supposed, was she . . . the first one without Little Mo, though not the first without Robert. There had been two of those while she struggled to make the day lively and cheerful for Mo and did not allow herself to admit to her own loneliness and grief . . . Well, it looked like being a repeat performance. Somehow it had got to be ordinary and unshadowed for Chloë if she could manage it.

"If I can bring Mark and his mother, too," she said, suddenly knowing that would help things to seem normal for all of them. "Chloë and Mark get on so well," she explained, "and Lucy's lonely, too."

Finn nodded. It was a relief to have that tacit admission from Beth. They were all lonely – well, they would all make the best they could of the difficult day when it came.

"I'm not much good at ceremonies," he admitted, smiling. "I left all that to Stephanie. But – but I'd like it to go right, for the kids' sake."

"Stop worrying."' said Beth. "We'll make it positively scintillating! Let's just get this trip to Beech over first."

So they waited patiently while Mark and Chloë demolished their sundae specials with extra chocolate fudge sauce, and then drove back to Ashcombe and climbed the hill to Beech's cottage with their purchases in their arms. Or most of them, for Corny had managed to chew a hole in the bag of nuts and they were scattered all over the car.

Beech saw them coming and stood waiting for them, looking a little apprehensive at the visitation.

"It's all right," said Beth, smiling at his puzzled face. "We've brought the animals their Christmas presents, that's all."

"I hope they're right," worried Mark. "You'll have to tell me if they're not."

"Nay," said Beech, smiling in relief, "there's not much one or t'other of 'em won't eat!" He watched gravely while Mark and Chloë laid out the various bags in front of him.

"Those are for Moses . . . and that's for the hens, and that's for Blackie . . . We didn't know what Juniper liked best, so we brought her some broccoli . . ."

They unloaded all their offerings and then went happily with Beech to distribute them to his hungry charges.

"Moses looks happier," observed Mark. "Doesn't he, Chloë? – Here, Moses, happy Christmas!" and he handed over an apple and a bright red carrot.

When they had finished going the rounds, Beech showed them where to store the left-overs for another day, and then said gruffly: "I got something for you, too. Remember, I said as I'd show you where the acorns fell? . . . I come across some yesterday – already sprouting, a few of 'em. Would you like to take a couple home?"

"Yes, please," said Chloë, sounding very polite and very definite. Then she put her hand firmly in Mark's and followed Beech down the path.

Beth and Finn glanced at one another, and joined the procession through the tall winter trees.

Beech led them to a different corner of the wood where several thick old oak trees stood in a rough circle around a curious open area of short grass laced with rabbit holes. It was almost like an ancient sacred grove, thought Beth, but clearly it was only inhabited by the rabbits now.

"Here," said Beech, stooping down under one of the oaks, whose massive trunk stood firm and strong above sturdy roots on the forest floor. "See?" and he pushed aside a few tufts of silvery dried-up summer grass so that Mark and Chloë could look down at the brown leaf-mould below. Mark bent down to see what the old, freckled hand was pointing at, and Chloë crouched down beside him, even lower.

196

On the soft ground in the hollow between the upthrusting roots, was a small pile of gold-brown acorns, and a few that were already blackened by the winter rains. As they looked closer, they saw that some of them had split open to allow curly pinkish sprouts to escape into the warm blanket of leafy soil around them.

"It be winter now," said Beech softly, looking down at the children's rapt faces "and things look mighty dead and cold, in the main . . ." He put out one blunt finger and touched a coral-coloured shoot. "But here, see, spring's already beginning . . . Things have gone down deep-like, but they're alive all right. They'm just waitin' for the sun to shine . . ."

The two intent young faces looked up at him silently.

"You put one o' they in a pot," he told them, "and come spring, you'll have an oak tree." He smiled at their awestruck expressions. "Small, mind, but a tree they'll be, no less!"

"Can you spare one?" asked Mark, almost afraid to touch anything so fragile and so miraculous – though he could not put such thoughts into words.

"Surely," said Beech. "One each." He straightened his back and looked away into the shadowy spaces between the winter-dark trees. "New life at Christmas . . ." he murmured, half to himself, "ent so far wrong, at that." Then he seemed to remember his charges, and turned back to smile at them. "Come up to the cottage and I'll find you some pots," he said.

"Can they have one too?" asked Chloë, looking from Beth to Finn. She was determined that everyone should share in this new magic.

For answer, the old man stooped again, picked up two more pink-fronded acorns, and handed them solemnly to the two adults who looked almost as spellbound as the children. "There!" he said. "Now we'm all fixed up." But there was a distinct spark of mischief in his faded eyes.

At the last moment, when everyone had been provided with pots and enough forest leaf-mould, and all the pink shoots had been successfully 'put to grow,' Beth suddenly remembered her Christmas cake and handed that over as a final offering. "Happy Christmas," she said, and added quietly, so that only Beech could hear, "and thank you for many things . . ."

Beech nodded, and did not attempt to reply. But the old eyes met hers in perfect understanding.

Corny, meanwhile, had gone back to talk to her mother and the two remaining puppies, but now she came out again on to the grass with a half-eaten paper bag stuck on the end of her nose, and ran off down the path with everyone in laughing pursuit.

Just as well, thought Beth. We were all getting much too solemn. Christmas does awful things to one's emotions . . . But there was no time to be sad now. They had to catch Corny before she ran out on to the road.

Beech watched them go, and his smile was wider than ever. "Keep it up, young Corny," he said. "You're doing fine."

Beth did not much like Christmas Eve. In fact, she did not much like Christmas at all – not this first one without Little Mo. It was going to be hard enough to get through it, she knew, and only the realisation that it was just as bad for Finn and Chloë without Stephanie made her stop feeling sorry for herself and resolve to be as positive and cheerful about it all as humanly possible. Finn, she knew, was trying desperately hard to be a good father, – to buy the right presents, remember the Christmas tree and the decorations, fill Chloe's stocking, and arrange with Mary for all the trimmings of a grand Christmas meal. At least, she thought somewhat bitterly, he has got something to do, and he has got Chloë – while I . . . But she wouldn't go on with that. Better not to look round at the empty rooms of the little Beehive, better not to remember too much about the loving warmth of those other Christmases . . .

Finn had actually asked her to come over and help them get ready, but she had refused – partly because she knew Chloë and Finn ought to do this together, it would strengthen the fragile bond that was slowly re-building between them. But she had also refused out of a perverse sense of panic because she was so inexorably being drawn into their lives, and Finn was so devastatingly attractive in his new grief and humility. He was already beginning to loom large in her life and she was sometimes a little shocked at the lurch of gladness she felt when he was near – the unexpected closeness of their understanding, and the sudden warmth of feeling that flared between them in unguarded moments.

Of course, it was only loneliness, she told herself. It was inevitable, really. They were both alone, both grieving desperately for someone loved and relied on who had filled their days with happiness. Only, of course, she had two people missing from her life. It was two years since Rob died – only six months since Little Mo left her. No wonder she turned to Finn for company – for comfort? But she shied away from that thought. It was too soon – too soon for anything but a grim attempt to get through the days, and much too soon for Finn who had only been without his beloved Stephanie for four short months . . . And then there was Chloë, too, whose recovery had somehow come to mean too much to Beth, and who was now beginning to show unmistakable signs of returning warmth and affection – directed almost as much at Beth as at Finn, and where on earth was that going to lead them?

Wasn't it all a bit too easy – a bit too contrived? Didn't she indeed feel 'manipulated', as Finn had suggested? Yes, Stephanie, she thought, a little fiercely, I do – and I know you saw very far ahead to a chance for Finn's future comfort. But it doesn't always work, does it? Human beings are not just pawns in a heavenly chess game, are they? . . . Or are they? I just don't know.

With these restless thoughts pursuing her, Beth decided to go out and walk, even though it was late and dark, and there was a bitter frost. The village was still very much awake, though it was after eleven, and many of the windows displayed glowing interiors and sparkling Christmas trees through uncurtained windows. There were people inside, too, cheerful families getting things ready and wrapping presents – and Beth hurried by, churlishly averting her gaze from all this cosy preparation, and feeling guilty for being so ungenerous. It wasn't their fault that she was left on the outside looking in, shivering in the cold night air. It wasn't anybody's fault except her own.

She passed the floodlit church with all its windows aglow with candles and the bells ringing for the midnight service. For a moment she hesitated. Should she go in? Sit comfortably in the warm, among the singing parishioners, rejoicing in the

Christmas story? But how could she? It wasn't possible for her to rejoice about the birth of a baby – not this Christmas . . . She knew, vaguely, that it ought to be – that most people found comfort in the ancient story – a renewal each year of all those promises . . . a baby born, a ransom given, a redeemer of all mortal sin, and a loving saviour who said: 'Suffer the little children to come unto me . . .'

But she couldn't – her heart rebelled against it. It simply wasn't possible, not with her own, loving little Mo so suddenly, so cruelly taken from her. I'm sorry, God, she said. I'm sorry – but not this year. Perhaps by next year I will see it more clearly – but now there is too much hurt.

She remembered Elkstone Church then, and the gentle old man she had met outside, and his voice saying: '*Remember the light* . . .' but even his quiet voice in her mind failed to comfort her tonight, and she hurried on, head bent, away from the friendly village up on to the starlit hills.

It was more than starlight by now, she realised, for the moon had risen into that cloudless frosty sky, and the curving slopes of winter grass looked almost white in its pure cold light. *Almost* white? She paused to look round her in wonder. For it had been foggy for most of the last two days, and now the frost had caught the drifting moisture and turned it all to a winter wonderland of shimmering crystal. Not a white Christmas in the true sense, she told herself, for there was no snow, but every twig, every blade of grass, every filigree spider's web and fallen leaf was etched in silver, sparkling and winking in the moonlight like a thousand jewels.

Drawing a deep breath of enchantment at so much fragile beauty, she began to walk across the crisp, silvered grass.

After a long time, when her mind was calmed and her body tired, she came back in a circle to the hill just above the village. She stood for a few moments looking down at the firefly lights below and the silver hoar frost on the tree-branches in the glow from the distant street lights. The moon was still bright in the sky, and the whole sleeping landscape lay bathed in the luminous whiteness of that glittering frost cover. It seemed almost too pure and pristine to bear.

She was just about to start down the hill towards the little Beehive, deciding at last that she must go home and try to sleep,

200

when she found herself looking at the dark figure of a man coming towards her over the pale, glinting hillside. A tall man, whose stride she recognised instantly, and who had been in her thoughts more than she cared to admit as she walked in the frost-transfigured night. Her first instinct was to turn swiftly and escape down the hill before he saw her – there were too many undercurrents and difficult questions to be asked and answered, and it was much too late at night to tackle any of them. But then she saw that it was already impossible to run away, for he had seen her and had quickened his stride to reach her, his face under the bleaching moonlight reflecting the gladness of recognition. She could not quench that look with craven retreat.

"What are you doing up here?" she asked, half-smiling at him in the silver dark.

"The same as you, I should think." Finn's voice was strangely rough. "Walking away from my ghosts."

"Not walking away from them." Beth shook her head at him gently. "More like – trying to find a way to keep them with me."

"Looking for 'Yonder'," said Finn, and though he was also smiling, his tone was quite serious.

Beth thought instantly of Chloë, and looked up at Finn with some doubt. "Ought you to be out here? What if Chloë wakes up and comes looking for you?"

"She won't." He sounded quite certain. "She and Corny were quite exhausted when everything was done. We decorated the tree, and hung up the stockings, and made the brandy butter, and iced the Christmas cake, and helped Mary to stuff the turkey . . . I couldn't think of anything else to do, and nor could she." He sighed, and then grinned at Beth in a rueful, apologetic way. "Honestly, Beth, we both tried so hard, it positively hurt!"

Beth laughed a little, but she did not miss the ache of sadness behind his flippant words.

"I'm glad I found you," he went on, brushing aside her laughter. "There's something I wanted to say to you, only somehow it never seems to be the right time, and tomorrow will be no exception."

Beth stood still, looking at him quietly. It was no good

201

trying to avoid things any longer. Whatever Finn wanted to say had better be said if they were ever to manage any kind of understanding.

"Well?"

But he seemed to hesitate, as if not knowing how to begin. At last he laid a deliberate hand on her arm. "Don't be angry with me."

"Should I be?"

"I don't think so – but I know you feel a bit pressurised. I understand why you fled from our preparations this evening – "

"I didn't exactly flee – !"

He kept his hand on her arm and gave it a little shake. "Be serious – I'm trying to apologise."

"What for?"

He sighed, almost with exasperation. "What for, she says! For dragging you into our lives whether you like it or not! For making use of you at every turn, for – "

"Be quiet," said Beth crossly. "You're talking nonsense."

"Am I?" he sounded relieved. "Then – maybe I can dare to go on?" But he didn't for a moment. He seemed undecided about what to say. He was a man more used to actions than words, and these were thoughts that he found hard to express. At last he drew a long, slow breath of resolve and began again. "What I'm trying to say is – I know we've been driven into a – a closeness we didn't expect . . . But it means a lot to me, Beth, just now, and I don't want to lose it." He paused, looking at her questioningly in the moonlight.

Beth did not know how to answer this, so she simply nodded. But it was a kind of acceptance. It meant a lot to her, too. How could she deny it?

Finn sighed again, and lifted his hand to touch her hair. It was a gentle movement, quite undemanding, but somehow unexpectedly tender. "Poor Beth, you've got so much to contend with – without my clumsy approaches!"

She smiled at him, a little uncertainly, in the sparkling white night. "It's just that – " she paused, sounding shy and tired.

"Yes?"

"I don't know who I am, Finn." She pushed the hair out

of her eyes in a childish gesture of bewilderment. "I mean –
you are an explorer . . ."

"An adventurer," he corrected grimly, "who is trying
desperately hard to be a father."

At least you have a rôle to play, she thought. And a child
to live for, whereas I – But she did not say it. She looked up
at him with a kind of bleak honesty and repeated: "I don't
know what I am or what I'm trying to be, Finn, or where
I'm trying to go . . . Not yet."

He nodded, accepting it quite calmly. "Well, then, that
makes my request even easier."

"Does it?" She sounded even more confused.

"It's just this," he said, sounding almost as shy as she was.
"Couldn't we, in the meantime, not worry about the future,
but accept what comfort we can bear and be glad?"

Accept what comfort we can bear and be glad, thought Beth,
a strange tide of relief washing over her tired mind.

"Of course we could," she murmured, and the tears glittered
in her eyes and made prisms on the frosted trees.

'*And be glad*?" he insisted, staring down at her.

She nodded again, not trusting herself to speak.

"Then – happy Christmas, Beth," he said softly, and drew
her close and kissed her under the pure white light of the
winter moon.

Somehow or other, it turned out to be a better Christmas than
any of them had expected.

Mark and his mother arrived at the Beehive armed with
mince pies and presents before walking over to Finn's house
with Beth in time for the mid-day, festive meal. Mark had
brought Beth a piece of soap shaped like a fish, to remind her
of the fisherman's solo in the school production. (And not to
remind her, Lucy assured her, that the little opera was really
just a glorified soap!) Lucy had brought her a new blue teapot
because Mark had told her that the old one had been chipped,
and she would have gone into lengthy thanks for all those teas
by the fire if Beth hadn't stopped her.

"I needed the company," she said, smiling, and then,
looking at Mark, she added: "And so did Chloë."

So they drank some spicy punch that Beth had concocted,

and Lucy began to look less pinched and tired even before they set out for the Mill House.

Then, it was cheerful chaos, with Corny tearing up all the Chrismas paper as soon as the presents were unwrapped (and sometimes before), and trying to run off with Mary's new scarf and almost fusing the Christmas tree lights on the way, and Mark and Chloë trying to catch her and prevent any further disasters, amid the general laughter.

Mark had brought Chloë a dog bowl on which he had inscribed 'CORNY' in bright red ceramic paint on the outside even though it said 'DOG' on the inside. "Only, I couldn't change it to 'BITCH' without sounding rather rude, could I?" he explained seriously, and everyone laughed again.

Lucy had brought more mince-pies and some home-made fudge for everyone, having asked Beth anxiously on the way if it would do, only she didn't like to come empty-handed, but money was too tight for presents all round. Beth had assured her that it would be perfect, and anything else would have embarrassed everyone, and then had wondered privately whether her own contributions would upset anyone. She hoped not.

She had bought a new blanket for Corny, though she suspected that the puppy would probably prefer the old scruffy bit that Beech had given her. For Chloë she had knitted a red woollen hat and scarf with bobbles on, to match the new boots that Finn had bought her (after anxious consultation with Beth). "She says she doesn't want toys or silly presents, she's got Corny, and she'd rather not have a lot of fuss . . . She seems absurdly grown-up about it all, but I must say I rather agree with her," he had reported. But the new red boots weren't silly, Beth told him, and in them Chloë would be able to go walking anywhere with him and Corny, and perhaps use the carved shepherd's crook he had brought home for her from the islands.

The present for Finn had been more difficult, but in the end she had found an old-fashioned glass prism in a local antique shop. It was meant to be an ordinary paperweight which would be suitable for Finn's new home-office set-up, but there was something about the light glancing through it that had reminded Beth of Elkstone Church and the strange conversation with the old man. *'You can't prove light. But it's there.'* She couldn't tell Finn what the prism meant, of course, but she wanted him to have it all the same. Maybe one day she would be able to tell him – she did not know about that. She wasn't sure if Finn was the kind of man to go in for abstruse conversations about light, though she had a lingering suspicion that he was. But when she gave it to him, he looked from the glinting prism to Beth's face and murmured: "It's like the moonlight on the frost . . ."

Finn and Chloë had arranged to hand out their offerings from the Christmas tree, and to keep them unembarrassingly simple. So there was a manly penknife for Mark, and a frivolous powder puff on top of a tin of talc for Lucy, (with Finn rightly supposing that she wouldn't buy anything so unessential and pretty for herself). There was a large box of marrons glacé for Mary, because she said they were her favourites and she could never afford them, really. For Chloë, there was a pair of bright red socks to go with the red walking boots, and the dolphin-headed shepherd's crook from the Spirios site which he had at last dared to give her. And for Beth, he and Chloë had found a small wrought-iron Japanese lantern with a candle inside, to remind her of Hamaguchi's Harvest and the children's own special triumph. (More instruments of light, thought Beth, and did not dare to say so.)

After all this excitement, it was time for turkey and plum pudding, and Mary and Chloë carried in the food together, both of them beaming with pride.

"She seems to enjoy it," murmured Finn, worrying as usual about whether he was expecting too much of his small daughter.

"Cosseting, remember," Beth replied, in an equally low voice. "It's important to her, Finn. Don't try to stop her."

He nodded understanding, and raised his glass. "To the cooks," he said. "God bless 'em!"

Corny blessed them too, when the scraps came her way at the end of the meal. She looked up at everyone with the utmost devotion and made it plain that everything was entirely right with her world, especially when there was turkey for dinner.

Corny had the kind of face, Beth reflected, that no-one could resist. She would tilt it to one side and cock those small velvet ears, and gaze upwards out of those huge amber eyes with an expression of intelligent understanding that it was impossible to ignore. 'I understand every word you are saying,' those clever eyes said, 'and I will do anything you want, if you will only explain it to me. Why is it wrong to chew electric wires?'

Not for the first time, Beth wondered if she ought to have taken one of Beech's puppies for herself. It would be wonderful company, though she shied a little from the thought of trying to fill the empty space left by Little Mo with a dog . . . So many lonely women did, and it somehow seemed hopelessly inadequate . . . and disloyal? . . . And yet – there was this enchanting little creature already winding itself round Chloë's heartstrings, and doing her nothing but good . . . Maybe, after Christmas, she would go and have another talk with Beech about it, and see if he had still got one of the puppies left.

"Beth?" said Finn, breaking into her thoughts. "Chloë wants you to play some carols."

Beth was afraid of carols – of anything that might shake her perilous calm today, but she agreed readily enough, and went over to Finn's beautiful Blüthner grand in the corner. It was a joy to play, and for a time she forgot to be sad.

One thing I must do, she told herself, is get myself another piano. I've missed it more than I realised. It will have to be a small one, though. The Beehive couldn't take a grand.

"Isn't there a piano factory round here somewhere?" she said, sitting with her hands spread out on the keys, and waiting for Chloë's next request.

"Yes. Bentley's. Why?"

"I need to buy one. A very small one – for the Beehive." She smiled up at Finn's surprised expression. "I sold my other one before I came down here."

He nodded. "Do you want me to see about it?"

"Oh no, Finn. This isn't for school. I'll fight for my own bargain his time!"

He pretended to look hurt. "Suit yourself."

She was instantly contrite. "Do you *want* to bother with it?"

"Yes," he said firmly. "And Chloë would like a trip to a piano factory – wouldn't you, Chloë?"

Once again Beth found herself drawn into the family net. She could only surrender with a good grace. "All right – why not?" she agreed.

Presently Mark and Chloë demanded to take Corny for a walk, so the whole party decided to go with them, leaving Mary to mutter about Christmas cake and building up the fire.

It was still very cold outside, and still a glittering world of white hoar frost, hanging like lace on every tree branch and edging each blade of grass with silver fire.

"Oh, isn't it pretty!" said Chloë, and ran off with Mark and Corny to inspect this crisp new winter wonderland. Her bright red boots and woolly cap stood out against the sparkling frosted grass, and made Finn smile.

"She looks like an elf," he said, and Beth and Lucy smiled too as Chloë's laughter floated back to them.

"I'm so glad she's well again," said Lucy impulsively.

Finn looked at her with sudden gravity. "Your son, Mark, had a lot to do with it, I'm told." Then his serious glance lightened as he saw the children turn and begin racing back towards him, with Corny at full stretch on her smart red lead. "Anyway," he said, before Chloë had quite reached him, "I'm enormously grateful."

Lucy did not reply to this, but somehow Finn's quiet word of praise seemed to soften her face and make her look much younger.

Beth reflected that Lucy did not get many warm and friendly words thrown in her direction lately, and the bitterness of the divorce proceedings were very hard to dispel.

"Time for tea," announced Finn. "Though I doubt if I can eat any more!"

"But Mary and me's made a cake!" protested Chloë. "You must eat some of it!"

"I'll try," groaned Finn. "And I'm sure Corny will help."

Corny looked up with liqud eyes and indicated with wildly-flagging tail that she would be happy to oblige.

The absurd cheerfulness seemed to continue without being forced, but Beth suddenly found herself beginning to feel extraordinarily tired – she could not understand why – and was glad when Lucy and Mark decided they ought to go home.

But here, Chloë, who up till now had been extra sunny and

207

co-operative for Christmas Day, suddenly became mutinous. "I want Beth to stay and say goodnight," she demanded.

Everyone looked at each other in consternation. Beth was already beginning to feel trapped in all this family cosiness, and now a screaming claustrophobia threatened to overwhelm her. She could understand very well why Mark had lain on the floor and drummed his heels and yelled – and she had an irrational desire to do the same. *You're not Mo!* she wanted to yell. *You're not Robert! You're none of you the ones I want! Why can't you leave me alone?* But Chloë was looking up at her with eyes that were growing dark with unshed tears, and she could not refuse them.

Then Mark, speaking in the curiously adult voice of one who had tried many times to diffuse family rows, said mildly: "Where does Corny sleep?"

"Upstairs with me," said Chloë, and the tears were getting nearer.

"Well, I want to say goodnight to Corny," he told her briskly. "So hurry up, and we'll *all* come up."

Chloë just looked at Mark's calm, cheerful face and went without a word.

The others smiled at each other and sighed with relief.

"She's tired," apologised Finn. "She's been up since five – and she was late enough last night, too."

Beth thought Finn couldn't have had much sleep last night himself, since he was on the frosty hill at one in the morning. But she made no comment.

In a remarkably brief time, Chloë called out, and they all trooped upstairs to say goodnight. Beth understood very well why the child was making such a ceremony out of it, trying desperately hard to fill the gap where her mother should have been. And, she suspected, Lucy understood too.

So Mark hugged Corny, and gave Chloë a brotherly tap on the head. Lucy looked shy, but accepted Chloë's lifted face for a Christmas kiss. Beth, feeling a dreadful reluctance and guilt, leant down and allowed those warm young arms to cling round her neck.

"It's been a lovely day," whispered Chloë in her ear.

And Beth knew she could not reject the appeal in that

208

anxious voice. "Yes, it has," she said. "Simply lovely," and hugged her back. And then she fled downstairs.

Then there was the difficulty of saying goodnight to Finn, but here Chloë's bunch of mistletoe in the hall came in handy, and Finn – being the only man in all their lives – kissed Lucy, leaving her all rosy and laughing, ruffled Mark's hair with genuine affection, and kissed Beth in another cheerful smother of laughter.

"I could run you home in the car?" he suggested.

"No," said Beth. "We'll walk. It's a lovely night."

They went out into the porch and stood looking out. The frost was holding, and the trees still looked dressed in diamond lace.

"It was a lovely day," repeated Lucy, looking up at Finn with gratitude shining out of her. "Thank you so much."

Beth said nothing – feeling more and more churlish. But Finn did not seem to notice, or if he did, he ignored it. He just looked at Beth and smiled, and murmured obscurely into the frosty night: "The magic is still there."

Corny was in the doghouse again. That is, she was in disgrace, but as there was no kennel to be banished to, she merely crept upstairs and hid under Chloë's bed. She knew she had done wrong, or at least she knew she had been shouted at, and since it hurt her sensitive soul to be scolded in loud voices, all she could do was hide.

First of all, it being so bitterly cold outside, Chloë hadn't stayed with her long enough in the garden, so she had been obliged to come in before she was ready, and that meant she simply had to make a puddle somewhere in the house. She had thought the best hall rug was a good, open spot, but Mary had disagreed. Loudly. So she fled upstairs. She was only passing Finn's door, she knew she was not supposed to go in, but there was this long, dangerous-looking snake thing hanging from a chair, and she thought she'd better kill it before it did any harm. It tasted of good chewable leather, though the metal bit at the end wasn't edible, but the rest was.

"Corny!" shouted Finn. "That was my best leather belt. It's a good thing you've eaten it, or I'd have used it on you!"

His voice sounded fierce, but somehow Corny didn't think

209

he was really very angry. In fact she thought he might be laughing inside, but she fled all the same. Unfortunately, the leather didn't really suit her, so she was sick on the carpet and that made Mary really cross. She even waved a broom at her and yelled: "Get out from my under my feet, you horrible dog!"

Corny was hurt. But she decided it would be better to make herself scarce – at least for the moment, and seek protection from Chloë who was really her friend and knew how she felt. But Chloë was doing something with pencils and paints and pieces of paper, and didn't want to be bothered. "I'm busy," she said, and went on making scratching noises on the table.

Corny tried eating a pencil, but it broke into sharp little bits with black stuff inside which tasted bitter, so she tried a square, white rubbery thing that tasted better.

"Oh Corny!" yelled Chloë – and she fled again.

This time she went into Finn's other room where there were lots of bits of paper and machines that went clack, and there was one in particular that kept on spewing out long thin strips of paper into a sort of tray thing just below. The paper kept falling off the edge, and Corny thought she ought to give it a tug or two and see if she could tidy it up a bit. It didn't get any tidier, in fact it got a lot worse, but it was a lovely game anyway, and Corny growled at it quite a lot to tell it to stop and shook the paper as hard as she could to teach it a lesson. But it simply would not stop.

"OH CORNY!" shouted Finn. "What *have* you done now? Look at the mess! Get out of here, you little horror!"

Corny got out, rather fast, and went and hid under Chloë's bed. She couldn't seem to do anything right somehow. Life was very puzzling.

But Chloë had stopped scribbling on the table when she heard Finn shout, and now she came in and rescued Corny from underneath the bed, and sat down on top of the duvet with the puppy in her arms. "It's all right, Corny," she told her in a soothing kind of voice. "He's not really cross. We'll go and say we're sorry in a minute."

Corny licked her hand and wriggled a bit closer. She was glad someone still liked her. Chloë could see she was still a bit hurt by all the shouts, so she held her tight and carried

210

her out of the room, meaning to go and talk to Finn about it. Perhaps if she reminded him that Corny was still only very little – eleven weeks wasn't very old – he would forgive her. She only need a pat on the head to make her feel all right again.

But Finn was talking on the phone when Chloë got to the door, and she hesitated just outside, not liking to interrupt.

"No," he was saying, "it isn't any good. I can't keep her."

Chloë froze, and went on listening in horror.

"My life has no room in it now for such distractions!" he continued. "I'll have to get rid of her . . . What? No, I won't change my mind. She's only an unnecessary burden – with too many unhappy associations. She'll have to go."

The tone of his voice was crisp and decisive, and brooked no argument. Chloë knew that voice – and, like Corny, when trouble was brewing her instinct was to hide. Clutching her beloved puppy tightly in terrified arms, she turned and fled.

Finn had vaguely noticed a flicker of movement outside the door as he talked on the phone, but he hadn't worried about it. Chloë and Corny came and went more-or-less as they chose, – and he was really much too indulgent to make too many restrictions. It was enough for him that they were happy together, and Chloë was continuing to blossom in the puppy's cheerful company. So he went on working for an hour or so, and then became aware that the house seemed unusually quiet. There was no scampering of small feet, no laughter on the stairs, no chasing or scolding or capturing, – in fact, nothing at all.

H got up and went to look in Chloë's room. It was empty. So was the little sitting room where she had been drawing. The paper was still there on the table, with pencils scattered about, but that was all.

He went downstairs to speak to Mary. "Have you seen Chloë?"

"No." Mary was cooking, and pushed the hair away from her flushed face. "I thought she was with you."

Finn frowned and turned away. "I expect she's upstairs somewhere."

But she wasn't. He searched every room in the house and there was no sign of her at all. "Perhaps she's in the garden," he said to Mary, and it was only then that he looked out of the window and saw the snow.

It wasn't just a few flakes falling, but a solid white sheet pouring out of a leaden sky, and slanting in a vicious curtain before the fierce north-east wind. "My God!" he said. "Surely she wouldn't be out in that?"

Mary also looked out in horror. "I hope not," she said fervently, and began to pull on her boots.

They searched the garden and the summer house, the potting shed and the wood shed, and every hidden corner. But there was no-one there. By now the snow was falling so fast that any small footprints would soon be covered, and Finn could find no trace of any, except a few vague depressions near the dry-stone wall that bordered the field. But even those weren't very definite, and might have been made by a rabbit or a passing fox.

He turned back to the house, and persuaded Mary to go inside, too. "You'd better stay here and keep the fires up. She may just have taken Corny for a walk." He shook his head in puzzled disbelief. "But I can't think why – in this!"

Then, all at once, the sound of his own voice talking to Theo Koussalis in Athens came back to him, and the words he had said took on a terrifying significance. "Oh, dear God," he muttered, "I believe she thought I was talking about Corny."

Mary looked at him, uncomprehending, but he didn't wait to explain. He went into the hall and rang up Beth.

When the snow began, Beth had made a quick dash to the village shop for extra supplies, knowing that her lane was very likely to get silted up in a heavy snowfall. She struggled home along a rapidly deteriorating road surface, skidding a little where other cars had packed the snow, and managed to get her own car safely into the garage. The wind was so strong by now that she had to fight to get the doors shut, but she managed it and made her way up the path with her arms full of carrier bags. When she opened the door, her phone was ringing, and she dropped all her parcels on the floor and hurried to answer it. Perhaps it was Finn. She had been waiting rather anxiously for him to ring her, after her shameful moment of panic at the end of Christmas Day. Maybe he hadn't noticed, but she rather

212

feared he had, and she didn't want to upset him. She was rather confused by the contradictory thoughts in her head, and would be glad, she told herself, to know that he was untroubled by her behaviour.

She picked up the phone, prepared to be extra co-operative and friendly. I was Finn all right, but a Finn she scarcely knew. His voice was rough with anxiety, his tone sharp and desperately upset.

"Beth? Is Chloë with you?"

"Chloë? No. Should she be?"

"No. She shouldn't. She should be here, but she's not." He drew a shaking breath. "Beth – I – I think she may have run away."

"Run away? Why?"

He seemed to sigh at the end of the phone. It was a despairing, anguished sound, and Beth was frightened by it. "I was talking to Theo Koussalis, about getting rid of Dancing Lady . . . I think Chloë may have overheard – and – misunderstood . . ."

"What exactly did you say?"

"I said . . . I can't keep her . . . I'll have to get rid of her . . . and something about . . . an unnecessary burden with too many unhappy associations, or something. She could have thought – ?"

"Yes, she could," agreed Beth grimly. And then returned to practicalities. "Where have you looked?"

"Everywhere," snapped Finn. But he relented at once, and sounded only tired and bewildered. "I don't know what to do . . . Can you think of anywhere she might go?"

Beth thought hard. "She might have gone up to see Beech. She's done it before . . . But it would be pretty difficult in this snow."

Finn groaned. "I'd better go up there and see."

"Finn, what was she wearing?"

"What?"

"Her clothes. Was she wearing those red boots? And her red bobble hat? . . . You'd see them very clearly in the snow."

"Yes," he breathed. "You would . . . I'll go and look."

"I'll hang on," Beth said. "Come back and tell me, Finn. We need to know what we're looking for."

"We?"

"Of course, we. Go and find out – and hurry, Finn."

The line went dead, and Beth waited, picturing in her mind a frightened little girl, clutching her beloved puppy in her arms, struggling through the snow to reach – to reach where? Somewhere safe where they couldn't be found?"

"Yes, you were right," said Finn's voice, close in her ear. "She's taken the red boots and your red hat and scarf, and –" his voice almost cracked here, "and her shepherd's crook . . . She must have meant to walk a long way . . ."

"Don't jump to conclusions." Beth's voice was crisp and practical. "Is Mary there?"

"Yes, she's here. As distraught as I am."

"Tell her to keep up the fires – and lots of hot water. I'll meet you up at Beech's cottage."

"But Beth – "

"It's obvious. We might as well try both ways. She might have wandered off the path in either direction."

"But is it safe for you to go out in that? There's a blizzard blowing."

"Chloë's out in it," snapped Beth. "I'll see you up there," and she rang off before he could make any further protest.

She put on all the thickest clothes she possessed, with two pairs of socks inside her wellington boots, and as an afterthought filled a thermos with hot sweet tea. Then, remembering Chloë's absurdly brave little gesture, she also found a walking stick to help probe the drifts, and set out into the storm.

It was blowing a furious gale by now, and the snow was driving across the hills almost horizontally, in a blizzard of blinding whiteness. It stung her face and got into her eyes and clung to her eyelashes and her hair, but she plodded on against the wind, and did not dare to stop. It was better to keep going in this whirling maelstrom, and not waste any time on worrying whether she would get there. But she did pause from time to time to look round at the snowy hillside, in the vain hope that she might see something red bobbing about ahead of her. But there was nothing in all that shrieking inferno but snow and more snow, and the dark shapes of trees cowering before the wind.

214

It seemed to take an age of climbing and fighting the relentless gale before she saw the final slope of the hill leading to Beech's cottage. The path had long since disappeared, but she had followed the line of trees with her eye, and now she saw with relief that she was only a few yards from the first of Beech's enclosures. As she approached, she saw the bent figure of Beech himself stooping over his pens and cages, battening everything down against the tearing north-easter. He straightened up when he saw her, and came hurrying towards her, instantly aware that something was wrong.

"It's Chloë," gasped Beth, against the wind. "She's gone missing again. I suppose she's not with you?"

He shook his head, looking grave and concerned. "Nay, I've not seen her . . ." He glanced round at his carefully-shut pens and cages. "You'd best come inside and tell me about it. 'Tis a bad day for a little 'un to be out."

He led Beth into the cottage, kicking the door shut behind him with a snowy boot. Beth hadn't realised how exhausting the climb up to his cottage had been, but now she felt her legs beginning to buckle, and sat hastily down in the nearest chair. Beech took one look at her, and hastened over to his old-fashioned range on which a blackened kettle was hissing quietly. "A cup of tea wunt do no harm," he said. "Why did she go off, then? What frit her this time?"

Beth sighed, and gratefully accepted the hot cup of tea and began to warm her hands around it. "I'm afraid it was something Finn – Mr. Edmondson – said . . . She misunderstood, and thought he was going to get rid of the puppy . . ." Or even get rid of Chloë herself? Beth wondered painfully, knowing how insecure and uncertain of her father's affections the child was.

Beech nodded slowly. "Not sure of their welcome . . ." he murmured. "It can make a crittur lash out . . . Fair wild, some of 'em are, when they're frit."

Beth agreed. It was clear that Beech, as usual, understood a lot more than he let on. It was also suddenly clear to Beth that the old man sometimes put on an even broader country accent than necessary when he wanted to say something important. It stopped him sounding so sententious.

But Beech was busy thinking about Chloë's whereabouts.

215

"If she wanted to hide Corny, she might go back to that old stump where I found her before . . ." he reminded her. "Remember?"

"Yes," agreed Beth. That certainly made some kind of sense. "Is it far? Could you find it in this blizzard?"

"Nay, 'tis not that far," he told her. "We can reach it through the woods . . ." He stared out of the window, assessing the state of the storm. "But we'd best hurry – 'twill be dark early this night."

"Finn is coming," Beth explained. "He'll be here in a minute or two . . . It's a bit further from his house."

Beech nodded and went across to his dresser where an old storm lantern hung on one of the hooks. He reached it down and lit it, and then looked round for a blanket or anything warm to wrap round a half-frozen child and a small puppy.

"I've got a thermos of tea as well," said Beth, "in case . . ."

In case of what? she thought, and did not dare to go any further in her mind. What might this piercing cold do to a small child crouching somewhere in the snow?

"Good girl," said Beech, as if he was talking to one of his frightened animals. Then he saw the tall figure of Finn Edmondson silhouetted against the snow, and went out to meet him.

"Is Beth here?" asked Finn at once, anxiety deep in his voice, and then smiled with relief when he saw her coming out behind Beech into the snow.

"Best get on then," said Beech, not waiting any longer or wasting any words on explanations, and he set off into the woods at once, carrying the lantern in one hand and the bundle of rugs tucked under his other arm.

Finn grasped Beth's arm for a moment in a hard, grateful grip.

"My God, I'm glad to see you," he muttered. "I never should have let you come out in this alone . . ."

Beth grinned at him through snow-caked lips. "You couldn't have stopped me," she told him, and ploughed gamely on through the snow at Beech's heels.

It was deep now, and drifting in places where the wind

caught it, so they had to walk warily. Twice Beth fell into a drift and had to be hauled out, and once Finn put one foot on what looked like level ground, and sank up to his thigh before he could drag his leg clear.

And the darkness was coming early, as Beech had predicted. Already the shadows were growing among the trees, and the light was fading behind the whirling whiteness of the snow, turning the winter world to an eerie wilderness of empty, darkening spaces . . . And in all that deepening twilight there was no sign of one small girl in a red hat, with a little dog at her heels . . .

Beech had moved with surprising speed through the snowy woods, and both Finn and Beth had found it quite hard to keep up with him, but now he slowed a little, and seemed to cast round him as if not quite sure of his direction. The snow had changed the dimensions of the landscape, making it hard for him to recognise the landmarks he knew. But at last he gave a quick affirmative nod, and set off again at right angles among the brooding dark trunks of the massive beech trees. He was near his destination now.

Finn and Beth pressed close behind him, breathing hard with the exertion of lifting foot after foot through the heavy snow, and Beth noticed that even Beech's hillman's stride was slower and his breathing was sounding stressed and ominously wheezy in the piercing wind.

But before she could begin to worry about the old man, he stopped suddenly, and pointed downwards. There was a large drift where the fallen beech tree had lain, and the snow seemed to have entirely filled the deep hollow beneath the upended stump. Beth's heart sank when she saw it, for surely no little girl could be crouching down there under all that weight of snow? But even as she thought that and stooped to look further, she saw what Beech had seen – a small flash of something red protruding from the snow.

"Oh God," said Finn, "she's gone to sleep in the snow!" and he began to scramble down into the hollow, afraid of what he might find.

But Beth forestalled him, leaping down past him and saying urgently as she did so: "No, Finn. Let me. She may have – " Gone back into retreat from Finn himself, she had been going

217

to say, but she knew that she could not. It would hurt Finn too much. She must just get through to Chloë quickly and explain, before any more damage was done.

The child was curled up in a tight ball of misery, with the puppy wrapped inside her coat for extra warmth. Beth could not tell if she was asleep or unconscious, or merely so cold and scared that she could not speak. But it looked as if the two small creatures had somehow kept each other warm, huddled together under the snow, for both of them stirred and opened snow-fringed eyes when she shook them.

"Chloë," she said, and wrapped her own arms tight round her for instant comfort. "It's all right. There's nothing to worry about . . . It was the boat – Dancing Lady – Finn was talking about. The *boat*, do you understand? Not Corny, *Not anything to do with you*. Finn wants to get rid of the boat – that's all."

She repeated it again several times, holding Chloë very tight in her arms until she felt the tension begin to drain out of the small, weary body, and Chloë's own arms slowly came up and wound themselves round her neck.

"Not – Corny? . . . Not me?"

Finn was down beside them now, clearing a way through the drift in order to lift her out, but he paused when he heard that and looked at Beth in horror. He hadn't quite realised how awful his words must have sounded to Chloë's doubting mind.

"*Not* Corny. *Not* you. Not anyone here," repeated Beth. "How could you think such a thing? Your father's been nearly out of his mind with worry – and so have I . . . Now, let's go back with Beech and get warm. It's too cold for Corny out here . . ." Talking gently, cajoling and coaxing, Beth got Chloë out of her nest of snow and handed her safely up to Finn's outstretched arms. For a moment the child seemed to shrink from his touch, but then she suddenly seemed to believe Beth's words and allowed herself to be held fast in Finn's thankful embrace.

"Oh darling," he whispered into the tangled hair under the little red bobble hat, "thank God you're safe!"

Beth climbed out then, carrying the bewildered puppy, and Beech came forward to wrap the rugs round both of them.

218

"She'd better have that tea," he growled, "afore we sets off agen . . . The cold can kill, if it ent checked . . ."

Beth agreed, and tried to unscrew the top of the thermos with frozen hands.

"Here, let me," said Finn, and gently took it from her, setting Chloë down carefully on Beth's lap.

"Well it's the first time I've had a picnic in a snowstorm," said Beth, and held the plastic cup for Chloë's nerveless fingers to grip. "Drink a little – it'll warm you up."

"C – can Corny have some?" Chloë's teeth were chattering now.

Beth offered a little to the puppy, but it was still too hot for her to drink. However, she had the sense to lean comfortably against the warmth of Beth's side, and did not seem to be badly affected by the cold.

"Best get back now," said Beech. "It's near dark."

And it was. The snow was still whirling, but black night was closing in, and it would be hard going even to get back to Beech's cottage. We'll have to stay there for the night, thought Beth. We'll never get Chloë down to the village through this . . . She could see the same thought in Beech's eyes, but he merely nodded his head at her and murmured: "'Twill be all right," as he picked up the lantern to lead the way.

It was a long, hard slog back to the cottage, and Beth was very tired by the time they got there. But she suspected that the old man, Beech, was even more exhausted, though he did not say so. Finn didn't complain either, though he had been carrying Chloë all the way. But he was tough anyway, Beth supposed, and used to hardship and endurance.

As soon as they got inside. Beech went into action. First of all, he pulled out the damper in his old range so that the fire began to roar up the flue and grow red and hot through the bars. Then he dragged an old tin bath in front of the glowing fire, and began to fill it with hot water from the big kettle on the hob. Next he fetched a pail of cold water from the sink, and went on adding to the boiling water in the bath until the temperature was about right for Chloë.

"A bath by the fire," he said to her, smiling, "like my Ma used to give me when I wus a little 'un. Now, you just get yourself in there, while I go and fix some soup." He winked at Beth, and stumped off into his back kitchen, where Beth was relieved to see that he had an old electric cooker which seemed to be in working order.

Finn stayed to help Beth with the bath, to which Chloë submitted with a rather alarming docility, but as soon as she was dressed again (the clothes inside her anorak were surprisingly dry) and wrapped in blankets by the fire, Finn announced that he must try to telephone Mary.

"Where from?" asked Beth, alarmed. "You'll never get down to the village in this."

Finn looked obstinate. "Mary will be going mad with worry down there. I've got to do something." He turned to Beech who was busy handing out mugs of hot soup.

The old man considered the question calmly. "Dan Briggs would be the nearest – down at the farm." He looked at Finn doubtfully. "You'd probably make it to there – if the fields aren't too drifted up."

"Which way?" demanded Finn, shrugging himself into his coat again.

"You drink that soup first," ordered Beth. "It'll keep you warm on the way. And don't you dare be long! We need you here."

Chloë looked at him out of drowsy, shadowed eyes and echoed Beth's words in a small, shy voice: "Don't be long."

Beech also began to put his coat on again, but Finn protested at this. "No, Beech, you've done enough. I can manage."

"I'll see you to the field gate," insisted Beech, sounding as calm and unruffled as ever. "You can see the lights from there – if the snow'll allow."

They went out together into the howling storm, which seemed to be as bad as ever. "'T'wont blow itself out till morning," said Beech, listening to the wind with an experienced ear. He led Finn down to a gate already half buried in snow, and pointed downhill through the driving blizzard. "There! Can you see it?"

"Yes," Finn said, peering ahead and catching a fleeting glimpse of light. "I think so . . ."

"Take the lantern," Beech told him. "And mind the drifts. 'T'ent far, as the crow flies – only you'm not a crow!" And he

220

laughed, and turned back to the house. Finn plunged on into the darkness, swinging the lantern before him.

When Beech got back inside, Chloë was already on the verge of sleep, but she sat up with a start when the door banged shut against the wind, and asked in a scared voice: "Is he all right?"

"Surely." Beech's soft old voice was full of comforting certainty. "He's a big, strong man, your father. He won't be fashed by a bit o' snow."

Chloe burrowed her head against Beth's shoulder in relief, but instead of settling down again and going to sleep, she suddenly began to cry.

In all the time that Beth had known her, she had never seen Chloë cry. In the sunny days with Stephanie there had never been any need – and when she was at her most shocked and grief-stricken she had seemed too remote and cold to cry at all. But now, suddenly, the floodgates were opened, and she wept in Beth's arms as if she would never stop. She wept for Stephanie, her mother, who was gone for ever, and she wept for Finn who she now knew was as sad and lost as she was, and she wept for herself because she was bewildered and frightened and lonely and had no idea how to tell anyone how she felt.

"I thought . . . I thought . . ." she sobbed.

"I know what you thought," said Beth, holding her close. "But it isn't true – you know that now." She brushed a gentle hand over the tangled hair and hot, flushed little face. "He loves you very much."

"And Corny, too?"

"Of course, and Corny, too."

But Chloë was till not quite convinced. "What's a *burden*, Beth?"

"Not you, anyway," replied Beth firmly. "But a boat like Dancing Lady could be – if you didn't want to be bothered with it any more."

Chloë was silent then, trying to work it out, but the helpless sobs still shook her. "He might want her – if he didn't have to stay here with me."

"No." Beth was quite definite. "He doesn't *have* to stay with you, Chloë. He came home because he wanted to. I think he needs you more than you need him at the moment."

221

"Does he?" It was a new thought to Chloë, and as she began to consider it, the sobs at last subsided. "I'm sorry I ran away," she said, in a small contrite voice, and leant back wearily in Beth's arms.

"It's all right," murmured Beth. "Everything's all right now." But before she had finished speaking, Chloë was asleep.

The old man, Beech, with exquisite tact, had left his own warm fireside and gone upstairs to potter about the cramped attic space, wondering where to put his unexpected guests. The upper floor of the cottage was divided into two tiny rooms, but they were icy cold, and one of them – the one Beech didn't use – hadn't got a bed at all, only an ancient broken horsehair sofa and a couple of extra wooden cages which he sometimes used as an overflow for small animals when the outside pens got too full. His own room had the same old iron bedstead he had slept in when his wife was alive, but it was shabby now, and the springs sagged, and he wasn't sure he could find any really clean sheets to put on it.

Now he came downstairs quietly, and put a cautious face round the door. When he saw that Chloë was asleep, he came over to stand by Beth and spoke softly in his gentle old voice. "I've been lookin' at the upstairs, Missus, but I reckon it's too cold for the little 'un, after what she's bin through." He paused, looking at Beth with a question in his glance.

Beth nodded and waited for him to go on.

"I wondered – there's an old settee up there – if her father'd help bring it down-like when he gets back – we could put it close to the fire, and she could stay warm all night, if you could make do with the chairs?"

Beth smiled at his anxious expression. "That sounds perfect, Beech. But where do you sleep?"

"Up there," he said, jerking a thumb skywards.

"In the cold?"

"Nay, I allus sleeps up there," he said reasonably. "I'm used to the cold, see? But the little 'un – and probably you as well – you're used to heated rooms and such." He looked at her hopefully. "You could keep the fire up for me – "

"Have you got a hot bottle?" asked Beth, being practical.

The old man laughed. "Never did have one o' they."

"Well, what about an old cider bottle? Have you got one of those?"

He scratched his head in puzzled surprise. "I might have – "

"Then fill it with hot water," Beth told him briskly, "wrap it in an old bit of blanket, and put it in your bed."

Beech began to laugh again, but Beth shook her head at him and spoke seriously. "I think you should, Beech. You got just as cold as the rest of us out there – and you were out in the snow far too long with a chest like yours!"

He looked at her with respect. "Yes, Missus," he said meekly, and began to go out to his kitchen to look for the old cider bottle she asked for.

But Beth held him back. "Stay by the fire a bit, Beech. You've had no time to get warm yet. It would never do if you got sick. What would your animals do?"

That was an argument that the old man couldn't resist. He sighed, shot Beth a faintly humorous glance, and sat down in the other chair by the fire. He had to admit he was tired when he thought about it, and the warmth of the fire made him want to close his eyes, but that would never do. He was in charge here at present – he was the householder looking after stranded guests. He must not forget his duty, however weary he felt . . .

"Why does everyone call you Beech?" asked Beth. "Don't you have another name?"

The spark of humour in his eyes grew bighter. "Well, yes, Missus – but no-one ever used it. I was 'prenticed to a gardener when I was fourteen, see? And it was Beech come here, Beech go there, Beech pick up that rake, Beech bring me that spade, and it sort of stuck."

"Didn't you mind?"

He grinned. "Nay, I liked it. Sounded kind of manly. And anyways, I've allus had a soft spot for beech trees."

Beth grinned too. "Not *Mister* Beech?"

He shrugged cheerfully. "Nay, I've never been much of a mister."

"What was your other name, then?"

His voice was a bit reluctant when he answered. "Zebedee – but don't you go tellin' folks that. I'd never live it down!"

Beth laughed, but before she could think of another way to detain him, the old man was on his feet again.

"I got another lantern out back," he said. "I reckon I'll put it on the field gate, then he'll see his way home."

Beth was getting increasingly worried about Finn out there in the blizzard but she had not liked to say so, or to admit, even to herself, how much Finn's safe return mattered to her. But now she said, as casually as she could: "How long is he likely to be?"

Beech shook his head doubtfully. "Nay, 'tis no great distance . . . but snow is slow-going stuff, especially if there's drifts . . . He might be an hour or so."

Beth sighed. He had already been an hour or so, and the wind was still howling out there, the snow was still falling on the shrouded hills . . . But Beech is right, she told herself, Finn is big and strong and used to hardship. This little adventure would be nothing to him . . . He'll turn up soon.

"I'll not be gone long," said Beech, swinging the newly-lighted lantern. "But it'll shine quite bright in the dark."

He went out through the door, trying not to let it bang in the wind, but Chloë was far out now and did not wake. Beth sat on alone, with Chloë in her arms, and waited for the sound of Finn's footsteps on the path. Waited, with the knowledge growing within her that her heart waited too, and for more than the sound of his footsteps . . .

And presently she did hear them – not one set of footsteps but two – and Finn's deep voice answering Beech's soft one as they came up the path, and the sound of boots stamping off snow at the door.

"Here I am!" he said, shaking the snow off his shoulders, and dropping two heavy-looking bags on the floor. He turned to Beech, smiling, but Beth could see that even he was looking exhausted now. "Mrs. Briggs sent you up some provisions for your uninvited guests."

"What's it like down there?" asked Beech, eying the heavy bags on his floor with interest.

"Pretty bad," admitted Finn. "Dan Briggs says all the roads are blocked, and they won't get a snowplough through till tomorrow morning at the earliest. A lot of the power lines are down, and the phones – but his was working."

"Did you get hold of Mary?" asked Beth.

"I did. She was mightily relieved. I said we'd get back sometime tomorrow, but it depends on the weather, and the roads. I don't want to risk keeping Chloë out in that wind for too long."

"I reckon it'll drop by morning," said Beech, and began to unpack the new stores.

There were two home-baked loaves, some farm butter and a round of yellow cheese, a solid wedge of home-cured bacon from Dan Briggs's pigs, a packet of tea-bags and a carton of porridge oats which, Grace Briggs had assured Finn, was a good way to start the day on a snowy morning.

"She didn't send milk or eggs," explained Finn, "because she thought Juniper and the hens would provide them."

"Quite right," approved Beech, glad that at least some of the provision for his guests could come from him. "And now I'll make us some tea."

Finn looked down at Beth cradling the sleeping Chloë in her arms, and his face softened. "You must be tired," he said softly. "We'll move that sofa down in a moment. Beech has told me all about it . . ."

Beth looked up at him and found that she was so glad to see him that she couldn't speak at all.

Presently, the old horsehair sofa was brought down and put by the fire, and Chloë was gently transferred to it, still wrapped in blankets. She scarcely stirred, and neither did Corny, who had fallen asleep in a warm corner out of harm's way. Then Beech brought in the tea and some of Grace Brigg's bread and cheese, and though both Beth and Finn thought they were too tired to eat, they found that they were not, after all.

"I did what you said, Missus, about the cider bottle," said Beech, looking both shy and faintly amused at the same time. "Will you be all right, all of you, down here?"

"We'll be fine," Beth assured him. "But have you got enough blankets left for yourself? Haven't you given them all to us?" She was still worried about the old man upstairs in the cold.

"Nay," Beech laughed. "There be plenty o' they. My missus was a great hoarder o' blankets. Cupboards full, she had." He gave an impish smile, and added: "I uses 'em fer the animals, too. She'd have a fit if she knew!"

He hovered for a moment, waiting to see Beth smile, and then said: "Well, then, if you can manage – I'll leave you to it . . ." and tactfully withdrew from his own fireside and stumped away up the stairs.

Finn stretched his long legs out towards the fire, and lay back in his chair and sighed. "He's a wonderful old man. I don't know what we'd have done without him today."

"I tremble to think," agreed Beth. But her voice was slow and vague. Exhaustion was fast catching up on her – that and the warmth of the fire . . .

Finn smiled at her dreaming face, and then leaned forward once more to have a look at Chloë. "D'you think she's all right?"

"Yes." Beth roused herself enough to sound firm. "She's not too hot – or too cold. Her breathing sounds all right. I don't think she'll suffer any ill effects."

"She looks a bit flushed." He sounded absurdly anxious.

"That's because she's been crying," said Beth deliberately, and went on to tell Finn what had been going on in his small daughter's mind.

He listened quietly to all she had to tell him, and then shook his head sadly. "I'd no idea . . . How could she know about *burdens*?"

"She overheard you, Finn, remember? And she understands a lot more than you give her credit for." She looked at him straight. "You must talk to her, Finn. I think you'd be surprised."

"I'm surprised already," growled Finn. "But of course I'll talk to her – if she'll let me." He still sounded doubtful about it, but when he saw Beth trying to summon up the strength to argue Chloë's case again for her, he looked at her tired face and changed his mind. "Go to sleep, Beth," he said softly. "You've done more than enough for us today . . . Let's talk in the morning.

"In the morning . . ." echoed Beth, and fell asleep in her chair.

Sometime in the night she woke to soft lamplight and a glowing

226

fire. Beech had left them an old oil lamp to burn when the bright main light was switched off, and it cast a gentle muted radiance on the old cottage walls. Finn must have made up the fire quite recently, for the coals were bright between the bars of the ancient black range, and flames from a couple of half-burnt logs cast rosy shadows on the ceiling. But now Finn lay fast asleep, his long limbs spread out and quiet, his breathing slow and deep. Beth leaned over to have a look at Chloë, who also lay fast asleep, curled up on the old horsehair sofa, with little Corny, who had crept out of the corner when no-one was looking, curled up even smaller at her feet. They both looked entirely relaxed and contented.

All is well, thought Beth. Everyone looks very peaceful. A sudden, extraordinary sense of well-being swept over her as she watched those sleeping faces. I love them, she thought, amazed. Of course I do. What am I afraid of? What am I running away from? We are already a family, whether we like it or not. Already dependent on each other, needing each other, caring about each other. Why didn't I see it? How could I be so blind?

I don't know how long it will take, she thought. A year? . . . Two years? . . . Five? We all have wounds to heal, Chloë as much as any of us. But we'll come together in the end. What else can we do? . . . I know it was what Stephanie hoped for, – and I know I still feel a bit pushed – but I think she was probably right . . . When Chloë was lost in the snow and we were so frightened, I knew I loved her . . . And when Finn went off and I waited for him to come back? . . . Yes, I knew I loved him, too. Why else would I have been so profoundly glad when he came back safe?

She began to think then, seriously, of Little Mo. You'd like Finn, she told him, and Chloë, too. And I know you'd like Corny . . . And if I have come to love them, Mo, I don't love you any less . . . How could I? You are still my son, my firstborn, my perfect companion, and the ache that you left in me will never be cured, the gap will never be filled, but somehow, I know now, I can find room for the others, too . . . It's the same with Robert, she thought. My tall Robert, are you listening? You were my first love, Robert, when I was still almost a child – my lover, my husband and my friend –

227

and I shall always love you . . . But I am discovering, Robert, that love isn't finite. You can't put it into boxes – some for Mo – some for Robert – sharing it out like a packet of cornflakes until it's all used up . . . Because it's never all used up, Robert, is it? . . . I'm new to this, you see, and I didn't understand. *It's never all used up* . . . There is always room for more, only I didn't know it . . . I was afraid, you see, Robert, afraid to let it happen. I thought I'd lose you and Little Mo. But I won't, will I? You'll always be there – always where I can reach you . . . I don't need to be afraid at all . . .

She stirred then in her chair, and looked up, to find Finn's eyes open and fixed on her face. He looked at her quietly in the firelight and then smiled with slow reassurance.

"Don't be afraid," he said.

In the morning, when they were just finishing an enormous breakfast that Beth and Beech had cooked between them, there was a loud, cheerful knocking on the door. When Beech opened it, he found two rosy boys smiling at him on the snowy step.

"Mornin', Beech," said the tallest. "Our Dad sent us up to see if you was all right?" His bright, inquisitive glance took in the family party round the table, and he spoke now to Finn. "And he said to tell you, the snow plough's been through and he's got the landrover out. So if you can get down to the farm, he'll run you all home."

"And we've brought the sledge for the little 'un," added the other boy, smiling even more broadly.

"What a grand idea," said Finn. "Chloë, how would you like a ride on a sledge?"

Chloë didn't know what a sledge was, exactly, but she thought anything those cheerful boys suggested might be fun.

"Makes sense, that does," approved Beech. "Her legs are mighty short for this snow." He looked enquiringly at the boys. "How was it coming up?"

"Pretty deep," said the eldest.

"Drifty," added his brother. "There's one the size of a house on the path to the village . . . Dad says you'd best go round by the farm till it's cleared up."

The old man nodded, and he and Finn went out with the boys to have a look, while Beth got Chloë into her coat and boots, and rescued Corny from the back kitchen where she had been visiting her mother, Jess, and the two remaining puppies who had been brought into the warm last night to escape the snow.

"Afore you go," said Beech, standing in the doorway, "I wants to show Chloë something." And he beckoned to them all to follow him over to the animal pens. He had already been out that morning to clear the snow, and Finn had gone to help him. Now, the path was swept, and the wooden cages were clean and dry.

"Here," Beech said, and stooped down by the last wire enclosure, where Beth knew he kept the injured hare. "I want you to let her go."

"Now?" Chloë protested. "In the snow?"

The old man smiled at her. "Hares don't mind the snow, little 'un. They can run in it, light as feathers, and they can curl up small somewhere in a hollow, like you did, and keep quite safe and warm . . ." He looked down at the wary, nervous creature with her sensitive, twitching ears laid back almost flat against her head in fear. "But she'm ready to go, see? . . . And fretting to be away, poor crittur . . . Each time I come, she looks at me kind of hopeful like, and when I doesn't let her go, she goes small and quiet . . . and sad, little 'un. She needs her freedom, see? It's time she was away."

"But what will she eat?" asked Chloë, still sounding anxious.

"She'll burrow down and find the grass," Beech explained. "And the snow's less thick under the trees where the roots are . . . She'll manage." He looked at Chloe's worried face, and added: "But I usually puts a bit o' food out, in case they comes back . . . She won't starve."

Chloë nodded then, seeming satisfied.

"What shall we do?" asked the boys, who were as fascinated as Chloë, though a lot more used to hares than she was.

"Just keep still," ordered Beech. "If we all on us keep still when I opens the cage, she'll go easy, and not be frit." He stopped again, and gently lifted the wire gate at the end of the pen. "Come on, now, my lovely," he crooned to her in his gentle old voice: "Time to go."

For a moment, the anxious eyes looked into his and the hare kept quite still, but her nose was already scenting the wind, exploring the different feel of the air by that open space . . . Then, cautiously, she moved, and the black-tipped velvet ears lifted to catch the new sounds of freedom on the snowy hillside. Just for one more breathless second she hesitated, and then she was out of the cage and streaking away across the snow, her light feet making pointed patterns as she went. But she did not immediately disappear from view. Instead, she paused for one final look back, and began to make curious zig-zag patterns on the snow with her dancing feet, leaping in the air in a sudden ecstasy of free flight. Once, twice, she zig-zagged and circled, – once, twice, she leapt and danced, and then she began to run through the snow, her feet flying over drift and hummock and curving slope until she was gone.

"There she goes," said Beech softly. His blue, far-seeing eyes rested thoughtfully on Chloë's face, and then moved to Beth's and last of all to Finn's. "'Tis not only cornfields they dances in, see?" he said.

None of them answered, but they all understood him, even Chloë. But now it was time to go themselves, and Chloë put her arms round the old man's neck and said, in her best party manners: "Thank you for having me. It was a lovely breakfast!"

The merry boys settled her on the sledge, with rugs round her to keep out the cold, and decided to let Corny ride on it, too, for her legs were far too short and she sank into the snow up to her ears with every step.

Finn and Beth scarcely knew how to thank Beech – for it was quite clear to them both that he had probably saved Chloë's life yesterday, knowing where to look for her. So Beth followed Chloë's example, and simply put her arms round the old, frail shoulders and hugged him hard, and Finn added his arm to the general embrace and growled in his deepest voice: "Bless you for all you've done!"

Then they were away, with the Briggs boys pulling the sledge and promising not to let it go too fast, and Finn, who was still a bit too protective this morning, keeping up beside them in case Chloë fell off, and laughing as his feet fell into drifts and potholes in the powdery snow.

Beth came on more slowly, watching the cheerful procession with curiously misted eyes. She stopped for a moment on the hillside and looked round her, still seeing in her mind's eye the dancing hare before it streaked away into the distance. It was a different world this morning, she realised, as she stood gazing out across the valley below – a pure, white, untouched world of breathtaking beauty, its contours smoothed and softened by the seamless blanket of unsullied snow.

Are you out there, Mo? she asked. You and Robert? Dancing about like the hare in the snow? . . . There were other children below her now, on the slopes near the farm, sledging and snowballing, tumbling and laughing in the sun. She could hear their laughter floating up to her where she stood, and she thought some of it was Chloë's and Finn's.

And among those dancing figures on the snow slopes, did she see another small one she knew? . . . The light was very dazzling on all those pristine crystals, setting the whole brilliant world a-shimmer . . . It's all right, then, she told herself, suddenly sure of it – sure of the rightness of everything in this new white world. Be happy, Little Mo, Be happy, my tall Robert. Keep dancing . . . I know you are with me now.

"Are you coming?" called Finn.

"Are you coming?" echoed Chloë.

They had reached the edge of the slope above the farm, and they waited there, holding out their arms to catch her if she ran too fast, and laughing up at her in the sun.

"Yes," answered Beth. "I'm coming." And she began to run through the snow.

231

PART VI – THE GREEN LEAF

After the snow came the thaw, and with it the doubts. From the euphoria of Chloë's rescue and the relief that everyone was safe, and the wonderful sense of rightness and certainty that came after, life ground down to the anxieties and problems of day-to-day existence, and it wasn't easy.

Finn had black moods when self-reproach and a kind of helpless rage at his own stupidity almost swamped him. He would shut himself up then in his new tiny study and try to work, and neither Chloë nor Beth could get near him.

And Beth herself still had moments of panic when she felt drawn into their lives more swiftly and finally than she wanted to be – moments of guilt when she thought: What about Robert and Little Mo? How can I let them be crowded out by these two demanding people? . . . How can I desert them? . . . And then she felt both guilty and disloyal – and did not know how to face Finn or Chloë when they approached her with some new demand – as they always did. And that made her feel guilty and ungenerous towards them as well. She was very torn, very confused.

At last the tensions between them suddenly blew up into a major row, and Beth was horrified to hear herself shouting at Finn: "You're turning into an introspective, self-pitying wimp!"

And Finn, shouting back, called her a self-righteous prig, and told her to stop preaching at him.

They looked at each other, appalled. But it was Finn who relented first. "I'm sorry, Beth," he said, holding out a hand to her in contrite appeal. "It's my guilty conscience speaking."

"That's what I'm complaining of," retorted Beth, trying to ignore the pleading hand. "You have absolutely no reason to feel guilty – and you *must* stop it, Finn. It's destroying you – and it upsets Chloë, too."

"I know," he said heavily. "I know." He managed to summon up a bleak smile. "And you have every right to lecture me."

"No, I haven't," Beth told him. "You've got to work this out for yourself." And she turned away, determined to escape from Finn's house and his private demons to a more neutral place where she could deal with her own.

"Where are you going?" Finn's voice was suddenly sharp with anxiety. He knew he was driving Beth too hard, and he also knew, with painful clarity, how much her presence meant to him.

"Just home to the Beehive." Beth's voice was weary. "I – I think we both need some space, Finn . . ." She looked up at him, also trying a tired, bleak smile. "I just need time . . . and so do you . . . Don't fret about it."

"But I – " He had been about to say: "But I need you!" and was suddenly ashamed of being so demanding. It was true that they needed space – or Beth did, anyway. She looked so tired today, and there were great shadows under her eyes. He had to let her go – had to let her find her own peace, just as he knew he must find his own, too, before they could come to a true understanding. He just had to let her be free to make her own decisions, and hope that they would in the end be the same as his . . .

"I'm sorry," he said again, speaking gently this time. "I didn't mean to pressurize you . . . Just – just come back soon . . . I mean, as soon as you can . . ."

He seemed to be going to stumble on into incoherent pleas and denials for ever, so Beth simply turned back and kissed him quietly. "*Wait*, Finn," she said, her voice soft with more love than she knew. "Wait . . . It will be all right . . ."

And she went then, very firmly, and did not look back.

So she was alone at home that weekend morning when Mark came knocking on her door. Since Christmas and the snow episode, she had not seen so much of Mark as before, and she felt a bit guilty about that, too. Really, she told herself crossly, it was absurd to be so riddled with guilt about everything – she was just as bad as Finn. And the rift with Finn lay like a bruise on her mind, and she knew she ought to resolve it soon. It was time she made some firm decisions and put her own life in order.

"Mark," she said, smiling. "I'm glad to see you." And then, when he still stood there, looking up at her in silent appeal, she added with sudden extra warmth: "Aren't you coming in?"

But he shook his head. "No. I want you to come with me." His voice was sharp and urgent. "It's Beech . . . I think he's ill."

"Wait while I get my coat," said Beth at once. "You can tell me about it on the way."

They set off together to climb the hill to Beech's cottage, and Mark at once launched into half-apologetic explanations. "I've been going up to help with the animals on my own a bit . . ." He glanced sideways at Beth. "I mean, Chloë's got her Dad back now, and the puppy, as well . . . She doesn't need to go and see Beech so much . . . ?" There seemed to be a faint question in his voice as if he was not sure he had done the right thing.

Beth nodded. And felt even more guilty. Had Mark missed Chloë and the cheerful Saturday morning outings? . . . Had even old Beech missed them, too? She had been up once to see him after the snow, just to make sure he was all right, and to thank him again for his help. He had seemed well enough then – perhaps a bit more wheezy in the chest than usual, but as active and busy as ever.

"But today when I went up," Mark continued to explain, "there was no-one about – no-one looking after the animals . . ." His concerned young face turned to hers in anxious appeal. "So I went to the cottage . . . to ask for some more food for the animals . . . but I couldn't make anyone hear." He was still looking at Beth, seeming almost to be apologising for something. "Jess was outside, whimpering to get in. She made quite a fuss . . . so I – I sort of looked through the window . . ."

"And – ?" Beth felt his hesitation, and knew she had to get past it.

"Well, he was there all right – kind of lying back in one of the chairs. And he was coughing a bit, so I knew he wasn't asleep – but he didn't seem to see me." He hesitated again, and then went on with a rush: "I – I didn't like the look of him much, so I – I came for you."

"Quite right," approved Beth, and smiled encouragingly. "If he's ill up there, he'll need help."

"That's what I thought," agreed Mark, somehow enormously relieved that Beth didn't seem inclined to scold him for peering through Beech's window.

"Could you manage to feed the animals on your own?" asked Beth, her mind busy with practicalities.

"Yes, I think so – unless there's anyone new or special . . ."

"Good. That'll take one worry off his mind." She glanced at Mark with renewed appreciation. Really, he was turning out to be a very responsible boy, someone to be relied on in an emergency. Then she gave up worrying about what she might find at Beech's cottage, and concentrated on climbing the hill as rapidly as possible. It had occurred to her that a tough old man like Beech wouldn't lie down in his chair and give up unless he was feeling pretty bad, and he might need their help fast.

Again there was no reply when she knocked at his door, and after waiting a few moments, she lifted the latch and walked in; Jess, like a faithful shadow, slipped in behind her. The old man lay in his chair, breathing fast and wheezily, and scarcely seemed to notice her coming in.

"Beech," she said, giving the frail shoulders a little shake to recall him, "how long has this been going on?"

He stirred, and opened bleary, dilated eyes. "Missus . . . ?" He seemed almost embarrassed at being found in this collapsed state, and tried to sit up in his chair.

"No," said Beth firmly. "You stay there. What you need is a cup of tea."

He seemed about to protest, but she went on swiftly: "Mark is here, too. We'll see to everything . . . Just lie back and relax."

She was a little alarmed when the old man did just that, seeming too tired even to resist being ordered about. He simply fell back in his chair again, and sighed and closed his eyes. Beth noticed then that his breathing was very rapid and shallow, with an ominous catch in it. I'll have

235

to get the doctor over here, she thought. He can't go on like this.

Then she went into action. "Mark," she called. "Can you find some logs or some coal? We've got to get his fire going."

Mark wasted no time in answering, and shot off round the back of the cottage to where he knew the log-pile was kept. Meanwhile Beth had managed to make some tea on the old electric cooker in the back kitchen, (there didn't seem to be an electric kettle anywhere), and she also found a tin of soup which she emptied into a saucepan to heat. Soon, Mark and she between them had the old range roaring up the flue and casting a rosy glow on Beech's huddled figure. He stirred as the warmth began to reach him, and obediently clasped his hands round the mug of tea that Beth held for him.

"Drink a little," she coaxed. "It'll warm you up. Like Chloë in the snow!"

He took a sip then, and managed a creaky smile. But with returning awareness, came the anxiety. "The animals – ?"

"Mark will see to them. He knows what to do. And if not, you can tell him!"

Once more a faint, creaky smile touched him, but a fit of coughing suddenly quenched it, and Beth was shocked at how much it shook those bent old shoulders.

"Beech," she said. "I think you need a doctor."

"Nay," he mumbled, "'tis only a cold . . ."

"It is *not* only a cold," she told him severely, "and you know it."

For a moment the faded, rheumy eyes seemed to glare defiance, but then they clouded a little, as if not quite sure of their own strength to resist, and Beth was quick to notice it. Her own gaze softened, and so did her voice. "It makes sense, Beech . . . You'd get a vet out to one of your animals if necessary – you told Mark so."

"Only in emergency," muttered the old man, still fighting.

"This *is* an emerency," said Beth. "And you need some expert help, just like they do. Be sensible!"

He looked up at her then, and shook his head in helpless denial. But he didn't say any more.

So Beth went outside and sent Mark off to Mrs. Briggs at

236

the farm. "She will know what to do and who to send for," she told him. "Just tell her what's happened, and I'm sure she'll help. They're all fond of Beech down there."

Once again Mark ran off, wasting no time on words. Beth went back and managed to persuade Beech to spoon down a little soup. But it obviously tired him, and he soon laid down the spoon and leant back in his chair again, with one hand resting on Jess's head as she lay curled up beside him.

Beth thought the best thing to do then was to leave him in peace, and tidy the cottage a bit as quietly and unobtrusively as possible. But presently the old voice spoke from the chair by the fire in a curiously flat and tranquil tone.

"'Tis no great matter . . . at my age."

Beth stopped in her tracks. At first she thought it was the faint reproach of an old man who felt ill and neglected. But then she realised that it was no such thing. It was a simple statement of fact – as he saw it. He was old, and if he was near to death, it was no great matter.

She went across to his chair, drew up a stool and sat down beside him, taking his hand in hers. "It may be no great matter to you, Beech, but it is to your animals, and to Chloë and Mark, and to me."

His cloudy eyes rested calmly on her face. "Nay, 'tis the natural way of things . . . I told 'em, remember? When you've got most of the corners knocked off and done all you can – "

"Yes," Beth interrupted firmly. "But you haven't."

He blinked at her, confused. "Haven't I?"

"Not by a long chalk," she said, and pulled the rug up over his knees with a brisk, determined hand. "There's Chloë, for instance. How would she feel if you go off chasing hares in cornfields? She'll think it's all her fault for getting lost in the snow."

Beech blinked again. "Will she?" He shook his head slowly, only half-convinced. "I'm tired, Missus,' he said, and again it was not a plaint but a simple statement of fact. "'Tis time I had a rest . . ." His mind seemed to drift to other, less simple events then, and he said suddenly: "'Tis different when they'm young . . . 'Tis hard to see the sense of it then . . ." His eyes fixed themselves on Beth's face again, with piercing awareness.

"Mortal hard . . ." he repeated softly, and sighed. "But this, now – 'tis only natural. Nowt to worry about . . ."

Beth simply looked back at him and shook her head, deciding not to argue with him any more just now. Probably it was the bronchitis talking, she told herself, and Beech's own sturdy spirit would revive when he felt better. But she was worried, nevertheless. She had never heard him talk like this before, sounding so calm and unconcerned about the prospect of imminent death. It troubled her . . . So she sat on beside him, saying nothing, and waited for the doctor to arrive.

And presently, he did, accompanied by Mark and Grace Briggs, who had come up 'to see if there was anything she could do, like?' and brought another bag of useful stores with her 'just in case'.

Dr. Forbes was oldish and kind, beneath a bluff no-nonsense manner, and he knew his villagers and their ways pretty well. He also knew that Beech was fiercely independent, and the idea of hospital or leaving his own hearthside simply appalled him. "Well, my friend," he said, after listening to the sounds in the old man's chest with careful attention: "I've brought you up some antibiotics, since you can't get to the chemist, – and you'd better take 'em. That chest of yours sounds like the church harmonium being sat on . . ." He grinned at the old man's obstinate face, and added: "You be good now, and do as you're told for once, and we'll soon have you on your feet again." He winked at Beth, snapped his bag shut, and followed her outside to have a quiet word.

"How bad is it?" asked Beth anxiously.

Dr. Forbes sighed. "Bad enough. But the old boy's tough. He's done this before and come through all right." He smiled at Beth and rubbed a weary hand over his face. He had been up most of the night with someone's late baby who had been unwilling to come into this sorry world (and he didn't blame it, either) . . . and old Beech was only one of his commitments today. "He would be better off in hospital, of course," he went on, "but you know Beech. He wouldn't hear of it. Last time he said he'd push his own daisies up, thank you, on a clean hillside and not some sooty town ones!" He laughed a little, but Beth was still too anxious to laugh.

"It won't come to that, will it?"

Dr. Forbes patted her arm. "Not if he behaves himself! But he'll need to stay put and keep quiet. I'll get Sally – the District Nurse – to come up and bully him!"

"I can come up in the evenings after school," Beth told him. "But mornings would be difficult . . ."

"I can do mornings," said Grace Brigg's cheerful voice from the doorway. "I'm up at five for the farm anyway, – and Beech won't want seeing to till long after that . . ."

"And I can feed the animals," volunteered Mark. "I know what to do now."

"That's settled then," nodded Dr. Forbes, smiling at them all. "I'll be up myself to keep an eye on him . . . With all that tender loving care, he should do all right!"

He went off then, and Grace Briggs, after a bit of bustling around and fixing some more soup and a thermos of tea, also went off to her busy farmhouse, promising to be there in the morning, and left Beth and Mark in charge.

"Don't need anything more," grumbled Beech, turning restlessly in his chair. "Go on home – the pair of you!"

But they didn't. Not till he was asleep and the fire was banked high, and the various hot drinks and pills and potions were laid ready to hand. Then they tiptoed out, leaving the watchful Jess in command, and smiled at each other like conspirators.

"He'll be all right now," said Beth, and hoped most fervently that she was right.

They kept it up for two worrying weeks, disregarding Beech's protests, and by that time the doctor's antibiotics were beginning to work and the noises in Beech's chest sounded a little less frightening. But the old man himself did not seem to recover any of his old vitality, and remained curiously quenched and listless, with his eyes far away and full of smoky dreams. He did not even seem to be much concerned about his animals, but merely nodded when Mark reported progress, and simply sighed and murmured: "Good lad . . ." and left it at that.

Beth was worried by this, and by the increasing signs that Beech's indomitable spirit was somehow slipping further and further out of reach. He had not said any more to her about what he considered the natural progress of old age towards

239

death, but she knew it was still a very real eventuality in his mind, and his tacit acceptance of the situation troubled her. For some reason that she could not explain even to herself, it became a sort of battle that she had to win. There had been too many deaths in her life – too many disasters – and though this one might seem to be the most natural and least distressing of them all, she somehow could not accept it, could not let it happen. If she could just stave it off, and persuade the old man to believe in the future again, maybe she would be able to believe in it, too.

And then there was Chloë – she had enough to contend with already, far too much, really, for one small girl, what with her precarious relationship with her father and her guilt about running away, and her own private grief about Stephanie which was still not altogether resolved in her young mind . . . How would she feel if Beech were to die as the result of that rescue in the snow? Guilt was a bad thing for a little girl to have, – and bad for Finn to have, too. There was already too much of it in their lives . . . No, – Beech had got to get well!

But was that a selfish wish, she wondered? He had said he was tired. Did he really want to give up and let go? No, she told herself. I don't believe it. He's a born fighter – the will to go on will come back soon. I'm sure it will . . . He's still got a lot of life left to live, a lot of things to do. He will begin to enjoy it all again soon, I feel sure he will. And besides, she thought, without much surprise, I've got really fond of the old man. He's done such a lot for me, and for many other people too, I shouldn't wonder, as well as all the animals he's saved . . .

For as soon as word got round about Beech's illness, there was a touching procession of children from the village, bringing him bowls of soup and pies from their mothers, and small offerings of cakes and sweets from the village shop, and sprigs of winter jasmine and bright-berried holly from their cottage gardens and the hedgerows on the way.

Beech accepted their offerings quietly, seeming a little bewildered by all this attention, but the dreamy distance did not quite leave his faded eyes even when he smiled at the shy young faces at his door. Come back! thought Beth, almost

240

wanting to shake him. Come back, Beech! Stop dreaming. You are needed here!

"Nay," murmured the soft old voice, interrupting her thoughts, "'tis hard to be sure . . ."

"Sure about what, Beech?" she asked, startled.

"Where you rightly belongs . . ." he said, and this time his eyes seemed to have lost their distance and to be gazing at her with piercing directness.

Beth did not know how to answer him, or whether he was talking of his own future or of hers . . . But yes, whichever way you looked at it, the choices were hard.

So far, she had not told Chloë or Finn about the old man's collapse, and she had given Mark strict instructions not to do so either, yet. She wanted to be sure that Beech was really on the mend and back to his own cheerful, optimistic self before she dared let them know what had been happening.

It had meant, of course, that she had not had the time to go over and see Finn at all during these weeks of anxiety, and the rift between them remained open and unresolved. But since she had asked Finn so desperately for some space, she supposed he would accept her continuing absence to be exactly that – a need for space, and not make any attempt to contact her. All the same, irrationally, she found herself rather wishing that he had tried to find out what was happening to her. But then, Finn was very scrupulous when it came to respecting her wishes, and very shy, as well. It would probably be a long time before he dared do anything now, and she would probably have to make the first move . . . if only she was sure what she wanted to do . . .

Peter Green, on the other hand, had no such scruples, and when Beth had refused several lighthearted invitations to go out for a drink, he demanded to know why.

"Beech is ill," she explained, "and I've been going up there most evenings to give him a hand . . ."

Peter's cheerful face looked concerned. "I'm sorry to hear that. Can I help?"

Beth smiled. He was always so ready and willing, young Peter. Nothing seemed to daunt him. (Not even Fuji-yama!)

"I think it's all under control," she said carefully. "They've

241

worked out a sort of rota system . . . And Mark's been very good with the animals."

"Well, at least I could chop up some wood or something," he insisted. "And then I could walk you home and buy you a drink on the way."

Beth sighed. "You're incorrigible! All right . . . I'm sure I can find you something useful to do up there."

"That's the idea," grinned Peter. "A Really Useful Person, – that's me."

So after Beth had got Beech some supper which he didn't seem inclined to eat, and Peter had banked up the fire and fetched in some more logs, they found themselves going companionably down the path to the village pub, where Peter insisted on both of them having a bar snack as well as a drink.

"Stands to reason," he said. "Working all day, and then dealing with Beech. You must be starving."

Beth gave in, admitting she was both tired and hungry. But then she suddenly noticed a tall, dark figure sitting alone in a corner, and suddenly found she had lost her appetite.

Finn had seen them come in, laughing, from the cold outside, and watched them morosely as they settled down at a table across the room. Now he looked up and smiled at Beth faintly, but made no move to go across and speak to her.

She sat, paralysed, while Peter went up to the bar to order, and did not know what to do, or how to ignore the wild racing of her heart . . . I want to go over and talk to him, she thought. No, be honest, you want to go over and put your arms round him. He looks so gaunt and grim. What has happened to him? . . . If this is what no communicating does to him, it can't be right . . . Can it?

But Peter had come back with the drinks, and was standing by the table, looking down at her curiously. "What is it? You look as if you've seen a ghost."

She tried a wan smile. "Not a ghost, exactly. It's Finn – Finn Edmondson."

"Oh." Peter put down the drinks rather carefully. "Shall I ask him to join us?"

"No!" Beth sounded absurdly fierce. "No," she repeated,

more calmly. "And if he comes over, don't tell him about Beech."

"Why not?" Peter was nothing if not forthright.

Beth looked at him helplessly. "It's a long story – I'll tell you later." But her eyes kept returning to Finn, longing to make some kind of contact, to bridge the aching chasm that seemed to yawn between them.

Finn, however, was not going to prolong things. He finished his drink rather too quickly and got to his feet. Then, with careful deliberation, he came over to speak to Beth on his way out. "How are you? We've missed you."

"I – I've been busy," said Beth, trying desperately to hold herself back from launching into justifying explanations.

"I can imagine." Finn's voice was dry. "Well, come and see us, when you have time to spare." He nodded coolly at Peter, avoided Beth's eye, and strolled with studied nonchalance out of the door.

Beth stared at his retreating back, with a face grown suddenly ashen, and could not say a word.

Peter watched her quietly, but made no comment just then. Instead, he busied himself with the food that had just arrived, and tried to ignore the fact that Beth left hers almost untouched. A little later on, he fetched her another drink and said abruptly: "Why mustn't he know about Beech?"

Beth had more-or-less pulled herself together by his time, and now she produced a slightly less painful smile and told Peter about Chloë and the snow, and about the absurd cloud of guilt that hung over both father and daughter and how hard it was to disperse . . . And if, in the process, she told Peter a bit more than she realised about her concern for the two of them, he was much too kind to remark on it. But, looking at the blazing pallor of Beth's expressive face, he drew his own conclusions, and stoically put away a lot of private dreams.

It was only when he left her at her own doorstep that he decided to speak. "Beth," he said, "the winter's nearly over. It's time you got your act together. You can't go on living in the shadows for ever."

She looked at him in astonishment. But before she could think of any reply, he had stooped swiftly and kissed her, and gone away down the path in the dark.

It was one morning soon after this that Beth suddenly noticed the little green shoot. She had left the flower pot with the planted acorn in it on the kitchen windowsill where it could catch the sun, and it had remained there all the winter, with its dark leaf-mould surface undisturbed and empty. But now, all at once, there was a thin green shoot thrusting up to the light, with two tiny knobs at the top of the stem that might turn into young leaves. Beth looked at it, breathless with wonder, and put out a finger to touch the new spear of green. So small – so fragile – but somehow already pliant and wiry, strong with upsurging life.

I must show Beech, she thought. Perhaps it will make him want to come back . . . I'll wait a couple of days, and see if those knobs develop into leaves. Then it will really look like a tree . . . I wonder if Finn's or Chloë's has come up yet? . . . And whether they'll be wanting to show it to me, just as I want to show it to them? . . . But that must come later, she told herself sternly. Beech must come first. It might help. It really might.

So she watched it each morning, and each evening when she went up to see Beech she hoped he would be starting to come back from the distant places without needing to be recalled – but he was still vague and quiet, with his eyes clouded with dreams and his gentle voice almost too soft to hear.

But one morning when Beth looked at the new shoot, the small swelling knobs had burst into two perfect oak leaves glowing with a pale, vibrant green, and she knew it was time to take it up to show Beech.

She went up in the morning this time, since it was the weekend, and found the old man still in his chair but bathed in a shaft of pale winter sunlight.

"Look, Beech," she said, holding out the little tree in its pot, "it's happened – just as you said it would . . ."

The old faded eyes looked from the transparent green of the new leaves to Beth's face, and the cloudy distance was suddenly gone from his gaze.

244

"Well now," he said to that ardent face beside him, "seems like spring's on its way . . . 'Tis time for new beginnings . . ."

"Then – ?" began Beth, meaning to issue a challenge he could not ignore.

But at that moment Mark came in through the cottage door, holding something close in his two hands. "Beech," he said, "I found this bird on the road . . . It's very floppy, but I think it's alive." He held the soft limp bundle of silver-grey feathers out for Beech to look at.

"Why, 'tis a merlin," said Beech, putting out a blunt-tipped finger to stroke the tumbled feathers. "Been hit by a car, I shouldn't wonder, poor young thing . . ."

"Is it badly hurt?" Mark's voice was anxious.

Beech's strong brown hands went firmly round the unconscious body and felt carefully along the fragile bone structure, gently unfurling each folded wing. "Can't feel no broken bones," he said at last, still speaking slowly and softly. "He might be just stunned . . ."

"How d'you know it's a he?" asked Mark, trying desperately to keep Beech's attention.

"The colour," said the old man shortly. "Grey on top – pale underneath. The female is browner . . ."

"What shall we do with him?" Mark persisted, sounding all at once curiously young and helpless. But he glanced sideways at Beth and she fancied there was a faint gleam in his eyes.

"Put 'im in a box with some straw," instructed Beech. "But open, mind. He's a wild thing, see? Mustn't be shut in . . . And you'd better put 'im in the flying pen – the one the owl had . . . Then he can try his wings a bit, if he recovers . . ." He stroked the pale, silken feathers again, and the bird gave a faint twitch of his tired head.

"I think he's coming round," Beech said, and clasped his warm hands more firmly round the powerful, unmoving wings. "You go and get that box," he said to Mark, his eyes still on the little merlin, watching for any flicker of movement. "I'll bring the bird . . ." and he got out of his chair on somewhat shaky legs and stood looking at Beth with a glimmer of mischief. "Seems you were right," he said. "'Tis time for new beginnings . . ." and his blue tired eyes, back from their distance, rested for a moment on the new little oak tree.

"Shall I leave it here for you?" asked Beth.

He paused, and then smiled at her, almost impishly. "Nay . . . Take it with you . . . There's maybe someone else you ought to show it to . . ."

Beth did not misunderstand him. The old man knew too much about her, and it was no good dissembling with Beech. "Do you think – ?"

"Go and see," he said, still with that faintly impish smile. "Like I said, spring's on its way . . ." and he gave her a real, Beech-like mischievous wink, and made his way out of the door, with the quiescent bird still in his hands.

Beth watched him go, to see that he was not too shaky, and saw him join Mark by the owl pen and stoop to go inside . . . The two heads were close together, talking quietly as they settled the bird in his safe new refuge . . . They both seemed entirely occupied and happy . . .

Satisfied, Beth turned away, with the little oak tree still in her hands and went down the path at the edge of the trees. But she didn't go home the usual way. Instead, she plunged deeper into the woods and took the steeper track that led down to Finn's house at the other end of the valley.

The pale winter sunshine had strengthened a little as the morning wore on, and now there was a hint of warmth in it, and an extra patina of bright gold lay on every twig and fallen beech leaf, and cast strange patterns of light and shade on the tall silver flanks of the trees. Beech is right, she thought. Spring's on the way. And she began to notice as she walked that there were already hints of new green among the winter tangle of dried grasses and shrivelled bracken – dog's mercury was thrusting up among the tree roots, and she suddenly came upon an early primrose struggling to flower in a sheltered corner.

Somehow, the sight of the small, pale flower with its face lifted bravely to the sun, made Beth's own anxious heart stir with hope. It was going to be all right. Of course it was . . . All the warm feelings of certainty that had swept over her that joyous day in the snow, when she had called out "I'm coming . . ." to Finn and Chloë waiting for her below on the snowy slopes, now came sweeping back. The agony of dark doubt that had kept her away from them these last weeks suddenly seemed to dissolve and disappear, as mist dissolves in the sun. It was going to be all right – she felt sure of it – and somehow Mo and Robert were caught up in this sense of renewal, too.

You are alive again, like me, she told them, smiling a little to herself in the strengthening sunlight. Aren't you? . . . Can you feel the spring coming? It makes my toes tingle. Does it make your toes tingle, too? . . . There'll be more dancing in cornfields than ever, then, won't there? . . . And she went on through the faintly greening woods, growing slowly more certain of her direction and her future with every step in that bright, glowing new world of early spring.

There was even a thrush singing, high up in a tall beech tree, to light her on her way. "Be quick!" he sang. "Be quick! Spring's on its way!" Beth smiled up at him, shading her eyes against the dazzle of sunlight, – and almost fell over the silent figure of Finn sitting with his back to her, gazing away through the woods at an empty world he could not bear to contemplate . . .

"Finn!" she said, sudden wild gladness surging through her, and she carefully set down the little oak tree before him, and then her arms went round those stiff, lonely shoulders, drawing him close.

"I thought you said you wanted some space," he growled, not looking round.

Space? she thought. With all these deep woods and wide hills around me? . . . Space for Mo and Robert – for Finn and Chloë – for Beech and his animals . . . and for me? What more could I want?

"This is all the space I need," she said, and laughed in the sun.